Praise for *Play*

"Jess Taylor's *Play* is at once haunted and haunting,
a frightening and ultimately compassionate story of
the painful and winding path one person takes in the lurch
toward healing. It's a novel full of light and heart even in
its darkest moments: a beautiful, compelling debut."
—Liz Harmer, author of *Strange Loops*

"In *Play*, Jess Taylor has created a uniquely gentle sort of dread,
weaving a story that is compelling and compassionate, and burning
with profoundly moving insight about trauma, the power of art,
and our deep need for connection."
—Jessica Westhead, author of *Avalanche* and *Worry*

Praise for Jess Taylor

Jess Taylor

AY

Book*hug Press
TORONTO 2024

Library and Archives Canada Cataloguing in Publication

Title: Play : a novel / Jess Taylor.
Names: Taylor, Jess, 1989– author.
Identifiers: Canadiana (print) 20230480985 | Canadiana (ebook) 20230481043
   ISBN 9781771668798 (softcover) | ISBN 9781771668804 (EPUB)
   ISBN 9781771668811 (PDF)
Classification: LCC PS8639.A9519 P53 2024 | DDC C813/.6—dc23

The production of this book was made possible through the generous assistance of the Canada Council for the Arts and the Ontario Arts Council. Book*hug Press also acknowledges the support of the Government of Canada through the Canada Book Fund and the Government of Ontario through the Ontario Book Publishing Tax Credit and the Ontario Book Fund.

Canada Council
for the Arts
Conseil des Arts
du Canada

Book*hug Press acknowledges that the land on which we operate is the traditional territory of many nations, including the Mississaugas of the Credit, the Anishnabeg, the Chippewa, the Haudenosaunee, and the Wendat peoples. We recognize the enduring presence of many diverse First Nations, Inuit, and Métis peoples, and are grateful for the opportunity to meet, work, and learn on this territory.

To the past,
goodbye!

The only secrets Adrian likes are the ones we have together. He's cutting sticks from trees, and I'm here to do whatever he needs. My hands are hidden in gloves so that he doesn't know my knuckles are torn up again. A secret.

"Okay, I'm going to hold the sticks steady and you're going to wrap them." I nod. The sticks are taller than either of us. I'm already almost as tall as Adrian, who has always been skinny and small for his age. I'm nine. He's twelve. We're at the edge of the age where the differences start to disappear and age doesn't seem to matter anymore. Although I've always been the one he wants to play with and be around. His thin bones and gaunt face make him look taller than he is, like he's a thin stick that's been cut from a tree himself. Neither of us can ever eat enough, always hungry, even back then, but I go through stages where I grow a little pot-belly: my arms, tanned and freckled by the summer sun, gain a layer of baby fat chub.

Adrian gathers the top of the sticks together, splays their other ends out to make a cone structure that we could fit in. I wrap the twine we took from Uncle Jim's garage around the top. "You've got to make like an infinity sign or they'll all fall apart," Adrian says. We switch: I hold the sticks, and he holds the twine and shows me how to wrap it, up and down and around.

The sun's hot on my black T-shirt, Mickey Mouse printed on the front, wagging his finger. The shirt used to be Adrian's. Most of my clothes were Adrian's, and my parents don't notice that I've faded into Adrian's family as if that's where I belong. Later, I'll think that maybe they just didn't understand what goes into making kids, raising them. I live as proof of their love, but proof doesn't feel.

"Go get some rocks, Paul."

I kick around at the ground, covered in long, dried grass. Every spring it looks like Adrian's backyard might go green—shoots appear through the dead grass of last year, but it always dies off again before summer even comes. I gather two, three rocks and bring them to Adrian. He lines them against the bases of the sticks. "This will keep them from collapsing inward."

"Are we going to cover it with leaves?" I ask. "To make walls like a real house?"

"That's a good idea!" And we're off, collecting leaves. We need a way to attach them, so I run up to the house, where Aunt Dot is making us peanut butter sandwiches.

"We need glue!" I announce.

She's cutting the crust off of Adrian's PB & J. I can tell she remembered no jam in mine. "And what for, Paul?"

"We're making a city!"

"A city?"

"Yes, a real city, and Adrian says we'll make it so it glows and lights up just like in the game."

"The game?"

"The Lighted City!"

We've been playing The Lighted City for years. Out of all our games, it's had the most staying power—the image of glowing skyscrapers and houses and a village for us to call our own. Some games just do that, reveal things about who you are and who you want to be.

The game has existed as long as we've played together, but it's twisted and evolved over time. Out there is a city that is waiting for us—both Adrian and me—and we know the place is perfect.

Adrian imagines a place with no parents.

I imagine a place where we are in charge and worshipped.

Adrian imagines a place where we can be together.

I imagine a place so beautiful it hurts when you look at it.

The game always starts the same—we are walking in the forest and we hear something call to us: the leaves hissing in the wind are carrying a message. First, they speak to me. Adrian does the voice: "Paul, we need you. Paul, we don't know what to do. Our people are dying. They are cold and hungry, Paul. Only you can save us."

Adrian is with me because he is always with me when I play. When I'm alone, at home, I draw, I sort my stuffed animals, and I think about the next time I'll play with Adrian. Any ideas I have, I save up for him. That's the way he likes it.

"Do you hear that?" I ask Adrian, who is no longer the voices of the people of The Lighted City. He is himself again.

"What is it?"

"People," I say. "I think they're in trouble. This way!" We cut through the forest. Adrian follows close behind me as we go deeper and deeper.

"Wait," he says. "I think I hear it too."

Now I become the voices. "Adrian, it's you and Paul we need. You were always destined to rule us. We need you to bring the light back to The Lighted City. Please, save us."

Adrian and I look at each other, ourselves again, and we start to run through the forest. As we run, the trees beside us burst into flames at the tips of their branches, lighting our way. The path ahead gets darker and colder, but our very beings bring the warmth and light.

We come to a clearing, lit by a circle of trees that hold flames. The fire doesn't burn the trees though. It doesn't work that way. "Look," Adrian says, and he touches the tip of a branch and the fire doesn't burn him; it cannot because he is its creator.

"Adrian," I say, because what is beyond the clearing is amazing. There are skyscrapers made of glass and twisted tree limbs and branches, the dark windows slowly lighting up as our presence fills the clearing. Tiny huts, just big enough to house a person or two, lead up to where the skyscrapers are, and in front of each house, a fire lights. People begin to come out of the houses, and the sticks they hold emit light from their tips as soon as they walk toward us.

"We're saved!" they exclaim, and warm their hands at their front-yard fires.

Adrian takes a backpack off and pulls out bags of rice, lentils, chickens, vegetables, all food we've stolen from the dinner table. The townspeople come and take the food, share it out amongst themselves, and begin to cook and feast. Music starts to play in celebration.

"What is this place?" Adrian says to a boy closest to him.

"Don't you know, Your Majesty?" the boy says. "You're home. You've reached The Lighted City."

And it's true, we're the king and queen, the way it was always meant to be. Adrian takes my hand, and we kiss. At the beginning, that's how the game ends.

Now

For a long time I didn't even let myself think the name "Adrian." Everything that happened with The Lighted City was only "what happened to me" or "the day everything happened." I hid all my bad experiences in a chest where they wouldn't be able to touch me. Any complicated feelings I felt, they went in there too. By keeping them tight away, I could continue to live. That was also something that felt hard for me. Sometimes it still feels hard.

But everything always came out in dreams, especially once I moved to Toronto. And then, in 2016, things got worse, the way they need to before they get better. That was when things started to change. When I started to really look at those things in the chest and wonder if I had any hope of becoming a person who felt at peace.

Dr. Johnson recommended I try writing everything down to see if I can make sense of it all. Selina, she prefers. To see if I can be more honest with writing than I am in our sessions together.

Not *it*. I have to stop doing that — I need to call things what they were. The Lighted City. Adrian. Everything that happened in 2016, when I was close to finally losing myself. The notebook I pick is black leather. When it arrives at the door, I peel open the cardboard and hold it in my hands. It suits the way I feel about my memories, I suppose. I open it and the spine creaks.

On the first page, I write instructions for myself.

You will talk about 2016.

You will talk about The Lighted City.

You will be brave and truthful.

You will get to the bottom of what happened.

I put a piece of masking tape on the cover and then write on it in black permanent marker: *How It Happened.* Because I realize that's what I want to figure out. Not just what happened, although that's important too. I don't always feel I can trust my memories. In some places, there are gaps, or things begin to blur and look different. And as I look at the cover, even it blurs and changes: *How Could It Have Happened?*

Sometimes it feels like I've been working so hard for the past nine years, and yet I still end up trying the next thing that promises to make me feel in control of my life. But I want to live, or at least I want to try to want to live, so that's something, I guess.

How It Happened
The Lighted City

In those days, we are a we: Paul and Adrian. Never lonely when we're together. For as long as I can remember, Adrian has said that we are a team, and I believe him—need to believe him. Around him is the only place I feel like I belong. We know each other inside and out. With other people that feeling is impossible, and we're each other's only friends. More than friends, cousins. Adrian tells me that cousins are like super friends because you can lose friends but a cousin is always your cousin.

I come over in the day and he smiles his eight-year-old's mischievous grin at me, his blue eyes bluer than the sky when it's freezing cold in January. He is so pale, almost see-through. The skin covering his bony arms looks pristine, but I know why he's wearing long pants even though it's so hot we had to be kicked outside by Aunt Dot. Normally, she has to find us out there before we can be called in. Sweat runs down his ankles, along his bare feet. I know what's underneath his clothes.

I wish I didn't.

Despite what we know about pain, our days that summer are made of play. We climb a pair of cherry trees that hang close to where Adrian's field turns to forest. We dig through dirt. We swing branches like swords. We are dragons, cheetahs, koala bears.

Walking through the forest, we find a small broken rock laying against a large one. The big one is half buried in the ground. Adrian pokes at the ground with a stick, dragging it in the dirt beside the big rock, seeing if he can dig it out. I point to where the small rock is cracked in half. "Why's it like that?" He picks the halves up.

"Maybe an animal dropped it from up high?" Adrian says. He looks up at the sky and his black hair falls back off his sweaty forehead. All that's up there is the canopy of leaves and needles creating the shade we've been desperate for. "Or someone threw it." He winds up like he's going to throw the half in his right hand, just to see how far and hard it will go. But then he looks at it and holds up the left. "Look, Paul." He slots them together and they are whole again.

He gives me one piece and he carries the other.

"This is important," he says. "You can't ever lose it." I nod. "It's like ... what do you call it? A pact. A pact to be together forever."

"Friends forever."

"Like this forever!" he says and takes my half back and presses it into his until the rock looks whole again. He gives it to me.

Everything between us is a pact. As the years come and we grow, the pacts have more details, but the core stays: Adrian and I must always be together. Or, looked at in another way: neither Adrian nor I can live without the other.

Now

I hadn't wanted to go to therapy at first, after everything that happened with Adrian. I was forced to by my parents. I began talking without talking. I moved my mouth, but I didn't say anything. Then, I turned eighteen and graduated and left home to live with my boyfriend. He told me he was the only therapy I needed, but eventually our relationship fell apart and money for college ran out. Instead of running home, I dropped out of school and moved to Toronto. I wanted to prove that I could be independent, that what happened hadn't messed me up the way they feared. I didn't need to continue to be their burden once I was old enough to be on my own.

Now, fourteen years have passed. Somehow it's 2025, and Selina appears on my screen every week, calling from a small office in the West Toronto PTSD Clinic. I've been waiting over a year for a psychologist, but it's still hard to begin. I want to do things right this time.

It's different from the type of therapy I went to in my later twenties, when I was trying to figure out what to say to Trevor or why I couldn't act the way I wanted to act. Why I couldn't be the type of person I thought was good and honourable and true, someone who said and did what they meant and who didn't want to hurt others. Someone who didn't get angry or want to make themselves bleed or engulf the world in flames. That therapist just sat back and waited for me to talk, and it was so easy to not say anything. When she talked, she spoke about "mirror neurons" and "interpersonal relationships." To her, my relationship with Trevor was a living, breathing thing, when neither he nor I could even acknowledge it existed.

Instead, Selina brings activities, like I do with students. I've never had a therapist like her, so structured. And she's close to my age, but stylish in a way I'm not, her black, curly hair kept cropped close to her head, gold-rimmed glasses perched on her nose. My outfits never look like they go together. At the beginning of each video call, we plan the session's schedule. I find it comforting, knowing exactly what we're going to do. Nothing unexpected, not pushed anywhere I don't want to go. I like being guided along, like thinking about Selina taking the time, as I do before I teach a lesson, to carefully plan the outcomes, to look up something new to go through, to send me the documents to print and use.

Today she says, if I'm agreeable to it, she'd like me to try to make a timeline. "I want you to make a timeline of your life, but you don't have to write down every little thing. Just those we'd classify as trauma. From there, you'll circle the trauma you feel has impacted you the most, the one that really stands out. We call that the *index trauma*. Then we'll work on processing your index trauma. For now, all you have to do is pick what you feel that is."

"Processing?"

"Yes, by writing and listening and talking through the events. If you write out the index trauma first, we can go through it together in session. Eventually, you'll record what you've written and listen to yourself reading it. The idea is to make the memory less 'hot.'"

The word *hot* already brings me back there. To the day everything happened. I stop being able to focus on Selina through the screen.

"We want it to become more like a regular memory. A significant memory, but not one that drags you back into the moment every time you think about it. Usually this will give you more control over the memory too—so that it doesn't pop into your mind at random times or come up in your dreams. First, though, we need to pick what to work on."

I open the document Selina has shared, which already has a line drawn along it, thick and black and ominous. The surface of my scalp starts to tingle. "Can I do it for homework?"

"Sure, why don't you do this one for homework, and we'll do something else for today's session. Next session we can begin by talking about the timeline."

"Okay."

After the session, I print the timeline and put it on my kitchen table. I go to the fridge and pull out a bottle of white wine, pour.

I know this is the point. To be able to talk about these things that happened and not be afraid of them and not let them control me. I've finally gotten to the point where my life feels more within my grasp. But the dreams, how I feel…everything is still so real to me no matter how far in the past it is.

I drink the glass of wine.

In a cabinet in my bedroom, I keep the markers, crayons, and art supplies I bring when I see students individually. I open the cabinet, releasing the doors from their fastener, gently, not wanting to cause them any distress, and grab a pack of fine-tipped markers. There. This will make this fun. Or I guess as fun as ripping yourself open can be.

At the top of the timeline are printed instructions, similar to what Selina told me. After all this time waiting for trauma-informed therapy, I know I want to do this. I want to take it seriously. I need to circle the trauma that impacts me the most.

Along the timeline, I use code:

1995, when I was five: *finding out*

1998–2007, when I was eight to seventeen: *The Lighted City/Adrian*

2007, when I was seventeen: *the day everything happened*

2012, when I was twenty-two: *the other Paul*

2016, the spring and summer I turned twenty-seven: *Adrian's death, money, the boy*

2020–2023, early thirties: *pandemic (world trauma, but nothing major happened to me)*

And then I'm pleased to see that the years that have followed have been pretty free from new things. I don't write anything down for 2024 or this year. Although the pandemic has continued to spike, and our health care system has sputtered along, I have been okay. It feels strange to think of that, and I write down underneath the timeline, *I'm okay.*

For a time, in my twenties, with all the heartbreak and the way things kept happening to me, I felt like maybe I was someone who just drew bad things to me, a curse or something about who I was, deep inside. Especially the things that happened with Adrian. But looking at the timeline, since my late twenties and early thirties, I've had a period of peace.

Of course, peace is relative and my stomach hurts when I eat and the nights that I don't have nightmares are less real to me than the ones where I do.

I circle all the things that have happened because I think it's funny; I mean, they've all affected me at some time or another. Continue to affect me. Then I begin to draw. I draw trees, creating a lush boreal forest around the edge of the paper in marker. And then I add flames. With the same colour, I star *the day everything happened* and then draw a smaller star beside *Adrian's death, money, the boy* because I need to talk about that year. That year was one where all the bad things felt fated and I didn't think I'd get out of it alive.

How It Happened
May 2016

The full moon. When I think about late spring in 2016, that was the first problem. The second problem was that the weather was getting warmer, warmer in a way that loosened everyone up and made us all stay out too late. Me, and then Trevor, and then Stef and Derek, and then Kayla and some guy she'd just met that night. I put my head on Trevor's shoulder, egged on by the moon, and also by the smell of him. I loved the feeling of the canvas of his khaki jacket, which his dad had made, he told me once. The sadness of his voice saying that—his dad gone, dead—little details I'd assembled until I had a full picture of his sadness, a raw, rippling grief that lived in his eyes and created an ache in me that grew and grew until I needed to fuck him for a few hours to make it go away.

As I got drunker, I pressed into him harder, the rough fabric creating its pattern on my face. I wanted to make him indelible on me. His smell: Camel cigarettes, the kind with a real stink, and some kind of cologne, and another smell that no one else noticed but that tugged at me in a sad, small way. But instead of letting me stay pressed against him, Trevor moved to the right and I had to catch myself against the table to keep from falling down, sloppy as I was, and then he just shook his head at me and took out a pack of cigarettes and knocked three out on the table, and then he gestured at Derek and the guy I didn't know, and then he was gone from the table, standing off to the side, passing around his cigarettes and lighter, my cheek still run through with tingles from pressing that rough fabric, my nose already missing his smell. I heard him talk about his brother, Max, complaining about something or other. Kayla bought me another drink because everyone knew the state of my bank account. Everyone knew.

That night, Kayla kept saying that it was "the first patio night of summer" and hugging us all. Her curly brown hair was set free as usual, her blue eyeshadow making her dark eyes even more bewitching. Her voice got louder as she drank.

Stef kept saying, "It's only May thirteenth," and checking her phone for news from the babysitter. She sucked her cheeks in the way she did when she was thinking, her high cheekbones making her face seem even more severe. Only I knew how her hazel eyes turned green in certain light, how her black hair looked after a night staying awake wondering if her partner, Derek, was coming home to her and Wynn. Tonight, her hair was pulled tightly back into a slick ponytail.

I couldn't focus on their conversation as they slipped into an argument about how Kayla meant "the Season," as in the party season, and Stef meant the season as in what season it was literally, and how Stef was no fun and Kayla was too much fun and could really tone it down if you asked anyone. Then they were hugging, and I wasn't sure why—all the history between them, longer and more complicated than what I had with either, smoothed over each of them like a balm. The half-hearted argument melted away under the light of the full moon that wanted everyone to be intimate anyway.

I watched Trevor talk with the two guys. He always patted guys on the back as he talked, but with me, or any woman really, he turned his gaze away, kept the conversation short and clipped. "Trevor's an asshole," Kayla always said, quick to label. To her, Trevor was only allowed around for the sake of Derek. And yet, I knew he was not the way she saw him. I saw how his grey eyes could slip into a blackness, how his iciness was often a case of not knowing what to say. I believed the ember from his cigarette was the most beautiful thing on a night like this. The cigarette went to his lips, and those lips were the ones that kissed my stomach and then lower, lips that covered teeth that bit my thigh, up to where it joined my pussy, waiting for his tongue. My wrists, ready to be bound.

We all left the bar at the same time, but he wouldn't go home with me, even though I subtly walked in his direction after parting ways with Kayla and Stef. "You always make everything so obvious," he said.

My scalp started to tingle and I took a step toward him. I needed to make him look at me instead of always looking away. I wanted to thread my hands through his dark hair and give him a tug like I knew he liked. "What's wrong with obvious?" I said, despite the fact that I, more than anyone, kept things hidden. "What's wrong with that?"

"Just go home, Paulina," he told me. "I'll see you tomorrow anyway." But I wasn't Paulina, not really. I didn't know how I could get him to understand.

"Tomorrow?" I said, because of course I was too drunk to remember that tomorrow we'd all be together again, moving Kayla into a new apartment because she'd been evicted. I was ready to start yelling, now that I'd remembered: Why didn't we just go home together and then go to Kayla's together, and why did he always act this way any time we were with our friends? But just when I was ready to start yelling, to really get into another fight—our main shared activity other than sex—Trevor ran up the street away from me and flagged down a cab, despite always complaining that, like me, he had no money. Even though I knew his dad had left him money, enough so that he never needed to have a real job. A writer, an artist, free to be who he wanted to be.

I walked home. The moon lit my way. The stars blurred in the sky. Rejected by Trevor again. And still, longing beat in me, the type of longing that only exists in your twenties when you're attached to someone who barely gives a shit.

My apartment was waiting, where I lived alone in the attic of a house. Most days I didn't mind the loneliness, craved my own space, my own walls. But that night I folded myself into my bed and then I hit the mattress again and again. I pressed the back of my hands to my face and lightly gnawed at the scars that were knotted along my knuckles as if I were scraping off the last bits of meat from a bone. I wanted to hurt, the rage beating in me like the blood I knew was just under the skin, but I stopped myself. I needed sleep. I would see him in the morning.

But May 13 was more than the night of another rejection. Looking back, one of the many things that frighten me is knowing that somewhere out there, a man was moving silently through a North Toronto ravine. A late spring, full of children missing. And across the country in Vancouver, sometime between when I left The Cave and when I was at home in bed, Adrian was alone in a room with a shotgun.

Now

I am in The Lighted City. Where Adrian and I always promised each other we would end up. Each tree illuminated by flames suspended in its branches. But unlike we'd promised, I'm alone. Where is Adrian? It's impossible to see the stars with all the light. How had we ever thought a place so bright with fire that you couldn't see the stars was beautiful? As I walk on the paths carved through the forest, toward the huts that I know are hiding there, the skyscrapers made of mud and branches that Adrian and I have carefully constructed over the years, branches lean in and grab at my face, at my clothes, but none of the flames on their tips burn me. Nothing can hurt me here, only annoy me, only grab at me, trying to keep me from getting to Adrian. So I begin to run. But no one is waiting for me when I reach the clearing full of small houses we've created. I am alone, and always will be.

I shouldn't be surprised that they've started again. My dreams. But the morning after I drunkenly filled out my trauma timeline, I wake exhausted. I let sleep engulf me again even though I had plans for painting, maybe even heading to my new studio. I let the morning slip away.

When I wake again, it's the afternoon. My first client meeting is in an hour. I tell myself there's not enough time. I can't get all my supplies out and work before. Even sketching, I reason, would be difficult, without the time to sink deeply into the images I want to create. So I work on my trauma homework. Maybe if I get all of it out of my head, the dreams will stop coming back. I need a break, a longer one next time. Those dreams aren't like regular ones, of flying or sex, imaginary landscapes. With these dreams, I can get a complete night of sleep and still wake up so tired, short of breath. They stick with me throughout the day. I can barely keep my eyes open as I dress, make coffee.

Each tree illuminated by flames suspended in its branches.
Too real.

I open my laptop just in time to take my first video client of the day. Jocelyn's smiling face fills the whole screen. Her glasses glare in the blue light. "Can you see me okay?" she asks. She moves the camera, and her frizzy, grey hair takes up most of the frame before the view moves back to her face.

"Yeah, I see you," I say. "How's the week been?" Jocelyn's in her seventies and is one of the first adult students I took on when I started offering online drawing and art lessons during the pandemic.

Before Trevor moved out east, we had a roster of tutoring clients, Trevor handling writing, grammar, and English, while I mainly did art. Sometimes I also helped little kids with their reading, taught them how to follow a story and love characters like I did. When the pandemic hit, instead of giving up and trying to find full-time remote work or just waiting things out, we shifted the clients who were interested online. When he moved in 2021, he still had a few, which helped offset the cost of relocating and getting set up for his PhD. And I found that more and more people wanted online art classes. They were home and bored and seeking out new skills. I began to offer small group classes online and virtual kids' parties. And what had started as a way to get a few years of stability solidified into a real business, separate from Trevor's tutoring. People actually felt that I had something special that they could learn.

Jocelyn's the one who's kept the lessons up the longest. In that time, she's produced several triptychs and submitted her paintings to contests, even placing once or twice. She says there's still more for me to show her, but I doubt it. Maybe the companionship is really all she's looking for.

"I have one more painting I've been working on for the show on Friday—you said you'd come to the gallery, right? Eight p.m."

"I'll be there. I wouldn't miss it for anything."

"This painting, it's been giving me trouble."

The screen shakes as Jocelyn picks up her laptop and carries it over to her easel. I feel disembodied until she holds her computer steady again. I can't see her. Only the painting fills the screen. It looks finished to me—it's of a subway car, a ghostly orb lighting up one corner. One of the spirits Jocelyn claims she can see. "What's bothering you about it?"

"Well, that's the thing. It's not the spirit—I think I've captured that perfectly—but something about the *feeling* is wrong. You know what I mean. When I close my eyes and imagine what I want it to look like, it looks different."

I want to tell her that sometimes you need to circle around subject matter, getting closer and closer to what it really was, what it felt like. That it's hard to recreate something until you can hold it clearly in your mind. So many burning trees. So many lost children.

Instead, I say, "Did you use any source images?" The subway interior is stylized, not precise, but maybe that's what she wants.

She laughs and puts her computer back down so I can see her. She holds up her sketchbook to the screen and shows me the pages and pages she's filled with photos she's taken of the subway, then printed, then practised drawing beside. "One or two." She laughs again.

"Well, one thing I notice is that the walls of the subway car, they are similar in hue to the orb—I mean, the spirit—to the light coming from it. I'm not sure if that's what you want, but it takes away the contrast. The spirit looks less like an otherworldly thing and more like a bright spot."

"I want the person looking at it to feel how I feel when I see them. The world is full of so much more than I ever imagined."

"Well, then maybe you need to bump up the contrast, make it something distinct that really doesn't seem like it belongs there. Make it more eerie."

"But the spirit does belong there. It belongs there more than everything around it."

"Then it still needs to be distinct from the background."

"Hmm. Okay."

"It can be as easy as darkening the walls of the subway car slightly so the brightness of the spirit really pops. Didn't you tell me their light is almost blinding?"

"Yes, exactly! Okay, I'll try that." Working with her, it motivates me too. I can imagine myself being like her one day, still learning, still growing. The idea makes something swell in my chest.

✧

Outside, it's already cold as the world creeps through the last week of November. Small pellets of snow, almost more like ice, fall through the air. Stef and Kayla are waiting for me across town, so I hop on the streetcar, tapping my card on the green sensor as I board. They always do this, pick a time to meet right when I'm finishing up with a client and then fail to account for the time it takes for me to get from Roncesvalles to Little Italy, but I know I'll feel good having gotten out of the house and eaten something. As a masked woman glares at me, I realize I've forgotten to put on my face mask in my rush to the streetcar, so I fish around in my coat pocket until I find it and then put it on. My face becomes moist and hot with my own breath. I've gotten my yearly vaccines for the flu and COVID, but it doesn't matter. No one can tell if you're vaccinated or not, and everyone has a different idea about how much they want to mask and what they think others should do. My own feelings shift with the threat, and I never know what's the right thing. With the most recent surge in the early fall, the restrictions tightened up for a bit, but now with the holidays coming and cases back down, a new booster dose in everyone's arms, things are easing up again. I fold myself into a seat near the front.

I think about Jocelyn's spirits and how it would feel to see one on the streetcar with me. When she talks about them, she speaks with confidence. If I hadn't also been haunted—didn't still feel haunted—I wonder if I would've been more dismissive when she told me about them. I'm not sure. The more I grow and experience the world, the more I feel I don't know anything about how it works and that there will be more surprises in store, even spirits riding the subway.

My phone dings. I have an email from Trevor, shorter and more to the point than he usually is.

Friday, November 28, 2025
Subject: Coming home!
Guess what? Received an early Christmas present: a plane ticket to Toronto! Mom says she doesn't want another Christmas over Zoom and we're all boosted up. So, I'm returning! Only for about a week or so, but I'd love to see you if you're around the same days I am (are you going to Caledon this year?). It's killed me not seeing you for so long. FaceTime isn't the same!

Let me know when you're around.
Or just text me, whatever.
I have so much I want to say to you.
T.

Even seeing *T* signed at the end sends my heart pounding in my chest. Sure, I've tried to date people here and there, but no one had the staying power that he always did, occupying a space in me that was normally only full of my own lonely thoughts. I'll be taking a bath and he'll pop into my head, and then I'll have an email waiting for me. Or I'll send him a message and we'll talk or schedule a FaceTime. He's in my dreams, and in them we talk about everything, but I can never say the things I want to say, just like in real life. And just like in real life, he's always gone, away across the country, probably fucking who knows who.

I flick over to his previous email.

Tuesday, November 25, 2025

Hey P.—

I can't begin to tell you how happy I was to hear about the PTSD therapy. I get why you didn't want to talk about it over FaceTime, but I'm here if you ever want to.

We never really talked about what happened to you after that big blow up (I know I know, you hate talking about that fight, but maybe we should?), but I've always felt it's existed between us: that we know all of each other better than anyone out there. I know I was an idiot back then, but, yeah, I still appreciate that you trusted me with this stuff. And I do mean that.

The rest was filled with newsy details about his life on the East Coast. It's taken us a long time to reach this level of friendliness, a friendliness we maybe even owe to that horrible year, 2016. That year cleaved me open and he became the person who knew me. We needed something like that. We decided to just be friends. *Friends*, a strange word, a ridiculous word, Stef and Kayla told me. But finally, Trevor and I had no secrets, and very little room for betrayal. And maybe that was good.

The streetcar pulls up to Clinton. I hop off, removing my mask as I walk, the cold stinging my face. There was a time when every part of Toronto filled me with wonder. Now, after fourteen years in the city, I yearn for somewhere new. The roads seem too dirty, the people too mean, and I'm too lonely. This wasn't the city of my dreams. Or of Adrian's.

I can see Stef and Kayla through the window. Twenty minutes past five and Kayla is already holding up a drink to the light, showing Stef its colour. So it's going to be one of those nights.

"Oh, look who's finally gracing us with her presence," Kayla says and laughs as I walk over to where they are sitting. Stef gets up and hugs me right away. The place is old-school, and the server gives me a menu instead of handing me a tablet to order.

"Sorry I'm late. I had a client till five. She's that one who's having the art show soon."

"Oh, cool, yeah, I think I'll go to that. I mean, we just survived another lockdown, I'm up for anything at this point." Kayla breaks into her charmer's smile, and Stef and I can't help but smile too. Kayla takes a sip of her drink and sets it down gently on the table. Back at The Cave, Kayla would slam her drinks down on the table, not wanting to do anything without energy, but as she's grown older, she's become more and more aware of the setting she's in, more able to camouflage her behaviour to what she feels is accepted. "It's the only way I'll get ahead," she'd told me once when she was drunk, telling me about this change that she'd gone through, gesturing to herself, her skin. "These are the things you don't have to think about."

I can see why Kayla is quieter here: This place doesn't have the magic of the places we used to gather. The drinks come in fancy highball glasses with complicated descriptions and cost three times what we used to pay for a beer in our twenties. But The Cave shut down. So many places have shut down, and only a few new ones have sprung up. The number of people we see in person is also different since the pandemic, but at least I still have the two of them.

"I was just telling Stef that I'm in love. There's a new manager in another department, and he's not going to know what hit him. Love is coming!"

I laugh. "And has he met the future love of his life yet?"

"Briefly. At a management meeting. With twenty other people. Today. But I swear I felt a spark! Our eyes connected across the room, and it was like BOOM! Magic!"

"And is this even allowed?" Stef asks. Her hands clutch each other and she looks even skinnier than the last time I saw her. Her dark hair is pulled back in a tight bun.

"Yeah! I mean, I think so. There's no power issue, if that's what you mean. Sure, I've been a manager for longer, so I guess I'm technically his senior." Kayla sits a little straighter as she says this, and Stef nudges me underneath the table. "But we'll oversee different teams, and he won't report to me. We'll only come together from time to time to make decisions as equals during the management meeting. It's perfect really. Finally, I'll be with someone who understands what it's like."

"It must be very hard to be a big fancy manager who has given up all memories of being a lowly employee," Stef says, grinning. She waves at the waiter and then orders four appetizers for us to share. Extra olives.

"I know you disapprove, Stef. I swear I'm not a class traitor."

"Hmm. Then what else would you call it?"

"Wanting to feel like my career is actually going somewhere? Not being stuck somewhere doing the same dead-end work over and over again until I die, while barely making enough to live?" Kayla stops herself from saying "like you guys," but it's implied.

Stef began teaching one or two college classes when her daughter, Wynn, was just born, and eventually went back for her master's and got hired on full-time. I saw the amount of work it took, nights I would go over there and prep lessons and occupy Wynn while Stef turned out another assignment. She never let herself slip at her job, despite what she had to balance. She would wake up early to finish a whack of grading before making breakfast for Wynn and getting her off to school. It took so much for her to get that full-time job. And me, while I know it's not the most lucrative, I like being my own boss, having control over managing my clients, and having the choice to seek out more short-term work at camps or centres if interest in my own classes start to dwindle.

"I'm happy with my life, thank you," Stef says. Her eyebrows come down over her beautiful green eyes—the only feature from her father, she says—which flash for a moment before looking away from us. "What a wonderful evening. I'm so glad I came out."

I slip my hand onto Stef's underneath the table and squeeze it. I'm here for her, even if she can't feel it. Kayla's Apple Watch beeps. "I need to stand," she says, and walks out the restaurant doors to smoke. We watch her shivering, pulling her designer sweater close around her.

"She's not trying to get at you. You know she admires that you teach."

Stef continues to frown. "Well, it's hard for me to understand how she can just slink her way into management."

"It wasn't easy for her," I say.

"That makes it even worse."

I want to tell Stef that we're all trying to find a way to survive, but I know Stef has a hard time seeing it that way. She thinks it would be more honourable to struggle than to be a manager, thinks the way Kayla loves the power that comes with her position is a sign of everything that's wrong with capitalism. Sometimes I can't imagine how these two people became friends, lifelong friends, until I think about how I met them, drinking and talking about art and acting and music at The Cave. Back then our jobs were only things we did because we were stuck, when our hearts were caught up in art. But it's not easy to keep going when your heart is one place and your time makes you spend all day somewhere else, and sometimes what people want changes.

The appetizers are put down. "I don't think I can eat these," Stef says and picks at an olive. She puts bread on her plate and just stares at it.

Kayla comes back in. "Awesome, food's here! Has everyone calmed down?"

Stef continues to stare at her bread as if she hasn't heard at all. She swallows. "I have something I need to tell you guys," Stef says. "But I don't want to make it a big deal."

"Okay," Kayla says, sitting down cautiously. "Look, if it's about what I was just saying, I'm sorry, I was being a dick. Please don't be mad at me, Stef."

Stef shakes her head. Remains silent for a moment. She knows how to build suspense. "I'm pregnant."

"Wow, congratulations!" Kayla says. "What'd Derek say?"

I hug her and ask about Wynn, if she's excited to be a big sister. "Are you feeling all right, Stef?"

The answers are Derek is happy, Wynn is not happy, and Stef is vomiting twice a day. "Let me know if I can do anything to help. Even just running an errand or bringing food by," I say. Kayla nods.

We chat a bit more about babies and mat leave and how life will be briefly different for Stef. "I don't even know if I remember all of what I did with Wynn. And Mamá helped so much. It's going to be so much harder to do it alone."

Kayla leans across the table, her shirt almost dipping into her drink. "Listen, you are not alone. One: you have Derek. Two: Wynn is a freaking teenager and can help out whether she likes it or not. Three: you have us. And we are immortal, so we're not going anywhere."

Stef laughs. "Maybe you all aren't the only ones. I feel Mamá sometimes, feel her around me."

Kayla grabs Stef's hand. "Like, you feel her cold, clammy hands around you?"

"No, not like that. Like in a way where I just feel her presence sometimes, like she's guiding me. Or earlier this month during Día de Muertos. We just did something small, since Wynn isn't that into it anymore, but it was nice to remember her and pray, even though you know I'm not praying to anyone when I pray, except maybe I am talking to her. And in a way, her way, she talks back. We went to visit her grave as well, laid out some food for her, set out some photos and marigolds. That part, Wynn was into. She flopped beside Mamá's grave and lay there for thirty minutes, even though the ground was hard and frozen. Derek said if she wanted we could see if we could find an empty grave for her! She was so serious when she lit a candle."

"So emo," Kayla says.

"I don't think she'll ever fully understand that it's supposed to be a celebration," Stef says. "She doesn't seem to be able to see death that way."

"I remember that age," I say. "You're sad and confused a lot."

"She's especially sad when she has to do family things," Stef says. "But I also think she remembers Mamá, even though she was so young when she died. And she sees death in the same way her friends at school do. A sad thing. I wish we could go down to Mexico and connect more with the culture. But I don't even know what family is left. Mamá didn't talk to her sisters by the time she died. And this baby will have even less of a connection. I wish this baby could have met her at least. All I can do is hope the baby will feel her like I feel her, like Wynn remembers."

"I know what you mean, Stef, about presence," I say. I think about Adrian, almost expect him to walk through the door. Or for an orb of light to appear in the corner of the restaurant. Spirit.

Stef leans forward, waiting for me to explain. But Kayla interrupts. "Paul, that's almost the first thing we've heard from you all night. What's been going on with you?"

I think about Selina, the notebook for therapy where I've been trying to explain everything that happened, to put it in order since it never feels clear to me—where, just like with my art, I'm circling, circling, never coming all the way to what's the truth. But I want to get there. "I got an email from Trevor. I guess he's coming home for the holidays."

"Derek never told me that!" Stef says.

"I just heard from him on the way here, so maybe he's just starting to get in touch with everyone," I say. "But it'll be good to see him."

"So you're going to get together?" Stef asks. She looks concerned.

"More like sleep together," Kayla says.

"I don't know. It's been a long time. At least we stayed friends."

"Exactly what you want with someone you used to hook up with," says Kayla, "friends."

Stef rolls her eyes. "It's different with them, and you know it."

"Oh, I know it. He's always been obsessed with Paul. Still didn't get her to move to the East Coast with him. Even though he begged." Kayla mimics the way Trevor's brows knit together when he gets really serious.

I laugh. "I wouldn't say he begged." But Trevor had said I could come with him, that we could move our tutoring business out east. But he still couldn't say it, what I needed to hear, about a future that glittered and shone. I'd still needed hope fed to me when he went away; I didn't know how to create my own. Maybe I was learning now. "Anyway, maybe that wasn't the best decision at the time." I swirl my drink in my glass, listen to the ice hit the sides. "I've been thinking lately that maybe Toronto isn't where I want to be for the rest of my life."

Kayla shakes her head. "No way. Paul, we know you. And you and Toronto, you're two peas in a pod. You're, like, made for Toronto. That's why you didn't leave before and you won't be able to leave now. You're not going anywhere. You're stuck in this city forever."

How It Happened
May 2016

Memories of the night before came to me, making my stomach burn. Fighting with Trevor after we left The Cave, again. My rage. My throat tightened. I didn't want to, I didn't want to ever, but I opened my eyes.

The morning was rude. I could tell by the way sun angled in through the blinds, how it tried to make sure it'd get my attention. A hangover pulsed behind my eyes, and I flung myself at the sink, filling glass after glass of water. There was no time to feel bad, no time to eat, even if I'd had food in the fridge. I had to get to therapy, and then I had to help Kayla—I'd barely have time to get from one place to another.

My therapist sat across from me in her office. One wall was lined with plants—hanging plants, a tall tree in a pot, a little wooden stand that housed pots of herbs on different levels. They could soak up the sun, which filtered through the windows that took up half of each wall in the office.

She liked to be silent until I said something.

"I saw him last night," I said.

"And how was it with Trevor?"

"Fine." Hunger rolled around in my stomach, my missed breakfast reminding me how awful I was. My headache had followed me into her office, not being able to escape the light. Even after showering, I thought I probably still smelled like the booze that was working its way through my pores. I was sure she could smell it on me.

She tugged at her sweater, pulled it around her chest, even though the heat in her office was incredible.

"It's difficult," I finally said, because that was one of the reasons I'd started going anyway. Because it'd been over two years of this nonsense with Trevor without anything really changing, without me being able to tell anyone about it, without having an easiness between us...I couldn't even say his name to my own therapist without feeling nervous. I'd tried swearing him off, avoiding him. I'd even tried to date someone else in the middle of all the back-and-forth nonsense. Sometimes things felt so good between us that anything seemed possible, that what was between us must be love—he'd even said so once when we were younger, after a bad fight where I thought I'd never see him again. But even that made me rage. In my life, nothing ever really changed. To me, life was a magnificent, terrifying beast that everyone else got to admire from afar, while I was stuck inside its jaws where it was rancid and impossible to move.

"How?"

"I wish I wasn't here," I said.

"What do you mean by that, Paulina? Alive?"

"No," I said, but my heart pounded and said YES. "I wish I wasn't here, in this office, in the same place I always am. That it wasn't always difficult."

"Well," my therapist said, and sat back in her chair.

I didn't say anything.

"Those sound like some really hard feelings. What are some things you could be doing to approach this difficulty?"

"I'm here."

"You're right, Paulina, you are. A great first step. So, let's start to really get into it. Where do you think this difficulty all stems from? What makes you want to keep working on things with Trevor?"

"It's not even just him. I think I'm just stuck." She waited for me to say something else. "I can't even imagine things being different. Maybe everything's just meant to be this way."

"You don't deserve difficulty, Paulina. No one does. Do you see any parallels to other men in your life? What was your relationship like with your father?"

"They were great. My parents were fine. They were happy together—they are happy together. I'll probably see them within a week. It has nothing to do with all of that, I told you."

"I know you told me. But Paulina, you tell me very little. I'm here to help you. To listen. And if there are things you haven't told me, that you need to talk about, I'm here to listen. No judgement. I know these things take time."

"Well, I'm seeing him today," I said. And I went through all of my anxieties about helping Kayla move, what I feared would happen when I showed up at Kayla's. I didn't want to hide my dreams from her, my past. I wanted to be open and brave and true and honourable. I wanted to be considered a good person. And when I thought of a good person, I thought of someone who had nothing to hide. But more than anything, I felt our sessions were showing me that you could be open while another part of yourself was still sealed up tight.

At the end of the session, we talked about money, how I didn't have any to pay her yet, but I would get paid soon, I would, and as she told me that was okay, her voice seemed choked, like she might be on the verge of tears, but the way she was sitting, the light hit her glasses so I couldn't see her eyes. She was the same age as Mom, and I often felt like she wanted to scoop me up and take me home, teach me about life in a new way, although I told her a million times that who I was had nothing to do with my parents—it was just the world and the way things happened.

She wrote the amount I owed down in her black book, where she sometimes jotted things down about our sessions but mostly just kept track of how much money I owed. She called her practice *equity-informed* and provided a sliding payment scale, the lowest of which was still too much for me. As she leaned back, the light moved from her, and I could see she hadn't been crying. I'm sure she felt very little for me.

Now

When Selina asks me to describe my family, I don't know what to say. Do I describe Adrian, the one person I felt was my family? Do I describe my parents, the way they have always been distant in the background? Aunt Dot, how she was there until she wasn't? Uncle Jim, how he started everything?

What does it mean to be family? Are you supposed to protect each other, love each other? A place of safety. But it's not true that you need to fear strangers the most, stolen children are often taken by family, and Adrian, he was hurt by family too. The boy was. And me... I was—

"How did the first assignment go, Paul?" Selina smiles at me through the screen. I imagine it to be genuine. I feel like I can relax with her.

"It was difficult," I admit.

"Did you just focus on your feelings? The impact and how you feel what you went through changed you?"

I'm sitting at my kitchen table, my binder full of notes from therapy beside me, next to *How It Happened*, my notebook full of writing about 2016 and the day everything happened and how it all twists together in my dreams. "I think so. How I feel isn't always clear."

"Has the writing been helping with that?"

"I think so."

"Do you want to share what you have? We'll come back to this and keep revisiting how you feel about everything, and how some of these thoughts change over time."

"Okay," I say and begin to read:

It's hard to say how I feel about the day everything happened. The thing is that everything between Adrian and me started when I was so young—our lives were one—that I don't remember a time before him, before our love and The Lighted City. I felt like it all was destiny. That I was meant to die with Adrian. That we were meant to be one together. It's hard not to feel that way for me. That the things that happened were meant to happen, that I'm some sort of lightning rod for them. And then, when things go bad in my life, I feel like it's deserved. Like it's because I'm a bad person, or unwanted. Sometimes it feels like if I'd let us both die that day, I would have saved us from all of the hurt that followed. I'd promised him to be loyal. If I'd stayed loyal, things would have been different. But I ruined it. I ruined it by thinking that I deserved more. And I continue to ruin everything around me. Bad things still happen. I can't stop being a lightning rod.

"This is one of those moments where I wish I could be in the same room with you. To hold space. I hope you feel that I'm holding space with you."

I hear her, but everything feels staticky in my ears. "It's fine," I say.

She nods slowly and purses her lips. She takes a moment to sit with me in silence and then breathes out. "When you read that, what part stands out for you the most?" she asks.

I feel shaky and raw. "I guess the line that I was meant to die with Adrian."

"What is it about that line?"

"Well, at the time, on the day, I had no idea that just under ten years later, Adrian would kill himself. We'd always promised each other that it would happen together."

"Did you say it in that way?"

"Well, no, it was all a game, until it wasn't. We were going to go to The Lighted City, walk into the flames, and go together."

"On that day, was that what was going to happen?"

"I have no idea. I can't remember all of it. But at the time, it seemed like it was just me."

"That you were going to be the only one killed?"

"Yeah."

"But then later you talk about loyalty. That if you were loyal to Adrian, things would have been different."

"I don't know. I know he saw it as a betrayal."

"What was a betrayal?"

"I'd fallen for someone. I was making a plan to get away from my family."

"And do you see that as disloyal?"

"I just think it was the cause of everything. His anger. That I hurt him when that wasn't my job."

"What was your job?"

"To love, to protect?"

"But you did love him. And 'protect'? Wasn't he three years older than you?"

"Yes, he was. But he had a harder life than I did. He needed someone to help him escape."

We continue to work through my assignment, questioning my thought process as we go. Eventually we make a list of "stuck points." Selina tells me these are beliefs about cause that have made it harder for me to recover. That everyone has some of these, but we want to see if processing what happened to me will change mine over time. We write them down in a log:

If I hadn't struggled, Adrian would still be alive.
If I was a good person, bad things wouldn't happen to me.
If I had continued to spend time only with Adrian, he wouldn't have hurt me.

With each one we add, I get more and more tired. In isolation, they all look ridiculous. When I say them out loud, I know they don't sound true. But when I look at them all on the page, my mind gets cloudy and I can't think anymore and all the fight goes out of me. And then I know, more than anything, what is really true:

If I try to move forward, bad things will happen.

How It Happened
May 2016

When I reached Kayla's, the U-Haul was already outside. I said hi to Kayla and hi to Stef, gave them both hugs, and then I gave Stef's daughter, Wynn, a hug, interrupting her collecting dandelions on the lawn. She hissed at me like a cat, so I left her alone to continue her game.

Kayla had lived in her top-floor apartment for two years and had been evicted, along with two couples. The landlord said they were moving in and going to renovate, but everyone knew they'd just renovate and then rent the three apartments for even more money. But there was nothing for Kayla to do except find an apartment that was further west and in a high-rise. She was still going to be paying more rent.

I helped Kayla organize the books and clothes she was giving away on the sidewalk, leaned a textbook against an old, broken kitchen chair. Kayla did nothing small, and the U-Haul was a long and high truck like I'd only seen families use. I picked up a lamp she said was going with her and started to move toward the truck.

And then I felt a shiver run through me. The sound of steps echoing against a metal floor. I walked over to the U-Haul, peered into its cavity, and there was Trevor, shoving a chair into the back.

"What, you're not going to say hi to me?" I said, leaning against the ramp. I forgot the lamp immediately, put it on the ground. My mouth began to twist into a smile, despite yesterday. *I'll see you tomorrow anyway*, he'd said.

"I'm just getting out," Trevor said. "I didn't even see you."

I looked around like I was already bored. I could see Wynn hissing even though I couldn't hear it from where I stood beside the U-Haul ramp. Stef bent down beside her daughter. Wynn crawled on all fours away from Stef, around the back of a tree, and then stretched her arms up the trunk, pulled a little at the bark with her nails. Stef laughed and licked her hands as if they were paws, putting one behind an ear in the clichéd way that grown-ups play. Wynn didn't mind though. She looked over at her cat-mother with interest, although in the next moment, she decided to flop sideways into the grass. A cat sunbathing.

My arms were stretched across the ramp by this point. I wanted to run down into the grass and flop beside Wynn, another sleeping cat, until my hangover and adulthood drifted away. Trevor started to walk down the ramp. "Hello?" he said, nudging my arm with his torn Converse. "Excuse me? I think I'm walking here."

I grabbed at the toe of his shoe. "Mine!" I said, laughing.

"Knock it off, Paulina," he said. "No one has time for your antics."

I lifted my arms and he walked down the ramp and then I was following him up the stairs into Kayla's apartment. "'No one has time for my antics'? Who even talks like that?"

"I was being facetious."

"Don't you think it's too early for that?"

"I think it's too early for you to berate me."

"Not even a little bit?"

Without discussion, we walked to opposite ends of the futon and picked it up.

"Careful," Kayla called from the other room, where she was rolling up posters: art prints, flyers for marches for racial and climate justice, noise artists she loved. "That futon has been in my family for decades. I'm pretty sure I was conceived on it."

"Gross," he said.

"I think it's romantic," I said.

"I'm going to put you two on separate duties if you can't get along," Kayla said, walking over to scold us. She put her hands on her hips.

I looked over at him and his eyes were dark and open. How could the light grey that appeared as he sparred with me be replaced by that other side of him in a moment? "We'll be good," he said. He nodded at me, and I wasn't sure what I'd done right or what I'd done wrong—all I know is that Trevor became different and got me to retreat, backwards down Kayla's stairs, giving me instructions gently, both of us laughing instead of getting angry when we bumped into the banister. When we got the couch into the U-Haul, he grabbed me into a hug, and he was so large and warm that all I could taste was his laundry detergent and all I could feel was his chest. No one could see us in there, and for a second, I thought this must be the way we both actually felt, like we wanted to move furniture together and hug and kiss.

My phone rang.

I pulled away from him.

It was Mom, and Adrian was dead.

How It Happened
The Lighted City

I was made for Adrian. This was told to me as a story as far back as I can remember.

I sit at Aunt Dot's kitchen table, barely five years old, dunking toaster-oven-cooked chicken fingers into cold, squeezed-out plum sauce pooled in the centre of my plate. "I knew you since before you were born," Adrian tells me.

"That's right," Aunt Dot says. "Your mom and dad sat here and told me and Jim and Adrian all about *you*. You weren't even making your mom big yet."

"Really?"

"Yep. And they called us when they knew you were a girl."

"I remember," says Adrian. "The phone rang and you said, 'Well, instead of Paul, it looks like they'll be having a Paulina.'"

"You were barely three, silly," Aunt Dot says. "I don't think you really remember. You just remember the stories."

"But I *am* a Paul," I say.

"But we didn't know that back then," says Adrian. "She means the name your parents were gonna call you. Anyway, you were born two days after my birthday, and Mom said that was because you were for me."

"I was so happy to have a child for Adrian to play with. I knew we weren't going to have any more, and your mom and dad weren't either. They were happy with their little girl."

"Did they think I was going to be a boy?"

"Oh, we were sure of it. She felt just like I did with Adrian, the whole time—the heartburn, the headaches, even down to the way she carried. We hoped you'd be a boy—just for a little bit—thinking it would be easier for you and Adrian to play. But as soon as I heard you were a girl, well, I knew you'd be perfect for Adrian too. We'd just need to make sure he didn't fall in love with you."

"Why not?"

"Because you're family. That sort of thing doesn't happen here."

"Oh."

"A long time ago, though, kings and queens were *only* allowed to marry family."

"Why?"

"I guess because they thought it kept the bloodline pure—also I think it was a way to keep money in the families. Marriage wasn't about love back then."

"Do you love Daddy? Is that why you married him?" Adrian asks.

"Get outside, go play. Paul didn't come over just to talk to me all day." And we run out the screen door, knowing Aunt Dot is too shy for our personal questions.

I can't imagine anyone loving Uncle Jim. He's the opposite of Adrian, big and mean. Adrian looks more like Dad did when he was a boy, from what I've seen in pictures. Slight. *Like a wisp*, Aunt Dot says. *Don't blow too hard or he'll float away.* And he has those same bright eyes you can't help but look at. Aunt Dot says Dad used to have girls follow him all over, at least until he met Mom and fell in love. I imagine it's how I would have looked, except blond, had I been a boy.

"I guess my mom is right," Adrian says once we're outside. "We can't get married."

"We can't get married *here*," I say. "We learned in school, there are lots of places where kings and queens still rule their countries. Maybe there's a place for us. Where we could be king and queen."

"A place just waiting for us."

"Yeah!"

We play kingdom. A lost city is out there, waiting for us. This is how The Lighted City begins. No fire, no suffering needed to reach it. Just a place we can call our own.

A car turns into Adrian's driveway. We watch from where we crouch in the long grass, still small enough to be completely hidden, like barn cats. Uncle Jim. Adrian begins to cry, silently. I pull him to me, even though he's three years older. He's all skin and bones anyway. I hold him and pretend all my skin is able to fall away until I am only Adrian, helping Adrian, making him not sad, comforting Adrian. This is why I was made. Yes, for Adrian to play with. But also for Adrian to love.

How It Happened
May 2016

Two Caledon houses were tied together by two roads, one coming straight at the other; kissing roads, Adrian and I called them. He would run from his and I would run from mine once we were both old enough to leave on our own—although if I'm being honest with you, our parents, especially his, never seemed to care about us being old enough. We'd meet at the edge of our roads, where pavement met dirt, and kick stones all the way up his dirt road until we reached his house. This house, more than mine, haunted me when I slept or biked to work. Thoughts rushing in again. Sometimes, depending on how I was feeling, that house drew me back to it. I've always had a problem with making myself hurt.

My parents came to get me and drove me north through the city and then through the country to our home in Caledon. "You need family at a time like this," they said to me, but in different ways. They couldn't help almost always being in unison. Two people stuck together so tight that nothing, not even a child, would break them apart. I didn't want to go back there, where we never talked about anything that had happened, or about how Aunt Dot and Adrian moved away to Vancouver just to keep us apart. Adrian had never tried to find me, even though I would have been so easy to find. I'd kept all my social media public. Sometimes I looked for him, but I never found him. He'd never liked computers or trends, never wanted to communicate with people our age except me. At least that's what I thought. And once I'd betrayed him, he was gone from me too.

Adrian had taken a shotgun and held it between his feet and used one toe to press the trigger while the gun was in his mouth. Aunt Dot had found him. But my parents didn't tell me that then. They didn't tell me anything then. They couldn't—Aunt Dot was always the only one to tell me anything, and I hadn't spoken to her in over nine years.

My parents tried to ask me about work, my friends. Usually they could get me talking about my friends, at least, but they didn't know any of their names, even though I'd told them so many times about Kayla and Stef and Derek. Even told them about a night or two at The Cave. They turned on the radio for the rest of the drive. A fragment of classical music played and then cut to an Amber Alert. "Aren't these supposed to be text messages now?" my parents asked each other.

"Amber Alert! Victim is Michelle Muñoz, seven years old. Missing since last night eight p.m. Suspect is Catalina Muñoz, last seen driving a white Toyota Corolla. Please contact Crime Stoppers, 416-222-8477. More updates to come."

"Is it always the parents?" my parents asked me.

I remembered a news story that followed me when I was a child. A girl had fallen asleep on a couch and someone had come in and taken her. She was my age at the time. Sometimes I fell asleep on our couch underneath the front window, like she had. But no one took me, even though more than anything I wanted to be carried away. She was murdered, though, by a family friend, not her parents. The story had made it hard for me to sleep at night, and I avoided dark windows, expecting to see someone on the other side, hunting for me. But for some reason, horrified as I was, I still wondered why no one had found me, scooped me up, and taken me away to a different life. Why no one noticed me. Not my parents. Not anyone. Except Adrian.

We pulled into the drive.

The driveway was flanked with lilac bushes, and birds darted between all the trees. There was a forest in the backyard. All of this had been my inspiration when I was younger, what would eventually lead me to paint and then to create sculpture. The wild turkeys pecking at their own reflections in windows or the sides of cars, singing frogs and stagnant lakes, the way a tree sagged before one of its dead branches was about to break. We walked inside, and I hugged my parents. I usually didn't hug either of them, but this day, I let them hug me for a long time.

"Paulina," they said. "Lina." My real name, Paul, never came out of their lips.

Even though I was born from my mother, Adrian made me. I couldn't imagine myself inside her, the thirty-eight weeks I was closer to her than she was to Dad, where she felt my every movement, my twists and turns. I came out before she was ready, she said to me; they hadn't decided on a name for a little girl.

But once I was out of her, equilibrium was restored. Mom and Dad thought and breathed and felt with the same mind again. "Paulina," they said, "not Paul. Paulina, Lina, our Leenie, teenie leenie."

But once Adrian and I were old enough to play, he saw me. Saw that I wasn't the stiff-dresses-in-school-pictures Paulina. "You're Paul," he said, and I nodded. I wanted to be like Adrian. Sometimes it felt like I'd been born in the wrong body: I had an image of myself with short, blond hair and a wiry body, climbing trees, exploring forests, being in charge. But then sometimes being a girl felt right. I spent nights picking at my skin when I was little, as I wondered who I was and why I was, until a little cut formed. This was before I discovered that punching things both released my anger and cut me up. I just wanted to be me. Just Paul. Someone who could dream full cities. Someone who could build.

"Paulina, what would you like to do?"

They showed me the flyer for Adrian's funeral, printed from a webpage, the URL still at the top of the page. The boy, the man in the picture, I didn't recognize him. His sharp, blue eyes hidden behind round framed glasses. His dark hair buzzed off, the softness gone. Only his thinness was as I remembered. His cheeks still looked gaunt. "Are we going?" I asked them.

"Us? No, no." I should have known. They never went on airplanes or travelled. Not because they were scared—something had always kept them homebound. Just as they couldn't leave each other, they would never leave Caledon. "But I talked to my sister," Dad said, breaking rank with Mom. "And she said you can come, if you like. If you want to come, you can stay with her, grieve."

"If you need to grieve," Mom said, sharply.

They joined again. "Let us know, and we'll pay for your flight. The service is Thursday."

"Okay," I told them. "I'll think about it." And then the morning's hangover and my sorrow caught up with me. The fact that Adrian— it was Adrian who was gone.

Before I went down to bed, my parents stopped me. "We know that Adrian... He was important to you. And I hope you understand why—"

"We really don't have to talk about it," I said. "I don't think you did anything wrong." But silently I counted the 107 months I'd been without any contact from Adrian.

My childhood bed moaned with my weight. Before I had moved in with my first boyfriend, at the beginning of college, my parents and I had moved my bedroom into a small room in the finished basement. It was fine for a while, and soon I was gone anyway. Now when I returned home, the same fear of the dark I'd had when I was four years old returned. I rolled over on my side. Even though I couldn't see it, I knew the wall in front of me held a Man Ray quote about Dadaism. I'd taped it there when I was seventeen. Adrian had never liked art, just making things, and while he inspired me, this world was my own. I reached out and felt for the tape and the paper, trying to ground myself in this room that felt no longer mine. I'd never believed in ghosts before Adrian died, but I imagined the ghost of Adrian flying in through the window and settling beside my bed, watching me. I grabbed my bedspread and walked upstairs. I slept on the couch until the living room windows were pierced by the light of early morning.

✧

May was always hard for me—the day that everything happened getting closer and closer until we reached the twenty-fourth. Prom week. Every year, I tried to run away from it and couldn't. I wondered if he felt it approaching every year too, just a couple weeks before our birthdays two days apart; if it pressed on him, like it did me; if that was what had moved him to death.

During the day, I tagged along with my parents while they bought things, and I tried not to think about that day or about our birthdays. But spending time with them just made me hurt in a different way. I saw the way money fell from their hands: wine, food, a new firepit for outside. Dad bent over and examined the tag on a new barbeque at a hardware store. I knew I should ask them, but I also knew what the answer would be. "You need to stand on your own feet, Paulina." My independence was another thing they required of me: I needed to ask very little of them.

✧

That evening, I slipped out the screen door, tying my shoes once I was outside. Little bits of sun poked through the trees. The days were getting longer and longer. Down my road, then along another winding dirt road, I walked to where Adrian had once lived, a sprawling run-down bungalow, opening up to a backyard and that field of long, constantly dry grass.

I climbed the wooden fence that bordered the property and dropped over to the other side. I didn't know who lived there now, but the house still looked the same, like it needed a new roof, like at any moment it would fall in on itself. I cut through the grass, crouching over so that no one could see me from the house. The large tree in the middle of the field was our main clubhouse. We climbed it and it shaded us. I needed to go to it. I finally reached the tree, tapped the trunk. Home free. The trunk had a split in the centre.

My brain was seared with memories. Playing in the yard, building up The Lighted City around the tree. The tree was so many things to us: clubhouse, hiding place, and, on that final day, the thing that kept me trapped, stuck with Adrian. I gently rapped the trunk with my knuckles again, felt how the scars created a barrier between skin and bark. I could so easily let go, rip my skin open, not feel what I was feeling, had been feeling since Mom called with the news. All the pain of Adrian, losing Adrian, losing Adrian again. I began to cry instead of hurting myself, beside the tree. I only wanted to remember our play, those good times together, but I always had the memory of the tree on fire, of me naked, of Adrian being taken away.

I heard the screen door to the back porch open, but with dark setting in, I couldn't see if a figure had emerged from the house. I crouched, quiet. Hoped the gathering darkness was enough to hide me. I crept along, steady and quiet in the grass, the way Adrian had taught me—heel, toe, heel, toe, silent—until I reached the wooden fence. The porch lights went on. Was someone staying there? I ducked under the fence and bolted down Adrian's road until I got to my own, safe. As I walked down the road toward home—my parents' home, never truly mine—my heart beat violently in me, the wildness I could never quite get out.

And I know it was my mistake, picking up when I saw the word *Home* on my phone's screen, my mistake that I'd only taken a step or two toward the U-Haul ramp, away from Trevor. "It's Adrian," she said.

His name enough to knock the wind out of me.

"What?" I said, but I said it again and again. I wanted the information, no matter what.

"Oh, Paulina, I'm so sorry. He's dead. He died."

"No."

"I know, Lina."

"How?" I said, but meant *why*.

She was silent for a moment. "He killed himself."

I hung up the phone and went over to my bike, picked it up, ready to bike away, get away from there. Nothing needed to be said—I could just go home and people would think what they wanted to, that I felt too sick, that Trevor and I were fighting too much. I didn't care. I just needed to be alone, away from there.

Wynn jumped in front of my bike. "Halt, demon!" she said, and I had to press my brakes so hard that I slid off my seat and my bike fell sideways on top of me. Trevor ran over and lifted my bike off me and Wynn ran to get her mom, and then I was in his arms. Only when I was wrapped up did I know I was crying.

"What is it? Are you okay? Does anything hurt?" he asked.

"It's my cousin," I said. Everyone had gathered around. "It's just my cousin, he died."

Then I had to hear everyone moaning and asking if they could do anything, and I had to explain, I just wanted to go, that if everyone just could let me go I'd be fine, that I hadn't even wanted to say anything, just when I fell I bit my tongue and tasted blood and then mentioned it, that he died, and could everyone let me go home, please.

"I'll probably go to Caledon for a bit," I said to Trevor under my breath. He just nodded and watched me bike away.

And it was unclear to me how the building up of these events allowed me to say the words "my cousin" out loud, as if the shock of his death was enough to will those words out of me. Now even Trevor knew. Normally, I wouldn't have told anybody. But I've never been convinced that I live the better way.

Now

When I read that part of my notebook to Selina later, she wants me to talk about it. About what I mean by living a better way. About why I mentioned that belief at the same time I described finding out about Adrian's death. "You used the present, 'live.' Do you still feel that way?" I tell her that I think there are many ways to live, but that, even if you are a person who lives with openness, eventually the world pins you in so that you are stuck with only one way of being.

"How would you describe openness?" she wants to know.

"I guess…I don't know that I would describe myself as an open person, in that I don't want to always share about myself. I'm fine to sit back while my friends share their news, and then maybe joke around or talk about that instead. But I mean, not thinking there is only one right way to be, being open to other ways of seeing the world."

"I find it interesting that you describe openness in this way, yet you also think that something about the way people are means they can't change. How did you describe it?" I see her glance off-screen, down at a notebook. "'The world pins you in so you are stuck with only one way of being.' Do you think that people can't change?"

"Well, I just find that a lot of the same things happen over and over. People get hurt. People see and handle the world or stress in the same way, again and again."

"What happens when they recognize that, do you think?"

"I'm not sure. I know that's how things happen, but it doesn't stop me from being the way that I am. I will always be the way I am."

"Do you think 'People can't change' might be a central belief for you?"

"I guess."

"Let's add it to the list."

I add *People can't change* to my list of "stuck points." I've learned that when we add something to the list, it means that Selina thinks it is a thing I believe but that isn't quite true. But I only believe things that I've seen, felt, experienced. I don't just make things up.

In this way, I'm more open, by my definition, than Selina is being—Selina who is prescribing that I should change my beliefs. I know that we see the world differently, and I'm okay with that. In fact, I'd love to continue talking with her about it, about what makes a person a person and what makes them believe what they believe and if she's ever truly met a person who changed. But I don't like adding things to the list.

"Can we end early today?" I ask. "I have a headache."

"Oh, of course, Paul. But I want to remind you that we still haven't discussed your index trauma. Have you written it yet?"

The day everything happened. May 24. The Lighted City. I still haven't gone there. When I write about it, it's not clear, just pieces of what it was like to play.

"No, not yet. I just think—the notebook, it's been working for me. I don't want to mess it up."

"Well, we have a certain process we go through for this treatment. It's been developed over time and tested with a lot of clients. We know it can work and help so that your nightmares, the feelings you experience, they aren't so bad anymore. If the notebook is working for you, that's great—we want to help you develop coping mechanisms that you can use on your own to feel better—but we also should be following the process."

"I just need a little bit longer. There's just so much."

"This week, try to write about it. You don't need to read it to me. It can just be for you. We want to make it so the index trauma has less power, less weight. You'll record yourself reading it and listen to it each day, record your feelings about it, journal if that works for you. But pay attention to what's happening in your body. Over time, it will get easier. The memory will have less heat. That's the exposure."

"So, I don't have to send it to you?"

"Only if you want to. Some treatments include reading together so we can work through it in session, but we're more concerned with the impact of what happened and working through that. But if you want to share it with me, I'm open to it. You can always share whatever you need to with me."

I nod. "I'll try."

After we get off the session, I open a new bottle of wine. I know I shouldn't, that maybe I should just call Kayla or Stef instead. Write Trevor an email or see if he's around to FaceTime. Prepare a lesson. Draw. But all I want to do is drink.

How It Happened
The Lighted City

"The Lighted City has been holding its breath this whole time, waiting for us. Once you get inside the city walls, everything glows, lit by a blazing tree in the town's centre. But they need you, Paul, just like we always knew. The city's people stay inside their houses, in the dark. They are waiting for us, Paul. Once their king and queen return, they will be able to leave their houses and take a branch from the tree and bring fire into their homes. They are so cold now. They are hungry, Paul. We can't let them be cold and dark and alone forever. You can't just let them starve. They need us, Paul, like I need you. I'm so happy I have you.

"You're the one they really want. That's why you can go alone. I'm nothing to them. But I promise, I'll come into the fire after you. You just have to go first. Once their houses are lit, you can help them. We'll build the city bigger and better than it ever was. We'll be able to take over whatever we want, and we'll always be safe behind the city walls. Nothing will ever hurt us, Paul. Nothing can, as long as I have you. You've become so good at building, you'll be able to teach them how to do everything I've shown you. You've always known how to teach them, how to explain things. I never can, not like you. You'll show them what I've shown you.

"Okay, step closer to the tree. Are you ready to go with me, Paul? Are you ready to be together, finally, forever? I never want to be apart. I don't know why you thought you could be with him, when I've always been here for you, it's always been us, Paul, I can't remember when it wasn't. Don't be afraid. It's just a little rope. I thought you liked it. You always liked The Lighted City. We've always wanted to go, and now it's time, Paul. I came into this world first, but now I'll leave it second, your turn to be first. Go ahead. The people only get light if there is a king and queen. The two of us. There together."

How It Happened
May 2016

My apartment hadn't changed while I was in Caledon. It was still what Kayla called a "one bedroom, barely," with no door separating the kitchen/living area from the bedroom. I'd tacked a curtain up to give the sense of division. My things still spilled from every shelf. Books were stacked beside my bed in a tower with a glass of water on top of it. You had to be creative when you had very little money. A relationship I'd had when Trevor and I were on a break had cleaned me out, as I'd always paid for myself and my ex whenever we went anywhere. While we'd gotten the cramped place together, soon I was living there on my own, covering the whole rent.

Other than drinking, I wasn't bad with money. I ate simply and efficiently. I didn't buy anything that I'd consider a waste. I swapped clothes with Kayla and Stef. Kayla brought me things she made— she knit and sewed with her uncontrollable energy. It was one of the ways she showed her friends she cared. But although I found ways to make things easier, I had rent to pay, which took almost all of my monthly money, along with therapy. But without money, I wasn't bored. My imagination entertained me most of the time.

Poster boards leaned against the walls with half-drawn things or photos of things I wanted to mix together to make something new.

The two years I had at Sheridan for illustration, before I ran out of money and hope and moved to the city, were driven by wanting to do something original. But classes were full of other people wanting to be original, too, and everything that came out of their mouths sounded the same. I wanted to help them break their bad habits. I wanted to help them become someone real, rather than only a fragment of who they thought they were expected to be. So I helped the others in the class create, forgot about my own work, found everyone materials or whatever they needed.

Away from school and in Toronto, I started creating again. I drew a boy who looked like a monster, his face flickering somewhere between mine and Adrian's, a row of sharp teeth protruding from his mouth, a body that became a blob that could morph into whatever the monster desired. In wordless comics, the monster went from one corner of a city to another, in search of someone to love. The comics weren't anything good, but at least they were something.

But when I started to teach, it seemed almost impossible to do both at once—the creating tied to my ego, the teaching tied to a desire for selflessness, to bringing other people up. Every day, the first thing I saw in the morning was my ego, bits of art I'd never completed. It killed me. It really did. I'd tried to throw them out so many times.

I sat on my bed and pulled out the printout that my parents had given me for Adrian's service. It would be Thursday, and I had work scheduled all week long, but the girl who covered weekends at Artastic! owed me a favour, and my boss at Drop 'n Draw was always willing to cover if it meant they saved a buck on my pay. But I didn't know if I could afford a few days' less pay. I was waiting for my cheque from Artastic!, which was already late.

I looked at Adrian's unfamiliar face. Even though he was twenty when it all happened, he'd still looked like the boy I'd grown up with then. Not like this.

Adrian James Tremblay

Adrian James Tremblay at 29 years of age, on May 13, 2016, passed away after a long and courageous struggle with his mental health.

    Adrian was loved by the Vancouver community and known for his work at his stepmother's healing centre and for his volunteer work with others experiencing complex mental illness and healing from childhood trauma. For the past seven years, Adrian volunteered every Saturday at a downtown food bank, where his leadership and dedication were noticed and appreciated, winning him a Civic Volunteer Award in 2014.

    With those he helped, Adrian was open about his own trauma, and his loss by suicide will be felt by those in his community, as by his doting mother, Dorothea Tremblay, and his stepmother, April Casey. A short service for Adrian will be held at the Sea Healing Centre on Quebec Street on Thursday, May 19, at 11 a.m. In lieu of flowers, please send donations to the BC Crisis Centre.

The Adrian I remembered only had me. He didn't volunteer or meet people or speak about what he was going through. Everything we experienced was a secret, and on top of that secret, I also had to keep the secret of what he was going through at home with his father. Who was this Adrian who was loved by a "community"? Who spoke openly about his past experiences as if they couldn't hurt him? And did he talk about me? Was there a whole group of people who knew about me and The Lighted City and everything that had happened between us? Eventually, all those things had hurt him, or he wouldn't be gone. Or maybe Adrian was just tired of waiting for me and had slipped off to The Lighted City on his own.

I'd dreamed of finding Adrian so many times, of having a way to contact him, but I hadn't been able to find him online and no one had told me where he'd moved to. Now I had a chance: a path to Adrian. I needed to go. I messaged Dad to let him know to book the ticket. I figured I could leave after work on Tuesday or on Wednesday morning and still get there in time for the funeral. Maybe I'd even stay an extra day or two. See where Adrian had lived. Maybe I could feel him there.

I put the obituary away and lay in my bed, forgetting to take off my clothes. My phone beeped, but it was Trevor, not Dad.

While Trevor had been silent the day and half when I was in Caledon, he could only handle silence for a certain amount of time before he'd reach out. Better if I never did. He didn't like me if I was too eager.

Hope you're ok. Come over if you're home.

I went over to his place in the Junction. He lived in the top two floors of a house, the lower floor rented out to a married couple. His main floor had a large living room, balcony, and kitchen, and the top floor had a bathroom and two bedrooms crammed into it, one taken by Trevor and the other by his roommate, Kyle. It would have been a great place for parties, but Trevor preferred solitude. "I need to preserve the quiet of my space for my writing," he said. And his roommate was often gone, staying with his boyfriend.

I climbed the steps I knew too well. When he saw me, he covered my face with kisses, breathed heavily into my ear and said, "I know how you feel," ran his hands up and under my shirt and touched my breasts the way he knew I liked. Together we walked up the steps from his living room to his bedroom and fell into his bed, and I actually didn't think about Adrian or grief. He held my wrists together and licked my nipples and all I thought about was pleasure.

In the morning, I stared at his cheek and the side of his face. I ran my hand along the thickness of the muscles in his arm. When he woke, he pulled me into him and I lay contained on his chest, although my thoughts were roving—through the grief to Vancouver and Adrian and back again, worrying about money and hoping he'd make us coffee and breakfast. Without my Artastic! pay, I was out of my monthly money and had no groceries at home.

Trevor pushed me off him and got out of bed, went to the bathroom, ran the shower. "Can I come?" I called after him.

"If you want," he said. I walked from his bedroom to the bathroom. His roommate had already gone off to work. Trevor didn't work, except on his writing. He claimed to have funding to work on his first book, and he sometimes wrote content for blogs, if he felt money was getting tight. Not that it paid much. He, like me, never bought new clothes and was constantly scrounging, trying to make it so that the money his dad left him would last. I was still worried about breakfast, my stomach churning with hunger, but I didn't want to ask.

Inside the shower, Trevor stared at the water faucet rather than at me. I stole little glances at his penis, which hung floppy and small in front of him. "Not turned on this morning?" I said.

"I'm taking a shower."

"Shower sex," I said, and wrapped my arms around him. I loved doing that, feeling how my arms could encircle all of him, even though he was so much taller and bigger than me.

He laughed and kissed my forehead and pushed back my wet hair, all the gold gone, damp dark brown now, and directed the shower head right at me so water ran down my face. "You know, I'm not much of a fan."

"I heard around town that you're a fan of me."

"Who said that?"

"It's in all the tabloids."

"What are you talking about, Paulina?" But Trevor was hard now and cupping my breasts in his hands and then his mouth was on mine and his tongue was on mine and I could taste the mineral sweetness of the water coursing over us. He flipped me around and I bent over and put my hand against the shower wall and he pushed his dick into me, and only I came like that, so then he picked me up, still dripping wet, and brought me over to the bed where he tossed me and pulled a condom out of his drawer and rolled it on over his dick, which was now perfect, and then we went at it until we were both spent and sore, having already had sex twice the night before.

"Fuck," he said.

"I know." I wanted to ask why things were the way they were with us when this part was always so right, when our good days were always the best days. But, of course, I didn't say anything, and we heard the sound of running water, the shower still on. He laughed, and it was so good to hear him laugh. Sometimes I forgot how sad he seemed most of time until he laughed and broke his own moody spell. He got out of bed and turned off the shower in the bathroom and came back in. He pulled on his briefs, tight and black, his T-shirt, his hoodie, his jeans. I cherished everything he put on himself, because it was his.

"You want coffee, or what?" he said.

"Yeah," I said. I got up and pulled on the same clothes I'd worn the night before, still too unsure of things to ever pack an overnight bag. This time had felt different, though. We'd watched a movie instead of going out drinking with everyone at The Cave and sneaking off home together. This left both of us less tense, and also, we drank less and woke up to a hangoverless morning. He'd also seemed careful with me, briefly asking about Caledon and hinting about Adrian and death, but trying not to upset me. I wasn't used to him trying to be tender.

We went down the stairs to his kitchen, and he opened the refrigerator and picked up the carton of milk. He checked the expiry and then opened the carton and sniffed.

"Milk's gone bad," he said. "That's how you like your coffee, right? I guess we could go out? Grab breakfast or something?"

"Oh," I said. I imagined the moment we'd be needing to pay, and me saying that no I couldn't pay, that I was out of cash. That it'd force him to pay, and this would surely annoy him. Especially since he always watched his money himself. "I'm good with black."

"Let's go out. There's a good place around the corner."

"I can't," I said. "I have to stop by Stef's."

"Why didn't you tell me before?" he asked. He took a big step back and looked at me, resting his hands on top of his head, like he always did when I said something like this.

"I forgot, sorry."

"Whatever," he said, and put on water to boil. He pulled out coffee beans and put them in the grinder. The grinder whirred and whirred, the sound the way my stomach was feeling, and my head. I was so hungry. He emptied the ground coffee into the Bodum, and we waited in silence for the kettle to whistle. The whistle finally let itself go, piercing the air, and he poured the hot water over the coffee grounds, stirred. And then, before waiting long enough, he plunged it. He took out two mugs from the cupboard and poured weak coffee into them and handed me the one I knew was his favourite. Then he went over to the bookshelf, scanned the titles, finally grabbed a book from a stack on the table. He walked past me and went upstairs, not asking me to follow. A punishment.

I drank my coffee quickly and washed the mug in the sink and then cleaned the Bodum and put all of his clean dishes away and wiped the counter and emptied the milk carton and flattened the carton and put it under the sink with the rest of the recycling. I found an old receipt hanging out on the corner of a table, smushed up beside books I wished were mine, in an apartment where I wished I lived with him, Trevor, my love to whom I barely knew how to speak. I wrote *Sorry, Trevor*, and I wanted to write something else, but didn't, and I put the note under the corner of the Bodum. Then I left.

In the middle of the night, Trevor had shaken me awake with his eyes still closed. "Paulina, you okay?" Normally we slept back to back, both being restless sleepers, but he pulled me over to him. Maybe he'd heard me call out with a nightmare. "Are you okay?"

"I'm okay," I said. "Are you okay?" But I whispered it into his chest. And we slept like that, snuggled up, until it was morning and time for shower sex.

I texted Stef telling her I needed to come by, and I needed to eat. She texted back that she was there. Wynn had already gone off to school and she was alone in the apartment and she would love to see me and have me distract her from her marking. I sent her an emoji of a balloon.

I loved the walk from Trevor's to Stef's. It was most beautiful in the fall with leaves falling down everywhere from old Toronto trees, but May had its own charms. Flowers bloomed in the small square gardens in front of people's houses along Trevor's street, the houses large and either divided up into apartments like his or full of rich families I could barely imagine. I walked north to Dundas Street and peered in the windows of shops in the Junction, dreaming of books and art supplies I couldn't currently afford.

When I'd moved to the city, I'd thought everything would be different. Every time we'd visited Toronto as a child, I would miss Adrian terribly, sometimes even calling him from the hotel Dad had a conference at. But I never told him that I looked at sun glinting off the blue glass of skyscrapers and it lit up a place where he didn't exist and his problems didn't exist, where someone didn't need me the way he needed me. That maybe The Lighted City, for me, was a place where he wasn't. Where I was free to discover who I was without him. I always felt so guilty after. When we were younger, he'd needed someone to hold and to hold him back and tell him he was good. Of course, that wasn't how it remained.

But the memories of my childhood were even in Toronto. I couldn't escape them. And the things I'd originally fallen in love with there, they were hard to reach. Most days, if I biked downtown, I couldn't even catch a glimmer from the skyscrapers. There were other things: the lake that stretched along the south of the city, which at times I'd bike along when my thoughts felt like they were pressing at every piece of my skull. I'd thought I would be painting in Toronto, but instead I was working for art centres trying to teach children to love art the way I did. Even working two jobs, I could barely afford anything and I always needed more hours to justify living in my apartment without a roommate. It left me with no time for anything creative, only for picking interesting things like necklaces or glass off the street like a bored magpie in hopes of making a project that was still unseen.

Stef was already making eggs and fried tomatoes when I let myself into her main floor apartment, toast in the toaster. "You're the best," I told her, and she smiled at me.

"Will you quit?" she asked after I told her about Artastic! and how I hadn't been paid this month. "What if they don't pay you?"

"I don't know what I could do. I don't get enough hours at Drop 'n Draw. It's two days a week right now, and only a couple hours. Barely worth the travel. But, like, I don't even think I could do anything else... I don't really have experience."

"Can I lend you some money?" Stef asked. Things were easier for her now that she was teaching more, even though the only way she made it work was by teaching at two separate colleges, sometimes getting up at four in the morning to prep and get to her first class in the morning and not finishing up until after dinner, or later. She'd spoken to her chair at one of the colleges about going on full-time, but he told her that without a master's, she didn't have a shot, no matter how great a teacher he thought she was. Her partner, Derek, was a software developer, one of the only people around us who had a career that was relatively stable and brought in money. Wynn cost more and more as she grew, and their rent kept going up and up, but between the two of them, they were making it work. They were at least able to pretend that they weren't entirely struggling.

"No, Stef, it's fine."

"You've done a lot for me, Paul," she said. I wasn't really sure what she meant, but I was glad that she thought that. I had only been a friend to her over the years, and that was something I'd maybe needed more than her.

She closed her laptop.

"You marking away?"

"Procrastinating away. I was reading this article about the '20 Big Questions in Science,' what is left for science to answer. The short summary is that we've come a long way, but when it comes to answering questions about life and existence, there is still a lot we don't know."

"Give me a question."

"Why do we dream? It's still talking about Freud as if he's valid, but the answer they give is that we still don't know why we dream."

"I think it's breaking through to another dimension," I said.

"Maybe! That could be a theory. Freud says it's wish fulfillment."

"Then what about nightmares?"

"Well, he thought everything went back to sex, so maybe it's got something to do with that?"

"You think my sex is full of nightmares?"

"Is it?"

"Hmm, my nightmares are full of sex."

"Other people think it's the random firings of the brain, but now they think it's about learning, replaying waking life in dreams, processing all the stimulus from the day so you can learn, grow, heal, do better at tasks."

"Kayla was in my dream last night." I'd had horrible nightmares, curled up beside Trevor, disrupted only when he stirred.

"Really?"

"Yeah. My nightmares are back."

Stef thought my nightmares were connected to a night out we'd had in 2014. A stranger had taken me home and roofied me. The really fucked-up part was that I'd liked him when I met him. We had the same name, Paul, and it seemed romantic until I woke up in the morning naked in a hallway, barely knowing who I was. One more piece of my past. We didn't talk about it much, but right after it happened, she'd suggested I see a therapist, had even found me someone with an adjustable pay scale. The therapist I was still seeing a couple years later, by then trying to figure out the way I felt about Trevor and why I reacted the way I did to his moods or something he said or something he didn't say. I'd sworn her to secrecy despite the way everyone else at The Cave talked about their therapists like they were their best friends. But she didn't understand the way that nightmares were rarely about one thing, and sometimes for people bad things happened again and again and again. At the time, I felt that I attracted these things to me like a magnet, that something about who I was made them happen, and that people who were different from me led a charmed life where nothing could touch them. I don't want to believe that anymore.

"They'll go away again, you know that."

"I was in this room, and I was alone and chained to a bed, and then all of these men came in to torture me. I strained to get away, but I couldn't."

"Jesus."

I left out the part about how Trevor had also been in my dream. I couldn't give away anything about our relationship, or he might not want to be with me for good. In the dream, he sat in the corner, watching and not doing anything, as if all his limbs were too heavy for him to lift. Adrian had come in, his bright blue eyes all I could focus on while thinking, *You're dead.* I also left out the part where I was naked.

"A woman came in, and all the men were gone, as if they'd never been there at all. No one was there anymore, except the woman. I couldn't see her face. She lit a cigarette, and for a second, I could see her face in the flame, and it was Kayla. She said, 'They're all lying to you, Paul,' and then she put her cigarette out on me and said, 'Especially him.' But she wouldn't tell me who she was talking about."

"Well, that's definitely a nightmare," Stef said, and got up to pour us both more coffee. "It's probably about what happened to you, don't you think?"

"Yeah, maybe."

"It's hard to lose someone," she said. "It can stir all sorts of things up." She waited to see if I would say anything more, sipped her coffee watching me. When it was clear that I was clamming up, she asked, "Do you trust Kayla? Do you think your dream has anything to do with that?"

"I mean, it was just a dream," I said.

"Sometimes I trust her," she said, "but sometimes I worry. It's like I can see her skating around this dark hole, and she keeps getting closer and she gets more excited the closer she gets, and she's the only one who doesn't know that if she falls in, she's gone forever."

"I know what you mean," I said, but Kayla seemed happy to me. If anything, she seemed too happy, obsessed with living her life as much as possible. She almost never talked about anything negative, unless you got her onto the topic of microaggressions when she was drunk. She could have a singular focus when she grabbed onto a goal, whether that was a date for the night or having as much fun as humanly possible, or even doing things differently at work, from what I heard of her reporting back about her "tedious-as-fuck desk job." I could see why that would scare Stef, though. Stef had always done everything right since having Wynn. Even at The Cave, she was careful—to not drink too much, to not say something she'd regret, to not stay out too late. The more she worried, the more drawn and thin she got, like each worry feasted itself on the food in her stomach.

We spent the rest of the morning talking. Stef was always my favourite to talk to, since she was interested in so many different things. She told me about how she'd started teaching Wynn Spanish, but she wished she could teach her Russian. She barely remembered any of the Cyrillic alphabet. Her father had emigrated from Russia to Canada, where he'd met Stef's mother, who was second-generation Mexican-Canadian. Stef often spoke of their love for each other and how it was able to bypass cultural differences. Stef's mother had sympathized with her husband's experiences, having seen her parents struggle in a similar way: with bigotry, the language, and not feeling a sense of belonging. He could belong with her and Stef now. He'd left too early for Stef to hold onto the language, fallen in love with someone else as quickly as he had her mother, and started a family elsewhere. But Stef still held onto those early days, where she loved her father and he loved both her and her mother, and they were a family like Derek, Wynn, and her. Someone passing by speaking Russian might stir up a memory of her father, of a grandmother and grandfather she never met in person, without any understanding but a feeling. But Stef's Spanish was as perfect as her English. She often taught courses in both.

Stef's original plan had been to only speak to Wynn in Spanish, wanting her to have that connection to her heritage, but Wynn's dad had been monolingual and so was Derek. Combined with

Wynn's reluctance to speak in general, the Spanish-language learning was only now beginning.

And I was learning from these conversations, too, always felt I was learning so much from Stef, despite us being right around the same age. Kayla only liked to talk about romance and people, the parties she went to, nights out that became days out that became nights out. That was good for me in another way, keeping me in the now, but Stef made me feel like there were multitudes to everyone I knew.

We ate as we talked, and finally I was full, and all the ideas we talked about filled my head up with things that didn't have to do with Trevor. Or how I'd disappointed him, made him pull away from me again. I didn't even think about Adrian, for a bit at least. Although as soon as there was a lull in the conversation, there was a prickling behind my eyelids, a heaviness in my chest.

"I have to run to No Frills. Come with?"

We walked down Dundas in only our T-shirts and jeans. Summer would be coming soon.

At No Frills, Stef crammed a quarter into the shopping cart release, and we entered the store. She picked up packages of hummus and muffins and tortillas and tomatoes to replace the ones she fried for breakfast. She bought sandwich meat and bread and three types of cheese. When we left the grocery store, Stef handed me two of the bags. "Here. Half of this stuff is for you."

I hugged her. Even if I wouldn't take her money, she'd still found a way to help me out.

After I put the groceries away at home and ate a sandwich, my stomach started to churn. Inside my stomach, a tree was on fire, trying to burn its way out.

Now

I do my usual ravine walk, this one along the Humber River. I want to walk all of them, no matter the weather. I've told myself it's about my art, gathering materials to create the installation I've been working on. But maybe it's also about leaning into memory instead of away from it, a pilgrimage through memory, honourable instead of horrifying.

I think about 2016, kicking at the ice that makes the path slick. I pretend that if I can chip it, the ice won't be able to make me fall. I think about the boy. When I think about him, I try not to think about finding him. What I want to do is let my imagination make him alive again. Where would he have been during May, during the part I just wrote down in *How It Happened*? At that point, the boy would have still been a boy. I imagine him being unlike Adrian and me, more like the kids I teach. A type of wholesomeness you either have or you don't. Maybe he was friends with the kid who lived next door. When they wrote about him in the newspaper, they said he was smart and had been doing work after school as part of a gifted program. He was known for a good imagination and being shy with kids, but kind.

At this point, he was still climbing trees. He was playing all afternoon and then coming home to dinner, to a mother and grandmother who loved him, who wrapped him in their arms.

They were asked time and time again, "Why didn't you notice when he was gone? Why did you wait so long to call?" The police figured he must have gone missing on the way home from school. But I don't want to think about that. In May, before I went to the funeral, he was somewhere very alive, connected to the world through thought and movement and play.

How It Happened
May 2016

I needed to get to work, and all I could find was nickels. It would take sixty nickels to pay for my subway fare. I opened my desk drawers and dug through pencils and notepads and half-drawn faces on paper I should have discarded. I threw chargers on my floor, tangled cords left over from digital cameras that were now broken. At the back of one of the drawers I found what I was looking for, an old change purse I always forgot about with an elephant stamped on it. Inside were two toonies. That'd get me to work and my paycheque.

I loved work—loved the kids. Artastic! was in a converted dance studio space above a children's boutique. Behind it, a parking lot stretched for all the parents driving their "little ones." The area and clients were bougie, but still, I loved it. Loved the way the kids' hands all reached for the back of my shirt when they needed something, surrounding me, "Paul, can you help me?" I showed them how to spread glitter-glue with a piece of paper if they didn't want to get their hands dirty. I showed them how to use the edge of a crayon to make a sharp dot of pure colour. I held down the piece of paper for a student as he erased. "See, teamwork!" I said. Everyone got a high-five before they left, and I felt all those high-fives on the way home each day. I took photos of their work for my portfolio, even though I knew no one really cared if some artist who was barely an artist made up some silly projects kids could do.

The last student left and I said goodbye to his mother and sister and to him. "High-five!" he screamed, even though we'd done three high-fives that day. We high-fived again and I locked the door behind them and went into the office. All the teachers had folders in a little filing cabinet for cheques and messages, and I opened mine, and there was no paycheque there. I got paid fifty dollars per class, and I was now owed more than five hundred dollars from this pay cycle. The last time I'd gotten paid was right before my rent came out, and soon, rent would be due again. I hadn't seen my boss in two weeks.

I messaged Artastic!'s weekend instructor, Lai. She was around my age, maybe a little younger. I guessed my boss figured that any-one with more experience than us would be able to work out what a scam she had going: we put hours into our prep and developing programs and were only paid for the couple hours a day we were in the centre. Still, at twenty-five dollars an hour and without having a completed degree, I'd never be able to turn down a job like that.

Hey are you looking to pick up extra hours this week at all?

Sure! I'm broke af. When?

Wed–Friday. I have to go to Van for a funeral.

Yeah I can cover for you, no problem. Are the cheques in?

No. Have you been able to get through?

Goes to voicemail when I call her.

Doesn't she know we need to eat?

The other instructor was typing. I saw her three dots appear and then disappear. Appear then disappear. She never replied. I locked up the centre and started my walk home. It would take hours. I should've brought my bike. Maybe if I had, I would have avoided so much: Nik, the ravine, the boy. But you can't change the past by looking at it.

The sun was setting, casting the parking lot in navy shadows as the streetlights decided whether they wanted to turn on. I began to cut across the lot. Only cars passing on the street shattered the quiet. "Hey!" someone called as I reached the edge of the lot. I turned to the voice, calling from near the centre doors. The dad of one of my students stood beside a black SUV. "Tammy forgot her sweater!" I walked back, even though it was getting later and later, darker and darker. I couldn't see his face where he stood. With my nightmares still in my mind, I didn't really feel like walking through the parking lot as the dark came. But as I walked up to him, he broke into an easy smile full of crowded teeth, and I relaxed. "Paulina, right?" he said. "I'm sorry, it's just I dropped off Tammy at her mom's. And she noticed that she didn't have the sweater, and I promised I'd go back and try to catch you."

I unlocked the door for him, and we went in and found her sweater, a green cardigan with yellow chick buttons, tucked underneath a chair in the corner of the room. Blue glitter-glue was smeared along the sleeve.

"I think I know why she forgot it," I said, pulling out the sleeve to show him.

He took the sweater in his hands and examined the smear. He laughed, and I started laughing too. A pain cut through my chest, guilt at betraying Tammy's shame. I knew it was the only reason why children hid anything, maybe adults too. "Well, I can wash this and return it to her mother next time I pick her up. I'll tell her I didn't have time to bring it back."

"Will she be upset with you?"

"It doesn't matter," he said, and smiled at the glitter-glued sleeve. "She really likes blue."

I locked up and we left the centre and he told me more about Tammy, mentioned he was divorced again, and I told him about the projects she liked the best and about the other kids in her class. But he wanted to know about me. I told him I'd gone to Sheridan for a little bit for illustration. I'd dropped out because I moved to Toronto, and almost as soon as I was set up in Toronto I ran out of money and started teaching on the side, hoping to one day go back to school. He'd grown up in Montreal. His parents had moved to Canada from Poland when they were both in their teens. "Then I moved here and did a postgraduate copywriting program at Humber, and now that's what I do. It's kind of tough. You have to be on your toes and switch jobs a lot."

He pulled a baseball cap out of his back pocket and put it on over his cropped blond hair. He extended his hand for me to shake, and so I shook it. I thought he was trying to meet my eyes. I looked away. "Nik," he said. "Tammy loves your lessons, Paulina. Lessons from a real artist." I didn't know why he was laying it on so thick.

"You can call me Paul," I said. "Thank you. I like having her."

"Where you headed? You want a lift?"

I worried about getting in the car with him, even though he'd given me no reason to worry, had only been being friendly. But the walk home would be long through the dark, would take me over an hour, maybe two. "I live all the way down in Roncesvalles," I said.

"No shit! The Polish neighbourhood. I used to go shop down there when I first moved to Toronto. I'll give you a ride," he said.

"It's a bit different now," I told him as I got into his suv. He drove down south through the city. We passed through Corso Italia and drove along Davenport, past the warehouses at Dupont and Ossington, and then over to Dundas West.

"Oh, I know, the whole city is changing, all the little neighbourhoods are getting lost. Not that I miss it or anything like that. If I had it my way, I'd be in a condo right downtown. I always wanted to be a downtown city guy, right down in the action, but after Magda and I broke up, I got a house in the Junction. A rental, but it's nice, and it's closer to North Toronto and Tammy."

"My friend lives in the Junction," I said.

"Oh yeah? Where does she live?"

I'd meant Trevor, where he lived on the second and third floor surrounded by his books, stacks of his favourite writers. A book loyalist, he called himself. But instead of correcting Nik, I told him about Stef. "She's right on Gilbert. She's got a daughter, too, a little older than Tammy."

"She your age?"

"Yeah. How old are you?"

"Thirty-four." He glanced at me from under his baseball cap. I could smell his clean aftershave, as if he'd taken a shower just before coming back to the centre. "You must be, like, twenty-five."

"I'm turning twenty-seven in June. You got married young then, I'm guessing."

"Too young." He drummed his hands against the steering wheel to music in his head. He seemed simple, grown-up, and well-adjusted, having left one life to start another. The type of person who made decisions about their life instead of having things happen to them. "We met in our first year of university at Concordia. It seemed suitable, you know. We were both Polish living in Montreal. Our parents belonged to the same church. They knew each other. Actually, they mentioned us, kept wanting us to go on a date, but we never wanted to be set up. We were teenagers! We wanted to do our own thing! We thought we'd end up with people who didn't have old-school parents. But then we actually met in class, after hearing about each other for all those years. So we thought it was fate, you know?"

"Really? Fate?"

"What else would you call something like that?" Hot Beast of Existence, I thought to myself. The Doom of Human Nature, always telling us something means something instead of nothing. Instead of being things that happened and piled up and up in the past, ready to play havoc with the present.

We passed the liquor store and Loblaws and then we were on Roncesvalles, getting closer and closer to my apartment.

"But then we had Tammy and realized we hated each other."

I told him to turn left on Westminster, and we pulled up in front of my house. "Thanks for the ride," I said. I gathered my bag of supplies, construction paper and scissors and stickers threatening to jump out at any moment, zipped up my jacket, pushed my sneaky golden hair out of my face, away from my mouth. "It was nice to meet you."

He reached out and took my hand. I noticed a white scar running up the side of his wrist. He shook my hand. "We will see each other again." This time I let him meet my eyes. Icy blue like Adrian's. His thumb rubbed the scars on my knuckles as our hands parted, perhaps by accident.

How It Happened
The Lighted City

The closet is usually locked, but Uncle Jim, red-faced, his blond hair so light it's almost see-through, fiddles with the knob. He takes out a key. "Adrian knows to never use this when I'm not there, and that goes for you too, Paul."

I nod. He inserts the key and opens the wooden door. The wood on the inside is weathered grey, as if it's been exposed to rainy day after rainy day, instead of hidden inside a house. Along its walls are rows of guns, their barrels long and black or the silver of polished metal, plastic and wood detailing, and butts in sienna, clay, and even a goldenrod that seems out of place. Hunting guns. Smaller black cases, locked, are stacked on the floor, which I can only assume contain smaller guns. More deadly guns. I know what Adrian's told me, about Uncle Jim and danger. But today, Uncle Jim wants us to use a rifle and Adrian is eager.

"What about that one?" Adrian says and points at one of the cases. "The one you showed me." Adrian stares his father deep in the eyes, and it's hard for me to picture the fear that I know is in Adrian, but we both know that Uncle Jim isn't drunk yet and he's excited about the guns, about putting the guns in our hands. We've gotten used to his moods, to knowing when he thinks we're good and when we need to stay out of the way.

"Okay," Uncle Jim says. "But only you can hold it till we start shooting."

Adrian nods and holds the case to his chest. Another way Adrian is special, because Uncle Jim has chosen him, and he is the son, and I'm only here because my parents wanted another afternoon free. I heard them tell Aunt Dot over the phone this morning, "Can Lina come over there? We need some peace." Even though I've been trying to be quiet, quiet, quiet, alone in my room, drawing. Not quiet enough, not gone enough.

Uncle Jim grabs a rifle off the wall. I'm still taking it all in: a machete hung off a nail hammered into the wall, bows and arrows, a spear that looks handmade. Some of the guns are ancient, others brand new, the best for hunting deer, for taking on the trips Uncle Jim never takes me on, that I hope he'll never take me on.

"You can lead, Paul," Uncle Jim says, and we are outside. He wants me to show the way to the forest, but with each step the hair on my neck is raised, feeling their eyes on me ahead of them. I imagine Uncle Jim raising the gun and pointing it at me. And, despite myself, I imagine Adrian taking the handgun from the case and shooting me first, one, two, while Uncle Jim is still lining up the sight like I'm a deer. Adrian knows I'm human.

"She's going too fast," complains Adrian. "Slow down, Paul, we're carrying everything."

I want to bolt into the forest, but instead I hang back and fall into step beside them, glancing at Uncle Jim to see if he cares that I'm no longer leading. He doesn't seem to notice. His hand is perched on Adrian's shoulder, almost at the same level as his own since this summer started. *It's just Adrian,* I tell myself. *He's not like his dad.*

But he already knows how to shoot; that's obvious when we reach a clearing in the forest. Uncle Jim takes out a piece of chalk and marks an *X* on a tree. "This will be our buck," he says.

Adrian and Jim put the gun in my hand first. "I want to watch," I say.

"But you won't know what you're seeing until you do it yourself," says Uncle Jim. "Listen. Lie down."

I don't want to lie down. Not with Uncle Jim there.

Adrian comes beside me. "I'm right here," he says.

I lie down. Above me, tree branches carve their shapes into the crystal-blue sky. "On your stomach, you idiot. I'm going to teach you how to shoot prone first. It's easiest," Uncle Jim says. I roll onto my stomach and lift my chest, resting my weight on my elbows. "There you go," he says. "Doesn't your dad teach you anything?" He knows that he doesn't. He knows that I'm always with Adrian. I reach for the gun that he passes me. He shows me how to brace it again my shoulder. My heart is beating so fast I worry I'll stop breathing. "Now," says Uncle Jim. I press the trigger, and the gun leaps against me, thudding into my shoulder.

"It went into the woods," Adrian says. I don't care where it went. My shoulder aches from where the rifle recoiled and slammed into it.

"Show her, Adrian."

We spend the rest of the day trading back and forth: Uncle Jim loading the guns, Adrian as the model, and me as the pupil. They make me prone again and again. They make me sit and shoot. I even take a shot standing, but it's too strong for me and the shot goes way off to the left, and Uncle Jim decides that position is too danger-ous for me.

Then Adrian takes out the handgun. "You really have to focus with this one," he says, and his voice is exactly like his dad's. "Hold it steady."

I try and try, but I never hit the X. Adrian shoots it again and again. "I've had more practice," he says. "You'll get it."

But every time I hold the gun, all I can think is about how it can kill. An image pops into my head of me turning the gun around, close in a way I can't miss.

$$\diamond$$

The walk home is lonely. Adrian stays back with his dad, drinking beers even though he's fourteen, even though he has his first day at a new school tomorrow. I want to tell him to hide. I don't know how he can act like this with Uncle Jim after everything he's told me, and everything we have.

My parents have left dinner on the table for me, and they are downstairs watching television. I grab my plate and bring it down-stairs, lounging on the carpet at their feet. "Good day, Leenie?" Dad says. "Ready for school tomorrow?"

I nod, but I'm finding it hard to swallow. "Dad, do you know how to shoot?" I ask.

He shrugs. "I learned when I was a boy, but I wasn't really into hunting. The idea of killing an animal didn't appeal to me."

"Why, Paulina?" asks Mom.

And I'm crying and I can't stop. Normally I wouldn't tell them, but I think about the guns, how I didn't want to touch the guns and there were so many of them and how both Adrian and Uncle Jim knew how and I couldn't figure out how and I describe shooting and shooting and the shots disappearing into the forest. "Paul," Dad says. "Jim probably thought you'd like it. Lots of kids do. Adrian does, and you guys do everything together."

"Maybe you're a bit young for it," Mom says.

"He didn't mean to scare you," Dad says.

"He probably was hoping you could join Adrian on a hunting trip," Mom says.

I start crying harder, saying no, that I don't want to go, that I'm okay with Adrian but not Uncle Jim, never him. "Please don't make me go."

Dad laughs. "You're so worked up, Leenie. Guns are toys for some people."

"Really," Mom says. "But you don't have to hunt."

"Not my thing either," Dad says. "And I guess you're my daughter after all."

He reaches down to where I'm still sitting on the carpet and ruffles my hair. I know, in his eyes, I've done something right. I flinch. I can't help it. Since I was eight, I haven't been able to stand when anyone touches me like that. He frowns and downs his glass of wine. "Bedtime," Mom says. "You've got your first day tomorrow. Sixth grade isn't easy, you know."

My tears aren't even dry yet as they shake their heads at each other. They ascend the stairs and I brush my teeth in the bathroom, stare at my face in the mirror. It meant nothing to them, my fear. It's like I don't even exist.

But the fear stays in me as I lie in bed. My shoulder is sore where the rifle kept slamming into me, and I press it. When will my bruise appear?

I can't take the fear.

I sneak out of bed and see that the upstairs light has been turned off too. There is nothing but darkness cast against the stairs. Beside the TV, the phone, attached to its curly black cord, waits for me to call the only person who can take this fear away. "Adrian, I'm so scared," I say, hugging the phone to me. "How do I know he won't kill us?" But I remember that I'd been scared of Adrian too. I want to hear something from him that reminds me that Adrian is still Adrian. That he's the sweet person who can imagine worlds with me.

"He'd miss me," Adrian says, as if it's the most obvious thing in the world. "Knowing how to shoot is good for The Lighted City," he says. "For if we have to defend it." I hadn't thought of that. I breathe into the phone, waiting for more. I need to hear more about our place. "They could help us get there," he says. "If fire doesn't work."

"I don't know," I say. "Fire seems...purer. Like we just walk in."

"A portal," he says. "And then we are in our world."

"Yeah, together," I say. I can see it now, the flames licking our bodies, yellow and red and blue and white light everywhere, and then us walking through into the magical world we will rule. People running to us. "Are you nervous," I ask, "about starting high school tomorrow?"

"Don't ruin it, Paul," he says, and I think his voice is meaner than he intends. He must need me.

"I'm sorry," I say. "I wish we'd had time alone together today." I know that will make him happy.

"Me too," he says. "I always feel better when it's us two. Come over tomorrow."

I say yes and then I say I love you and then I hang up the phone. I start a new school tomorrow, too, a middle school with grades six to eight. All summer I've been bound tight with Adrian. I can't imagine walking in and pretending to be a normal eleven-year-old when my real world is in the forest with Adrian.

I know I still won't be able to sleep. I slip out the back door. I go to the edge of the forest when my parents are asleep and I see Adrian and Uncle Jim, Uncle Jim's hand on Adrian's shoulder, and I feel sick, I feel sick, I start swinging at the trees, imagining Xs marked with chalk. First I only feel my fear and then I feel my rage. I swing and I swing, and then my hands are wet, my knuckles torn again, tomorrow they will be bruised as well, and pain begins to smart and throb. I suck at my hands, the metallic sweetness of my own blood.

How It Happened
May 2016

It's hard to write about the time just after he died, the grief I felt, still feel. Because if I'm honest, no one around me would have thought I was affected by it much at all. I worked, I was present for the kids I taught, I talked to my friends about their lives. But inside me, Adrian was free and a tree was burning like a voice calling my name. My whole body ached as I biked to work, as I tried to be the same old Paul for the kids and the parents and my friends. As I tried to hide my sadness and this wound, torn open, dripping crimson fresh.

On Tuesday, at Drop 'n Draw during the day, barely anyone came. The company had rented a room in a strip mall in the hope that parents would drop children off while they shopped. Stef brought Wynn once, to be nice, but later told me that from a parent's perspective, it was a charge for glorified babysitting. "Not that you aren't great at what you do, Paul," she said in a way that made me wonder. And what was wrong with babysitting? But the owners paid me no matter who came, mailed cheques regularly, unlike Artastic!, and were well-intentioned despite being bad at business.

I waited, alone, for children to come. Sometimes, during the morning shift, a team of mothers with strollers would appear, toddlers strapped in and straining to get out and scribble. But from noon until two, all the kids in that age group were at home taking naps, and all the older kids still in school.

Finally, around three, a mother came by, ready to drop her boy off. "Where are the other kids?" he asked.

"Not everyone gets to miss half a day of school because they had a dentist appointment," his mother said.

The boy didn't say anything, just nodded slackly and then nodded again and again, allowing each movement to become more exaggerated. He began walking around the room as if he had bricks for feet, bumping into chairs and tables like they'd been getting in his way on purpose. He wanted to hear noise ricochet through the emptiness.

"Stop that," his mother said. "Or we'll go home without McDonald's." Her son reluctantly slid into a seat. "Not a lot of kids getting dropped off with all those kids going missing lately, huh?"

"I'm not sure what you mean," I said.

"You know, all those Amber Alerts. I swear there's more of them."

"Maybe we're just paying more attention. It's safe around here," I said, although I didn't know if that was true.

"Well, if someone tries to take him, tell them he'll eat three times his weight in groceries," the woman said, and laughed. "Tell them he's more trouble than he's worth." The boy looked miserable.

"Don't worry," I said to the woman. "We'll have fun. I have stickers."

His interest in stickers and the activities I set up kept him busy for a half hour, but he didn't stop feigning clumsiness. "It's just that my hands and feet are so *big*," he told me. "I can't help it." He held up his hand to me, a little bigger than the size of my palm. "I'm going to be tall," he said. "I think I'll be the biggest in the class by the end of the year."

"Six weeks," I said.

"Yup," he said, and stood his glue stick up on its end and knocked it over.

✧

I signed out when my two hours were up, and on the sidewalk outside of Drop 'n Draw was a lost barrette, made of hard plastic, teddy bears in crimson red. I'd had barrettes like this one when I was a kid, still kept a few in a tin in my desk, even though I didn't have any reason to wear barrettes anymore. I would have thought kids were more likely to have little metal butterflies now, fake diamonds, gemstones, clips like their mothers wore or headbands and bows ordered from boutiques with sustainably sourced fabrics. But maybe this was only true of the children I taught at Artastic!, whose parents had the money to pay for the lesson packages. Children privileged enough that McDonald's wasn't a treat and art was education and not something to keep a kid busy while their parent shopped. I put the barrette in my pocket. It was time to head to Artastic! for the afterschool program.

Nik didn't bring Tammy to Artastic! that afternoon, and so I studied her mother. I wondered what she did, if she was a copywriter like Nik. They'd met at Concordia, but I couldn't remember if he'd said what she'd been studying there. Her hair was bobbed at her chin, sitting straight and flat, as if she went to the hairdresser each day. Not like the wild gold mess on the top of my head, the blue eyes that always seemed a little too full of panic instead of perfectly chilled. We must've had so many brief, nothing conversations.

Tammy's mother was the one who usually dropped her off. She told Tammy to behave before leaving, but Tammy always behaved. She was one of the best-behaved kids I'd ever seen, but her mother said it like Tammy was someone who needed to be watched. Her mother wore a cropped, black blazer and black work pants, a sleek white tank top. Just in from the office. The way she spoke to Tammy made my scalp start to tingle. She barely said hello or goodbye to me. Then she was gone, the sound of her high heels clicking down the hall.

I handed out the construction paper to my students. By this time, I knew everyone's favourite colours, Tammy's was blue. She sat on her hands and swung her legs back and forth as she waited for her paper, crayons, and pencils, which I knew she wanted to get at. When I was a kid, I used to sit on my hands like that. Mom had always said I had fidgeting hands, hands that wouldn't stop tearing things up. If I tore things up, she noticed me. "Little hands of destruction," she said to Dad, holding up one of my hands, always covered in marker, to show him. She taught me, if I didn't know what to do with them, to sit on them. She was right. The pressure made them numb, and then they didn't want to do anything anymore.

Tammy had her green cardigan on, yellow chick buttons. "Nice sweater," I whispered to her as I passed her a piece of paper, and she gave me her biggest smile.

I bent over to grab white paper to hand out from the cubby in the wall where we stored it, and I felt a hand tug my shirt. I turned around, and Tammy was up and out of her seat, standing behind me. "My daddy thinks you're nice," she whispered up at me.

I walked her back to her seat. "I think he's nice too," I whispered back at her. "And I think you're nice." She gave me another Tammy smile, and I was smiling too, but it wasn't my regular awkward smile, it was my true smile, the smile only those kids could make me do. Tammy spent all session drawing a boy. When I asked her to explain to the class what he was doing, she said, "He's playing in the leaves."

✧

I packed that night, getting ready to fly out early the next morning. I still hadn't told Trevor I'd be out of town. Part of me wanted to keep our silence going—he could think I was still waiting around in Toronto if he wanted. But the thought of him texting me to come over and me telling him *then* that I was in Vancouver...well, I knew that would make everything worse.

Hey I'm going to Vancouver for a few days
If you don't hear from me, that's why
Funeral

He texted back almost immediately.

Okay. Let me know when you're back?
K.
And I'm here. If you need anything.

What did being "here" mean to him? The silent treatment since I'd left his place? The way Trevor always was, sincere and ready to be close one moment and far away the next? Well, now I could put him far out of my mind as I actually went far away. I doubted he would have even noticed I was gone if I hadn't told him.

I rolled my clothes the way Kayla had shown me, the way that kept all the wrinkles out when you travelled. She'd lent me her suitcase that had been all over the world with her—to Jamaica to visit her grandmother, to Bali to find herself, to Germany to take a language course, hiking in Peru. "I know the reason why you're going is a bit of a bummer," she said as she hauled the black, wheeled carry-on up the steps to my attic apartment. "But sometimes it feels so good to be somewhere else." I couldn't imagine it, but soon I would be somewhere else. A shiver went through me. I left the lights on when I went to bed. If I turned them off, I was sure I would be confronted by Adrian's ghost.

Now

I am meeting Stef and Kayla, and Stef is holding her baby, but it's not alive yet. Kayla is smoking inside. "What's it like being a coward?" she asks me.

I drift away from them and see Trevor, shivering outside in the cold. I go to him, but he's frozen stiff. I can barely see his face because it's encased in ice. I brush at his face, and his hair peels away as my hands touch it. The face is revealed, thinner, gaunt, delicate, not Trevor. The eyes open, and they are blue. They belong to Adrian.

I'm hungover and ragged the next morning, my dream still clinging to me. Unless things get really bad, usually my nightmares are pieces of my childhood, things that happened with Adrian. Sometimes they are echoes of 2016, as if I never escaped that terrible year. When they start to include my present, that's when I know I'm heading toward trouble. In the dream, I was with Stef and Kayla in the restaurant we were at the other day. Trevor/Adrian breaking into my night out, disrupting me.

There are other signs too. Signs my memories are sucking me back in. Signs I'm trying to ignore. Things are getting bad again. I've started the treatment, so shouldn't I be starting to feel better?

Not constantly stuck in this cycle of spending all day remembering my past and being scared of my present?

I try to take care of myself. I drink water. Make toast. I still hurl into the toilet.

It's Jocelyn's show tonight.

I crawl back into bed.

But when I close my eyes, I can see Adrian's.

How It Happened
May 2016

It was dark as I pulled Kayla's suitcase along Bloor to the UP train, which would take me to the airport. I joined other travellers, sleepy commuters, nodding off with headphones over their ears. I took my printed boarding pass out and smoothed it against my lap, double-checked I had everything I needed to fly. My first time.

Although flying was supposed to be new and exciting and Stef had told me I was off on an adventure, I still felt like thinking was impossible, my movements slow and heavy. Adrian. I turned and looked out the train window and thought I caught a reflection of him behind me, but when I turned, only another passenger was there.

Even though it was four thirty in the morning, Pearson Airport was crowded with people, dodging around each other. The sound of suitcases rolling along the ground and then along the ridges of the flat conveyor belts filled the air. I followed the crowd toward Departures, checked my flight and gate against a large digital screen, which was bigger than my wall at home. I did a breathing exercise as I walked in the direction the arrows pointed, toward my gate. I counted, I breathed, I walked.

I'd seen airports in movies, and one time I'd gone to meet Kayla after she'd returned from travelling for a month, smelly, skinny, and full of stories, her usually pale brown skin deeply tanned. But I'd never gone past the pick-up area. I was struck by how mall-like it was, combined with an authoritarian energy, so many rules, to filter people from one place to another. Was there a line for grieving passengers—one that would allow them to slink off without being seen by other people?

My parents had given me some pocket money for the trip, in case I needed to grab food or couldn't eat with Aunt Dot, but I'd be staying with her. This was always how their help was given, pressed into my hand without meeting my eye, slid into birthday cards with *Paulina* written in cursive, but never a response to a need, a question, a plea. I reached my gate with time to spare and grabbed a breakfast sandwich with egg and cheese from a coffee stand. I was always hungry back then and never eating enough, and the sandwich disappeared quickly, leaving me wanting another. But I knew I needed to stretch out the money my parents had given me. I couldn't afford to run out of money before the week was out.

While I waited, fixating on money gave me something to think about that wasn't Adrian. Other than my rent, which I'd stashed away in an account I used for that, I had about thirty dollars in my bank account. This would have been enough if I had gotten my biweekly pay from Artastic! on the thirteenth as planned. Then I was due for another paycheque from them on the twenty-seventh. But without the money coming in, I was screwed. My rent was $1,300, which I couldn't afford next month unless I figured out something fast. I went through a mental checklist of possible jobs I could apply for. I had no administration experience, so I couldn't get an office job like Kayla. My typing speed was low, so I couldn't look for work doing transcription. I hadn't finished my degree, so that cut out a lot of jobs. Serving was a possibility, but I had no experience, and it seemed like everyone who served had already broken into it when they were younger or by hanging out with a cooler crowd of beautiful people who acted or played in bands. Last time I'd applied to restaurants and cafés, I hadn't gotten any calls.

I knew how to do only one thing: teach kids about colour and shape. How to transfer emotion into a picture, how to express themselves.

The gate agents called for my zone to board and I lined up. I checked my phone, but no one had messaged—it was too early. I typed a message out to Trevor and then deleted it before sending it. Then I typed the same thing to Stef: *Boarding now. Wish me luck. If I die on the airplane, tell everyone I love them.* Then I put an emoji of a plane and a scared face.

She messaged back right away. *You are an adventurer! Good luck! I'm sure the flight will go great. I hope you are able to still have a bit of fun in Van even though I know it'll be hard.*

Hard didn't begin to cover it. Now that I was away from working and my usual life, heading toward Adrian's funeral, I felt like I was wading through fog. *Thanks.*

Wynn will want to FaceTime if you're up for it.

I sent a thumbs-up emoji and then fumbled to get my passport out to show the gate agent. Most of the time, no one cared who I was or where I was going, but here they demanded to know every step of the way.

I found my seat beside a woman knitting. "I hope this won't bother you," she said as her needles clicked together intricately. She didn't even need to look down. She was older than me, maybe in her mid-forties. Kayla had taught me knitting was cool—she made gifts for me and a lot of her own clothes back then.

"It's fine," I said, and rearranged myself in the seat, trying to find a comfortable position. The cabin's stale air made me sick and anxious, so I opened a vent above me. I closed my eyes as the cool air hit my face.

"Do you get nervous flying?" the woman asked me. Her needles clicked.

I opened my eyes. "I'm not really sure. It's my first time."

"I get nervous. Even though I fly all the time. I fly to Vancouver to see my brother, and every year, I fly to Grenada to see my parents and grandparents. Does anyone fly to me? Nope. So I knit. It's good for distracting the mind."

"Maybe I'll draw."

"Are you an artist?"

"I used to be."

She laughed. "You're too young to have used to been anything."

Maybe she was right.

The screen embedded in the back of the seat was broken, but when the flight attendant came around to offer me headphones, they cost ten dollars anyway. I pulled out my sketchbook. The plane's engine began to run, and above me the seat-belt sign lit up. I buckled myself in. My chest and arms ached with nerves. Beside me, the woman knit contentedly, but I noticed even she was sitting a little more rigidly. I took a deep breath and began to draw.

Although I never felt like I really worked on anything, I was always sketching. Sometimes only the world around me, how I saw it, the way it was alive and could influence the actions of the people in it. Drawing was the only thing I felt I had time for, was something

I could do between things, as long as I always had a sketchbook with me.

Most of the time, rather than draw the real world, I planned what I would make with all my collected materials. I wanted to feel like the pieces I gathered when I was outside were meant for something, like it wasn't an empty compulsion. Like maybe I was saving up inspiration, ideas, and material for my next big project. I was dreaming of sculpture. But when I drew what I wanted this to be, I came back to the same images. A burning tree. A field of long, tall grass. Little huts scattered around, built of twigs and mud. A child's game.

The plane moved forward and started to roll on the tarmac. The woman beside me began to pray, in time with her knitting needles. I glanced over at her. "I still am afraid," she said to me and then reached for my hand, which was shaking. The plane lurched forward with increased speed, and we bumped once, twice on the tarmac before lifting into the air.

I couldn't help but say, "Wow," looking out the window past the woman as we went higher and higher. Below us, Toronto and the GTA were reduced to squares underneath a sky slowly being lit by the rising sun. The clouds were tinged with pinks and purples and oranges.

"It's amazing, isn't it?" the woman said. "A few minutes ago, we were down there." She let go of my hand.

Now

My alarm wakes me at four in the afternoon. My phone is full of messages from Kayla on our group thread with Stef.

where is this thing

do you think it's ok if I just wear my work clothes? I don't think I'll have time to change.

or too fancy

not fancy enough?

what do you wear to an art opening?

Paul

Paul

Paulina

Heloooo

Hellooooo*

I quickly type to them that sorry, I was away from my phone, working. I cringe at my own lie, but keep going. I know if I mention that I was sleeping, Stef will have a lot of questions for me about how I'm feeling and if I'm okay, and I'm not ready to get into any of it. I tell Kayla to wear whatever she wants, that some people might dress up, especially if it's their show, but many others will be coming right from work as well.

I pull on a sweater Kayla made me last year. Emerald-green wool yarn, so soft. It took her six months, and she said it would have taken her longer if it hadn't been so chunky. "I think it looks great with your hair," she said. And when I look at myself in the mirror, she's right; there's something pleasing about the way my frizzy, gold hair looks against the green of the sweater. The scattering of freckles across my nose is more noticeable. I hope they look cute— Trevor, at least, always loved my freckles. But I still look hungover, dark circles under my eyes. I cake on concealer.

It's snowing outside as I leave my apartment. Thick flakes. My dream comes back to me again. Wiping the ice from Adrian, dead.

The grief has always been there. I thought it would go away, but instead it changed: sometimes it swells up and takes me over, and others, it's quiet in the background, like a jazz record someone forgot to turn off. I want to say that it began when I lost Adrian, the day I was tied to the tree, the day he did it to me—tried to send me to The Lighted City—but it didn't start then. The grief started when I realized the way Adrian and I were together was wrong, when I realized he was in pain due to his own family and we didn't have anywhere safe, no one to turn to.

Other kids, they had parents who brought them to movies, who asked them what had happened at school, who wanted to know where they were going and when they'd be home. But there wasn't any of that for me. And other kids, they had parents who kept them out of harm's way, who protected them as much as they could. They didn't inflict that harm, didn't turn a blind eye to their own child's suffering. Adrian wasn't so lucky.

We never had a chance to learn a better way.

I catch myself, think purposefully, *But I can still learn.* I add *maybe*, because I still am me and I still doubt, but I repeat it to myself as I walk, blocking out the thought of Adrian. *Maybe I can still learn, maybe I can still learn.*

The wind whips the flakes into my face, and I fight against it as I walk to the coffee shop. Inside, some people wear masks, especially as they line up for the refreshments table. The rest keep a little more space between them than we would have before the waves of the pandemic. To make up for it, everyone is almost yelling. The noise with my headache is almost unbearable.

"Paul!" Jocelyn runs over to me, and she, too, is dressed in green, a dress made of silk that has lilies embroidered on the back. Her green eyes are ringed in dark eyeliner. "It's so good to finally meet you in person!" Jocelyn is unmasked but embraces me. She holds a sleeve of her dress against the shoulder of my sweater, compares the shades. "Looks like we got the memo. I'm so happy you came. I would have never been able to do all of this without your help."

"That's not true," I say and gesture at her paintings, which take up two walls and a corner of the café. "You've done so much, and that takes time and dedication. You've done more here than I have in five years."

Jocelyn beams hearing my praise. I mean it. None of my other students have worked as diligently, produced anywhere near as much. Although Jocelyn turned to art after already having a life-long career as a public health administrator, she dedicated herself as fully to her new passion as if it were a full-time job.

"I hope you'll get to meet the other artist," she says, gesturing away from her paintings to the other wall, covered with dull, styl-ized paintings of streets of Toronto. "Enjoy yourself, don't let me keep you." She squeezes my hand, and I want to stay close to her, to feed off her warmth and energy. I still feel coated in fuzz, on edge.

But I can tell she needs to work the room, and at that moment, Stef and Kayla walk into the café, knocking snow off their boots. "There are my friends," I say. "They are so excited to see your paintings." I leave her, walk over to them.

"It's freezing out there," Kayla says, rubbing at her arms.

"Maybe you should buy a warmer coat," Stef says, adjusting her scarf. She looks a little better than the last time we saw her, but not by much.

They take off their coats. Kayla flings hers onto the coat hook by the door and Stef gently places her own wool navy coat beside Kayla's, fishing around in her pockets to retrieve anything valuable before leaving it. I see her slide a library card into her pocket.

"Don't want that to get stolen," I say, poking fun. She frowns at me. "Are you feeling okay?" I ask her.

"I've been better," she says. "I'll have to get home before eight."

"What happens at eight?" Kayla asks.

"Projectile vomiting."

We grab snacks, and Kayla and I pour ourselves big glasses of wine, full almost to the brim. "We need to be prepared," Kayla says. "For the art." Stef looks miserably at both of us, pours a glass of water, and we begin to circulate, looking at the art.

Before the pandemic, I never worried about going to a café. People have started to say the waves are over now, but then again, no one ever expected it to last half a decade. It's hard to know what to believe—we've had periods of time where life went back to the way it used to be and then everyone got sick again. At this point, normal feels like going to a café and not knowing if I should wear a mask or not, or who to talk to, and then spending the week taking tests to see if I picked up COVID.

Since the last spike died down, I'm getting the feeling that people are ready for new life again, that they want to go out and mingle despite the cold weather. The art show has a great turnout. The brick walls of the café are the perfect space to hang art, and more than anything, people want to experience art, be around other people experiencing art.

"If only this wasn't bad," Kayla says. The painting in front of her is of Roncesvalles, covered in snow. "If I wanted to see Roncey, I'd walk outside."

Stef laughs and we all move on to Jocelyn's.

"Wow," Kayla says. "Just wow."

It's true that seeing them all together is a little much. Spirit after spirit. In some, they appear as halos of light. In others, they are more star-like. In comparison to the other artist's lifeless Toronto, they seem fake, overblown, and new age.

"I thought you were helping this lady," Kayla says.

I stand in front of a painting that Jocelyn has never shown me. The spirit is behind trees in a forest. The light illuminates the branches of the trees, spills over the leaves on the ground. Light presses against the green and brown colours. My forest. I can't feel my hands. My lips are cold and I can't stop looking at the painting. The sounds around me are gone, I am gone.

Someone touches me and I hit at their hand. "Get away from me!" I say, but then I see Stef's face, confused. My heart is pounding. I take a shaky breath. I'm not in a forest. My feet are on a wooden floor, not a bed of leaves, twigs, moss, and mud. I'm in a café. Adrian isn't here—Stef is at my side. Jocelyn is at the front by a microphone, waiting for everything to quiet down. Her eyes lock on mine and then move to Kayla, who is taking photos of Jocelyn's paintings and laughing, probably posting them to Insta ironically. To Jocelyn, I'm sure we look like children.

"What happened to you?" Stef whispers to me as Jocelyn again speaks into the mic, asking for everyone's attention.

"It was that painting," I say. "It creeped me out."

"Have you been okay?" Stef asks. Other than Trevor, she's the only one who knows I struggle with nightmares, with things haunting me and creeping up. She doesn't know all the details of my childhood, though, just as I don't know every single thing about hers. We've kept a boundary up that feels comfortable and safe. I could still walk away from my friendships without someone knowing all my secrets. "I haven't heard much from you."

"Yeah, I'm fine."

"I just thought, after our dinner, I'd hear from you . . ." She places her hand below her belly button.

I know I should say something to explain. I should tell her about the treatment, about what it's doing to me, but my skin crawls and itches. More than anything, I need to get out of there, but I have to wait for Jocelyn's speech. Jocelyn who painted something that I'd only ever imagined in my games, in my dreams. Realized in her painting. Why hadn't we worked on that one together?

"I see spirits," Jocelyn begins, and Stef quiets. A few people in the crowd titter. "I know that sounds funny to many of you."

Stef and Kayla exchange a look, rubbing their lips together, suppressing laughs.

"Especially the younger crowd. But when you've lived as long as I have, you begin to realize the universe doesn't work the way you expected. You lose people. Friends. Children. Parents. Slowly everyone around you goes. And you begin to think, when you enter a space, about all the people who came and went through it, going about their day, centuries and centuries of people who had lives, some short, some long. But all were living and then weren't. This careful consideration and respect of what has come before, of the way life works, it changes the way you see things.

"I was a child when death first happened to someone I knew. My grandmother had died and I was devastated. My parents sent me to play in the parlour while they took care of business in the other room, not wanting to expose me to what death really is for the living—an administrative hassle."

A few of Jocelyn's friends in the audience laugh.

"But I couldn't play. How could I? It'd started to sink in. Nana was gone. Gone for good. *Heaven?* I thought. I tried to imagine such a place, the way it was taught to me with golden arches and up in the clouds, but I could only think about what was around me and her. She'd been sick for a long time, but we'd still spent time together. She'd snuggle me into bed beside her when she wasn't well and make up stories of faraway places, mystical forests, and every story had a brave girl going on adventures in it. We didn't hear many stories like that back then. So I began to think about her stories rather than playing with my doll. And that's when the light came. I knew it was her spirit. She hovered over my toy box. I understood immediately. She didn't want me to give up on being a kid. She wanted me to keep playing.

"I knocked on the door where my parents were. 'Nana's in the parlour,' I said. Well, let me tell you, they had me in bed before I could even think about it. They told me I was imagining things.

Ever since that day, whenever I mention the spirits, people tell me I am imagining things. As I got older, it changed. I was a con artist or a kook, for not seeing what others wanted to see, for telling people what others didn't want to hear. That the boundary between life and death is thin.

"Painting has allowed me to show others what I see, to open that door for them. People are afraid to engage with such ideas without art. That's why painting is necessary.

"I began this series during the first lockdown in 2020 and took up virtual art lessons with my instructor, Paulina, who is here at the back." She points at me. "Wave, Paul!"

Eyes on every inch of me. I give a quick wave. People nod, turn back to Jocelyn at the front. "Over the past five years, we've created a lasting bond as she encourages me to explore these thoughts in art, but to focus on the technique, to keep experimenting when I think I've done everything there is to do. So thank you, Paulina, for your understanding and care, and your valuable instruction."

Stef nudges me. Kayla gives me a thumbs-up. The audience applauds and Jocelyn steps aside to let the other artist speak.

"That was absolutely ridiculous," Kayla says.

"No, I think I get it," Stef says. "It's like magic realism."

"No, you heard her, she is trying to show something she believes one hundred percent exists when it one hundred percent does not." She downs the rest of her wine.

I've had enough. "I wish you guys wouldn't be so rude. She's a client. I can't do anything to piss her off or I'll lose her." Stef points behind me and I turn. Jocelyn is behind me. Our eyes connect for only a moment, and hers are red at the edges, fighting tears. I don't know how much she's heard or what she's taken offence to or if I've lost a client of five years over all of this. I'm too sick to deal with the fallout. The painting she never showed me, I can still see it.

"Let's just go," I say to Stef and Kayla, and I know this is as bad, worse, than what their insensitivity has done to Jocelyn, but I can't stay. I just can't.

And we are the ones who are wrong, who aren't seeing things as they are, not Jocelyn. I know this. We have it all wrong. Her speech was right. The boundary between life and death is thin.

How It Happened
May 2016

As the plane descended toward Vancouver, we flew over mountains, their snowy peaks. I'd lived somewhere with large, emerald hills, gentle-curved even when steep. I was unprepared for the way mountains jutted into the air and how their tips gathered mist around them as they pointed at the clouds. So big that they made you gasp as you tried to pin down their colour; depending on the sky, they looked grey, blue-black, forest green.

The wheels skidded as we landed and I glanced at my seatmate, but somehow, she'd fallen and stayed asleep, her knitting resting in her lap against her slack hands. When she stirred, we didn't talk. She rubbed sleep from her eyes and began to gather her things, pulling a shawl around her. I threw my backpack over my shoulder. The morning airport was crowded, throbbing with people. Brown carpet stretched down long hallways and the signs were in English, French, and a Chinese language. The glass on the ceiling and the windows revealed grey skies. I had no idea where I was supposed to go.

My stomach ached. I was hungry again after the flight, having decided the in-flight snacks were too expensive. Aunt Dot hadn't been able to meet me, since both she and her partner were working morning shifts, so I was supposed to take something called the SkyTrain and a bus to her place. They promised to be home once I got there. But I was all turned around. Navigating Toronto's airport for the first time had been hard enough, but at least I had my gates to guide me. I needed to find the train. I finally asked a volunteer in a green vest, and they smiled at me and walked me over to where a sign overhead marked the direction to the train. I walked along long brown halls until I found the train, on a platform outside. Immediately, I got goosebumps. I'd only brought one sweater, a black oversized hoodie, and I dug through my backpack until I found it at the bottom. Toronto's heatwave hadn't prepared me for this. It felt like March, not May.

The train ran along an elevated track over highways and trees and suburbs. It clicked upward like an old wooden roller coaster. One time, Aunt Dot had taken Adrian and I to Wonderland and we rode a roller coaster that climbed a mountain and then plunged inside of it, stopping close to a robotic dragon that spewed fire. It all seemed so real to us and we went through again and again, even though the way the wooden and metal tracks creaked scared us and the climb before the cars were released downwards made our stomachs tight with fear and anticipation. It was worth it for the fire again and again. But this train plunged down over the ocean, and behind everything I could see the mountains. Their magic was as real as—realer than—the dragon's mountain.

As the train hummed along, I wondered what Aunt Dot's house, Adrian's house, would be like. I felt my breath catch in me when I remembered he wouldn't be there, that I was going to his funeral. Why, in grief, was it so easy to have these little moments of forgetting, only to have the reality of death sweep in?

Dad had said that Aunt Dot was doing okay when he spoke to her about me coming to stay, but that her partner was handling most of the arrangements because she couldn't. Maybe I shouldn't have come. I had enough nightmares—I didn't need to walk into one.

Once I got off the train, I walked to the bus stop. My hunger had turned to nausea. I'd written on a piece of paper the bus number to look for, the one that would take me to the house Aunt Dot was now living in. The ride was short, and I counted my breaths as I got closer and closer. Rain started to drizzle down as soon as I got off the bus, and I pulled my hoodie over my head, dragging Kayla's suitcase along faster. And there it was. What had been Adrian's home. A small, squat house with white wood siding. A green lawn, kept short and neat. Flowers blooming in the front garden, tulips and daffodils. The rain strengthened, pinged down on Aunt Dot's yard and the roof of her small house.

When she opened the door, I was faced with a woman who looked very much like me, but older and wider, her golden hair frizzed up like mine would be if I stayed out too long in the rain and then let it dry. Her face was rounder than I remembered. She had my soft cheeks, but they continued and gathered under her chin. But when she saw me, she smiled a smile of relief, revealing the dimples I knew. Another woman floated behind her, as if she were tethered to her. She was tall and thin with short, dark hair swept back. She nervously looked out at me.

"Hi, Paul," Aunt Dot said, and hugged me. With my face buried in her shoulder, I had no time to feel pain. I had no time to feel anything at all, except this woman I hadn't seen in ten years surrounding me. She smelled the same, and I felt a sense of recognition.

She was the only adult that had ever paid attention to me. She let me go. "This is my partner, April."

"Oh," I said, since I'd never heard a thing about April except pieces from Dad. "Hi." April and I shook hands, and she smiled at me, revealing a gap between her teeth. Wide, full lips. So much easier to describe, to name, to see someone for the first time than it is when they are close to you. "I've heard a lot about you, Paulina."

"Paul," corrected Aunt Dot.

"It's nice to meet you," I said. Aunt Dot watched us to see if we liked each other, but we didn't say much.

The house was small and crowded with furniture. The living room had a couch with a weaving loom crammed in beside it, half a shawl completed, a basket of yarn stowed under the shelf in a coffee table. The mantle was crowded with figurines of angels. These had been in the house in Caledon as well. I assumed the weaving was April's. Aunt Dot had never done anything with her hands; too clumsy, she said. The walls were almost all bare.

Aunt Dot was already tearing up. "So, Paul, I wish we had a room for you to stay in, and when I offered for you to stay here, I stupidly was thinking we had the space, and we do, but we don't have a room. Because it's just our room and Adrian's—"

She stopped herself.

"Adrian's room isn't ready," said April. "One day, maybe we'll have it for guests. If we stay here. But for now, I hope you're good with the couch."

Adrian's room. The room he'd died in, or at least that was what I imagined. Were the details of his death—the shotgun, sitting at the edge of the bed, were these things made up, filled in by my imagination later?

"Oh, that's fine," I said, looking around the living room. The kitchen was separated from it by a doorway without a door, the hall to the bedrooms straight ahead.

"It folds down," explained April.

"We're planning to move into something smaller, as soon as we find something cheap enough. It's all a lot to think about right now," Aunt Dot said. "Maybe a condo, close to the hospital and Healing Centre."

We went into the living room, and I sat on their beige couch. April hid in her room, I guess to give me and Aunt Dot a chance to talk.

"How are you feeling?" she asked me. And I could see her hands were shaking. "I can't believe how long it's been."

"Like no time has passed," I said, although I didn't know if it was true. I did feel comfortable around her. Even her sadness seemed familiar, had always been there with the way Uncle Jim had treated her, had treated Adrian. Aunt Dot was the only one there, other than Adrian, when I was lonely or afraid, or wanted to know things. She kept stories about Dad and how he'd met Mom, about what it was like for them growing up. One story she told me was about a horrible guy "getting a little fresh" and Dad going after him, saying he would break his neck. She told me she always remembered that phrase, "break his neck," and that she'd used it to get out of a few jams herself. The father I got through her stories was different from the man I knew, who was meek, contained, and never showed much emotion.

My parents lived in a world of their own. Bound by their love in their own Lighted City, maybe. A place where their Paulina didn't exist. I knew all these things about my parents, the things I learned from Aunt Dot's stories, but couldn't see them. I knew both my parents always tried to do the right thing with every choice they made: they talked about duty, they stressed following the law, they always filed their taxes on time. Closeness, outside of romantic love, was different. Complicated. They were terrified of a child's questions, so eventually I stopped asking.

You can love someone and still make it so that they never feel it. You can even make it so that they know it, say it from time to time, but by making them feel a bother, you make it so they never understand that they have a place with you. That you want them. I never felt so unwanted as when I was in my parents' house.

The things that wanted me were trees and grass, were insects and the birds singing, the still moments where I came face to face with a deer—those told me that I was loved by the world and would be safe in it. Adrian's embrace told me that another human could see in me what I saw in myself when I was alone and outside, that I wasn't an alien, I just needed the right person to recognize what I had in me and understand the good. But then that wasn't enough to heal either.

Even now, Aunt Dot was willing to sit down and talk to me, despite everything, but she was also the one who'd taken Adrian away, who'd disappeared from my life and Dad's life without thinking what it would do to me.

"I'm happy you're here," Aunt Dot said. But I was thinking about the day I first lost Adrian, and my scalp was starting to tingle again but my stomach growled in a way that we both could hear and we laughed awkwardly. "Let's get you some lunch. It's been hard for me lately, but I know the whole world looks better on a full stomach."

I watched Aunt Dot as she chatted with me and April as we ate. In some ways, she seemed calm and content in her new life. A life without Adrian. Even when he'd just died. I knew I'd never be able to talk to her about him. Not when I remembered him being stuck in that old house in Caledon with Uncle Jim and no way out except through me.

✧

After dinner and glasses of wine, April talked nonstop about the things we would do in Vancouver before I left. To her, Vancouver was about exploring outside, hikes and beaches, and maybe once you were tired from the outdoor air, dinner at a restaurant downtown.

"I shouldn't have had that," Aunt Dot said, pushing her wine glass away.

"Do you need to lie down?" April asked her, hand over hers. Aunt Dot nodded. "Sorry, Paul, I think that will be it for us tonight." They went into their bedroom, April on Aunt Dot's arm, guiding her.

I pulled out the sofa bed, wrapped in a quilt April had made. With the door to their room shut and no streetlights on the street, the living room was pitch black. I tossed and turned, kept awake by heaviness in my bladder and fuzziness from the wine. I got up to try to find the bathroom with the flashlight from my phone, not wanting to turn on lights and wake Aunt Dot and April.

Down the hall, the door was plain, white, uncovered. I knew it wasn't the bathroom, but I opened the door anyway. I needed to see him. Adrian. Adrian's bedroom door in his home in Caledon had been something we decorated. He'd asked me to paint the carved, dark walnut panels, but the wood still showed through, despite the thick forest I painted, the flames at the top of the door, burnt orange eating at the edges, ochre threaded throughout the flames, and at the centre, white light, another world.

But inside, despite the plain door, the room was him. I pointed my flashlight all over the room. On the walls were photos of Adrian, of us as kids, their house in Caledon, of him when he was older—an Adrian I'd never met, the same glasses and shaved head from the picture in his obituary. This Adrian was in a group of people. He had a medal around his neck. This Adrian paddled a canoe with two kids in the back, his shirt the kind of cheap material and unreal bright blue of a camp counsellor's. *He wasn't alone*. And other things too: flyers for community centre events and soup kitchens. I thought I recognized his cartooning style in some of the event flyers. Along the tops of the walls of the bedroom, he'd pinned up photos of birds and wildlife torn from magazines. Photos and drawings of trees. I even recognized one or two I had done, all those years ago. Maybe I wasn't the only one of us to become an artist.

Then I looked at the bed. The bedspread was new, black, but my stomach rocked and my scalp tingled. I thought I couldn't breathe. Adrian had died here. I knew it. The thought began small and then circled and wound around me. He'd died. I shut the door.

The bathroom was at the end of the hall. I peed and then found my way back to the living room.

The sofa bed dug into my spine, and Adrian was in the bed with me. "It wasn't so bad here," he said. "Promise." Rather than being frightened of seeing him, I was drawn to him, relieved to see him again. Even in death he had a hold over me.

"What happened to you?" I asked him. I looked for his eyes and found them staring back at me. Crystal, piercing blue. "Why did you go?"

"When I got here I pressed the phone to my face. I wanted to call you. When I got here, I couldn't call. I fell asleep with the hard plastic phone digging into my chest. When I got here, I called my father only once, or maybe he called me. I wouldn't speak but I heard him breathing."

"Adrian, why is the world the way it is?"

"We need to build our own."

"Do you want me to find you?"

"The Lighted City is nothing without you. We always needed the two of us. When I got here, I was so lonely, I walked around by myself for days."

I reached out to Adrian to pull him to me. But I was alone, in a living room on a sofa bed that dug into my back, watched by a row of figurine angels.

I was awakened by the sound of a kettle in the kitchen. The quilt was wrapped around one of my legs, like it was preparing for the eventual moment when it would strangle me in the night. Returning me to Adrian. I untangled myself and straightened my PJ bottoms, my T-shirt. "Good morning," I called out.

April popped her head out of the doorway. "Want coffee?" she asked. I nodded and went into the kitchen, stood awkwardly until she gestured at the table. She poured coffee into a mug and plunked it in front of me and then grabbed a small tin out of one of the cupboards before sitting down. "I need my other morning pick-me-up," she said. She took out a little metal pipe and unscrewed the lid off her weed tin. She chugged half her cup of coffee and set to work packing the bowl. "Dot won't be up for a while. She's on medication," April said. She lit her pipe, inhaled. Blew it toward the open window. "To help her cope. Makes her drowsy. You can't imagine what it was like...how difficult it was for her to find him. And it hadn't been easy in general—I mean, you knew him, you know what he struggled with...and you know, what happened. Your family was ripped apart."

I tried not to think much about that word—*family*. I had never really felt like I belonged to one. Aunt Dot was Adrian's mom, Uncle Jim was who we avoided, and my parents were the people I lived with but who didn't really know me. The only person who knew me was Adrian. "Yeah, I guess so."

"You probably don't want to talk about all that. Sorry, I have a way of trying to look at things straight on. Makes it easier to be alive, I think. And it helped Adrian, helped Dot."

I drank my coffee. So this woman who I didn't know had all that Aunt Dot knew in her. She wasn't bad—I liked April and her relaxed way of talking, the way she didn't pry into what I was thinking or feeling. But it made me uneasy. How much else had Adrian shared about me? How many people in Vancouver knew all about me?

"We'll probably be seeing a lot of each other over the next couple days, Paul. Dot, she's got a shift tomorrow at the hospital even though I told her she's got to rest, but I think she thinks if she stops for a minute, it will all be worse. We have to get out of this house as soon as we can. But it's not so simple. You know how it is. We have a mortgage, we need to decide if we want to rent a while or buy something new. Anyway, I don't have to work until later tomorrow, and I thought I could take you with me to see the meditation centre. Dot will meet us there when she's done work, but the two of us can spend the day tomorrow exploring Vancouver. We can go to the beach, Stanley Park, downtown, wherever you want to go."

I hadn't expected to spend such little time with Aunt Dot while I was here. And then to spend most of my time with a stranger. "I'll see her today, though, right?"

"Yeah, well, once she gets up, we should head over to the centre and make sure everything's ready for the service. It's going to be a long day...for all of us."

The service. I'd been trying to put it out of my head, memories of Adrian's room last night pushing ideas of his death from my mind. But that was what we were going to do today. Celebrate his life and come to terms with his death.

The Sea Healing Centre reminded me of a small community centre back in Caledon and was filled with folding chairs. Generic and empty of anything remarkable, the room seemed devoid of anything but this purpose, to collect people. At the front, a podium and mic had been set up and people took turns talking about Adrian. That picture of him, the one I didn't recognize, was taped to the podium. The service was full of people around my age, some teens, and men with beards. The men with beards looked important and wore full suits. They all seemed to know each other and shook hands when they met. I hung toward the back. My dress was the only black dress I owned, the one Kayla had nicknamed my "manslaying dress," and it was too tight, too short and revealing. I knew my boobs were hanging out, and I pulled my grey cardigan tighter around me, but it was no use.

"It's always hard to lose a patient. It's even harder to lose a person who was as special as Adrian..."

"When I met Adrian, I was totally in pieces, man. I wasn't ready to talk about, like, my life, or like my mom, or any of it. I just wanted to get high and disappear. But the moment I walked into Adrian's group, that guy changed me. He changed the way I could talk about myself, see myself…"

"Adrian was the type of person who had vision, hope. Even if you couldn't see the good in yourself, he could see it in you…"

"Everything he did was for other people…"

I wanted to stick close to April and Aunt Dot, but once the speeches ended, they were immediately surrounded by people, talking about Adrian, how remarkable he was, how he'd helped them. No one seemed to know the Adrian I knew. The one who, yes, had vision, but also violence. The one who could heal and hurt at the same time.

The surface of my scalp began to tingle and I knew I was angry, but I couldn't tell at who or at what. Was it only death, lurking around, making all these people remember a person in fragments, when he'd been different from that, both more and less than that? We'd been the most important people to each other, and now I was barely considered a part of his life. Maybe the anger was with my parents, who, despite what I had told my therapist, had made it impossible for Adrian and me to be in touch. I hadn't known how to reach him, how to find him. My parents had even cut Aunt Dot off for a while, until Dad knew that Uncle Jim wasn't calling her any- more, that he'd signed the divorce papers. And Aunt Dot, I was angry at her too, as much as I tried to pretend I wasn't. That she'd agreed to all of it, hadn't given Adrian and me the chance to clear the air before he was yanked away across the country. Adrian and I had some- times joked as kids that The Lighted City must be in BC because it was as far as you could get from Caledon without emigrating to a new country. We thought we might go there together.

And Adrian. Of course, I was mad at Adrian. For the years and years of all of it when he should have known better, when we both should have known better, when we should have realized it wasn't only a game. And that what we were doing needed to stop in order to give us our own lives. That The Lighted City didn't exist and we needed to abandon it instead of trying to make it real. It didn't have to end the way it did.

And he didn't have to leave, stop living the way he did. If only he'd tried to find me, then he'd have known that while I was angry, I also knew everything had been messed up, we'd both been messed up, and it was okay to know that and keep living, as long as we had each other again.

But there was nowhere for me to put my anger. I couldn't yell. I couldn't run as fast as I could in the other direction. I wanted to be a storm. I wanted to rip my skin open by punching something hard. I wanted to bleed until the tingling on my scalp and the blood pulsing in my ears were gone and I was at peace.

I tried to focus on breathing. I counted as I breathed, slowing it down.

The speeches were over. People mingled now. I kept floating, trying to make myself small. "Paulina!" April came up to me, her face tight. "Do you want something to eat? Are you doing okay?" She handed me one of the two wraps on her plate. Egg salad.

"I'm all right," I said. "He's just not like I remembered. There was all this time I hadn't seen him."

"I don't think I'll be able to eat much today," April said. "Do you want to get out of here? Go exploring? I could leave for a bit, drop you back home to get changed and then bring you back downtown if you wanted to walk around. I need to run back to the house for a jacket for Dot anyway. It's getting cold out there."

"Shouldn't I stay?" I said, and my throat became choked and tense. I thought I should stay because I was family. But I wasn't Adrian's family anymore. He didn't know me. These people had been the ones who knew him. The teens that were sobbing into their moms' shoulders. The people he'd worked with at the food bank, the people he'd led in healing circles and support groups. Gone was the anti-social Adrian who'd only had me. The Adrian who'd died had left an impact.

"Actually, yes, I want to go, if that's okay."

At Aunt Dot's, April gave me a key. "You can let yourself in when you get back, if we're still out taking care of things." She grabbed a coat off the hooks by the door and then took a piece of paper from her pocket. "Here. This is the bus that gets you downtown. I should run back. Is it okay if I don't give you a lift down there?"

"I'll have my phone anyway," I said. "I'll be fine."

"Okay, well, here's twenty bucks, and here's some change for the bus. And here." She drew me a map and marked where the library was, the seawall, museums, and bookstores. "Call my number"—she pointed at it scrawled at the top—"if you need anything, or get lost, or for whatever, okay? Sorry things are so hectic today."

"It's fine," I said. And then I was alone in Aunt Dot's house. Adrian's house.

I changed out of my dress and into a T-shirt, hoodie, and jeans. Walked to the bathroom, makeup-remover wipes in hand, and once again, I paused by Adrian's door.

I went in. The world I had discovered last night in the dark was still here, not dreamed up. Did that mean that Adrian was here too? Maybe? Somewhere?

Pieces of paper were scattered across his desk. Pencils, gnawed like a child's. I picked one up and felt the indents, put it in my pocket. I noticed his handwriting, fragments of his thoughts— maybe the beginning of poetry, a diary—written in pencil. *The locket. Step one two three, pivot, dig. Secret hiding spot.*

To anyone else, this would have made no sense, but the image of a locket came clearly into my mind. It'd held a school photo of him and a school photo of me, and it was another secret we had. I'd have to go back to his old house in Caledon and look, see if I could find it.

I know now it wasn't a message to me, but at the time, seeing his words, having his pencil in my pocket, he felt closer to me than ever.

Leaning up against a picture frame propped on his desk was half a rock. I ran my hand along the edge. My own half was long gone. After I left home for college, my parents threw away anything I'd had that showed a sign of Adrian. I hadn't known that they understood what the half-rock meant.

I was about to pocket Adrian's half when I heard a creak in the kitchen. I flinched and dropped the rock. The pencil was enough. I didn't need to steal too much from the dead.

Once I got on the bus, though, I was crushed by a loneliness I'd hoped to leave behind in Toronto. I took out my phone and checked for messages. Nothing from Trevor. I sent a quick text:

Funeral is over. I'm just going to hang out downtown by myself.

I waited for a reply and considered sending another, but I knew the double-text always sent him hiding from me for a few days.

I messaged Stef: *Down for a FaceTime later? Service is done, I'm by myself.*

Her response came right away. *Sure! Give me an hour?*

I leaned my head on the window, watching as we moved from residential roads to downtown. I'd often imagined what had happened to Adrian, after everything that happened. Aunt Dot took him away, after he was released from the hospital. One person I'd dated had had a mental illness and was in and out of hospitals, and I imagined that Adrian most likely was treated the same way— aspects of them were the same: the periods of inspiration and activity, the visions, followed by periods of despair. For three months in grade eleven, Adrian had refused to go to school, sleeping on the back porch on a bundle of blankets like a dog. He'd been close to being kicked out for a series of fires he'd set, and this was the only school he hadn't been expelled from. He'd told me about the fires, that they'd be something that would transform the world. By then, I knew that Adrian needed more from me than I could give. I doubted I'd be able to walk into the flames. Adrian had crashed after he'd been caught, as if a different version of him had lit the fires. He told me it was all so stupid.

"What about The Lighted City?" I asked him, and he told me he didn't want to talk about it. So I came over after school and cuddled him, read to him. I stroked his forehead and his eyebrows and nose. I traced his lips. There was something beautiful about Adrian like that, all his fight gone out. I'd already thought up the way that Aunt Dot would have kept him in Vancouver, and thought it would be similar to that period: watching him, making sure he took medication to dull his imagination, not letting him out to walk around where he could see the city, where he could be free. Trying to make up for all the time she hadn't protected him by locking him up tight.

But I knew that wasn't the way to take care of Adrian. He needed the wind. He needed to walk around as if no one owned him, needed to live in a place where his father couldn't find him. I had a feeling that if I'd been able to get Adrian away when we were teenagers, or even before that, we would've been able to make something of ourselves. But he wasn't mine to raise.

I'd been wrong, though. Adrian hadn't been kept locked up. And while it sounded like he'd been in treatment, he'd found a world, people who respected and cared for him. He'd made a difference in people's lives—not like how he did in mine, but in a way that opened people up instead of closing them off.

Then, why, Adrian, did you need to die?

I walked around downtown Vancouver imagining I was retracing Adrian's steps. That he'd looked up at the skyscrapers in the downtown core and thought of The Lighted City, walked past people who were homeless and thought they could have had a place with us—they were only missing a place they felt they belonged. That everyone could come and be safe in our city. Remembering the imaginary life Adrian and I had constructed for ourselves only reminded me how little I had to show for my life.

I wanted to do good things for people, to help them, like Adrian had. There was so much emptiness in my life. Aside from my students, my friends, I never gave anything of myself. I was aware of the tensions underneath everything, that there was a reason life was so hard—for myself, for Stef, for Kayla—a reason none of us had stability, although we craved it. That everyone was broken and couldn't get things together. That the opportunities we were told would exist didn't exist. Anything that happened in our lives was carved out of our sheer desperation and willpower and endless nights of work—and even then, everything often went wrong. Jobs were lost, too few contracts gained, evictions served. And things were even harder for Stef and Kayla than they were for me. I knew they felt like they had to play good, good, good around white people to get the same things. Stef, especially, played down her heritage at work and around white people, tried to make sure everything would be seen as perfect and proper in a way I never had to worry about. It wasn't like with me, where I was able to walk into Artastic! and Drop 'n Draw and people immediately trusted me enough to hire me to work with their rich, white kids, even if my hair was wild and my smile not quite right.

I didn't want to waste the pocket money April had given me on lunch at a restaurant, so I went into a supermarket and bought some bread and peanut butter. I sat on a bench, looking out at the sea, and ate. Before I finished, rain started falling, coating me in its drizzle.

✧

Stef FaceTimed me while I was out there. I told her I was having a good time. She seemed to feel that the words were wrong, the way Stef always could, but as was usual for her, she didn't push it and ask about my life, the funeral, or my family. Instead, she told me about the new things that Wynn was learning—that just this week Wynn was talking more, communicating with other kids more, now that they all were able to understand how to play properly, inside a story with a beginning, middle, and end. She told me about a soccer league Derek had joined and that he was already getting excited for the World Cup this year. She told me about how she wasn't able to get any work this summer, despite teaching college for the past five years, almost full-time. She said if she got hired on full-time, she'd get a salary instead of getting paid course by course, and the summers wouldn't feel this way anymore. She said she was thinking about going for her master's like her boss had suggested. She said the summer approaching wasn't as she expected, filled with light, but instead was a path winding into a forest where she feared she and Derek would get lost—that it was good for Wynn to have her at home, but there was always that question of money, money, money, and even with employment insurance how were they going to manage to support a family on so much less. Maybe there were other jobs out there, a different way. But we both knew that wasn't the case.

She said everyone kept asking about me at The Cave. I wanted to ask, *Trevor too?* But the words stayed within me.

A brown-haired head bobbed into view and then bobbed out again. A plastic T. rex waved across the screen. "Roar," the dinosaur said.

"Hi, Wynn," I said.

Wynn sat beside her mom on the couch. "Can I hold it?" Wynn asked and reached for Stef's phone. I flipped the camera around and showed her the ocean. She only held the phone a minute or two before she got bored by my questions about her day and passed it off again.

"Well, she obviously misses you," Stef said. "She's been asking when we're going to FaceTime all day." This touched me, how I was a big enough part of Wynn's life that she noticed if I was away for a bit.

We got off the phone. Trevor still hadn't texted.

Although I'd been lying when I told Stef I was having a good time, there was something magical about being out here, especially near the sea. Something about the sea made me feel freer, and, looking out at it, I thought about how memories of Adrian also opened up a sea in front of me. And I thought about what he had done, how he was gone. Maybe that was what I longed for too— a sweeping erasure of self. Death, the last sea I would walk into.

How It Happened
The Lighted City

We are hiding in the forest, inside of a lean-to we've built together. I'm almost thirteen. He's fifteen. I've been ranting, and so has Adrian. My parents forgot to sign a form that would let me go on the class trip to Montreal. Then they had said it was too expensive, that I was too young. "I never went to anything stupid like that," Adrian says. "I didn't even tell them about it."

"But didn't you want to get away from them?"

"Well, sure," he says. "But I didn't want to get away from you."

I smile. I'm larger than life when he says things like that to me. Like even though I am just a girl who has no power over school or my parents or the decisions people make for me, I have power over him. But fury still burns in my stomach. "We were going to go to a cool museum and get to go shopping and eat in restaurants. And everyone already thinks I'm a freak, and now it's going to be even harder."

"So what? They are the freaks, not you. You're perfect. You think all those idiots would get to go to The Lighted City?"

Adrian leans on his side in the lean-to and smiles at me. His black hair falling over his face.

I look down. "But, Adrian," I say. "Like, The Lighted City, it's not the same as Montreal or something."

His eyes become sharper.

"I mean, like, it's not like we can just hop on a bus to get to The Lighted City." I stop myself before I say the thing that I know will set him off. *The Lighted City isn't real.*

"Are you feeling really angry?" he asks me, and he's watching me like how I see him watch animals in the forest sometimes when he wants to creep up behind them, bucket in hand to trap them. He's registering every movement I make.

"Yeah."

"Here." He takes out a lighter from his pocket. He turns it on. He pulls me closer to him. We're both wearing shorts, caught in the end of summer, warm September days. He holds me against him. "Watch." We both watch the flame. "The way to The Lighted City is through there. Just like it always has been. One day, when we're both ready, we'll just step into the flame and then none of this will bother us anymore, you know? It's all an illusion, and the real place is where we're away from all of it, together. But you have to be brave enough to let go."

I am afraid but I also like his warmth near me. He's holding me so tight and I'm still angry and I watch the flame like he says. "Yeah, okay," I say.

"You'll go with me? Promise?"

"I will."

"Pull up my shorts." I pull the fabric of his shorts up, exposing the white of his thigh, never tanned by the summer sun. He's still holding me, holding the lighter in front of my face. He lets the lighter go, flicking it off, and presses it to his thigh, the way I've seen kids press lighters into the vinyl bus seats on the way to and from school. He winces, tears come into the corner of his eyes, but he doesn't cry. "Your turn."

I can feel his heart beating faster. I pull my shorts down and point at a place beside where my underwear starts on my upper thigh. Where I know my parents won't see. He flicks the lighter again, and we watch the flame. "Ready," I say. And I can't wait for the pain to shut everything else out. The metal presses my leg and it's like when I use the trees to rip my knuckles open, like when I punch and let everything out, but it's different, too, because Adrian's here, and I'm not in control. I bite my lip till it bleeds. He pulls the lighter away from me. We both look down at our welts and lie back together, hold each other, hearts beating and out of breath. I'm not angry anymore. The pain pulses through my thigh, and I can't feel anything else.

"Those are our tickets," Adrian says. "We'll know when the time is right, that we'll go. We don't need stupid permission forms or a bus to Montreal or money. We only need each other."

And the rest, I can't remember.

How It Happened
May 2016

I got lost in Vancouver on the way back to Aunt Dot's from downtown by myself. Now, I would double-, triple-check the way. I would have someone to check in with, but back then, I didn't care what happened to me. The bus number was correct but went in the wrong direction, weaving through the city and unfamiliar suburbs, getting darker and colder as we went. I checked my phone and knew by the time that I'd gotten it wrong. When I asked him, the driver told me to get off and stand at a stop across the street. I couldn't even see the mountains against the dark night sky.

Once I finally made it back, no one asked where I'd been, and April made dinner for the two of us. She said Aunt Dot was sleeping, worn out from the service, but I had a creeping feeling that I was being avoided.

After April went to read in their room, I curled up on the sofa bed with my sketchbook and started to draw—pieces of The Lighted City, but when I let myself relax and draw what I was feeling, I only drew a hut where a figure of a boy crouched in hiding with a figure of a girl. A dark, starless sky, a night Adrian and I had run away, only getting as far as a hut we'd made during the day, but enough to know that we were alone and protected from his father.

That feeling of love, of wanting to hide and protect someone because you know where they hurt, was almost desperate.

Even all that desperation and love couldn't get us beyond a few metres from his house. And it never would. We'd never leave together, only apart.

My phone lit up: *We miss you!* Kayla texted.

Who is we?

All of us! We're at the cave!

Who's there?

Stef, Derek, Trevor so far. We ALL miss you. Even Trevor.

I miss you guys too.

What's happening in Vancouver?

Not a whole lot. Just wandered around downtown after funeral.

Don't forget us!

I won't.

I was cold again, on the sofa bed. The heat never seemed to kick on at night, and I actually missed the heat wave in Toronto.

I still had so many questions for Aunt Dot, but I wasn't sure I'd even get to see her. After everything had happened and Aunt Dot took Adrian away, it wasn't just Adrian who I lost, but her too. I was happy to never see Uncle Jim again, but her absence was more unsettling. Now she was doing it again. As if she thought I also had done something wrong, when Adrian and I had been found. And maybe I had . . .

I texted Trevor: *Maybe I shouldn't have come here.*

I waited and waited, but he didn't text back. Probably still out at The Cave, drunk. Too drunk to type or care about me.

✧

In the middle of the night, I woke as a body moved past the sofa bed and into the kitchen. A glass of water filled at the sink. Movement again, past the bed, down the hall into the bedroom. For a moment, I thought the person went into the second room, but of course it was Aunt Dot, returning to April. My soul ached for Adrian.

I half woke to the sounds of Aunt Dot in the kitchen again, morning this time. April was with her. "I need another day," Aunt Dot said. "It's harder than I thought it would be."

"So it's up to me to take care of her? You're the one who invited the girl. She flies back tomorrow morning."

"I know, I know. I wanted her here, I need some answers, I thought it would help. But nothing helps." She started to cry. "I wish my brother had come." I heard April move toward her in the kitchen. Gentle sounds. Maybe of an embrace. The feeling of not being wanted filled me up, but was so familiar, a painful coziness I could wrap around myself. I fell asleep again.

I woke and looked outside—a light, misting drizzle, grey skies. Aunt Dot was no longer in the kitchen, but April was making breakfast. "Do you have a rain jacket?" she said, instead of saying good morning.

"No."

"Hmm." She put eggs and bacon on my plate, set down toast, and then went to rummage around in the front hall. She came back with a red waterproof windbreaker. "Here," she said. "This will do for today. Dot's not feeling well, so we'll let her sleep till she needs to get up for her shift. I'll take you to Stanley Park today."

"In weather like this?"

"Hey, you wanted to see Vancouver. It's warmed up a bit too." We ate in silence and then crowded into the front hall, putting on our jackets. Hers was a bright yellow slicker. "I like it because it's classic," she said.

While April drove, the mountains appeared again as she crested a hill. Adrian and I had never dreamed of mountains, but seeing something so magnificent each day must have been comforting. Or at least I hope it was comforting for him.

At Stanley Park, we grabbed a park map at the information post and followed a trail through the forest instead of going along the waterfront. And there was Adrian. My Adrian, his hair shaggy and black and his face gaunt. Blue eyes like ice, not hidden behind glasses. Eyes looking for me. He walked with us in the forest, enjoying the trees that looked like something fallen out of our imaginations. I saw his long, pale hand wrapped around a trunk. His shadow sliding along beside April. I widened my eyes at him, behind April's back, hoping he would come to me, that he wanted to talk to me again, but soon he was gone.

How could he not have been happy in a place like this, with moss and ferns and a light drizzle of rain making everything green pop out even more? It seemed like the perfect place for him, yet he'd covered his room with photos of the past, allowed Caledon to become the place he yearned for, even though we'd always dreamed of living in a city, of getting away from his dad and off to somewhere where he could just exist.

April brought me to a path that led along the ocean and then we walked for a bit into the forest, along the path. That's when she started talking.

"I know it's probably sucked being here and not spending time with Dot, just getting stuck with me. But she hasn't had an easy road. And losing Adrian, it's the worst. For both of us. It was really hard for her, you know, coming here." She put both hands into the pocket of her rain slicker. "Along with everything else, she had to leave behind her first love."

"Uncle Jim? He's no prize."

She looked at me with her dark, startling eyes. "No, not Uncle Jim," she said, and laughed. Growing up, I'd always wondered how Aunt Dot had been married to someone like Uncle Jim, but I'd never really thought about her private life, how we all had one. Even as children.

"It hasn't been the best year, obviously. This has been a terrible time, horrific. And a lot of stuff was brought to the surface again. But I think overall Dot is happy here, with who she is at least. I don't want you to worry. Or to feel bad about any of it. I'm sure you have a lot to deal with already...and I'm sure as hell not going to say that it happened for a reason, because I think that there's too much fucked-up shit in this world for things to happen for a reason. Or it'd be one fucked-up reason. But she's happy here."

"How is that even possible?" I tried to catch the anger beginning to spike the edges of my words, but I couldn't help it. "He's gone!"

"I know," April said. "But things were different before that. We'll heal again." The path forked and April followed the one to the left that became paved and twisted toward the waterfront. I could hear the waves. "We have each other. She's being true to herself out here, and nothing against your father, but it took her forever to tell him about me, that she's queer. Apparently where you grew up, it's not the easiest to be out. But now she's just herself." Dad had never really talked about Aunt Dot at all, or mentioned that she came out to him, just let us know one day that she had a partner out in Vancouver named April, a woman, and that was that. I didn't know if it made him uncomfortable to talk about or what their conversation was like when he found out or if he didn't think it was anything of note. I'm sure he talked to Mom about it. "And we both love this place. She loves her work, loves taking care of people and has to do it somewhere because I sure as hell don't need her taking care of me."

I didn't say anything. I was still stuck on the word, "happy," that Aunt Dot was "happy."

I was going through an internal checklist—what I needed to be happy. I knew I wasn't happy, but I'd always assumed it was sort of the way I was. Or that I was like that now because of everything that'd happened to me. I didn't understand how a person could experience bad things and not have them cling to them, that an emotional state was something fleeting instead of permanently carved.

"There are good days and bad days. She needs to grieve right now, but she also needs to learn to accept a lot. But I think she'd like to stay in touch, if you would. I think she wants to understand everything before she moves on from it. She wants to heal the parts of her that she can, wants to reconnect with the family she has. I want to get married. But there are things that need to wait till someone feels ready, till someone's healed. At least she's living freely. Sharing our life with you, even with everything fucked up right now. I never was in the closet as long as she was, never had another family either, except for my parents. And they were great.

It wasn't easy, of course, but I was lucky, mostly. I don't know what it's like to be Dot, I tell her all the time."

I nodded, but April wasn't even looking at me. We reached the seawall. She stretched and a smidgen of sun was sneaking out from behind the clouds. "What do you think? Beach next?"

With the sea in front of me, I only was able to think about Adrian. But unlike in Toronto, my thoughts were able to roll out in the waves and break against the rocks.

April went toward the water almost right away, peeling off her windbreaker, her jeans, her T-shirt. She wore a black two-piece underneath, the top a halter that exposed a slip of her tanned skin. "You should swim!"

"Isn't it too cold?"

"Not comparatively." Compared to what, I wanted to ask, but she slipped in without even looking back, one, two steps and her body began to disappear beneath the surface.

"I didn't bring a suit," I said, but I was already pulling at my jeans that were too tight for my legs, tripping over them as I pushed my socks off my feet.

Despite how terrible that time was in my life, these were the moments, looking back, when I saw myself begin to break out of the shell of who I had been as a child. I was somewhere I'd never been, stripping off my clothes in air that still had a chill, ready to move into the water in my underwear. I think more than recklessness, I'd reached a point where I needed to change something in order to keep going on, that, although I constantly thought about joining Adrian, there was another force, pushing me to see what life had to offer.

Moss clung to the rocks closest to the shore, and as I walked forward, I stepped on one and began to stumble, twisting my ankle.

More slippery than it looked. My ankle throbbed, but I kept going. The cold water around my ankle calmed the pain. A heron watched us from a few metres away like a spectre. It took off as I moved forward clumsily.

"I've never swum in the ocean before," I said, but truthfully, I'd barely swum at all—not really in Toronto lakes or in summer pools. Once or twice, I'd tagged along with Kayla in a big group to Toronto Island but always found myself walking in until the water was at my knees and then walking out, kicking water at the edge of the beach, listening to a new friend tell me their woes.

My summers as a child had been taken up with Adrian, and the lakes and rivers in Caledon weren't clear enough to swim in—we were sure leeches or fish or snapping turtles would get us. And that if they did, we'd never recover. No pinch of salt would send Caledon leeches shrivelling and shrinking; we'd be doomed to blood diseases, Lyme disease, poisoned. Aunt Dot had told us about West Nile disease, and we feared mosquitoes and ticks, so much that summer smelled like DEET and sweat. Our mouths tasted sour with the spray of OFF!

If we'd only gotten into the car, been driven by a parent, we could have been at a beach at the nearest conservation park, swimming. Eating a hot dog from the snack stand. Meeting other kids. But we never even asked our parents, falling deeper into our own world.

"Adrian came here with us too," April said, turning to me and waving with her hand, gesturing to come closer to her, deeper into the water. "It was his first time swimming, he said."

"Did he like it?"

"He loved the beach. He'd smile. Every time he swam out further. The water helped him unwind a little."

"I have this image in my head of him being miserable all the time," I said. As I spoke, I moved closer to April, deeper into the water. She was right. It wasn't cold, comparatively. Compared to what, I still wasn't sure—some archetype of what cold was, melting snow in January, sneaking inside of your gloves, down the top of your boots when you least expected it. "Like, once he was here."

"Why? Was he like that when you knew him?"

I thought of Adrian and felt his presence beside me, breathing on my neck. His lips so near to my skin. And he began to move, I could see him leaping into the water, swimming out further and further until I could only see his head bobbing in the distance. Although I couldn't see it, I could feel his smile from here. His energy that was never still, constantly in motion, showing me things.

His long hands weaving together grasses until he had a boat we could float in. Stones collected and built until he made a cave where we could store our snacks and belongings we didn't want washed away.

So much of him was what I imagined, not what was.

"No, he wasn't miserable," I said.

At school, he hadn't had many friends. Other kids stayed away from him, as if there was an invisible force around him that repelled. I didn't understand this. He was the most compelling person I had ever met. This compulsion to be around him kept me from having a lot of friends myself, and anyone I got close to proved to me that I couldn't trust them, eventually ruined things with me. All I ever wanted, as we spent our days apart in different classrooms, at different schools once he got to high school, was to get home to talk with Adrian. Not even to play, but to talk, to comfort.

"Dot, she said he always was troubled. And sure, I saw that side of him, the way anyone is when they've gone through what he did. But he also gave so much to others, drew them to him."

How had he become so opposite?

I dipped under the water. I wanted to open my eyes, but fear kept me from doing it. I thought I'd see Adrian's corpse, floating, only half-drowned. Once Adrian had been kicked out of the school I went to, he'd gone to an alternative high school for a bit that allowed kids with problems to learn a trade, because even when he was a boy, Adrian had problems. But he only had problems because of Caledon and because of Uncle Jim and because no one would help him. Not my parents, not Aunt Dot. Even I couldn't, no matter how hard I tried. Even once he went to that other school, even once he was kicked out of there, too, I never said anything about what had been happening to him. Because I'd promised, and Adrian told me that secrets kept us closer together. As long as he had me to talk to, to be with, he'd be okay.

The air felt colder than the water, burning at my cheeks.

"Come on out," April said. "You don't want to be in it too long when it's like this. You never know what could happen. It sneaks up on you."

After we got out, I pulled my hoodie from my backpack, shivering, and put it over my soaked bra. I slipped my arms out of the sleeves and undid my bra behind my back with my arms still encased in their hoodie shell and then dropped the bra to the ground. Arms went back into the hoodie sleeves and I scooped the bra up and put it in my backpack. April laughed. "I guess modesty isn't dead," she said, and turned around, staring at the water. I slipped off my underwear and pulled on my sweatpants, crammed my feet into their shoes again. It'd stopped spitting, so I carried the red jacket in my hands.

As we walked back to the car, every shadow was too close. "What do you do at the centre?" I asked April.

"That's our next stop. I run it, keep everything going smoothly. We have a bunch of workshops, support groups. I run the meditation groups. My background is in psychotherapy, but then I became more interested in mindfulness and decided to look into nontraditional forms of healing. I was sick of working with organizations and institutions. Mainly, I'm interested in how the body connects to the mind." She pawed at my hand, using a gruff, short movement.

Instinctively, I pulled it toward me, scar-side pressed against my legs. "Right."

"It can connect explicitly, or implicitly. I had a cough for years, but it was only after I came out and went to a shit-ton of therapy that it went away. Once I met people who accepted me. And when I'm somewhere where I know I'm not safe, where I know people are looking at me, or where I know I have to watch myself, the cough comes back. But it's not something I think about, not something I know. I went to an ENT and was constantly on allergy medication and nothing helped. Until I figured out my body was telling me something."

"Oh." I wondered if touching my hand meant she knew.

Knew how I got when I was angry. Somehow could understand that the first time I'd run away it hadn't been from Adrian or from Uncle Jim, but from my parents, from the feeling of being unseen. I'd gone into the forest and when I was there, my hurt turned to anger, and I couldn't think. I wanted to bash my head against the tree trunk in front of me, but I thought about school, thought about walking in when people already thought I was weird, and walking through the halls and the way the other kids would look at me with a huge gash on my forehead, and instead of my head, I swung my fist. If I didn't let it out, something much more terrible was going to happen, and I couldn't let it. I didn't feel the pain, only that what had been aching in me was now silent and that some new form of life was pulsing in my hands.

That's how it felt the first time I swung.

The blood on the tree was terrifying. And then the pulsing in my hands—that red, dark stain that spread over the maple tree's bark, rutted and rough. The blood on the tree took up the whole length of my torso, about two feet. I hadn't expected there to be so much. It was the first time I'd ever terrified myself, made a connection between the way I felt—that black pit in me growing deeper each day, the trickle of anger along my scalp and in my shoulders, my neck—and what I could do, to myself or others. I was so young, only eight. There was power in this, a new way of seeing. There was control in being out of control.

But April walked away from me and didn't look at my hands, the gnarled scars on my knuckles from years of being ripped open and healing. I still felt exposed. Like no matter what I did, the most complicated, dark parts of me that I tried to keep hidden, somehow those came out and were the parts of me that everyone could see.

✧

April's Healing Centre had transformed, back to its original purpose. A sign at the front advertised that it was only for women-identifying and nonbinary people. Inside, there were big shelves against the walls, like at a yoga studio, full of cushions and blankets. On the back wall, a huge bookshelf was stuffed with titles like *How to Be Yourself*, *The Compassionate Breath*, and *Healing from Emotional Abuse*. Near the shelf, red, plush reading chairs were scattered.

Two women sat across from each other with cups of tea, talking. One seemed like she might even be crying, and the other one pressed her shoe against the bridge of the other woman's foot, to comfort.

As soon as I entered, I became short of breath and a rocking began in my stomach. And more than that, pain. As I watched the grief or confession pass between the two women, my own grief hovered in my chest. But the act of sitting there, and being honest— even if it was with Kayla or Stef or Trevor—was impossible. The only place sharing could happen was in someone's bed, in a little cave or hut made only for two, not out in the open in a designated place for it. It was false to share yourself when it was expected of you.

An arm flung itself around my shoulders and my body folded in, each shoulder trying to escape from touch. "Paul, what do you think?" April asked. Aunt Dot was with her, and she looked at me squarely in the face, as if she wasn't the one who had avoided spending time with me all day long.

"What did you get up to yesterday after the service?" she asked me, as if no time had passed since then. "Did you go to the science centre? Or any of the restaurants April told you about?"

I didn't want to tell them that I couldn't afford it—that I couldn't afford barely anything and wasn't sure why I was even there. That I'd come here on a ticket bought for me because it was the only way I could come and that I thought coming would make it so Adrian could finally leave me, but instead he was around me more and more. Or maybe I'd wanted to understand. "I was just walking around and taking in everything," I said.

"Do you like it here?" Aunt Dot asked. Her face was pained—she so badly wanted me to be enjoying myself, wanted me to feel no bad feelings. I'd forgotten that about her. That Adrian and I hid from her if we scraped a knee or bumped our heads, even though she was the one with the skills to make sure we were all okay. We couldn't stand seeing the expression on her face when we were in pain.

"I love it," I said. "Especially the sea." I hoped she couldn't see inside of me to where I felt raw about being ditched by her this whole trip.

There was this song I had liked as a kid: *Everyone you love will betray you*, it went. But perhaps I was remembering it wrong. I'd thought it was extremely adult, and wise. I still think about it sometimes, even though my parents were never willing to buy me the album, and I was too young to keep track of the name of the singer, or of the song. On rare occasions, when Adrian came to sleep over at my place, we'd huddle in my room in a blanket fort, rolling the dial of an old clock radio Dad had given me, searching for even the last few seconds of the song. We'd listen for hours through country and pop songs just trying to find it playing again. I don't know why I felt those words so strongly. What made my feelings the way they were back then and the way they were now.

For some reason, those childhood memories were much more real to me than anything that had happened to me in my twenties. My experiences as an adult faded so quickly—things that happened one year ago, two years ago, felt much further away than that. They were shed from me in the daylight until they came back stronger in the middle of dreams.

Everyone you love will betray you, even people you haven't met yet.

April told us the meditation class was about to begin. "You should join us, Paul. I think it'd be good for you."

"It will be good for all of us," Aunt Dot said, and put an arm around my shoulder.

An image came to me: Aunt Dot, putting her hand on my shoulder in the kitchen. My uncle making coffee in the morning, his right hand bandaged. "You know what that's from," Adrian whispers to me, once his mom leaves me and sits down at the table. He says it so quietly, maybe not even at all, just thought it so I thought it too. Uncle Jim chops an overripe tomato with the bandaged hand.

"I bit right through the skin."

Out the door, to hide and play, to escape.

How could she not have known?

April handed me a meditation cushion. The women who had been talking in the reading chairs approached the shelves that held the meditation pillows and blankets, took one of each. More people streamed in. April greeted each one—she didn't alter her brisk personality, but I realized that she was consistently open with each person, observant. Many were regulars and knew April by name. About twenty people organized themselves in a circle. I sat down, squatting roughly on my pillow. It was stiffer than I'd imagined.

"Hi," April said. "Let's begin."

She closed her eyes, and everyone around her closed their eyes.

My eyes closed. I'd never done this before, except before sleep, or in the depth of the darkness that had been coming for me since Adrian died. All I could hear was my breath. Every so often, April would interrupt the silence with a gentle encouragement to "focus on your breath."

I remembered walking with April over the gravel when we went to the beach, how she'd reached for my hand, my scars.

April's voice told me to focus on parts of my body, slowing, going through them one by one: my neck, my lungs breathing, in and out, God, I felt such a pain in my lungs, in my chest, it was like I couldn't breathe at all, but I was breathing, I pulled in air, and it was smoke, and I was tied to a tree and I needed to get out of there and Adrian was just watching, he didn't help me, he was naked, half-amused.

I thought we were going to do it together.

I opened my eyes.

I left.

Outside, I could hear the ocean. Wind was whipping up waves along the seawall, and I walked toward it, where I could look down into the sea. It seemed lonely, the way it reached up toward the shore, trying to press closer to where people lived. It would be easy—for me to slip off the pier here, to disappear into the water below. A better death than Adrian had maybe, slower, gentler. The water looked so dark green it was almost black without light shining down on it from above. The sky was grey, and it would be dark soon, another day passing away with me in it. Unless I finally made a decision.

How It Happened
The Lighted City

To build a shelter, first you need space. You clear the space of anything that would be too rough to lie on to avoid getting poked. Sometimes you can mat the grass down to make a soft floor, especially if the grass isn't all dry. Sometimes you need to pull the grass from the ground, to dig out the roots, pat down the soil. This is best when it's hot because then you have a cool dirt floor to lie on. Then you can bring in a rug or blankets. A tarp. Whatever you need. Depends how long you need to be hidden.

Then you need saplings or long branches. You can do it two ways. If you want to make a house with a flat roof, you can use stiff branches. Can use them for a lean-to as well. Need saplings for a dome. Saplings work best in general as long as you bind them tight. You can use vines to bind the dome, if you like. You can cheat, use rope or twine to tie the branches together into a frame instead of only relying on what you can find in the woods. For a dome, the branches all meet at the top, bound in place. For the others, you make a box, or lean your branches against trees and lash it to them. Take bundles of grass. These will be your sides. Take handfuls and bind them with twine or vines. Attach these to your frame.

You're hidden. You're safe.

How It Happened
May 2016

On the seawall, the wind picked up into a howl. "Paul!" Aunt Dot came running to me. "Oh my, Paul!" She pulled me into a hug when she caught up with me. "I thought we'd lost you for a second," she said. "That you were really gone." *Gone.* Hard to know if she meant back home, off downtown, or gone, like Adrian, gone. The sea still called to me, but my back was to it. Each wave was a breath in my ear. I didn't say anything. "What happened in there?"

"It was just too much," I said.

Aunt Dot sat on a bench and looked across the harbour. "I'm sorry I haven't been more available," she said. I sat beside her and one of my hands found the other in my lap, the fingers of my left running and bumping over the dips and rises and knots of scars on the back of the other. "Things have happened quickly for me, although I know that it must seem so slow for you. That I should have reached out to you to let you know about Adrian or even talked to you after we moved out here. But I didn't know how much damage had been done, and your parents didn't want me to say anything at all—just wanted Adrian gone."

"They always wanted everything gone," I said. "What happened barely made a difference."

"You know that's not true, Paul. They were really worried for you. It isn't... It was hard for Adrian being here, and I'm sure it was hard for you. You kids never had enough time apart—that was wrong I think, now—but also we needed you, Paul, you know that. I needed to talk to you, I wanted to know what you knew... if you knew... And I know it's not about me, it's not, I mean, Adrian..." Her eyes shone in the dusk light. She couldn't look at me. "It was better once we got here. For me, but for him too."

"But he was away from everything he knew."

"But it was an adventure, Paul. He was happy very often. He made friends. You saw all the people he touched. More than he ever could have if we'd stayed in Ontario. I don't think going through treatment there would have done him as much good, because he would have stuck to what he'd always known." Me, she meant. He would have gone back to me, tried to find me. I was what kept him stuck.

"But it didn't make a difference," I said. "He's still gone."

"Adrian was sick, Paul. He had days that were good, but he was still sick."

"I just never saw him that way. I can't help but feel like if I had been able to talk to him, things would be different."

"I really don't think they would have been."

"I just think maybe he felt guilty, maybe it was all my fault."

"Paul, what happened to Adrian, I don't really think it had much to do with what happened with you two. Of course, he missed you greatly, I know that. And he never had wanted to hurt you. But there were other problems, I mean, I think you probably know, but other things Adrian needed to work out. That we all needed to work out. It's hard to talk about. We did try though."

As she talked, Aunt Dot began to fold over. Her words became thicker, and I knew she was crying, although I couldn't bring myself to look at her face. I must have seemed cold in comparison, but tears couldn't come with my heart beating in my chest like this, the burning along my scalp. I knew my face was red.

"We went to family therapy, and he was doing well on his medication. We all were doing well. The last few years, it was like a different life. We were a real family. Not like before. My fault, not yours.

"What happened was that Adrian went off medication cold turkey, in secret. I only found out after. I didn't think I needed to monitor him. I didn't want to. He's an adult—was—and God, I shouldn't even have kept a gun in the house with all the heavy healing work the three of us were trying to do, and how uncovering all that stuff is also so much pressure. But I was afraid all the time, not of Adrian, but that Jim would come one day, even after all that time had passed...I shouldn't tell you all this.

"He just, he didn't like himself, Paul. He didn't feel good about himself and then going off medication like that, the chemicals, there was nothing we could have done."

"But what if he'd been able to call me? I would have talked to him."

"It wouldn't have changed anything," Aunt Dot said, but I didn't think she looked so sure. "I think sometimes it helps to get away. Once I did, I found April, I was able to make more of a life. Adrian's passing is a tragedy, but maybe it's brought us together, maybe that's what Adrian would have wanted. For us all to heal."

"No," I said. The Lighted City had never been about healing. It had been about freedom, escaping family, not strengthening it. "That's what you want, what April wants."

"It may not be like how you remember, but Adrian wanted that too. He put his whole life into it." His life after me. "He wanted to help others heal too."

I didn't say anything.

"I know you're supposed to go home tomorrow, Paul, I know we haven't had enough time together, to talk, to talk about everything. There is so much I want to say to you. And I don't know if you have a job or a partner, things you can't leave, but if you had the time, you could stay. I won't feel better overnight. I won't be able to tackle all of this with you right away. But I'd be willing to try. You could have a whole new life here. If you didn't want to get a place with us, we could help you with an apartment. Help you get a job. You could work with April until you found something…"

A life away from everything I knew.

It was tempting, being able to slip away, no more problems with Trevor, no secrets. People who knew who and what I was, a new city, people to lean on. A chance to finally not be hidden. It also made my skin crawl.

Truthfully, from the moment the plane took off to the moment it landed, I felt like I was making a mistake going back to Toronto, back to Trevor who hadn't texted me, back to Artastic!, which still hadn't paid me. I'd been given a chance to leave everything behind, to be with Adrian again, away from everything that happened in Toronto, but I couldn't do it. I would never be brave enough.

As the plane landed, I turned my phone back on. A message from Trevor: *Derek told me you get back today. Welcome home.*

How It Happened
The Lighted City

Uncle Jim's home, and he hollers for us to come inside for dinner. Normally when he's there and he smells like beer, we grab our plates and bring them back outside with us, where we eat engrossed in our own conversations, about our games, about our feelings, about a new bug or toad we've trapped and hope to tame. As we watch the sun fade away and the night sneak in, it's easy to feel protected. Everyone who could hurt us—my parents by ignoring me, or his—is inside, and out here, we are our own little unit, family. But Uncle Jim tears us away from that feeling tonight. We load our plates with potatoes and slices of beef, and he says, "Sit down instead of running off like little shits." He's got a beer in front of him. The counter is crowded with empty cans.

We sit. Aunt Dot doesn't say anything, brings us glasses of milk and sits down, too, and begins to eat. I hate drinking milk with dinner, but she always gives it to me anyway. It's too thick to wash down food, doesn't refresh me. Usually Adrian brings me a glass of water outside and chugs down my milk for me.

Their sick cat walks over to its dish and eats a few bites and then makes a low meowing sound, walking off to the living room where I know it'll throw up. I want to do the same. Trapped with these hunks of meat in front of me, milk. Uncle Jim watches Adrian, waits for him to eat. "Adrian," he says, as soon as he takes a bite. "What kind of name is Adrian? Why did we name our boy Adrian, Dot?"

Aunt Dot doesn't say anything, ignores it like it isn't even happening.

"Adrian. Aren't you going to eat? Why're you stopping?"

I'm old enough to know that Uncle Jim's drunk and we should go outside. I kick at Adrian's foot. He tries to keep eating, looking down, only focusing on the food. He swallows hard. I press my foot against his. At least I'm there. If he doesn't want to quit, run outside, I'll stay with him.

"Why didn't you take any beans? Huh? You think you're too good for our beans."

Aunt Dot says, "Please, Paul is over. Come on, Jim."

He turns and looks at me. Those red-rimmed blue eyes, Adrian's eyes in the face of someone I hated. I look back at him hard. I think, *I know you, I know what you're doing.* He isn't surprised by this. "And I guess you think you run the place?" he says to me.

Adrian jumps up and grabs my hand and we go out the back door, letting the screen door slam. We run. I don't really know why we run because I don't remember being that afraid. Only angry. We go back to my house, even though that's not a proper escape either, and make pizza pockets. Dad phones Aunt Dot to make sure Adrian can stay, Mom hovering beside him so she can hear what his sister says. He pauses for a long time, and I imagine Aunt Dot is telling him something, something important, that she wants to talk, but Dad reaches for his glass of wine that's out of reach on the table and Mom hands it to him and shakes her head in his direction. I know what it means. They don't have time for Aunt Dot, the way they don't have time for me.

Adrian sleeps on my floor in a sleeping bag. Normally we keep it in a basement closet that my parents swear is infested with rats, and Adrian sniffs at it, says it smells like something dead mixed with mouse poop. Somewhere in the middle of the night, either I have a nightmare or he does, and so we both end up on the floor, curled up in the sleeping bag, together.

Now

I take a bus north, on my way to another ravine pilgrimage. A man sits down beside me, unmasked, and begins to cough. He turns and looks at me, waits for me to notice him, then smiles and coughs deeply again without covering his mouth. I feel myself flush with anger. I lean away from him and look out the window. Light flakes coming down. I go over Jocelyn's email in my head.

Sunday, December 7, 2025
Subject: The opening
  I must say that I was quite surprised by your behaviour at my show on Friday. You weren't only a guest, but a guest of honour, and I did not expect someone I hold in such high esteem to ridicule me with others. We have had a working relationship for half a decade, and I've cherished our relationship—I'd felt it had moved beyond teacher-student to one of equals, despite the fact that I have continued to pay for your services. Now, I see that I am only a "client" to you, that you hold little to no respect for me or my art. I think the time has come that we cease our lessons, as I am able to work effectively on my own and am no longer in need of an "instructor," especially one who does not appreciate my art or what I am trying to communicate.

Thank you for the past five years. Until this point, they were a pleasure.

Jocelyn

The email makes me think that maybe I've been slowly slipping into 2016 not only in *How It Happened* but also in my actions, that part of me is in my twenties again, more concerned with Trevor coming back and my dreams than staying afloat. I've finally gotten to a point where I prioritize my survival over other things, and I don't want to be who I was before, where each day felt like a struggle. I know that part of what's allowed me to maintain my business is having more of a focus, more quiet in my life—fewer fights, fewer struggles. I've been trying to get my reactions under control.

Most days, I don't want to hurt myself anymore.

I do now, reading Jocelyn's email. I know she's right, that I acted childishly and I have to pay for it in the end. No matter how far you come, your past self comes out to create problems with your present.

The bus stops at St. Clair and I hop off, walk over to the entrance of the ravine. I've made it a goal to walk all of them, as much as possible. There's a whole network in the north end of the city, spanning west to east. When something happens to me, the places where those things occurred call me back, like part of me will always be stuck there.

I use the time walking to think about the boy.

I walk down cement steps, holding the railing in case the steps are icy. Off the side of the path is a Rubbermaid container with a heavy lid. Someone has spray-painted on it, *Please take.* It's for the people who live in encampments or on their own in little tents throughout the ravines. Since the pandemic began, people started leaving bins around, ready for donations. I pull my backpack off my back, unzip, and pull out cans of food, granola bars, juice boxes, matches, pads, and toothpaste, and lay them inside the container, nestled up beside other donations. I feel Adrian with me then and know that the person he grew into would have done the same, or more. He would have been the one who put these bins here in the first place.

But then I stop thinking about Adrian.

Think about the boy.

It's harder to connect to the memory when the weather isn't the same. Snow clings to the tree branches, and footsteps have mashed the snow on the path down with the weight of people strolling, or dogs on walks. Not like the beginning of June, wind whipping the branches around. A kite in the air as I realized we needed to go to the ravine...

After the boy was found, it made things harder for the people who lived here. Cops were around more. A violence became associated with living in the ravines, as if hiding a body and living were the same things. I didn't like needing to talk to the cops either, having them show up and ask me questions about finding him, asking me what I knew. They hadn't helped me with Adrian. They hadn't helped me when that man at the bar took me home. I didn't want to tell them anything.

I feel sorry, for everything. For discovering the boy, for changing things for the people in the ravine encampments who wanted to be left alone. But most of all, when I come walking down here, I feel sorry that I was too late. That I wasn't able to help anyone.

Adrian, another boy I couldn't save. Everything I tried to do to help making things worse, more confusing. The Lighted City, the fire that burned there, a fire that hurt instead of illuminating. Unable to heal.

I bend and pick up sticks, fallen from the trees along the path. Sometimes I have to kick off snow to uncover them. I make a bundle of branches, and when my arms are full, that's when it's time to start heading home. I try to fit them into my backpack, the zippers snug against where the sticks jut out of it, too long.

✧

When I'm back home, warmed up in front of my computer, Selina asks me about what I've written about Vancouver, about my first week of grieving Adrian. "I'm wondering if I can ask you about something I've noticed when you write about Adrian," she says.

"Yeah, sure."

"You mention this idea of protection, of what happened between the two of you, your bond, as being a way you were trying to protect Adrian, yet it had this impact on you that still bothers you now. I'm wondering how those two things work together and, when you think about those experiences now, how you see the impact."

"Well, yeah," I say, "I know that now. Obviously, it all went horribly wrong and just messed us up more. And I wasn't able to protect him no matter how I tried. I had no power to. I was too young, and then by the time I was older, I really felt like I couldn't make my own decisions about any of it. I was just caught in this thing the two of us had created. And by then, Adrian was different, angrier, scarier. He was a lot stronger than me and if I ever tried to stop things... well, I just couldn't.

"And with the kids too. I mean, with the ravine and everything. I couldn't protect them either—I couldn't get there in time, and maybe if I'd just realized everything wasn't a damn game all of the time, maybe I could have stopped things—"

"And what about protecting yourself, Paul?" Selina asks. "About younger Paul, do you think about that too, wish you could have protected her?"

I try to imagine what I looked like as a child and I can't.

"No," I say. "I don't think of her much at all."

I am one of Jocelyn's spirits. I know this because all I can feel is warmth all around me. My light spills over the floor of a forest. The forest is dark, other than where I illuminate, but I see another patch of light coming toward me through the forest. It's bigger than I am. As it comes closer and closer, all the darkness disappears, and I can see the trees, their bark smeared with non-spirit-Paul's blood.

I'm afraid, but it still comes to me, comes into me, and this is sex, I realize, and then I'm in my human form, tangled limbs, leaves everywhere, my heart beating so fast, breath against my face.

How It Happened
May 2016

When I was a child, there was no time to reflect. I had to be immediate. I hadn't felt in danger, although I guess I was. Instead, I had felt a need to lose myself in whatever was happening, to not question or think too deeply. So little had changed in 2016: I still moved like something would catch me if I stopped. Like thinking was what would cause the past to wash over me, and then I'd never be able to get away.

But I did think about it for a moment, as I waited for Dad to pick me up from the airport. Vancouver. Or even just reinvention. What the type of "healing" Aunt Dot and April claimed to be doing might do for me. How would it change my life to give myself over to something new?

But I wasn't ready. As soon as I saw Dad's sedan pull through to the pick-up area, I knew I wasn't ready.

Dad threw my bag into the back seat like it didn't weigh a thing and then we were off to Caledon. He was silent for the beginning of the ride. The radio played jazz until that was interrupted by another Amber Alert. "I can't listen to that," he said, and clicked it off. "So. How was it? How's Dot doing?"

I couldn't tell if he actually wanted to know. I couldn't really remember him or Mom having actual friends, but he had always been a little different when it came to his sister. I'm sure her moving had an impact on him too. "She's good. Her partner is really nice." The word *nice* didn't really fit my experience of April, but I didn't know how else to describe the caring way she treated my aunt, the type of relationship they had, different from any relationship I'd seen. Balanced. "April showed me around Vancouver a bit. Aunt Dot was working a lot, and she's, you know, grieving."

"And you? Are you okay? Was going out there okay?" He said this all very quietly. It was the first time he'd ever checked on my feelings. That was supposed to have been what the therapy was for, what keeping Adrian away was for.

"Sure, Dad." I looked out the window. "It was fine. Can we put on some music again?"

But ten minutes into the music, the Amber Alert repeated.

I returned to Adrian's dilapidated bungalow, close to night again in case someone was staying there. Over the fence, through the tall grass that scraped at my bare arms, warm with southern Ontario heat again. I walked away from the tree directly toward the back of the property, counting my paces—*one, two, three, pivot*—Adrian's note fresh in my mind. After five, my shoe hit a rock, and I crouched down, pulled out the stone, long and flat, and started to dig. Every so often, I paused to listen, to hear if there was someone opening the screen door of the house. I dug until I thought I'd gone too far, but then my trowel scraped the edge of something, and I kept going until it was fully uncovered. A metal tea canister that we'd stolen from Aunt Dot and stashed things in.

I swear to you that when I unscrewed the lid, it wasn't what I expected to find. We'd last filled the tin with our treasures, notes about where we wanted to be in ten years, several stones we'd collected from the dirt road, the cap from a bottle of vodka, the stem of a flower he'd given me, and the locket that had been his mother's that he'd put our pictures in. It was silver with roses etched into the metal. But when I unscrewed the cap and reached my hand in, there were no stones or notes or caps or lockets. I pulled out a gun. I wasn't sure if I'd seen it before: the guns from Uncle Jim's closet blurred together in my memory, gun, gun, gun along the walls. As I held it, I finally recognized one as something beautiful. The gun was heavy in my hand, metal with a wood handle. Someone had burned a design of twirling, leafy vines into the polished wood. In the tin, there was also a box of bullets.

I'm unsure about the idea that everything happens for a reason, but after Adrian died, I thought maybe the reason was that whatever was up there wanted to see everyone squirm. I thought about putting the gun back into the hole, but then I put the gun and bullets into the canister and screwed the top on and slid the whole thing into my backpack. It had found me. Like Adrian, the gun and I were fated for each other.

✧

The next day my parents drove me back to the city, not knowing what I carried with me. A piece of Adrian. Only he could have hidden it. Once I got home, I sat on my bed and pulled my backpack up beside me. Took out the tin, unscrewed the lid. The gun. Bullets. I put the gun beside me on the bed. There was always something in me that had been looking for it. A way out. But I pushed it under my mattress, where it made a hard lump. I liked that. I wanted to feel it as I slept.

That night I texted Kayla, and she texted *Woo! youre home!* and said she'd be over in two minutes, that there was a show she wanted to go to that night if I was down. I didn't care. I needed to be out, away from the gun. *I haven't been paid yet*, I texted her.

Don't worry, I got you, girl.

She showed up with a bottle of wine and a rant about some guy she was supposed to go to the concert with but who had blown her off. She'd twisted her brown hair into braids, and her eyes were smeared with blue and that mascara she knew made her brown eyes look round, round, round, so that she could find someone else's eyes to stare into and hypnotize, at least for a night.

"I see how it is," I said. "I'm just your backup."

"No," she said with a laugh and gave me a little push. "No, of course not, but for real if I had stayed home I would have gone insane." I was silent then, remembering the gun underneath my mattress. Thought about Adrian, coming to me in dreams and in the middle of the night. "Paul? What's up? Are you okay?"

"Can we put on some music or something?" I said.

Kayla nodded slowly and watched me as she pulled my laptop across the table to her, found something to put on. A slow hiss and moan came out of my laptop's speakers. "This is my roommate's band," she said. "What do you think?" I just nodded. The sound fuzzed into existence and then fell back again, leaving gaps without any noise, but then returned with a rhythmic thump. Feedback looped through the speakers, a hiss, a pop. "They're playing tonight," she said. I went over to the kitchen, poured myself more wine. "Did I say something? Are you okay? Is it about your cousin, you know…?"

"Can we switch the music? Is that okay with you?" Kayla flicked on something more upbeat, a girl rapping over synth and drums. We stretched out on the carpet, just lying there, not talking. She finally reached out a hand toward me and put it on my elbow.

"Were you close?" she asked me.

"We were," I said, and then I turned my face away from her, so she'd know I didn't want to talk about it anymore. Outside, it was finally dark. Dark made me afraid, but Kayla sat up and stared out the window, her face becoming more and more animated. Her excitement passed through her and into me, any fear I felt making room for Kayla, who stood and reached out her hand. "Come on," she said. "Time to go out."

✧

Kayla was pressed into some guy against the bar, and all you could hear was the growling of the band's music, how it hissed and popped. The way the bodies moved together—how could so many people fit into a space? I was repulsed and also wanted to dive right in, feel those arms pushing back my hair, completely surrounded. But I hung back by the bar, trying to catch Kayla's attention. As usual, when there was a guy involved, Kayla was gone.

I focused on the band on stage and then noticed the familiar broad frame, the beard and curly, dark hair. Those grey eyes, alive and joyful for once. Trevor was playing drums. He was one of those guys who had an acoustic guitar in his living room in a professional stand, but I always thought it was for show. He never talked about music, and it didn't seem like something he'd be able to do, the working-with-other-people part. His hands clutched the drumsticks and smacked the skins while the guitars hissed with fuzz. The sound of those guitars coated my tongue, but Trevor, of course, was the one I was watching.

When the band took a break, I looked for someone to stand with, so I wouldn't seem like I was waiting for him, but he actually smiled at me as he jumped off the stage and moved through the people pushing past each other to smoke outside. He was fighting his way to me, and my stomach clenched and my heart began to beat, the way it always did around him, so that I couldn't think. He gave me a hug, even though anyone could see—there were people all around us. Then he ordered two beers and handed me one. "I'm surprised to see you here," he said. "Did you catch the whole set?"

I said that I had and that Kayla was really into the next band and she'd dragged me along. "I didn't know you played drums," I said.

"Yeah, I guess those guys are pretty good." He drank down half his beer. "I thought you came to see me."

"You didn't tell me about it."

"I put it on Facebook. I invited you there."

My scalp starting tingling, and I wanted to tell him to pick up a phone for once and I would've been there, I would've been there early, I would've helped carry in amps and drums, I would've stood up at the front, watching, cheering him on. But even though he sounded offended, his grey eyes were still fixed on me and he was smiling. It always felt so good to see him smile. I swallowed. My scalp cooled. "Next time, text me. I'd love to see you play again."

"I guess you really want to see the next band, eh?" he said, stepping closer to me.

I stepped to him too, closing the space between us. The people around us had no faces, and they were talking all at once. "I don't even know their name."

"Let's go," he said, putting a hand on my waist. We chugged our beers and I texted Kayla, *Sorry. I had to get outta there.*

We laughed all the way to the cab, and he paid for our ride home. We didn't even make it to the bedroom.

After it was all over, I stretched on his futon, my arms in the air, and then I tried to climb on top of him, snuggle my head into his chest, an orphaned animal who just wanted love, love, love. It wasn't even midnight. He picked me up like I weighed nothing at all and set me sitting upright on the futon and handed me my clothes, which I put on. I thought that was my cue to leave, so I started to lace up my shoes, but he said, "Come outside with me while I smoke." He pulled out a crushed pack of cigarettes, and I wondered if he was turning into a chain-smoker, but I didn't ask. We slid his patio door open, and I sat on a chair he'd put out there, hugging my knees.

"I never knew you were a drummer," I said.

"Oh yeah. For a long time." He leaned on the patio railing and blew out smoke. "I think I must have been in grade seven? Or grade eight? Middle school. I played piano when I was younger."

"And the band?"

"I'm just filling in for those guys because I like them. I tried it for a little bit at the beginning of high school and kept it as a way to blow off steam. Nothing serious though—it was too much of a distraction from my writing."

"So, you were always about writing, even back then?"

He finished the cigarette. "I was always serious about it. Since I learned how to read. It was one of the only things I was good at, remembering words, being able to manipulate them and put them into a story." He put his hands on top of his head. "What's with all the questions?"

"I've just never heard you talk much about yourself," I said. "It's nice."

"You never asked."

"I thought I did."

Trevor shook his head slowly and laughed. He put his arm around me, and even though the night was hot, I wanted his warmth. I wanted to feel even warmer. "Well, what about you?" he asked.

We went back inside, although I knew my heart would ache, missing all those stars and the gentle hand of the night.

"What do you mean?"

"What were you like as a kid?" He went to the fridge and pulled out two beers and brought me one. "Tell me something I don't know about you."

Hit by his A/C with the cold beer in my hand, I shivered. We'd pushed the blanket he kept on the couch to the floor during sex, and I rescued it, pulling it across my legs. I traced the pattern, interlocking triangles. "I was like any other kid," I said, and I hated lying to him. I tried not to lie, even if I didn't often talk about the past. Lying was different, I felt then, more deviant than not telling someone something. I'd heard of lies of omission, but still didn't believe that they fell into the same category as a purposeful invention. Omission could be created by the loyalty that came along with keeping secrets. No one could force you to say anything you didn't want to say.

"I find that very hard to believe," he said. "Why won't you ever talk to me?" He still hadn't sat down. Sipped his beer by his wall of bookshelves and leaned against one, carefully.

"You're the one who doesn't talk to me."

"No, Paulina. That's not true." He walked around the apartment huffing and sighing like he was about to collapse with a heart attack. He always had to be so dramatic. "Okay, let's try something," he said. "I'll ask you a question and then you have to answer it. Then it's your turn. And I have to answer as well. No excuses from either of us."

"That feels so high school," I said, and kicked the blanket to the floor again. "Once you said I talk too much and now you're saying I don't talk enough."

"When did I say that?"

"You know when."

"Well, I don't remember, but I must have meant the kind of talking. Like when you get all chatty when you're drunk and talk about the moon and the stars and how big the sky is." He even held his hands out the way I did when I was drunk, reaching for someone, anyone to hold on to.

"I've been told it's endearing." Kayla and Stef had told me that, one of the first nights we all hung out at The Cave, shortly after I moved to Toronto. It'd formed a new belief about myself, something positive about my personality, and I held it close to me as I downed drink after drink all the nights and years that followed, designed to make me more chatty.

He gave me a half smile and my heart fluttered. I wanted him to touch me, but he said, "Even if it is…it's not *talking* talking." The smile faded, and he seemed determined not to look me in the eyes. He sighed. "I don't want to fight tonight. You can go if that's what you want."

I was trapped. I did care about him, I thought perhaps more than anyone else. Even if we were still a secret, even if sometimes he was so distant I didn't know how to find him. I wanted to hold his sensitivity carefully in my hands, wanted to crawl into his brain and see out his eyes. I desired the way he seemed to be about to cry or to rage, or the special, still way he could become removed. He was always watching the world. Sometimes I feared him. I was waiting for him to turn, the way I knew men did, no matter how much you loved them. Sometimes I expected to say the right thing to make him hit me. He never did. Despite my fear, I don't think he had it in him, and that was almost more frightening because then he channelled all his hurting into hurting people in the same place he hurt, in their open wounds.

"Fine," I said. "Ask me a damn question." I softened my swear with a smile, charmed by his interest in me. He lowered himself onto the futon, his leg pressing up against mine. I leaned into it, erasing any possible space between us.

"What were you most interested in as a kid?"

I'd been expecting him to push the vague question *What had I been like?*, which was a lot more complicated for me to answer, because back then I'd been both very loving and very afraid. I guess I was still the same way. None of us really outgrow our childhood selves. We just get better at masking them.

Everything to me when I was a kid was colour. That's what I was interested in when I was on my own, away from Adrian. My childhood was loving everything about colour. Taking paper after paper and using markers to fill the paper to the edge with a blend of purples and then greens, run over each other, the papers soggy with ink. My fingers covered in colour, the tips and sides, my multicoloured hands. Then playing at preschool with my hands in a bin of cars and trucks pushing through sand, raising my hands and losing my balance, falling backwards and my hand shooting out, crashing into a wall of blocks. Two fell and pinched the skin of my pinky finger and ripped it open. Blood was everywhere, all over the blocks. The supervisor took me to the washroom to wash the cut, jerking me and steering me roughly—I couldn't move fast enough—and told me I was so dirty with my hands covered in colour. I'd secretly thought the mess all over me was powerful, that it showed proof of how much I loved colour, of how much I drew. That was until I bled. The mess I'd made could infect the cut; I should always wash my hands and make sure to not get colour on them. I was so dirty.

"I was into drawing," I said.

"Obviously," he said. "But what else?"

"I don't know. Okay, building huts. I used to make these little shelters and forts in this field and in the forest behind my house."

"Really?" He stretched his arm out behind me and began to shake his leg up and down. He moved over a little bit so he could see my face. I loved the way he talked with his body. "How'd you make them?"

"It took a long time, a lot of hunting for the right supplies. But mostly imagination. I mean, they didn't look like houses or anything like that. They were little lean-tos and shelters and hollows."

"We made a lot of snow forts growing up, but never anything like that."

"All kids want to hide, I guess." I drank the rest of my beer and wanted to cry. Adrian had taught me how to weave a roof that was almost waterproof. He'd always had the idea for the structures, needed to hide away more than I did. "My childhood was kinda fucked up. I don't like talking about it too much."

"I want you to feel like you can talk to me," he said.

I realized he hadn't answered a question yet either. "Tell me about your first kiss."

"That's what you want to know? You really are peculiar, you know that? Okay, it was Kristy Patterson. We were at a pool party, and we were playing truth or dare. I was in grade five. And I picked dare and they dared me to kiss her. So I did."

"That sounds so normal."

And he laughed. "That's because you've never seen Kristy Patterson." Back to being an asshole.

We put on a movie, and I ended up falling asleep on his shoulder on the futon. When he nudged me awake, I jolted, my heart smashing and my stomach rocking with nausea. I clawed at him and he batted away my hands until I was totally awake. "What's wrong?" he asked. "Were you having a nightmare?" We walked up the stairs to his bedroom.

"Yeah." In my dream, I couldn't stop talking, and he was listening, and soon he knew about the gun and Adrian and he knew all of it, all of it, and his sullen mouth opened and his lips spread and he laughed.

Now

When I'm finally ready to write my first index trauma, the way I want to record it, I decide to do it outside of my apartment so that I don't think of those words every time I try to sleep. I decide that I need to be purposeful about this if things are going to change. I don't drink with dinner and I turn off my phone, hide it in a drawer. I pick up a true-crime book and read myself to sleep, my alarm set for early in the morning. I wake, sober for the first time in a while, and brew coffee in the dark. I peek outside and I can see blankets of snow covering the street, the branches of the tree outside my apartment window, cast in the streetlights.

I tuck a Thermos into my backpack and then wade through the snow to the streetcar. *I see another patch of light coming toward me through the forest. It's bigger than I am.* I keep looking behind my back, but on the sidewalk by the streetcar stop, it is the dark of an early December morning. A couple commuters walk up and wait beside me as the streetcar rolls up. They hold the collars of their dress coats together with their hands, hide behind scarves. The wind is sharp today.

Since last year, I've had a shared spot at an artist's space that comes with a locker and gives me enough space to work on my projects. My old sculpture studio closed down at the beginning of the pandemic, but in between waves, this new spot opened up and a client referred me. It's expensive, but it's been worth it to get out of the house and have the space to bring this new project to life.

But today isn't about art, although in a way, I can feel it feeding what I'm working on. As I get closer to the truth and to understanding everything that happened, it's making my project clearer. I'm alone at the studio and set up on one of the communal plastic tables. I take out my Thermos and drink the coffee. Then I put my notebook out. I touch its black, leather cover. *I'm not a spirit*, I tell myself. *I'm not light.* When I put it that way, I know it sounds illogical. *I'm not being chased. I'm alone.* My fear is still there, but in a way that I think I can handle.

Okay. Let's do this.

I write.

We are in a hut that Adrian has built. I've decided that I want more than living in Caledon and that I want to go away to school. I've fallen in love, with someone who is not Adrian. He can tell almost as soon as he sees me . . .

I write and write and write until it is all out of me, every last ash of the day everything happened, floating away as if caught in air. I'm loose and jangly after.

Keep going.

I press *Record* on my phone and try to read what I've written, but my words catch. I breathe. I count, but I can feel my heart quicken in me, and I feel hot all over, hot from flames. I need to stop. I start to dig my left thumbnail into the scars on the knuckle of my index finger, pressing until I start to feel its sharpness.

Someone comes in the studio door—Adrian, his hair long and limbs lanky. No, a guy that works in wax, but I still jump even when I know it's just that guy, that guy I see almost every time I'm here.

"Hey," the guy says. "Sorry, didn't mean to startle you."

I cough. I can't even catch my breath. Finally, after what I know is too long, I say, "No, it's okay, my mind was somewhere else. I have to take off anyway." I finally press *Stop* on my phone, which has continued to record this whole time, and then I slam the notebook shut. Head out the studio door without even looking back.

How It Happened
May 2016

Back home after spending the night at Trevor's, alone again. The gun lay in the centre of my duvet, and I could almost pretend that Adrian had been the one who put it there. In my imagination, I was always with him, he followed me from room to room. I could see, in my mind's eye, when he'd left the gun in the field for me to find. I remembered him as he was on the last day I saw him, tall and lanky, black hair falling into those piercing blue eyes. I leaned against the tree, and he pulled out all of our treasures and offered them to me, and I shrugged and shoved them into my back pocket. Then he pulled out the gun and pointed it at me and then he pointed it at himself and then he laughed that laugh Aunt Dot used to say could charm birds out of the sky. Instead, I'd always imagined fish leaping from lakes, rivers, oceans, gasping in the toxic air, contorting their bodies to flop an inch or two closer to him. He slid the gun into the tea canister and buried it. I watched by a tree, its bark pressing into my back. His long hand reached out to me and looped around my wrist. "Just in case," he said.

But none of that happened, and the way it seemed so real, his blue eyes sparkling with mischief, made all my memories seem misremembered. As if my entire life was something fabricated in retrospect.

I had to remind myself—not mischief in his eyes, but danger. He'd never used the gun on me, never threatened me with the guns kept by his father. But there had been pain, things he did to me. Rope on the final day, the day everything happened, but nothing like the gun.

I held it in my hands. It would be fitting, I thought, for me to die the way he had. I put the gun back on my duvet.

✧

On Monday, as the kids filtered out of Artastic! and were scooped up in their parents' outstretched arms, Nik was waiting. He pushed his cap back on his head and gave me a little wave. Tammy ran to him and shoved her picture into his hands. A boy, hiding behind the branches of a tree. "His name is Colin," she'd told me, pointing at scribbles across the page. Nik picked her up. I continued to say goodbye to the other parents and students. "Hey there," he said, waiting until there were no more parents left. "Long time no see."

"I was away for a few days. Funeral."

"Oh, damn, I'm sorry. You doing all right?"

"I guess," I said with a laugh, like nothing could bother me in this world. He immediately smiled too, crowded teeth straining to get over lip.

"I wasn't around either—Magda had Tammy. I had to take a trip for work. To L.A. Almost time to look for a new job, so had to get a good work trip outta this one first." He lowered Tammy to the ground, and she bent to study an anthill built up between two slabs of sidewalk, swarming with ants.

"I wish I had your life," I said.

"No, you definitely don't. You want a ride?"

"Sure."

"I had fun at least, in L.A."

"What was so good about it?"

"The strippers, duh," he said, and grinned at me.

I laughed. "You're joking."

He lightly punched me in the shoulder. The sudden touch made my stomach tense. "Maybe I am."

"Will I get to see Paul's house?" Tammy asked as she was buckled in.

"We're dropping you off first," Nik said. We both got into the front, and after I put my seat belt on, I turned and smiled at her.

"Colin's lost," she said. She was still holding her drawing in her car seat. "He's far away from home."

"Her new friend," he said, and then gave me a wink. "You ever have an imaginary friend as a kid?" He started to drive.

"Kind of," I said, thinking of Adrian. "My imagination transformed everything that was real into something else." I hadn't thought of it that way before, but as soon as I said it, I knew it was true. Some*where* else.

Nik grabbed my hand casually while his left hand lazily steered. He gave me a side smile, like all he was doing was goofing around. I peeked into the rear-view mirror to see if Tammy was watching, but she was staring out the window, distracted from the tablet in her lap by the landscape, the way the neighbourhoods slowly fell away until there was nothing but suburban houses and lawns. I felt like kids never really saw things anymore, and I was happy that Tammy was in my class, that she was special. Wynn was like that, too, that thoughtfulness already present in someone so young.

That connection to a future adult self that was able to reflect and be distant, but also still immersed in imagination. I had been like that. Still was like that.

I wasn't sure I liked the feeling of Nik's hand on mine, and I couldn't tell if it was because of who he was, that he wasn't Trevor, or that any unfamiliar hand would make me feel this way.

"Colin lives behind my house by the water—what's it, Daddy? What's the water?"

"It's the ravine," Nik said. "You're not allowed down there."

"Jason lets me," she said, and Nik squeezed my hand. "Jason and Mommy are going to get married soon, Paul. Are you going to get married?"

"I doubt it," I laughed, and I thought of Trevor. He'd have to admit we were together first. Nik watched my face out of the corner of his eye and gave me a half smile. A dimple appeared in his right cheek and I thought maybe I was attracted to him after all. A job, a kid, a house, work trips, and money without worry. An unshaking, relaxed hand holding the steering wheel with smooth, unscarred skin.

"Maybe Daddy and Rachel will get married," Tammy said.

Nik shook his head. "There she goes with her imaginary friends again. Honey, Paul doesn't know Rachel isn't real."

Tammy started to say something, but then Nik turned to look at her, hard and long and steady, even though he should have been watching the road. Tammy sucked in her bottom lip and stared out the window, breaking his gaze.

We drove up the long driveway to Tammy's house, the sun setting behind the trees in her Mount Pleasant neighbourhood. She unbuckled herself, climbed out of the seat on her own, and Nik bounded out of the car in a second. His smooth movements revealed an athleticism that made fear run through me. Tammy pulled on her backpack and held her sweater in her hands and looked up at Nik and hugged him. For a second, I thought she'd cry, but then she was running hell-bent to her mother's legs, wrapped herself around them. Her mother pressed her hands to Tammy's back and then stared out at the car, directly at me, her eyes hard. She didn't say anything to Nik, but she knew I was there, and that's all that mattered.

Nik walked back to the car and climbed in. "Fuck, I hate dealing with her," he said, but he was already smiling. We hit the highway. "What about you, Paul? Any exes I should know about?"

"No," I said. "Not in any real way."

"You must have some at least. Everyone knows how it is. By the time they're our age. We've all watched it all fall apart." He shot a look over to me, I think to watch if I was impressed by him confiding in me. "Good, bad, ugly. To know that things can start out so amazing and then become shit."

I wasn't impressed, though what he said was true in a way. But I'd heard it before... from Stef's partner, Derek, one night when he was drunk, from Kayla, from the bartender at The Cave. Everyone thought things were linear, that if it started good and got bad, that meant it would get even worse. Or they were startled when things got bad or became stagnant in the first place, had expected an upward climb toward ecstasy. But that wasn't how things really were—maybe they hadn't experienced something bad enough to stick to them. Back then I knew everything was cyclical, that what was bad would always come back, but now I thought the good would too. A plot to keep us trapped, alive, flies stuck to flypaper or swimming in a glass of orange juice.

"You're right," I said.

"I feel like I can talk to you," he said. "I feel like you know me." We were on the Gardiner now, and then we were cutting up Parkside and down my street. He parked and turned off the engine. "Let's exchange numbers? Then I can let you know the days I can give you a ride."

He handed me his phone and I put my number into it. He texted me so I had his: *Come here.* He put his arm around me, rested his head against mine. He stroked my shoulder with his hand. And despite wanting to pull away, another part of me convinced myself to relax and see what would happen.

He gestured at his pants to show me where his dick strained, hard, against the fabric. He took my hand and put it on his crotch. I could feel it hot underneath my palm and a pull toward him stirred in me. I rubbed it through the fabric, once, twice, tempted.

"What now?" I said. Not an invitation, but almost.

"Now, you go inside," he said, placing my hand back in my lap. He moved away from me and looked in my eyes. "And we will see each other again very soon." He kissed my forehead then, and I got out of the car.

A pit grew in my stomach, hard and black. Sometimes I could convince myself it was attraction. Like I'd stumbled off a cliff. But other times that pit was exactly what was wrong with me, that I couldn't tell what it meant.

My phone buzzed in my hand. *Come over if you want.* Trevor. The sun had just set, and I could see the red tail light glow of Nik's black SUV as it drove down my street.

I went over to Trevor's place, and once again, we talked on the balcony, and instead of ordering pizza, he made me food. He barely had anything, so he made some boxed macaroni and cheese and put broccoli in it. "For colour," he said. When I laughed, he said, "Hey, at least it's the organic white cheddar kind."

And I said, "Because it was on sale?"

And he smiled at me, the edges of his mouth hidden by the whiskers of his beard. He told me a little about his book, how he'd been writing it for about three years, and I was interested only because he was telling me and it was important to him. But mostly I was thinking about sex and Nik's hard dick in his pants and what it meant and if I'd done something to destroy a boundary meant to exist between the two of us. Or how if Trevor made me his girlfriend instead of having things always be like this, things with Nik probably wouldn't even be an issue. And did I even want Nik? I wanted to get to the heart of how a person could be attracted and repulsed at once. I could turn these ideas over while he told me about his work-in-progress, like turning over a stone secretly in a hand.

We fucked standing up in front of the bookcases. One of his hands clasped both of my wrists together, held them above my head, forcing me to arch my back, breasts pointed to him, squished against his chest. When he finally released me, he flipped me around, so that I faced the shelves, his arm across my neck making it hard to breathe. My hands reached out and pulled books down with them, so that once we'd both come, the floor was littered with paperbacks. We put them away together. It was nice, doing something like that together, making believe that it was my house too. I'd always thought he was touchy about his books, but he didn't mind that I stopped every now and then to read a back cover, to touch the pages, read a paragraph or two.

"You staying?" he asked me.

"No," I said, sliding another one onto the shelf. "I've got to plan out some Artastic! material for tomorrow." But really, I needed the bike home to think about the change in us, that he wanted me around, needed to decide if I liked it or not.

✧

At home, I lay on my bed and let an arm fall over the side. Then, like it wasn't a part of me, it searched under the mattress for the gun. All the confusion, all the pain, like swinging at a tree, it could be over in an instant. And over for good.

Then a text came through, a ping disrupting my thoughts. *Sup?* said the text, and that word became a charm against the darkness of my room, against the changes in Trevor, against the gun and my own self-loathing. Yes, self-loathing. Not grief, not sorrow. The hate, hating that my own hate was stronger than my grief or sorrow, hate so strong I couldn't bare it. *Sup?* spun through the air and chased away all that dark, the blue of my phone's screen hurting my eyes but fixing everything else. The message was from Nik. I didn't reply.

✧

When I woke up, my phone was still clutched in my hand, Nik's text message on display, but I wasn't in my bed anymore. I was in my kitchen, curled under my table, the curtain to my bedroom down. I must have tried to get away, to hide from the gun.

I'd picked up a lunch hour shift at Drop 'n Draw's new school program. For the last few months, they'd been running lunchtime programming, hoping to get kids hooked and then redirected to the drop-in centre in the strip mall. "We want to be the McDonald's of art," my boss had told me during my interview. I'd told him that he inspired me.

I went straight to the classroom we usually rented. The classroom door was locked. I tried to pull it open and push it, but nothing. This had happened before—the school often forgot about Drop 'n Draw—so I walked down the hall to the office. The ceilings of the elementary school were low to make the students feel comfortable. I felt like a giant, worried I would scare a kid if I went around a corner too fast. A secretary sat behind the counter at the office, poking at a computer. She didn't even look up at me.

"Hi," I finally said.

"Yes? Who do you need? Is someone coming down to meet you? Do I need to call them down?"

"I'm not a parent. I'm a teacher. I mean, I'm doing the program, Drop 'n Draw? I need the classroom opened."

"Oh," she said, and shuffled through some papers on her desk. "I thought I saw something about that last week. Let me check." She dug through another pile, clicked on her computer. "Yes, here it is. The program has been discontinued."

"What?"

"We discontinued the program. Has anyone from Drop 'n Draw gotten in touch with you?"

"No, they haven't."

"It hasn't been successful. We haven't had students sign up in a few weeks, so we've decided to discontinue it here. Most of our students, they want to play outside in the summer, and it's been such a warm spring. We might try again in the winter if enough students are looking for activities."

Before I left, I stooped to drink at a water fountain. It barely came up to my waist.

✧

I called my boss at Drop 'n Draw, and he told me they couldn't afford to keep the facility open either. He was sorry, but they only paid rent up till the end of the month and they were going to discontinue it there as well. "I'm sorry, Paulina. We were hoping the school program would drum up more business, and it seems to have sucked more money away."

"When will I get paid for the month?" I asked.

"Don't worry, we already have a cheque in the mail for you. You'll get it soon. I wish we could keep going, but it seems like there isn't the market for it anymore. Parents just aren't interested in art. Can you do math? It's all about STEM now. We're going to open a math centre, so if you know anyone who wants to be a tutor, let me know."

I was down a job and down money, and who knows what I was supposed to do.

I texted Trevor. *Got fired.*

I typed a crying emoji and then erased it. I sent a sad face.

Want a friend? he sent back. *Where are you?*

I was only a twenty-minute walk away, so, I went to him. I walked up the stairs of that old house to find his apartment door left unlocked for me. "Paulina," he called down the stairs. "Is that you?" I practically ran up the stairs and flopped beside him in bed. He loved sprawling in bed and called it "lying down" or "having a rest," which, except for right after sex, was never a hobby I'd been used to.

I was usually busy trying to hold the pieces of my life together, and if I wasn't doing that, and I had a moment to think, to rest, I spent that time reading books or drawing. Reading gave me access to something I hadn't lived, let me feel for others in the way I craved, but safely. When it got to be too much, I could close the book and put it away. In those moments, I was aware that life was beautiful, that the world was beautiful. Even the fact that there was so much suffering, that the world was still something so divided, where people killed each other because they looked different, or because they were convinced that only they saw the world in the right way, or because they were afraid—even that could be beautiful, in a devastating way. And in fact, that was the way I was most used to things being beautiful. I mean, we were all so similar, yet couldn't figure each other out, enough that we needed to blow each other's brains out, or our own. It was like an abstract painting, lines and colour everywhere, the way everyone went nuts. The other way I expressed all this, or used to, was by falling into the meditative state that art created for me. Just paying attention to the textures of the pencils or pastels, the grain of paper, until I created something new from the chaos.

But Trevor sure seemed to like to lie around a lot. Most of the time, we'd be silent, maybe napping occasionally or starting up sex again. But sometimes, something about lying together made him start talking, and lately he was talking in a way I'd never heard him talk before. As if, in certain conditions, there was a stopper that'd been pulled out of him. Trevor and I had been on and off for years, but I'd never seen him open like this. He'd never wanted me around so many days in a row either.

"What happened with the job?" he said, after we'd lain in silence for a while.

"I guess they've closed down. Or, basically, I have to learn math? That's the gist of the conversation."

"That totally sucks," he said. "But I bet lots of places would want someone with your skill set."

I rolled my eyes. "First I have to grieve," I said. "Then I can plot my next move." At the word *grieve*, Trevor became sullen again.

I thought he was asleep, but then he started to wrap me in his arms. "I heard from Max today," he said. I stared at the ceiling, still on my back, while he curled into me. "He's having a baby. Or Kim is."

"Uncle Trevor," I said, getting a little thrill from saying his name, which I tried to avoid speaking out loud around others so they wouldn't detect my feelings. "Are you excited?"

"Not really." He gave a sigh and pulled me closer. I rolled onto my side and let myself be spooned. "I am, but it just always feels like he's trying to live this life that will make Mom happy. And I'm not like that. And he has a good relationship, I guess, but he fools around on her, maybe she knows, I'm not sure. But I'm not like that either. He seems to think I spend too much time dwelling."

"Really? Has he said that to you?" His breath warmed my ear as he spoke, and I felt myself begin to be turned on. As long as he spoke, my mind stopped wandering, and I could feel him, close to me.

"Not in those words, but he thinks I should go back to work because he doesn't think my writing is work, and he's told me quite a few times that I need to move on from losing Dad."

"How can you?" His beard was now tickling my neck. I tried to move slightly without pulling away, so that he wouldn't think I was trying to reject his embrace.

"I know. Who I am is different forever now. And he doesn't see it that way. Especially because he doesn't understand that writing is what I need to be able to keep going. It's different for him. He's one of those people who doesn't have to think very hard and everything just falls into place."

"I'm sure that's just how it looks on the outside."

"Maybe. But I do think life is easier for people who aren't constantly thinking about art—some days, I feel like writing and painting and music are the only important things. We're all going to die anyway, so we might as well say something about the way we see the world. To be remembered."

"But then is it all ego?" I asked. "Is it all about being remembered? Cheating death?" I certainly didn't see art that way. For me, art was the only place I could be myself, say the things I needed to say. It was the place where I was separate from Adrian, separate from my friends or Trevor. Just Paul, just colour and shape and movement.

Lying there like that, I always lost track of time. We would wake up and bring snacks back into bed with us and hours would pass talking, having sex, and sleeping. I didn't know if it was still night or if we were creeping toward early morning, but now I didn't even work till the afternoon, so what did it matter.

"I mean, on some level it probably is. So much of it is. But I think it's something else too. Like, why do you paint?"

"I don't know. It was just something I always did. To convince myself."

"Convince yourself of what?"

"That I was real, the world was real, what I was experiencing was real. Or to make things real, or to make another place that I could exist in and think about. At first, a lot of my art was based on our games."

"Like what?" He pulled away and rolled onto his back. He was staring at the ceiling. I wondered if he wanted me to keep talking, and I almost stopped. "Like what kind of games?" he prompted.

"My cousin and I, we played all sorts of games. We created whole worlds in our imaginations. More real than real. Like we'd been kidnapped and forced to mine rocks all day and dig them up. But the game just became what we did. We'd dig for rocks all day long, and we'd have a certain quota to fill. Usually he'd come up with the stuff like that; he was three years older."

"You don't have any brothers or sisters, right?"

"No. There just was him. I mean, when I was a kid, I didn't even really have a lot of friends. Most of the other girls were mean to me. I was always thinking about other things than they were... I could see how they might think I was stuck up or something, but I wasn't. I wanted to play. I just lived far away from most people my age, and my cousin lived close and he didn't really play with anyone else either, so we just had each other."

"Max and I got on okay as kids, but we didn't play a whole lot together. I had some neighbourhood kids I was close with though. I was happy to have that. We played ball hockey and stuff. It was fun."

"I feel like I'm not explaining it well."

"No, I get it. You were tight with your cousin, you played, you made art based on the games."

"I was lonely," I said. "I guess that's what I'm trying to explain. I'm still lonely. He was all I had, you know? And I felt like I needed to preserve it. I still feel like I need to preserve it. It feels realer and truer to me than anything."

"I know how you feel," he said. His eyes were dark and soft and tried to stare into mine.

I rolled over and pulled the blanket around me, hoped he'd get the hint and finally fall asleep. He reached out and with one big, beautiful hand started to stroke my back. I held the blanket tighter, but I didn't tell him to stop, and eventually I fell asleep.

$$\diamondsuit$$

My folder was still empty at Artastic! when I got there. My boss still wasn't answering her phone, and by Friday, when I called, there was only a dial tone. The kids didn't know any better. They ran to me the same way, they asked me to cut paper for them, they listened when I showed them how to make orange with red and yellow and how to make it brighter with more yellow or paler with white or red-orange with more red.

Before I'd left Trevor's that day, I'd printed pictures on his colour printer of animals. The kids created their backgrounds, trees and water and that awful sun wearing sunglasses that everyone started to draw at seven. They pasted their animals overtop. Tammy asked me if I had a picture of a raccoon. "No, but I have a lemur."

"What's that?"

"It's a primate like a monkey, but he has a little mask like a raccoon." I took out the picture cut-out and showed her. "See?"

"That doesn't live here. Do you have any animals from here?"

"I have a dog."

"Wild animals."

"I have a polar bear."

"No, polar bears live on ice. That's wrong. Can you bring me a picture of a raccoon, please?"

"Okay, I will tomorrow. Do you have something you can work on right now?"

"I can draw Colin."

She sat back down and began to draw Colin, the way she always did, in the middle of dark brown lines that reached up to the top of the page. Green all along the top.

I know it's wrong, but part of me was angry to have to answer to their cries of "Paul! Paul!" Part of me wanted to walk out of there and make them work on their own. Keeping up the job without getting paid was unfair—I continued to open and close along with the weekend instructor, maintaining responsibility for the whole centre together. She also didn't know what to do. But the alternative didn't make much sense either. All those pencils and papers left untouched, all the glue unused, the kids stuck at home or showing up to a locked facility. I could already feel the parents' anger, which felt bigger than my own desperation at the injustice, at not being able to afford food, my rent coming due the next week, but having little time to make more money or find another job.

Parents' anger was always bigger than mine and could come out at any time. There were so many triggers it was hard to keep track: if their child was ignored, if another child wasn't treating their child one hundred percent the way they expected their child to be treated, if anything deviated from the life they'd carefully curated for their child—like a life was something easy to shape and mould. If anything went wrong, the order that had been set up had been violated. Their kid must only be happy, not experience any conflict, be able to play exactly how they wanted, and create only works of excellence. I thought maybe that this anger was a mixture of fear and anger for how the parent had been treated themselves. By avoiding a childhood like their own for their kid, the parent believed they would be able to undo their own childhood, even though I knew from experience that wasn't the way it worked at all. Life involved a series of disappointments and traumas, and it began as soon as the lights from the hospital scorched your new eyes. Not that there wasn't plenty to love, of course there was, but to expect any sort of fairness was ridiculous.

"You know what's crazy, Paul?" Lai whispered to me that Friday, the only day our paths crossed. Part of me felt as if our boss tried to keep us separate so that we wouldn't compare info. "Sheila deleted me off of Facebook."

"Are you serious?" I pulled out my phone and checked mine too, despite using up all my data and having no money for more. Our boss had also deleted me. "I think she blocked my number as well."

"I kind of thought you were overreacting before, but this is fucked."

"No cheque?"

"Nothing."

But I spread glue, cut out shapes, answered questions, and held hands. I went through the motions, trying to be present for the children.

But of course, with my boss disappearing on us and no money, and Drop 'n Draw closing down, it was unclear to me how I would survive. And then I thought about the gun, taunting me, as if survival wasn't what I wanted at all.

Now

This time, I'm going to walk in Rouge Park. I always put off going to that one because it's so far east, but I want to collect wood from all of the ravines. It's the only way the project will be complete.

I've booked a rental car in the area and once I find it, I tap my phone to its door. It clicks unlocked. The sun is shining, no snow, but there's that kind of fierce, blue-sky cold that chills you to the bone. I hop in and drive. I begin to think about the boy once I'm on the highway.

It was around that time the boy was taken—while I struggled to figure out a way to live. And although my own problems had seemed so important at the time, while I worried about money, a boy was being ripped away from the only life he'd known.

According to the articles I read about his disappearance later, he normally walked home with a group of other kids, but his best friend had gotten a ride with her sister instead. He broke away from the pack of kids, telling them he was going to go to the store for milk for his grandma on the way home. At least that's what the kids said when questioned.

This wasn't unusual—the convenience store was right there—but everyone saw it was dangerous once he went missing. The boy wasn't the type the pack protected. They went off home without even thinking about him. Separated from his friend who had gotten a ride, he was alone. He had no one. Like Adrian. Like me.

A black suv had been reported in the area before he went missing. A couple of the kids from the pack had told their parents about it the week before, how it slowed down as it drove by. A rumour started in the pack, rippling down from the oldest kids to the youngest: Someone was inside, watching. Looking for kids. Parents dismissed this. "Get a bunch of kids together and their imaginations run wild," they said, but a couple of the more cautious parents had reported the suv to the police. Nothing was done.

And the boy was alone that day. The pack had more or less forgotten about the suv of last week, and if they remembered, they didn't think anyone would want the boy. They didn't want him, so why would whoever was in the suv? But the boy got into a car, or maybe he was scooped up. Maybe it was a sedan or a black suv or a different car entirely. Either way, he ended up far from home, where I would find him.

A car cuts me off as I merge onto the highway, causing me to lean on my brakes. A black suv, filling me with rage, speeding off under an unforgiving, bright winter sky.

✧

That night I dream of money.

I enter my bedroom, and it's stuffed in the mattress. I rip the fabric of the pillow-top open until I get through to where the entire mattress is made of money. Kayla enters and she parts her legs and bills flutter to the floor. Trevor follows closely behind, money in his hands, fists of cash clenched. Then Adrian comes in, and I rush to him and his mouth opens and bills are there too, wet and soggy and crumpled. I pull them from his mouth and his head lolls back. The money is covered in his blood, and his skin's cold, he's a corpse; Adrian is dead.

When I wake up, I'm covered in sweat.

I go to my notebook and begin to read, to immerse myself in the events of that day. I read my index trauma and have to stop myself. It's just making it worse. The dreams. What happened with Jocelyn. Feeling constantly on edge.

Before I drift off to sleep, I tell myself that tomorrow I'll tell Selina I'm done. That it's just not working for me. Maybe I'm someone who just can't be healed.

✧

"I can't do it," I tell Selina during our session. "I can't read it out loud. I can't just listen to it and relax."

"You don't have to relax, Paul," she says. I know she's trying to read my expression through the screen. "You can pay attention to how it's making your body feel, what thoughts come up for you. You can reflect."

"But it's living through it again and again. When I tried before... it wasn't good. And it's just making everything worse. My dreams..."

"Have you been having flashbacks?"

"Not really flashbacks, not in the day. But at night, I can't get away from it. I think about it during the day, I write it down, and then it's there when I dream, all mixed up with now."

"I'm sorry, Paul." She leans forward and I can see the dark freckles across her brown skin. I'd missed them before. Through the screen, I realize, I only half know what she looks like. She adjusts her gold glasses and takes a deep breath. I find myself mimicking her breath, and I feel calmer. "That can happen with this process. It's not always straightforward. But I promise, people see a lot of improvement with this. We just need to keep going. The exposure to the memory will be what really helps. You should have fewer and fewer of those dreams. Maybe you'll even stop having dreams like this at all.

"Would you be open to trying together? We can make the recording together, and then I'm here to help you centre yourself after. You don't have to go through it alone."

"But I'm always alone," I say, and I can't help it; I feel a sob start to rise in me, but I fight it back. That loneliness that made me fuse myself to Adrian, feeling so unloved by everyone around me.

"Is asking for help hard for you?" Selina asks me. She puts the end of her pen in her mouth and chews on it. I find it endearing. Sometimes she seems almost superhuman to me, the way she's navigating the darkest parts of me.

I nod.

"Why do you think that is?"

"I want to be the person helping others, teaching and things like that," I say, but I know there's more than that. Something I still can't quite say.

"I'm here to help you," Selina says. "Like you teach, I teach. Helping you is my job, and I'm here as your guide through this."

"I don't know if I can do this."

"*You* can. *We* can, together. I'll be here to lead you through some grounding techniques if it gets too painful, okay? And if it's too intense, we can stop, focus on the first chunk and do the rest another day."

"Okay."

"You don't have to be alone, Paul."

"Yeah," I say, and it doesn't feel real to me. I'm the one who is stuck, trapped there, in The Lighted City. But I need to believe I can find my way out.

"Let me know when you're ready and I'll start recording."

"Okay."

"Go ahead."

"We are in a hut that Adrian has built. I've decided that I want more than living in Caledon and that I want to go away to school. I've fallen in love, with someone who is not Adrian. He can tell almost as soon as he sees me..."

How It Happened
2016

The Cave was empty, too early for the night crowd. The bartender slid candles across the table as I came in, and I hugged my sketchbook to my chest, a little shield against being awkwardly early.

I chatted with him for a moment and ordered a beer to sip as I waited, resting my head against a hand for only a moment—the reality of no more Drop 'n Draw and no cheque from Artastic! and the cost of the beer weighing me down. I'd promised myself that I'd only buy one, since that was all the money I'd brought, and I was out of the groceries Stef bought me before my trip. I'd already eaten the last couple potatoes and an egg, boiled together and slathered in hot sauce, lunch. I'd heard somewhere that drinking a pint of beer was like eating a loaf of bread, and I tried to imagine it, but only the bubbles filled my stomach.

I opened my sketchbook and began to draw, a charcoal pencil moving slowly across the paper. The sketches I'd worked on in Vancouver and on the plane were beginning to become a cohesive plan for a series of paintings and sculptures about The Lighted City. I felt I owed it to Adrian to make it real any way I could, since he'd never been able to find it in life, and I was now sure that he wouldn't find it in death either. I wanted to use some of the objects I'd found on the streets of Toronto and transform them into something new and beautiful. But whenever I began to work, my current situation and my past crept in. Stuck in Toronto. Stuck being myself. The drawings were unfinished, sombre, full of nostalgia. The motivation to finish the project, or even truly start it, was far off and impossible, as distant as The Lighted City itself.

The glow that was in The Cave now that the candles were all lit became the glow from the tree branches in The Lighted City. I could feel Adrian's presence there. I wasn't alone, he was looking down at me as I worked.

"Working away, eh?" I heard Trevor's voice, and then I looked up and there he was, sliding into the chair across from me. He put his notebook and a couple paperbacks on the table, their edges gnawed from use. A pen. A pencil for taking notes in the margins. Only yesterday, I'd sprawled on his couch while he bent over the kitchen table, chewing on the end of a pencil, his eyes looking for secrets in a book. I'd touched Adrian's gnawed pencil, which still lived in my pocket.

"You're here early too?" I closed my sketchbook.

"I'm always the first one here," he said. "Didn't you see me sitting at the back?"

"No."

"Oh. I thought you didn't want to sit with me. Wanted to force me to come to you."

"Why would I do that?"

He shrugged and flashed his own notebook at me, flicked through it so I could see all the pages he'd filled. "I come early to read or write," he said. "I'm writing again."

"You'd stopped?"

"I guess I was doing a little less than usual. Not because of you, don't worry. Let me see what you're working on." He tried to grab my sketchbook from me.

"Stop!" I pushed him back. "I didn't get to read yours, so you don't get to see mine."

"You wouldn't be able to read my penmanship anyway—it's different with a picture." He yanked it from my hands and spun it around to face him. I felt nauseous, and my scalp started to tingle. My hands were already feeling raw, like I'd punched something and ripped them open, even though it'd been more than two months since something like that had happened. I was trying to keep the will to hurt myself at bay, gun excluded. He read through the notes, flipped through the pages. "What's The Lighted City?"

"None of your business."

"You'll tell me one day," he said. "I know you will."

"And what makes you think I'm dying to tell you all my secrets?"

"Because of our connection," he said.

My hands were shaking even though they never did anymore when we were alone. I didn't know what I was supposed to be doing, how to look at him, talk with him like we were just two normal people who'd bumped into each other at a bar. I grabbed my sketchbook back and flipped through it myself so I could look at it instead of him, as if I had many thoughts I still needed to tease out about the work I'd done today.

"Do you want another beer?" He gestured at my glass, emptied down to a couple suds, guzzled as an excuse not to look him in the eyes.

"Sure." But then Kayla and Stef walked through the door. I could see Derek smoking outside and some guy Kayla dragged along out there too. Trevor jumped up and walked over to the bar, but once he got the beer he walked right by Stef and Kayla, who were now sitting with me, and said hi to Derek, who'd just entered. He drank from the beer himself.

All night, he stuck close to the guys, barely saying a word to me or Kayla or Stef. Warm May rain started to come down outside where he smoked with Derek, and when he came in for another drink, his black hair had a new frizzy energy, and his dark grey T-shirt was speckled with rain drops. The guys laughed about it, did another shot. "I guess you got stuck in the rain," I said, making it seem like I was casually waiting by the bar and that I didn't want to talk to him more, when I wanted him to give me any sign that what we were when we were alone in his bed, on his balcony, watching Netflix, any of that, could also be here.

"Uh, yeah, I did," he said, like I was in grade eight again and my crush was surprised I could speak. I did a shot that Derek handed to me and walked over to Stef and Kayla without saying anything else to him.

I started to tremble again, but not from nervousness, from rage. And then, the way I did back then, I lost myself, or became the self I was always trying to outrun but couldn't. I was drinking another drink, I was doing shots at the bar with Kayla, and she'd gotten paid so the shots kept coming. He watched me from across the bar, but didn't come over, didn't say another word to me. "That fucking coward," I said to Kayla, gesturing toward him. Stef had already gone home to the babysitter. He saw my gesture and widened his eyes at me. Telepathically trying to tell me to shut up. "I should have stayed in Vancouver. There's nothing for me here."

"What? What did he do?" He turned his back to us, continued to talk to Derek and the other guys. "Stayed in Vancouver? What do you mean?" Kayla was tugging at my arm, but I just continued to glare at Trevor, seething. I felt all lit up, and powerful, ready to tear him limb from limb. I knew it was late, but I wasn't going to go home without him. Or without some sort of explanation from him.

I didn't say anything, even though Kayla had now wrapped her arms around me. "What is it, Paul? Come on, talk to me." She pulled away from me and tried to look me in the eyes, but something was happening to me and I couldn't look at her, or anyone. "You never tell me about it and it pisses me off. Then you expect me to take care of your drunk ass whenever you're upset at him."

I can't remember too much after that. I remember talking to a guy up against the bar, watching Trevor's reaction from behind the guy's back. His eyes getting darker, but still pretending he didn't even know I was there. Kayla was gone, I couldn't find her, and there was this guy's face in front of me. Then Trevor and I were outside in front of the bar and we were the only two people left and I was yelling at him, asking what the hell he thought he was doing with me, what the hell he was trying to pull. "I'm not the one trying to fuck some random," he yelled back. "I'm not the one playing games."

"I know you'd miss me!" I said, and then I didn't remember anything, except yelling again and again at Trevor's back as he walked away from me, despite begging, crying for him to wait. The night disappeared as if I were staring into the hole in the barrel of a gun.

In the morning, I was alone in my bed. My phone had six outgoing calls to Trevor, only one of which had been picked up. And four calls to Nik, who'd texted in the morning. On the floor, my sketchbook was open and all the pages were ripped out and torn up. I even found one in the kitchen sink. It was when I was pulling the soggy pages from the drain that I saw my knuckles. The water hit the torn skin as I washed the rest of the pages down the drain. Each front knuckle was torn in an almost perfect way, circles of flesh exposed to the air. I wondered if I had done it in front of him, if I'd accidentally shown him that side of myself in a blackout state. I couldn't remember a thing. I blew gently on my knuckles. I wanted to feel them sting.

I put ointment and Band-Aids around each finger, grabbed a glass of water, and then climbed into bed. I didn't have anywhere to be, a Saturday free from lessons and commitments, and despite all the time we'd been spending together, I knew I wouldn't be getting a call from Trevor. Who knew if I'd ever see him again, or if I wanted to after the way he'd acted, keeping me a secret even though everything was different. Or I'd thought everything was different.

Hours went by with my head pounding and dreaming about the gun. My hand at one point slipped underneath the mattress and held it, felt its cool metal against my skin, my knuckles aching where the mattress pressed down, but then I had to get up and vomit. I didn't quite make it to the bathroom, and puke spilled from my mouth all over my apartment's floor.

Tylenol in my system, I tried to get my life together. I collected the pages still on the floor. Each one was destroyed. The Lighted City. Paintings and sculptures I'd never make. After the pages were deep in the garbage, I filled a pot with water and got to work on the vomit-covered floor. The soap was this pomegranate dish soap I'd bought because it was easy on my hands and smelled great. I loved the shade of pink they'd chosen, and I mixed it into the boiling hot water, erased my puke from everywhere it touched. I wanted the whole apartment to smell like pomegranates and not my insides. And then Nik was calling me.

"What, you don't answer your texts?"

I laughed sadly. "Sorry, I was sleeping. I'm not feeling too great."

"Not sounding too great either. I guess you had quite the night, eh?"

"Yeah. Sorry, for calling last night. I hope I didn't wake you up."

"Don't worry, Paul, I screen all my calls and keep this baby on silent."

"Oh."

"Was something wrong? Did you need somebody?"

"Everything's fine."

"You sure about that, Paul? Huh?"

"I lost my job, okay?"

"At Artastic!?"

"No, another one. But Artastic! is all messed up too."

"Oh, no. All messed up. We can't have that. I guess you're in quite the state, huh? What about dinner? My treat? Would that cheer you up?"

He didn't know I had no food, that I would've said yes if he'd invited me to a hot dog stand. I was glad he didn't know my desperation, that this was a friendly dinner, not a handout. "When?" I said.

"I'll come to you. Be ready in like an hour."

I glanced at my hands, covered in Band-Aids. What would he think when he saw me all bandaged up? I remembered the way his fingers had brushed my scars as we shook hands, his own scar on his arm.

I grabbed the manslaying dress from the hamper, dumped after I'd gotten home from Vancouver, and gave it a sniff. It smelled all right. I changed and looked at myself in the mirror. Dark circles under my eyes, a few pimples floating underneath the surface of my skin. I definitely looked like I'd had a bad night, but my cheeks looked flushed and my hair was wild the way I liked it. He had to see what was beautiful about me; he was always so happy to see me, not constantly morose like Trevor.

I ran up the street, a couple minutes late, and into the nearby Italian restaurant Nik had suggested. He was there, waiting, ball cap on even though he was indoors, his mouth already smiling mischievously. The restaurant was washed in orange dimmed lights, each table decorated with a glass oil lamp, its thick wick keeping a steady flame.

I already knew there was no potential for love with him. Knew as soon as I walked in and saw him sitting there. But perhaps the feeling I had for Trevor, whatever made me qualify it as love, was actually pain, a lack in me, screaming. Like with Adrian, a need to hug and be hugged. Maybe not feeling that pain was a good thing. Maybe this was what I needed. To start in a different place.

"Whoa, you look nice," he said. "All dressed up."

I pulled out the menu, but met his eyes and laughed. He was wearing regular lounging clothes, an old T-shirt and jeans. I couldn't tell which of us was more embarrassed or which of us was supposed to be embarrassed.

He ordered for both of us. "Let's get two appetizers and a bunch of mains so we can sample everything and share?" he said to me in front of the waiter and then pointed at things on the menu that looked good to him. I usually got one main course, at less expensive restaurants, and did something my friends all called strategic eating, where you only ate half and saved the rest for tomorrow's lunch. "And don't worry," he said. "This is on me, of course."

"Thank you," I started to say, blushing, sipping the wine the waiter brought.

"I mean, at least one of us isn't a deadbeat."

"Hey!" My cheeks flushed, and for a second, I thought of leaving, but then he'd know that it was true.

They brought us a caprese salad, which Nik picked away at as he chatted to me, mostly about Tammy and movies, asking me if I'd seen them—I hadn't. Nik wanted to know things about me, as usual. He asked me to describe my parents and asked if I had a favourite. I found the question ridiculous and couldn't explain why. He asked about siblings, and I said no, I didn't have any. He didn't ask about cousins or aunts or uncles, so I didn't mention Adrian, and Nik wasn't Trevor, hadn't seen me break down hearing about his death, so Adrian could remain private, close to me. I said, "I was very lonely," and this part was true.

"Aw." He put his hand over mine. "I hope Tammy doesn't feel that way. I wonder sometimes if that's why she's always making shit up, like Colin."

"Tammy's different," I said. "She's practical. You should see her in class. She always asks her friends to make a plan before they all start. They're five, most of the kids want to squeeze out paint and move it around. She wants to think about it."

"That doesn't mean she's not lonely. Haven't you ever gotten lonely, like, building Ikea furniture or something like that?"

"Yeah, of course. But some kids, they have too much going on in their minds to get bogged down with it. And then other kids..." *were like Adrian and me and came into the world with that loneliness*, I kept myself from saying.

"Okay, so I have an idea," Nik said. "Tell me if this is crazy or isn't something you do. What about if you started to watch Tammy?"

"Like babysit?"

"Not just babysitting. Like, you could teach her art. Read with her, play with her. Weeks when she's at my house. Tutoring. Her mom might be into it, too, have to talk to her about it." The candles on the table flickered, as if laughing. My manslaying dress, put on for a pity job offer. But then I remember the taste of my lunch the day before, everything boiled and going bad. "She hasn't been too crazy about the art centre lately. She doesn't like the other teacher and she doesn't like the kids. I think she feels restricted by the way they only want to play. I was talking with her mom and we were thinking it'd be nice to get her in something a little more specialized to her needs. She's a smart kid."

"She is," I said. "But I'm not sure. I mean, I'm still working at Artastic!"

"Didn't you say Artastic! was all fucked up?"

"Yeah," I said. The people at the next table felt so close. A romantic dinner for two. I lowered my voice. "They are a bit behind on paying me. That's all."

"Quit. I swear I'll make it worth your while, and I'll pay you on time unlike those idiots." Thirteen hundred bucks in rent due in a week. Money owed to my therapist. Food. I needed this job.

"My boss just sort of disappeared. It's messed up."

"So, you'll do it?"

Our pasta arrived and I stabbed noodles with my fork. "I just hope this isn't some weird charity," I said.

"It's not! I promise," and he held out his pinky to me. I took it and we pinky swore on it. He met my eyes and winked. In that moment, I wanted to get close to him, and he could see it.

"All right. I like Tammy, I think it'll be fine," I said.

"Let's drink to celebrate." As we drank, his foot found mine, his knees brushed mine underneath the table that was too small for all of our food.

I got a text from Trevor as I ate a tiramisu: *Please tell me you're okay.*

And another: *I don't care if you're still mad at me, Paulina, I'm getting worried.*

Nik reached over and picked up the hand that held my phone. He gently pulled it from my hand and placed it on the table, screen down. He pulled my hand close to him, and my stomach snagged as I knew what he would see. He held it up in front of his face to inspect my bandages. "Interesting," he said. "Very interesting."

In the morning after my date with Nik, I went straight to Trevor, texting to say I was on my way. Of course, he was home. Unless he was out at The Cave with all of us, he was always home. He texted back a single letter, *K.*

The heat wave hadn't broken. If anything, it kept getting hotter. Sweat trickled between my boobs, and my backpack stuck to my shirt. As I walked, I practised what I was going to say. That I couldn't believe it had come to that at The Cave. That I was sorry. My knuckles had barely started to scab over, and I'd freshly wrapped them in Band-Aids. If they got to the point where they were healed enough, just looked skinned, I could leave them uncovered—people asked about them more if they were hidden by Band-Aids.

I climbed his steps. The door was open for me, and Trevor was pacing around the room. Wads of Kleenex were scattered across the table. "Hey," he said.

"Hey." I stood by the door. I wondered if he would ask me if I'd fucked the guy at the bar or if I'd fucked anyone or if he'd tell me he was fucking someone else now, or that he always had been and that was also all I was to him, obviously, a way to get laid. I started to get angry, standing there by the door. My scalp started to tingle. I was having a hard time breathing. All the usual signs I should get out of there, that I'd make everything more of a mess than it already was.

"I'm sorry," he said. "About the other night. I always say the wrong things."

He still didn't understand that it wasn't what he said but always what he didn't say. What he couldn't admit to others, or admit to me, so that I was stuck in between.

But then he walked over to me, and I could smell him. I hadn't even known I'd missed him, that I wanted him, until he was right beside me and I could smell his body. And I'd only been away from him for a night. Disappointment with how we both had been flooded through me, and my nose stuffed up with potential tears. He normally wasn't one for hugging too much, but he hugged me. The floor beneath me fell away and I had to swallow hard to not cry and had to fight to make sure it didn't all make me angrier. I folded my arms in front of myself so that they weren't around him, his arms wrapped around me. "Let's have sex," I said into his chest, because I couldn't stand the way he was hugging me, I couldn't, not after everything, not after going out with Nik and the way I'd been feeling.

When we had sex, I felt my pleasure could go even deeper. My skin tingled all over, especially my cheek as he kissed it. "Could you be rougher?" I whispered. Because my mind was still going and pain was the only way I knew how to quiet it. "Please."

He thought I wanted to dirty talk. "Oh, is that what you want? Do you want me to tie you up? You'll have to beg for it."

"Please, slap me."

He slapped my ass gently and laughed. We had sex two more times before watching a documentary and eating leftover pasta straight from Tupperware.

✧

Nik had walked me home the night before. "We could drive," he said.

"Don't bother, I can walk myself. It's just around the corner. I'm very brave and independent, most of the time," I said.

"Maybe independent. But brave?"

"Don't be such a dick."

"Then let me walk you home."

Nik was now my boss, wasn't he? And he was still flirting with me—maybe I shouldn't have called someone who was going to be my boss—was my new boss—a dick. Although he could be one, in a different way than Trevor. Nik seemed to be a dick because he thought it was funny to be a dick. With Trevor, well, I knew why. His sadness dug into every part of me until all I could see was his eyes when they turned from grey to black.

As we walked down Roncesvalles toward my street, Nik reached for my hand, touched the Band-Aids. A light touch, but enough to make me wince. Then he moved his hand to the small of my back, my waist. I stepped forward. "This is my street, I can go the rest of the way. I don't want you to have to walk too far from your car."

Nik looked at me, at the space I'd now put between us. He looked up the street, to where he knew my apartment was, closer to the end. Of course he knew; he'd dropped me off. "Okay, Paul," he said. "You probably need to sleep after last night anyway."

"I'll see you…"

"Right away, if you can. I'll text you the address, and we'll start right away, on Monday."

"Okay."

"Don't miss me too much," he said, and tugged the bill of his hat down. Underneath the streetlight, I couldn't see his eyes. His whole face was in shadow.

"I'll try," I said, and began to walk down the street.

"I'll miss you so much I won't be able to stand it!" Nik's voice snaked after me, and I quickened my steps until I was at my front porch. It was hard to tell, but I thought he was still standing there at the end of my street. Would that really be such a horrible thing? It was warm out, summer was almost here. Things were different when the weather was like that, there was no pressing need to go.

✧

But the morning after the date, if that's what it was, it was Trevor who called to me, who I needed to see to make things right. After we ate lunch, we went back to bed. "Let's nap," he said, and was asleep before I even had time to respond. He draped his arm across me, and although I couldn't sleep, I was careful not to move, not wanting to wake him.

Trevor started talking before his eyes were even open. "You kept telling me you were going to move to Vancouver," he said. "When you were drunk."

"I did?"

"Yeah. You kept saying you were going to disappear, vanish from my life." He put his hand on mine, resting on my belly. "You're not really going back, right?"

"No, I'm not," I said. I didn't say it was because I couldn't imagine being away from him, being away from my friends, everyone I knew. "I was just tempted while I was there."

"I get it," he said. "Vancouver's a pretty chill city."

"Yeah?"

He opened his eyes. "I went there a couple years ago, to visit a writer I struck up a friendship with."

"You have friendships?"

"You're mean sometimes, Paulina."

"I'm only kidding," I said, and I rolled over into his side and playfully swung my arms around him. Clung to him hard like a monkey who had found its mother. "I'm just a little kid."

He shook his head and removed me slowly. My limbs were nothing to him. He easily took my hands off him, one at a time, and rolled me over until I was on my back staring at the ceiling. "I have to get some stuff done," he said, "but you don't have to go. I mean, unless you want to."

I decided to stay and try to work as well. I wondered if I could sketch in his apartment, or if I'd feel like he was always watching me.

We showered together and kissed underneath the water. I didn't tease him and we didn't start up anything, just were playful together. I used my hands to cup water and dumped it onto his chest, slicking his chest hair to his skin.

While Trevor worked, I phoned Artastic! The weekend instructor picked up. "Hey, Lai, I'm not going to be in for my shifts next week. I got another job. Is the cheque there?"

"Still nothing."

"What should I do?"

"I think my dad is going to help me sue them unless they pay. We're sending a letter from our lawyer. Do you want us to make one for you?"

Lawyers meant money, money I didn't have. "No, that's okay."

"You sure? It would take him no time, and probably having you involved would help our case."

"It's okay," I said, again. This time Lai stopped talking, but she didn't hang up, rustled around on the other end of the line. "Listen," I said, "I can't get through to anyone there. Can you tell them I quit?"

"Sure, but I'd send a letter of resignation if I were you. Cover your bases. You don't want them to act like there is a reason to withhold your wages."

"Yeah, you're probably right."

"And let me know if you change your mind about the lawyer."

"I will."

"What was that all about?" Trevor said after I hung up the phone. "Did you just quit your job?"

"Yeah," I said. I went over to the fridge and pulled out cheese and bread. "Would you eat a grilled cheese?"

He nodded. "What's going on, Paulina?"

"It's a crappy job. I got a new one."

"You did?"

"Yeah. Tutoring."

"Is that going to be enough money?"

I turned and looked at him, saying it so casually. Enough money. Like he even understood what that meant. "Should be."

I turned on the burner and buttered two pieces of bread and put them down in the pan. He bought the type of cheddar that was pre-cut into slices, only six pieces to a package, not caring that it cost more. The cheese made me rage. This was why he would never understand me; he didn't know what it was like to bounce from job to job, or why I couldn't stay at Artastic! for another month not knowing if I would ever actually get paid. When his dad was alive, they had taken trips, blown money on all-inclusive resorts. He had a fucking family cottage, yet he still got to play poor artist in the city. And maybe he didn't have a lot of money anymore, but it was hard for me to see that as something that wasn't a choice. He'd chosen to focus on his writing because he didn't need to worry about money the way I did or Stef did. Or even Kayla, who spent her days in an office rather than hunting down acting gigs like she'd once wanted to. The person who had the most money and time got to be the person considered the most serious about his art. The damn cheese.

"What are you thinking over there?"

"I'm going to use all this cheese, that cool?"

"I don't care. It's my roommate's, I'll just get him more."

One side of each grilled cheese was burned. "Here." I put it down in front of him.

He ate it without even looking up.

What made attraction the way that it was? Why could you be attracted to someone in one moment and then lose it? And then with others, like Trevor, it only seemed to grow, no matter how they treated you or the bits that didn't seem to be quite compatible. I thought about Nik, standing at the base of my street. In another version of that moment, I would have invited him up. If there hadn't been Trevor, if Adrian's shadow wasn't always hanging around. I thought of the scars, the way Nik smiled that first struck me as cute, struck me as something kindred. But it'd gotten all twisted up. The first time that Nik gave me a ride, he'd seemed like the kind of person I should have been with. Solid. With a kid, a family already, maybe looking to start over. Interested enough in what I did and my problems to offer a solution. A laugh to almost everything he said instead of a glower like Trevor. But remembering Nik standing in the street, the hand he'd put on the small of my back like he needed to guide me to my own house, it disgusted me. The black pit inside of me continued to grow.

Later, we sat together on Trevor's bed after streaming four episodes of a new show. One second he was fine, but the moment the show ended, he was far away and melancholy.

"What's wrong?" I asked. "Did I do something?"

He slowly came back into his eyes, that softness appearing, making the grey change colours. "What? No. Why?"

"You just seemed different for a moment." Of course, this wasn't true. Trevor disappearing into the black of his eyes was so typically him, and it made me want to run home and hold the gun in my hands and dream about flying away to where Adrian lived.

"Oh. Yeah."

"What's up?"

He got up from the bed, walked around his room, picking things up from the floor: pieces of paper, receipts, his clothes, mine. He picked up my shirt, but he didn't give it back. Instead, he folded it and put it on top of his dresser. One big hand smoothed any remaining wrinkles, and I wanted to be caressed like a shirt left on the floor and found by him, tidied until it was perfect again. "It's my dad, I guess?" His voice trailed up as if it were a question. He rarely talked about losing his father like it was something he had gone through, only spoke briefly about his dad as if he were a person who was very much present. Things he'd made, something he'd said. It had taken me a few months of knowing him and listening to the little bits that came out when he was drinking to know that his father was gone. He'd seemed so vivid to me.

"What about him?"

"I don't know if I ever really said it, but he died a few years ago, I guess maybe four now? But it's still so close."

"You've mentioned it, once or twice. And your brother, how he thought you should be dealing with stuff. But you've never really talked about it to me or anything."

"Yeah, well," he said.

"Did it affect you a lot?" I asked, and I knew how it sounded, hollowed out and not enough. It was the same as when Kayla tried to understand about Adrian dying and couldn't. No one could. But I wanted Trevor to feel like I was trying, like he could talk to me.

"Well, of course. We were close. I loved him," he said, and this profession of love came out so easily. "He suffered...The prostate cancer, he had it for a long time. We had a couple years where he was in remission, great years, but it came back and metastasized quickly. It was hard seeing that. It affected both me and my brother, but my brother, Max, he doesn't talk about stuff like that. He's much more, like...if he keeps going, it doesn't hurt him. He doesn't really understand how I am the way I am."

"You mean like, feeling sad about it still?"

"Yeah, I guess. I mean, lots of my friends had good dads. I saw it. Their families laughed together, they did things together. Their dads showed them how to do things and were supportive of what they wanted to do. Those guys grew up to be happy, well-adjusted people. And well, I can't. And it's not that he wasn't a good dad. That's not it. That's part of the problem. It's that he was the best dad, and then I had to watch as all of who he was degenerated. My friends got to experience more things, different things with their dads, and what was happening at home for me was witnessing a slow death. My mom taking care of him. The whole house revolving around taking care of him before he went into palliative care. And I never resented it, and I don't think Max did either. I feel guilty even saying that. He was someone with an irrepressible spirit. I wish I was like that. Everyone who met him was his friend, even his kids, especially us. And that makes it even worse because I know I'll never be like that. I'm incapable." He was silent for a moment. "In a way, he was all I had."

"But what about your mom? And Max?"

"We were all going through it together, of course. But my dad was the one who read and encouraged my writing, he was the one who understood when I had days where everything felt...he told me the German language had a word for how I felt sometimes, *Weltschmerz*, that heaviness that comes with knowing that all over the world there are wars and famines and injustices and we are powerless. Days you feel so heavy, you can barely move."

I looked at his face, his large, straight nose, the forehead that was slightly too long and wide, that already wrinkled. For a moment, I could imagine what that face would look like old, his grey eyes the same colour as his hair, the places where more wrinkles would appear. I knew I'd be able to still love him, would love everything about that big head, even when he was ancient.

"I guess you understand," he said, "with everything you've been through recently."

Adrian was in the room again, putting his long hands around my wrists. "What do you mean?"

"With your cousin dying. You don't have to talk about it, but I don't know...It's been nice, lately, Paulina, having you around, because I know you get it."

"It's not quite the same. I hadn't seen my cousin in years...With your dad, it must have been hard, having him there one day and then gone the next."

"Yeah. We knew it was coming though. Which made it easier in some ways and not in others. I guess, I felt like I got you better, after you got that call...we're simpatico."

Simpatico wasn't the first word that came to mind, although I was against using words like that on principle.

"How come you've never talked to me about it before?"

"You never asked. I don't know. I talk to the guys about it a lot. I mean, it's not a big secret, like how you are about everything. I think it's healthy to talk about death and talk about losing people. Max thinks I can't let go, but that's not it. For me, I have to express it."

"Oh," I said. I hadn't meant to never ask. I'd held the pieces he'd told me when he was drunk like they were something special. A coat his dad made, that he'd left him money, that his brother was getting married and having a kid and obsessed with moving on, that his love for his father, both a friend and parent, would never leave him. That he'd spent hours and hours talking with his father, and doing things. Like with my friends, I knew almost everything about him now, the way he felt about different things, his past. But I'd still been holding back from him. My secret beat in me like it never had before. Adrian hovered in the air between us, the memory of his cold eyes a barrier to intimacy. "If I tell you something, will you promise not to tell anyone?"

"Paulina, I don't even tell anyone that we hang out."

"Never mind then," I said.

I stood up from the bed and grabbed my shirt from the dresser, pulled it on, and left. Outside, the air was still and humid, and the sun was hovering around the horizon, barely visible past the town-houses that lined the street. I walked down his street toward the bus stop, but when I reached the corner, I turned right, and when I reached the next corner, I turned right again. I walked all the way around the block and came back and walked back up the stairs. He was sitting at the kitchen table looking miserable, in front of a notebook filled with rows of his curled letters, looping in on each other. I heard his roommate move in his room above us.

"That's a first for you," he said without looking up. He was flipping the pages of his notebook, over and over, back and back.

"What is?" I said.

"Coming back after you storm out like that."

"Do I do that a lot?"

"Yeah, you do. Do you not even realize these things? That one second you're saying you'll tell me your darkest secret and I'm telling you how I actually feel about my dad dying, which isn't fucking easy to talk about, and then you just storm out like you don't give a fuck." As Trevor spoke, he hunched closer and closer to his note-book, to the surface of the table. "Just because I don't say what you want me to. I'm a person, Paulina, I'm going to say the wrong thing sometimes. I can't read your mind."

I walked over to him and touched his shoulder. He didn't flinch under my touch, and I could feel the stiffness in his back relax a bit. I wrapped my body around him, bending over and holding him, the way I used to hold Adrian, imagining all of my little molecules were pressing against his, trying to meld with his, that the skin alone was too much barrier between us. He put his hands on my arms and held my arms around him. We went up to his room in another moment.

In the middle of the night, I woke up and slipped myself into his arms. "I love you," I whispered, and his eyes opened.

"Same," he said, his voice phlegmy with sleep. "I mean, me too." We fucked then, although we fell back asleep lazily before either of us finished, and in the morning, I started talking. He let me lie on his chest as I told him about Adrian and how he'd killed himself, and I even told him about that final day—the rope, the flames— told him about everything except the gun. I also kept Adrian's secret because he was unable to tell me it was okay to tell someone, that it was okay, now that he was dead, to release what had gone on in our family. Somewhere through it all, I started crying. I'm not really sure why...maybe it was because Trevor's judgment was always what I was most afraid of. He'd constantly rejected me and I thought that maybe it was because he saw this part of me, saw where I'd come from and what I was made of and that I was marked by these things in my past. But he didn't see it that way at all.

"It's okay," he told me as I cried. "I understand." And he told me about these dark games he played with family friends—a series of dares that escalated through perversion. One time, he and one of the girls pinned down a cat and smashed it with rocks until it wasn't a cat anymore. That was when he understood that the games were real, but only once the cat was already dead. How can you take something like that back? He felt it was fused to him and said something about who he really was; he'd felt that way for a long time, until he got a little older.

"And your cousin, he sounds sick."

"No," I said. "He was hurt." And I wanted to say it wasn't like his games with his friends, it was more, it had taken me over, but I was so tired from talking already, I couldn't explain it.

"But you slept together," he said. "He forced you. It was rape." Trevor's voice caught.

"Not all the time," I said, and felt sick to my stomach. "He was hurt. He needed me," I said, but I couldn't stop crying, seeing Trevor's eyes get darker and wetter until tears were on his cheeks, seeing him cry about *me*, who deserved nothing. "You must think I'm so disgusting." The words barely released, choked through tears and phlegm.

"No," he said, and pulled me to him. "Never. These things aren't you," he said. "I mean, like, they aren't the whole you." And I knew then that I could give him all of myself. That hot spring would soon become summer, and it had already been a few years with him, hadn't it, off and on and all over the place. If he loved me and was ready, maybe we could finally make a life together, even if it was confined to his bed, his apartment walls, the balcony where he smoked.

✧

Those days I spent more time at his place than my own. My attic apartment was now home to the gun. Those walls had watched me as I failed in my life again and again. Every meltdown remained in the space, out of view. The vomit that had coated the floor, the fear

I felt in the dark where it seemed like my only option was the gun, the temptation of being just like Adrian again—all of it remained in my memory, and it couldn't reach me at Trevor's.

While we'd had many fights in his apartment over the years, it pulsed with energy, and sunshine spilled through the window that led out to his balcony with warm benevolence. It was also bigger, had many books I could look at, and a real kitchen we could cook in. His roommate either remained in his upstairs bedroom or was out with his boyfriend. I also thought that if I hung out enough, maybe one day he'd invite me to stay for good. Make his place mine. I thought maybe I could make him happy and maybe he could make me truly kind again, the way I'd been with Adrian, the way I'd felt when I was younger, as if the power of my love could fix everything.

Sometimes I'd show him a plan for a sculpture, like the one I hoped to do that would probably take me a year. It was a human heart, hollow inside, made of thick plaster. I would install hinges that allowed it to open, and inside the heart would be a miniature house. There were rooms divided the way someone would divide rooms in a dollhouse, miniature beds, a miniature fridge, all carved from wood or stone or put together out of things I'd found. He didn't always understand my drawings and plans, since they took a little bit of imagination to piece together, but he asked the right questions, and while he usually didn't seem to be interested in much but Netflix and moping, he was interested in this—me as an artist, I guess—or at least liked that I was an artist. "It's great that you're getting into it again," he said after I showed him. "I should get back to work on my novel."

"But you write all the time."

"I slack off more. And I get distracted, writing pieces about my life, people I know." He ran his hands through his hair and made it stand straight up like it was trying to escape from his forehead. "I like having you around, it inspires me."

It was one of the nicest things he had ever said to me.

"I wasn't doing much for a while either," I said. "Sometimes it's hard to get motivated when everything seems to be falling down around you, and your art seems so small."

"I know what you mean," he said.

He convinced me that I was talented, that I could do whatever I wanted. Together we wrote a Craigslist ad for tutoring clients. "I'll take on writing clients and you can take on art clients and the little kids," he said. He made me think that this new change in my career, it didn't have to be confined to only teaching Tammy, that there were people out there who wanted to learn from me.

I made a brochure, and he helped me pick the photo of myself for the front cover. He proofread the whole thing and talked to me about the best coffee houses to leave them in around the Junction. I folded them at his kitchen table, and he sat on his futon and read. From time to time, he'd look up at me and smile. He'd never really smiled much, ever. A rainstorm came in, and wind whipped the rain against the balcony doors, and his apartment felt like our own little refuge, like we were in a tree fort or a boat, totally secluded and safe.

✧

Sunday night, before starting work with Tammy, I was in his arms and he kissed me, once, twice, right where my cheek met my ears. "Why are you all like this today?" I said.

"I'm going to miss you tomorrow," he said, rocking me as he hugged. He brought me over to the futon, and we lay down, bodies pressed together, tighter, the tightest it could go. I remembered Adrian's ribs pressing into mine, and pushed away. "What's wrong?" he said.

"I just needed to breathe a second."

"You can breathe down here with me."

"No, I can't."

I know now that although it was one of my happiest days, I couldn't feel it. The thought horrified me—to know that an emotion was there, slightly outside my grasp. That what I yearned for was missing, not because he was withholding but because of something screaming inside my chest.

Now

I'm in The Lighted City again. There's a child trapped there, but Adrian can't see her. He takes my hands and I know where he's leading me. "Please stop!" I scream. Please. Please. But it's the child who's yelling, not me.

There's rope in his hands and he brings me to our home base tree. All I can see then is The Lighted City, Adrian and I together, the tree blazing, flames licking everything. Rope binds me to the trunk, flames lick at my feet. Once I know what's coming, I slow my heart down, breathing slowly. Once the fear's gone and we enter the light, Adrian and I are able to be together again.

I wake to my alarm at five in the morning. Although the dream was terrifying at the beginning, I still feel the sense of peace from the light, from slowing down my breath. What it would mean to die. In the dream, it was the way things were supposed to be. The way I would find peace. But I don't want to think like that. It's been a couple years since I've thought like that.

The studio is almost always empty when I come this early. My ideal work time, when I can get my shit together, is six. Everyone else tends to filter in between ten and eleven, so usually I can get a good amount done before anyone arrives, and then, when things get too crowded, I can go home and begin my workday.

Today, I would've had Jocelyn at eleven.

The studio, before anyone gets there, always seems too clean. The tables, big, plastic, and white, always have too few stains for what I imagine a studio should look like. Under the bright lights, with everyone's projects and supplies sealed away in their lockers, art seems like the furthest possible purpose of the room. Only a couple drying racks crammed in the corner give it away, and even these are pristine. Strict cleaning rules are stapled to the wall, but I think it must be because the place is relatively new and hasn't had enough time to accumulate drips and stains or hunks of glue.

I put my backpack on the table and pull out the latest bundle of sticks I've collected in the ravine. I scatter them across the table, line them up. Then, with a tiny key, I unlock a cabinet against one of the walls marked "Tools" and take out a small hacksaw. I begin to even the sticks out, cutting them down so they are all the same size. It takes a while, but I have to use what they have here. It's already enough to chip in for the studio fees without buying a bunch of tools, and I like the way the saw chews up the edges. I put the pieces I've removed off to the side.

I go to my locker and pull out the beginnings of a structure: sticks bound together with twine and glue. I've already made four of these, but figure I'll know when I'm ready to stop.

One of my studio mates rented a space to set up an exhibit at the beginning of January before the holidays are over. She wants everyone to include their pieces as part of the show. So I try to come almost every morning, to finish.

I have a large Tupperware container where I keep the little bits of wood that I trim off the branches. I'll use these for another purpose. I begin to wrap the sticks with twine, again and again, securing every so often with glue. I'm making a shelter. I'm making a place children love to hide.

✧

I see the wax guy locking his bike outside through the window. A papier mâché artist stops by his bike and begins to chat, waving their hands in the air as they speak. I start to pack up, hoping I don't have to interact again when I'm still feeling raw. As I leave, Trevor messages: *I'm in TO! I should be free tomorrow if that works for you. When are you going to Caledon?*

I write back, *Not until Christmas. Tomorrow works. Leaf Café?*

Can't wait!

It's nice to see Trevor use an exclamation mark. In fact, since he moved to the East Coast, everything about our interactions has been *nice*. Not complicated. Not confusing. Pleasant. As if the sea air has changed him to his core.

How It Happened
May 2016

I sat in my therapist's office, before going over to Nik's to tutor, and tried to describe the things I was feeling about my trip and how things had changed with Trevor. Not hearing from Trevor while I was gone and the texts from Nik once I landed. The way Nik had looked, standing underneath the streetlamp, how he'd touched my scars, inspected my hands. I was trying to present evidence to her, but I didn't know of what. And then the *I love you*s with Trevor, talking about my past with him.

She asked me if I'd told Trevor how it felt when he didn't text while I was away.

"How could I tell him? He doesn't acknowledge me. It's not like we're together," I said. "I mean, I don't think we're together. We've been spending more time together, but nothing's been said about being in a relationship or anything like that. It's still a secret." Her mouth didn't move. She just watched me. A plant beside her seemed to angle its leaves to listen to me better.

"But haven't you been able to tell things to Trevor recently? Wasn't that what you wanted?"

"I thought so." She didn't know what had been told, and I couldn't tell her how telling Trevor had released something, the way he had described what happened between Adrian and me. My dreams had been more vivid, and it was harder, unless I was with Trevor, to get through my days without thinking about Adrian, without thinking about the gun. Although I didn't say it, I also felt the approaching anniversary of the day everything happened, just a few days away. That it was growing increasingly difficult to keep it off my mind.

"Do you think this relationship makes you happy? That it could make you happy?"

"Don't know if I'll ever be happy."

"What would you say if one of your friends told you that? Would you believe them?"

I ignored her. "I think that as soon as I was born I was unhappy, and that everything that happened made it worse, and now he's gone."

"Do you mean your cousin?"

"Yes."

"Do you want to talk about that a bit?"

"Not really." I just sat there, silent. I wanted to leave, but felt like it'd be rude. That then she'd think I was more fucked up than I was, or be able to see into me, see that I had a gun waiting for me, always, in case it got too hard.

"I'd really like to talk about how you're doing a little bit more. Are you sure you don't want to talk about your cousin?"

"No. Not really. I don't really want to talk about him all the time."

"Okay. Well, then we can wrap up, Paulina." She took out her little black book and opened it in her lap. "I've been wanting to talk to you, Paulina. We're three sessions behind now."

"I know, I know, I'm sorry."

"If you absolutely can't pay, Paulina, there are things we can do, but you have to tell me."

"No, I'll pay you. Next time. I promise. I'm just waiting on some cheques. Here. I have cash for today." I pulled a few crumpled twenties from my pockets—what was left of my spending money from Vancouver. I'd been planning on using it for groceries after I finished tutoring.

"Thank you. When can you come for your next session?"

"Um, since I'm starting a new job, I'm not sure when I can yet. Can I just contact you with my schedule?" She stared at me. She knew my schedule was for after-school tutoring, that I would be free most days for therapy. But she never called me on a half-truth.

"It would be good if we could schedule something next week. There's been a lot going on I'd like to follow up on."

"Okay, I'll let you know."

"Don't fall into your old traps, Paulina," she said. "Don't stop talking."

I got out of there as fast as I could, running down the steps and grabbing my bike. If I owed her for three sessions, I owed her close to two hundred dollars. And that was with her discount rates. I biked home quickly, fell into my bed I'd missed so much, spending so much time away at Trevor's, and reached my hand under the mattress to touch the cold of the gun.

Tammy acted shy when she saw me outside of the structured environment of Artastic! Nik was there, hovering by the doorway to the living room, where he'd set up the table with markers, paper, and a couple workbooks Tammy had for school. "Can I show Paul my room?" she asked before Nik left the doorway.

"Of course," he said. "Show her the whole house! Grand tour."

"Come on the Grand Tour," she said, and reached up to take my hand, shyness disappearing now that she had a task and was in control. "This is the kitchen." She brought me into a wide room with stainless steel appliances and an island. The fridge was likely full of food, and everything was clean. Nik didn't say anything, but I felt him standing behind me, close, the heat from his skin.

We walked by a closed door in the hallway. "Don't show Paul my room," Nik said.

"But it's the Grand Tour!"

"It's too messy," he said to me and winked.

Tammy lost interest in a second and ran ahead to her room, but I was imagining what was beyond the closed door, where only Nik was allowed to go. "Come here!" Tammy demanded. She'd always been quiet at Artastic!, making friends slowly and kindly with those around her, waiting for my approval as if she were scared what would happen if she did something wrong. But her "Come here!" was the way I often heard kids yelling at each other in class. She spread out her dolls in front of me and told me their names, showed me where their clothes were kept, opened her closet and explained things about it to me. She even crawled along the floor and dragged herself under the bed to pull out a bin of mixed-up Legos. She wanted to show me everything she had, wanted to tell me about everyone she knew. Instantly, she'd decided that more than a teacher, I was going to be her friend.

The imagination can do almost anything. For me and Adrian, it created a place, it created rules that we could live freely by, created so many games where we could escape from our families and finally feel joy. For Tammy, it created people: Rachel and Colin. She told me that Rachel was an adult with a job, like me, that she was nice and took care of her when she was there. She told me all of this in front of Nik, and he said, "Kids and their imaginations, huh?" And Tammy looked hurt because she wanted her imaginary friend to be respected, I guess. She didn't mention Rachel much after that, instead fixated on Colin. She went over the same details I already knew. Colin was hiding, and he couldn't be found. Nik paid me in crisp twenty-dollar bills.

After tutoring I went over to Trevor's place, and I picked up a few groceries we could use to make dinner. "What took you so long?" he said when I showed up, and instantly folded me into his giant arms. He kissed the side of my face with the same tenderness he'd given me before I left. "My roommate's home," he said quietly, placing my grocery bag on the counter, and led me up the stairs, even though I was starving. He pushed me back onto the bed and climbed on top of me.

"From behind," I said, and he flipped me around and I got on my knees. One of his hands gathered my hair and held it, like he'd thought I'd be too hot. He wanted to let my neck breathe, but then he was kissing my neck instead, biting it, and then I couldn't think and I couldn't be hungry, only his bed, his hands, his dick in me.

When it was over, I asked him, "So, what did you get up to while I was gone?"

"Not a whole lot," he said. "Just wrote, mostly." And then he was pulling on his clothes. "I heard about a cool show we should watch, I think you'd like it. I think Kyle left, if you want to head down." And he went downstairs without waiting for me, leaving me still undressed on his bed. My stomach gurgled. I wondered if the meat I'd bought was already beginning to go bad on the counter.

I put on my clothes, checked my phone.

There was a message from Nik. And a photo.

In it, his dick was hard and red and pushed up to the side.

Want it?

I didn't ask for that, I wrote and sent an angry emoji.

But you wanted it, he replied. I deleted the message thread and closed my phone. Did I want it? All I wanted was Trevor. I thought of Nik as a friend, a flirty friend, but a friend. But teaching his kid was now the only job I had, his twenties the only money for food and rent.

Trevor cooked pasta with the ingredients I brought, and we watched TV for the rest of the night. He asked me to stay over. Before we fell asleep, he ran his hands through my hair, the way he did to his own hair when he was trying to calm himself down. His hand moved from my hair to the side of my face and then perched on my shoulder. "I'm sorry," he said to me, once we'd both been breathing half-sleep breaths. "For everything." I didn't know if he meant about Adrian and what I'd told him, or the death, or the way he'd treated me over the years. And it didn't even matter. I felt like there was a little tunnel running from the centre of him to the centre of me. When I felt like that, I thought maybe he did understand all of me.

There was another part of me, too, part of me that I knew existed outside of what I had with Trevor, or at least wanted to. The part of me that dreamed of an ideal place, that knew there could be more for me than what I was experiencing then. The part of me that became the me I am now, the part of me that I hope will continue to grow, change, maybe even one day become someone I can love. The part of me that taught, that liked to go out with my friends, the part of me who listened to other people, the part of me that could find peace looking at the branches of the trees or a snowfall, the way a flower bloomed. The part of me that was growing. I worried that this part of me, perhaps the most beautiful part, was a part he'd never be able to see.

✧

The next day when I was over at Tammy's, I ignored Nik, focused on teaching and Tammy, and only said *hello* and *goodbye*. He'd already paid me in full for the week on Monday, and I'd show him that I could be professional, even if he couldn't. He mostly stayed in his office, leaving Tammy and me to draw, talk, and write.

In the middle of the night: *I'm sorry. I didn't think it'd put you off.*

It was just out of nowhere, I typed. *It'd be different if we were together or something.*

Do you want to be together?

I don't really know you.

But I feel like we do know each other, don't you?

I guess.

I like you, but I think it's complicated.

Yeah.

I'd do whatever you wanted me to. I think you're so hot.

The offer hovered beside me in the night. Despite the part of myself that was repulsed, another part of me was waking up.

Like what?

We could get rough. Do you like that?

Curiosity took me over. And something that was missing with Trevor. Had Nik been able to sense it? *Yes.*

What do you like about me?

You're a good dad.

1. I'm not. 2. Seriously? that's what turns you on?

Kinda.

What else?

Your scar.

What are yours from?

I used to hit things when I was upset. Not anymore. Urs?

I fell down a hill when I was drunk. Broke my arm.

Oh.

Why did you hit things? Why were you upset?

I just was. All the time. And it felt good.

Is that why you like it rough?

Ur so nosy.

You like it. You talk to me.

So? I talk to everyone.

No you don't.

I do.

Come over. I'm alone.

Not tonight. But maybe.

Soon.

Maybe.

I regretted the texts in the morning. They weren't from me—somehow Nik had figured out how to open the door to the part of me where the gun, Adrian, and my violence lived. I deleted the texts. I promised myself I would go into the house and teach Tammy and then leave. And that's what I did. When I got a *Sup?* in the middle of the night, I didn't answer. I spent more nights with Trevor. I tried to forget about the gun. The twenty-fourth, the day everything happened, passed like a regular day of work and time with Trevor. Perhaps I was finding a new normal, even if I still found it impossible to relax.

Once the week was over, I went to Tammy's mom's with her. Tammy led me to the edge of her backyard, where brush grew up and then abruptly fell away down a steep slope, studded with trees. A wire fence barely divided where the property stopped and the brush and forest started. "There's a river down there," Tammy said. "Jason says it's the ravine. He's gonna build a big fence."

"I guess it's kind of dangerous," I said.

"But I still like to play down there. That's where Colin lives."

From where we stood, I couldn't see the river. "It seems like you could fall. Maybe Colin can come play up here instead."

"He can't come up," Tammy said, and led me inside.

The next morning, I got up early before Trevor. Every day I woke up earlier and fell asleep later, my body pumping with adrenalin as soon as the light went off. I wasn't having bad dreams anymore, but terror sunk into me unless I pressed up against Trevor, and he told me it made it hard for him to sleep. So, I got up and made coffee. I checked and there were some eggs, so I could make him breakfast. I pulled a book from a pile on the coffee table, flipped through it, but nothing interested me.

On the kitchen table were sheets of paper scattered all over, Trevor's laptop close by. His work from the day before. Normally I was good, I swear, I was good, and I knew I shouldn't do it, but I started to flip through the pages. Paul. Paulina. Paul. Paulina.

He'd been writing about me. About how I stormed out and left him wondering, about our conversations, pages and pages about who Trevor thought I was and about my past, the bits I revealed to him, and what I hadn't revealed to him he filled in, made me into someone who was very much like me but missing those parts of me I knew he'd never understand. And of course, over several of the pages, was my secret. On them, Adrian was transformed into a monster, like everyone always saw it, not the little boy I'd grown up with, the boy who'd been my best friend and, in many ways, my only true family. And he didn't understand the man Adrian had grown into because, of course, how could I explain it to Trevor when I barely understood myself? He'd left an impact on so many who grieved his death. Yes, there had been violence, and yes, he'd hurt me in ways that I couldn't get out of my head, that made me afraid of almost everything, but there was more to it than that. I wasn't the only one who was damaged. I knew he couldn't understand.

All the love and loyalty I felt for Trevor fell away. I lay the pages out one by one across his table. I walked up to his bedroom and picked up my clothes and packed my backpack. He stirred. "Where are you going?"

"I'll be back," I said. "In one second."

And then I left Trevor's. I walked down the steps of his apartment, walked down to the front door. I hadn't brought my bike and didn't think I could face dropping in on Stef—she still didn't know about Trevor, despite what she and Kayla both suspected. I walked all the way to my apartment in Roncesvalles. It only took forty minutes, and it gave me time to think, about how the pain was growing in me again, how I felt like I couldn't breathe, how I knew I didn't want to hear what Trevor had to say about his pages of writing, how I didn't care if they were his novel, his journal, or what. All that mattered was that he'd failed so completely to understand me, to give me what I needed, that he kept me contained and secret even when I'd tried to be loyal despite Nik's texts and flirts, I'd tried to be open and honest and true—not that either of us had said I *love you* again or spoken about it.

I felt different—like there was a little click going off inside of me and it kept clicking. I didn't know what it meant at all. The old rage, the one that made me want to punch and yell and tell someone exactly what I thought of them, or to hide until I was somewhere alone where I could open up my knuckles again—that was all gone. All I could think about was the gun, and even that, God, I was feeling so sick and defeated, like maybe I'd lie in bed and not even have the strength to touch the gun where it was tucked between my box spring and mattress.

Obviously, I didn't kill myself during that dark year. But what made me want to put my mouth around the gun was also an impulse to shoot.

How It Happened
The Lighted City

Adrian asks me if I've ever had a secret. I am five years old and everything that happens to me is controlled by someone else. Other than a drawing here and there of naked bodies that I shove deep into the garbage cans of our home with shame, nothing is hidden. My parents wake me up in the morning and bring me to kindergarten and then the teacher tells me what to do at school and then I get picked back up and brought home and then I get dropped at Adrian's. The long grass sometimes holds a bit of lime green before it fades to a dusty brown in autumn. We love to play and hide in the grass, using our bodies to mat it down into little hollows and nests.

Adrian is turning eight. Eight seems so grown-up. Of course, he has secrets. "Sometimes," I say.

"Well, you know you have to keep them, right?" I nod my head. He pulls up his shirt and shows me round bruises, blossoming like flowers, purple and blue. Their edges start to run into a green and then yellow.

"Ow, what happened?"

"He did it." I know he means Uncle Jim. "He does that if I don't want to do what he wants. He does other stuff, stuff I don't like."

I don't know what he means, and Adrian explains about how when people love each other they touch each other, but he doesn't love Uncle Jim but he does it anyway. And if Adrian doesn't, Uncle Jim hurts him.

As he tells me, Adrian begins to cry, and I hug him like he's my teddy bear, I hug him like I can make him feel better with one hug. "Let's run away," I say.

"Yeah?" he says through tears. And we're off. We take Adrian's school bag and slip inside. Uncle Jim is out at work and Aunt Dot is in the living room reading. We go to the pantry and fill the backpack with cookies, crackers, packaged processed cheese slices. And then we slip back out the door and run to the forest.

"My legs are tired," I say, once we've walked far enough that I don't really know where I am.

"Okay, let's camp here," Adrian says.

We play. The Lighted City already exists as the game King and Queen. We construct crowns out of sticks. Adrian helps me find a way to hold mine together. "You're my best friend, Paul," he says as he puts the crown on my head.

"You're mine!" I say. "No, you're my king!" And I bow down to him, my own crown falling off my head. "Nothing bad can happen to you here."

"Nothing bad can happen while I'm with you," Adrian says, and he leans against the tree.

We try to stay until it's past dark, but as soon as the sun sets, the forest gets spooky. We hear animals shift through the darkness. "Is that a bear?" I say.

"Dad says there's no bears here," Adrian says. And I think about Adrian's secret again and feel sick.

"Do you think it's a mountain lion?"

"I think we should head back," Adrian says. His skin is puckered with goosebumps. He always feels the cold before me. "We need to go home."

On the walk back through the forest, we're both quiet. I jump every time I hear a noise, but Adrian barely notices, caught in thought. "You can't tell anyone what I told you," he says to me.

"I promise."

"And we probably shouldn't say anything about running away either. Say we were playing and couldn't see the sun and forgot the time, okay?"

"Okay."

We walk in silence a little more. I jump over every desirably hoppable log. "Paul," Adrian says once we catch sight of the house, "I know you don't know a lot about secrets... But once you start to have them, a lot more come." And we walk in through the screen door to Adrian's home.

How It Happened
June 2016

Without the escape of Trevor's apartment, night after night it was only me and the gun. Using it became more realistic, even after my last cheque from Drop 'n Draw came in the mail and, along with Nik's pay for the coming week, I was able to pay my rent. But by Saturday, I had nowhere to go. Tammy and I took weekends off. I stayed in bed, mostly, my comforter wrapped around me, trying not to feel the pain in my chest that I'd felt every morning since Trevor's betrayal. He'd used me. My story.

That night, I couldn't be alone with the gun, so I went to Kayla's. I could have dropped in on Stef, Derek, and Wynn, but Stef would have known I was upset as soon as she saw me and then Derek would tell Trevor. I didn't want him to know I was thinking about him at all. Since the beginning of June, my birthday and Adrian's had been on my mind. The joint parties we'd had as kids. He wouldn't have his this year. And here in the world, I remained.

Kayla and I talked and laughed and watched a reality TV show about a dried-up actress who'd been a child star. The whole time we hung out together we drank, and finally Kayla told me that she needed to dance, that I should leave my stuff there, pull on a dress of hers because we were going OUT. Kayla's shiny purple dress barely fit me, bagging at my butt and my boobs, places Kayla filled it out, and tugging tight over my stomach, where Kayla was always muscular and flat from hitting the gym first thing in the morning. I tried to see it as a sign I was no longer wasting away now that I finally had money for food. The heels she gave me were so tall I thought I'd fall over as we walked, but they were black and covered in glitter. "Perfect for you," she told me, and when I looked in the mirror, if I forgot how Kayla looked in the dress, the purple and black did seem to suit me. "One more thing," she said, and took a necklace, heavy with little pendants of each astrological sign, and clasped it around my neck. "A good luck charm for the only Gemini I like," she said. "Birthday girl next week."

When I'd first met Kayla, dragged to The Cave after meeting Stef at a Mommy and Me art class I was teaching when I first moved to Toronto, she'd seemed skeptical of me. Over beers, she asked me, "So what's your background?"

I'd laughed awkwardly. No one in Caledon, where most people were various shades of pale peach, had ever asked about my background. Instead, they asked if you were Catholic, or Christian. And in Oakville, where I'd lived with my partner and commuted to school, no one asked you anything at all. "Um, Canadian?"

"No, like, where are you from?"

"I've always lived here."

"But your people. They aren't *from* Canada. Unless you're Indigenous?" She smiled, knowing she'd caught me.

"Oh no," I said. "At least not that I know of. I guess it's some sort of mix? Mostly Irish, I think."

"You're new to Toronto?"

"Yeah," I said, feeling more and more embarrassed by the conversation.

"You have a bit of learning to do." Stef was listening to all of this and laughed and nodded. But she put an arm around my shoulder.

I felt so naive. Around me, artists moved in and out of conversations, and at the front of the room, a DJ was setting up. I was only twenty-one, and overcome in that moment with how I'd made the right decision to move to Toronto, to try to be an artist away from school and my past. "What about you?" I asked. "Where's your family from?"

"Some Irish and Scottish here, too, but my grandfather was Jamaican, but he was half Black and half Chinese. So, I have a lot of everything. Anyway, this is my Cave," she said. "My collection of friends, who I love, love, love."

Her brown eyes were open, yet assessing me. "Can I be a friend?" I said, after drinking the rest of my beer down in a gulp. I knew I sounded like the toddlers I taught, like the mommies introducing baby Liam to baby Teddy, *Do you have a new friend, Liam?*

But Kayla broke into a huge smile, the way the toddlers did. "Yes! Shots!" She ran to the bar and came back with a tray of tequila, which she handed out to everyone. Even Stef did shots on nights she had a babysitter back then. "To new friends!" she said, and raised her shot glass. All of Kayla's friends raised their glasses.

"Friends!" they shouted.

We all threw the booze back, and then I began to talk, talk, talk.

✧

Out on the street, I tottered behind Kayla, her good luck charm around my neck. Since June had begun, a chill had set in, like May and June switched places, or like June didn't want it to be summer yet. Even with the cool night air, out one place turned into out another, and we went from bar to bar. I smoked a joint with Kayla in an alley and drank from her flask. The night started to fade away. Trevor started to fade away. And even Adrian faded.

I followed behind Kayla, drunk, and high from the weed she'd given me, down streets that glowed with lights that blurred through the night. She was smoking a cigarette and talking to a boy up ahead and I knew I couldn't lose her... My memory jolted and I was transported to another night, years ago when I'd gone out with Stef. I was in another bar meeting a man, losing sight of Stef. And then waking up in a hallway. Kayla had never heard that story, and I knew she wouldn't look out for me. Good luck charm or none, I couldn't have anything else happen. I quickened my pace to catch up to her, even though I was unsteady in her heels.

The terror that I experienced in the city felt almost magical. Nothing could touch me—I had a resiliency that was like a superpower, but maybe it was the weed and the tequila I sipped from Kayla's flask. Still, I was nervous to be wandering along behind a friend who I knew wasn't watching out for me, didn't really care where I was going or what would happen to me. Kayla was always so caring until the night came and swept her away. Even though it was one or two in the morning, the streets were crowded with people.

I tried to call out to her, but she couldn't hear me.

Sometimes as I lay in bed, remembering a night where I'd been lost in the city, I thought to myself that life like this had a wild beauty. A beauty that could make the world into its ideal self. I wanted so badly for it to be its ideal self. I wanted to be my ideal self, too, a perfect me in a perfect world—and wasn't that what The Lighted City had always been about? A future where everything was real and true, dreamed into existence.

In the darkness, lost behind Kayla, somehow these things all shared a significance—an empty folder, a locked door, texts in the middle of the night, news of a suicide, a gun in a tea tin, a manuscript left forgotten, collected pieces of trash from the street, a night stretching onward, a friend not looking back to see if I was following, the ember from a cigarette, a scar on an arm, an invisible friend.

Sometimes I thought that everything was connected, but it was only going to lead you to eventual harm. If I thought about it logically, it made sense: we are all heading toward death, and it's this that gives us our kinship with everything—the sun in the sky and the grass and the trees, the insects and dogs and babies on the street in their strollers. Everything exists for a time and then does not.

I was terrified in the dark with only the streetlights to guide me. And they did guide me—I stumbled onto the night bus that ran from Roncesvalles to the Junction. Dug through my purse until I had enough change to hand to the driver. Then I was on my way. I cut down Trevor's side street once the bus stopped on Dundas. I started yelling "Trevor!" as soon as I was outside of his townhouse apartment.

I can't tell you why I was doing what I was doing. I was drunk and all I felt was my anger, coursing through me. It had taken hold of my hands, my neck ached, and a tremor passed through my whole body. I was so angry with him. Didn't know how he could've let me feel safe and then take everything from me like that, all of my experiences. By taking what I felt and lived, he'd transformed me into something sensationalized, disgusting, and wrong.

A light flicked on. The main floor. "Who's out there?" I heard a woman say. I heard her ask her husband if he'd heard anything.

"I thought I heard a woman's voice," she said.

"Fucking Trevor," the man said. By the time the man who swore came to the door, I was already running down the street in bare feet, my high heels now held in my hand, wondering why he hadn't woken up, why he didn't seem to care about me anymore, why he'd never cared in the first place.

✧

After that night, I didn't want to be away from the gun anymore. I knew I needed my escape close by. I slipped the tea tin into my backpack, underneath a change of clothes that I carried in case I got splattered in paint at Tammy's. When I walked, my backpack was heavy, reminding me.

✧

Tammy wasn't an odd kid like Wynn, who was always in her head, quiet, and could only be drawn out with play. Instead, she wanted to talk and share ideas. Mostly about Colin. I tried to teach her, I really did, but right away it seemed like what she needed was a friend. I'd been like that, too, but I'd only had Adrian, and once he was gone, this desire had left me with a rawness that was easy for others to exploit. I wanted to help her. To teach her how to live a life of honour and truth. I wanted to show her the world had beauty. And it really did during that time, as trees and flowers were blooming, only a couple more weeks until summer. We'd go for walks frequently and I'd show her the plants I knew how to recognize and we'd bring some flowers home and draw them. Teaching her gave me purpose, too, somehow. I always had something to look up once I got home, the name of a wildflower that seemed both purple and blue at once. What to call that exact hue. One day Tammy brought me to a light bulb and wanted to know how it was made, why some were white and some were clear and what that little thing on the inside did, what it was called. "Filament, I think," I said.

"Filament," she said slowly and stared at it harder. Then I had to go home that night and find out everything I could about light bulbs. I made worksheets and diagrams and found a book at the library that I brought in. Tammy did all the worksheets, quickly and incorrectly with her huge uneven printing, and then ran off and came back with an LED light bulb. "What about this?" she said. And so, I had more homework. This work, while it meant I wasn't drawing or creating or doing anything for myself, opened me up raw. I felt it in myself. I was interested and growing and struggling to keep up. I liked it. It made it seem like the gun in my backpack was the furthest thing from my thoughts. Adrian. Who had he been to me really? All that was left for me were Tammy's questions. All that was left was trying to teach a child to grow in a way I hadn't, with a natural knowledge of honour and truth.

But what did I know about honour and truth? Once Nik got home for the day, he moved around me in their house like he was afraid to touch me, like if he brushed me I'd either crumble or stick to him like epoxy. Although he was friendly, he left me alone to teach his daughter if he was home, briefly asked me about the day's activities if he'd been at work all day. Then he would pay me, and I'd go home with a wad of cash. Nik didn't believe in writing cheques—he wanted to give me the bills folded up and thick. By the time I got home, I usually had a text from him waiting for me.

✧

There is nothing more dangerous than a child who knows too much. A child who is a little adult in a child's body. And not dangerous for others—dangerous for themselves, however that knowledge falls on them. Part of me felt like I'd come into the world screaming and wounded, knowing all the heartache that would fall on me and those around me. That I knew the unseen heartaches, that everywhere in the world there were people going through pain, and that I hummed with a painful, invisible empathy for them that I was unable to turn off. As a child, I'd channelled all of this into Adrian because he was the person who had the most pain.

This was what worried me about Tammy. I couldn't tell if she'd changed because of me or if, as I spent more time with her, I was simply learning who she really was—the Tammy who was always smiling and shy in class was naturally a tiny adult in a child's body. Like me, like Adrian. Maybe the classroom setting had prevented me from seeing past the surface level of children to the people they were and would grow into.

I first noticed it through her art. Every day, she began to draw the same place, a scribble of blue at the bottom of a cliff or sharp hill, with trees spreading up. She learned to draw the trees overtop the hill so that they covered up the grass and mud and brush. It looked more realistic. She always wanted things to look exactly as they were. My art was always about drawing things that didn't exist, capturing my imagination. But Tammy wasn't interested in that. She didn't show me at first, and so, I didn't ask. I let her play and explore her ideas as I prepared part of a writing lesson or another activity we could do together. I'd needed my own space with art as a child, and I figured she did too.

One day she asked me how to spell it when she was done the picture. *Ravine*. She wrote the letters at the bottom with a black crayon and then brought it to me. "It's the ravine," she said. I understood the way she drew it now, as if she was looking down the hill toward the bottom, trees interrupting the clear view of the water. More realistic in its chaos, more precise to her perception. She'd drawn a little hut by the water and a little boy was beside the hut, I thought. But he was so small how she drew him that he was barely a figure, more like a dark shadow, waiting to go inside his hut. "I can only go when Jason's home. It isn't fair. Colin gets lonely when I can't come."

"Why don't we let Colin come here?" I said.

Tammy stopped colouring and put down all of her markers. "Really?"

"Sure. He's here right now. Didn't you hear him come in through the door?"

I'd never seen a kid's face crumple like that. One moment she'd been bright, alert, and the next second she was wailing and crying. Sometimes Wynn did this, and Stef and I were always able to calm her down with touch, with hugging, with comfort, but Tammy wouldn't let me near her. "Nik!" I ran up the stairs and down the hall, although I knew I should be the one to fix it. But since leaving Trevor's house, ignoring his calls, I really couldn't do much of anything that was hard. "Nik! Tammy's crying."

He poked his head out of the office. "Is she hurt?"

"No. I need you. She won't listen to me."

Nik pushed past me and went down the stairs. "What's wrong?" he asked her. He got down on his knees. He didn't touch her, just talked to her. "What's got you all upset, eh?"

She moaned out a word that I couldn't understand. "Colin?" Nik said. "What about him?"

"Paul said he could come here, but she lied."

"She lied?"

"She said he's here. But he's not."

I walked into the room. Nik was still down on his knees, talking to Tammy. I couldn't hear them anymore as they conspired in lowered voices, and I wondered what it was that they were saying. My shift was done anyway, and Nik had already paid me for the week, so I slipped out the door, onto their Junction street. The sun, which was hanging around longer and longer these days, was setting, but the air was so cool. The beginning of June. Time always confused me. I wished it would never move.

Now

It's impossible to have secrets from children. Even the sneakiest child is naively direct and can see who a person is underneath their kind smiles and distant voices. I never lost that childhood part of myself, and even if I shut it up behind a door, it grew a garden there that was overgrown, beautiful, and terrifying. This is how I'm able to understand other people. How even before Trevor and I were close, I knew he had pain in him. How I was able to look at Tammy and tell she was sad. But it went both ways. Tammy was also able to look at me and see through my skin and muscle and into that painful garden. She was able to understand because she also was sad. I worried about it, though, back then. Every kid I taught, I respected their private lives, but I also knew that if only I paid the right attention, I could keep them from turning out like me, like Adrian. Our secrets controlling us, almost all the way until the end.

Selina wants me to talk a bit more about childhood. She asks me about how I described Tammy as a tiny adult in a child's body, how I said I had been the same way.

"Do you think that everything you know as an adult, you knew as a child?" she asks.

"Not everything, of course. There are some things that come from experience. But, you know, I understood the way the world works, in its essence."

"And how does it work?"

"It's a trap, I guess," I say. "Terrible things happen to people who don't ask for it, and sometimes those people go on to be terrible."

"Do you think what you and Adrian did was terrible?"

"Yeah, I do. I mean, it's not supposed to happen for a reason."

"But did you have the knowledge of that at the time?"

"Well, no. But I did eventually. And then things got more complicated."

"Why?"

"Well, because Adrian didn't want our games to stop. He couldn't let them stop."

"And how did this impact you, Paul?"

"I felt like I didn't have a choice. I didn't have a choice about anything. And . . . it hurt me."

"It's okay to acknowledge that. Even though you cared a lot for Adrian, he hurt you."

"Yeah," I say. I don't want to talk anymore. This is where my feelings always get confused and my head gets cloudy. We end for the day.

✧

I set aside ten minutes of every evening to listen to my recording of what I've written about the final day. " . . . I see that he has the can of gasoline in his hands, and I beg him not to pour it on me, I beg him not to start the fire. I tell him I don't want to go alone, this wasn't how it was supposed to happen. We both are naked and I know if we get found, everything is ruined, that I will have betrayed him, but I don't…I don't want to die. Even if I did sometimes before, when we talked about it, I don't want to go in that moment and I'm so scared and I stop asking Adrian not to do it and instead I call for help…"

I stop listening even though it's playing. Part of me floats away and I think about other things, seeing Trevor, plans for the future.

Because I have a plan now, even though I never really let myself have one before. I want to go back to school, finish what I started when I moved out of my parents' place. I want to move forward.

The last time I had a plan like that was before the day everything happened—it was *why* everything happened. I can't help but have a sense of dread as I dream.

But it still feels good to dream again.

Since I started taking on more clients and running my online classes, I've been stashing money into an account, dreaming of going back to finish my degree in art. After that, I imagine taking a master's in education with a focus on art education, taking everything I've learned over the years teaching kids and grown-ups in groups and one-on-one. Maybe one day, I'll teach college like Stef. Or maybe I'll continue to own my own business or open my own school of art.

The recording ends. I jot down a few observations. I try to be honest about when I stopped connecting with my own words, when I couldn't listen anymore.

I kick through snow and slush on my way to see Trevor. It'll be Christmas next week, and when I arrive at the café, I see he has a gift, wrapped in front of him. Up close, I see he's wrapped it in pages from the *New Yorker* and used too much tape. "I didn't get you anything!" I say. He stands to hug me, and it feels so good, to be where I belong again, surrounded by his smell.

"That's okay! I just saw it before I left and it made me think of you, so I bought it."

I open it, struggling through the layers of tape. It's a book, of course. An *Encyclopedia of Colour*. "I love it!" I flip through the pages, and he's right, it's the perfect gift for me. Each page says a little bit about the history of colour and includes swatches. It's the type of book I'd want to make, if I made a book. It's the type of book I'd want to buy, if I ever spent money on things like that. "It's perfect."

There are tablets for ordering on the table. We explore the menu together, scrolling through the options, but decide on the typical: boring old Americanos, although we wonder if we should be decadent and order a waffle and ice cream and split it. We order a couple of cookies instead.

I didn't get involved with anyone while he was gone, not because I love him, although I know that I do. It was that after he left, I couldn't imagine going through it all again. That every person would need the same answers about why I was the way I was, and how I came to be. It was hard enough to sit with that myself, look at my past from different angles, dealing with it when it collided into me.

When he left, part of me had been relieved. I could pretend love wasn't an option for me, at least for a little while. Trick myself into thinking that maybe it would never happen for me. Everything with Trevor, it had been adolescent. All I needed was the city, my apartment and space, and my friends. If I had those things, I'd be okay.

But faced with Trevor, the wrinkles forming beside his eyes as he smiles at me, I still feel the pull toward him. Feel it even more.

His smiles come more easily now. For a moment, I look at him: Trevor and the dark curly hair I can never get out of my head and the largeness of him crammed into the tiny café chair. Three years apart, and still I feel like this. He's learned how to take care of his beard better, while he's been away; it's groomed now to a perfect not-too-bushy length. He's also gained weight. It sits well on his broad frame. A bell dings at the front and our number flashes on a screen by the counter. Our Americanos and cookies wait for us on a ledge, contact-free. Trevor gets up and heads over, but I stand too, carrying the cookies so he doesn't need to make an extra trip.

"I've been taking meds," he tells me as he sips from his coffee. "I would never say I'm cured. I mean, that's not really what it's about, right? But life feels so much more…I don't know, I don't want to say *vivid* because sometimes I feel like the pills flatten everything out, but I can really think and feel a bit better. Maybe *manageable* is the right word. Like finally I don't have to battle myself over everything. I've been doing therapy, too, but it's different with the meds. I feel good. For once."

I reach for his hand, something I would have been afraid to do before. "I'm glad," I say. And between us hangs the moment he left, when he asked me to come with him and I told him I couldn't. That I had too much here, my friends, my parents, work. I did regret it, during lonely nights, but I also saw how the space left room for me to grow, to work, to create.

His smile gets bigger and he continues to hold my hand. His fingertips trace the scars on my knuckles. It's hard to remember what things were like when everything between us was a secret. "Doesn't it feel good to be around someone who really knows you, inside and out?" he asks me.

But Trevor doesn't know that the process of him finding out about everything was so terrifying it almost killed me.

I want to talk to him more about my PTSD treatment, but we start talking about his thesis instead, and then we walk from the café to my apartment and up my stairs and we kiss and kiss and lie down in my bed together. He runs his hands through my hair. "I always miss you," he says, and I start crying for no reason except I realize I must have been extra lonely lately. And I realize how good it feels to cry instead of getting angry when I don't understand why I feel the way I feel. I can't even remember what it was like to be angry the way I always was. "We need to pick back up where we left off," he says, and I start to separate from myself, especially after thinking about how bad things were between us back then. I don't know if picking back up is what I want, but I do want his body, close to mine, so the me that thinks disappears.

The sex is different, slower. Part of it is that it takes him longer to get aroused even though he wants to start, and he explains it's the medication, so he pets me, remembers all my places, and he's warm and safe, all my nerve endings slowly come alive with his touch. "I want to make you feel good," he whispers before he goes down on me, and when he's finally hard after hearing me moaning, it's a relief to have him enter me, I've wanted him so much, but also he looks into my eyes, which he never did much of before, and instead of being afraid, I'm right there, I'm present, and I never want to leave the feeling of him.

After, while I lie with my head pressed against his chest hair, he tells me, "I've been thinking a lot about why we didn't work before."

"You have?" I'd been feeling so calm, but I begin to shake.

He strokes my back. "Like in a good way. I want to get to the point that I'm not always making the same mistakes. I think, I thought there was this coldness to you. Or distance, that something was holding us back from totally moving forward. But then we became friends and everything was easier. And I still wanted you all the time, but I thought maybe it wasn't what you wanted, that it was too much."

"But we still slept together if we were drunk," I say.

"Like two times," he says. "Anyway, I've started to realize lately how shit I actually was. That a lot of it was me. I was going through a lot, still carrying a lot of grief and feeling a lot of judgment from my family about being a writer and all that. And you were going through your own stuff…I never really understood PTSD before I met you."

"Yeah," I say, but then I pull away from his chest, prop myself up on my elbows. "Also, you always were calling me Paulina back then."

"I didn't know how important it was not to," he says. He tries to kiss me again, but I pull back. "But now I know."

I take a deep breath. "Trevor, it was really that you didn't acknowledge me."

"What?"

"You never would tell anyone that we were dating."

"I thought you didn't want to be together, so I kept it on the down low."

"All I wanted was to be together." But I think about how after a period when we got closer and closer, I'd panic and drink too much, not knowing what to say or how to act. Always rushing into a fight. Feeling the anger even though all I wanted was his tenderness. But still. "You should have made it obvious to other people that you liked me. That you weren't embarrassed of me."

"I would never be embarrassed of you," he said. His eyes start to get cloudy and dark and he pulls me into him. "Never, never. I'm sorry. I want to try again. I want it to last this time. I think we can."

I'm not so sure, but part of me has been more hopeful lately, so, engulfed by him, I nod my head. Yes.

How It Happened
June 2016

By the time I got to Stef's house, my stomach was on fire. I hadn't even texted, I just hoped that she'd be home. Stef opened the door for me, and I came in. She hugged me in greeting.

Her plush, grey couch was strewn with papers she was marking. A basket by the couch overflowed with Wynn's toys. Stef always said she needed something handy to keep Wynn busy when she was marking. It was so easy to get distracted.

"What is it?" she said as soon as she saw my face. No one was ever concerned about me in the way I was for others except Stef, and I began to cry. She was too kind. I'd been feeling angry... I hadn't even noticed until I was crying and my clenched fists relaxed. I didn't know who or what I'd been angry about.

Stef led me to the couch, pushing unmarked papers aside. I put my backpack beside it carefully, setting it down slowly so she didn't sense the heaviness that was inside. Soon I was talking, about how Vancouver had left me feeling awful instead of healed, all pent up, like I had decades to go before I'd get close to feeling normal, and I didn't know if I'd be able to take it, if I could last all that time. I told her in detail about Adrian dying and, finally, about Trevor, how we'd been seeing each other in secret and I'd told him something very special to me and he'd betrayed me.

"You know I'd never do that to you, Paul," Stef said. "You can tell me anything and it will stay between us. And that stuff about Trevor, we all already knew."

"You did?"

"Maybe not when it started, but Derek noticed you guys left together once, and I think Trevor said something to him about it or he got all protective over something. I think he cares about you."

"I'm not so sure. He always wanted us to keep everything hidden. Sometimes I think that...I don't even really know why I like him."

Stef laughed. "He's my friend, but I know, he's a bit of a jerk."

"I know."

Stef had left the radio playing. She was one of the only people I knew who still listened to the radio, rather than podcasts or watching documentaries over Netflix or something. She liked to listen to the news, and as we headed toward an election in America, she listened more and more. Even without knowing family in Mexico, it hurt her, the things they were saying about building a wall. She'd already started cursing 2016, and she didn't know then what was still coming. "My father, my nana, and my tata were immigrants. That was the thing that united my family even though they had different cultures. I don't get how a person, a country...how can they say things about people like that, people who risk everything for a better life, for a place where they'll be safe and have a family or be free to be who they truly are?"

"It's disgusting," I said, and Stef looked sad.

The radio said there was an Amber Alert, that another kid had been abducted. Bradley Anderson, eight years old. The vehicle was a black SUV.

"I used to be obsessed with stories like this," I said to Stef.

"Why? Isn't it scary? I get so fixated, thinking about what if it happened to Wynn."

"Yeah, I think it just scared me." But I remembered the feeling of wanting to be taken. I'd also feared that my uncle would disappear with Adrian in the middle of the night and we'd never see either of them again.

"Ugh, this is honestly the worst part of being a parent. I want to scoop her up from school right now," she said.

"We could," I said. "We could just do nothing but play."

"Come on, Paul," she said. "I'm surprised you're not sick of playing all day already."

Her partner, Derek, walked in through the door and gave me a wave. He retreated to their bedroom.

"So I got in big trouble today," I said. "Or I've been slowly digging myself into more trouble."

"What happened?"

"Has Wynn ever had an imaginary friend? Like, one she'd cry over?"

"Hmm, no, but then again, you know, Wynn does her own thing. Half the time I don't hear anything from her and then all of a sudden, she's telling me we exist in prehistoric times and we're going to get burned by lava or something."

"Okay, but like if you tell her that's not real, does she freak out?"

"Not really, but we go with it. She likes it better if we go with it. She will get upset if we cut the game short. We have to slowly transition from one activity to the next."

"Okay, because the little girl I'm tutoring, she had a total melt-down when I told her that her imaginary friend was there. She said she could tell I didn't think he was real or something."

"How old is she?"

"Five?"

"Yeah, maybe. I could see that."

"Do you think she'll hold it against me or get over it? I didn't stay to fix it. Her dad took over."

"She'll be fine. You know how kids are. They're upset for a moment and then they can't remember."

"I can't get fired from this job. It's all I'm living on now." I'd distributed the brochure I'd made with Trevor and gotten a couple hesitant emails, planned a few sessions with kids for the following weekends. But nothing else steady like my work with Tammy.

When Wynn came home, I paid special attention to the way she spoke and moved and wondered if it was different from Tammy or the same. Different from me or the same. I guess in some ways I assumed that all kids were like me, even though I hadn't felt similar to anyone as a child except for Adrian. Wynn wasn't like Tammy. She wasn't wise the way Tammy was. She was imaginative differently too. Tammy already seemed close to Wynn's age, despite being two years younger, and Wynn just wanted to play, whereas Tammy wanted to learn. Aside from her imaginary friends, Tammy really didn't seem imaginative at all. If you gave Wynn a piece of paper, she'd draw something you'd never seen before, but Tammy drew ravines, she drew her father's house, she drew me, she drew Nik, she drew her mom and her mom's boyfriend. The only thing different was Colin. Sometimes she drew her other imaginary friend, Rachel. She said Rachel was my age and that, like me, Rachel listened to her very closely. I guess she felt as if her dad and her mom ignored her.

"I understand," I'd told her that day. "I was a lot like you when I was little."

But maybe that was incorrect. I saw the world through art. With Adrian—who needed imagination to be more real than reality, or else he wouldn't be able to handle his life—I built the world of The Lighted City, and believed in it too. With our minds together, it was easy to create another world, so easy for me to get sucked into a world more interesting than this one. More forgiving and accepting. A place where neither of us would feel like we were wrong.

I stayed for dinner, which Derek and Stef made together in the kitchen while Wynn and I played. We pulled the cushions off the couch and used a sheet to make a fort. Wynn had recently discovered dominoes and insisted on teaching me the right way, not just setting them up and knocking them down like I knew how to do. Stef's old cat, which she had adopted before Wynn was born, woke from a slumber. She jumped to the windowsill and looked at the sun setting outside. She put her head back and chattered, almost mechanically. "Look," Wynn said quietly. "She's calling the birds."

"Is there a bird or a squirrel out there?"

"She wants them to come to the window," Wynn said, as if time and darkness didn't matter, that her cat would chatter away no matter what, able to lure whatever she wished to the window. "Sometimes you need to ask politely."

✧

At home later that night, I heard a gentle knock at my door. That someone was inside the building, having passed the front door, made me uneasy, but despite the silence from Nik since I'd left his house, I knew it would be him. And I already knew what would happen: I'd be fired. I walked down the stairs, and I opened the door. Nik was there inside my shared apartment hallway.

"The building door was unlocked," he said.

"Why didn't you text me?"

He came a step closer, and I remembered his face hidden by his hat underneath the streetlight. I'd left my job for him, but now I'd never work with Tammy again, would be broke again. The world had so little to offer me except my own desperation, and I already could feel myself getting out of control. My hands shook.

He walked closer to me, and my heart started to beat faster in my chest. I've always known that one type of fear is love. But he wasn't my love. He bent his face to me and kissed me. I could already feel the heat from his body pressing into me. His mouth was all over mine, and it felt different from how it did with Trevor, how with Trevor, we were like two snakes trying to share the same skin, but with Nik, it was like something heavy pressing down on me, and I wanted to run away, but then he was in my apartment, and I was closing and then locking my door.

"What do you want?" he said, and lay on my bed. I could see his dick, long and hard, straining at the cloth of his underwear, but I couldn't remember him taking off his pants.

I want to be safe, I thought, and it popped into my head and I had no control over it.

"I can make you feel good," Nik said. "Whatever you want."

But I stood there, looking at him. His blond hair was cut short, like he'd gotten a haircut before he'd come over, and he'd thrown his cap on my desk, on top of drawings I'd done. The room appeared hazy, impossible to bring into focus. I'd had a glass of wine or two at Stef's, and my head was pounding with the sugar. "Is Tammy okay?" I said.

"What?" he said. He got up out of my bed and walked over to a reusable Whole Foods bag he'd left by my desk, pulled out a bottle of white wine. "Glasses in the kitchen?" he asked as he walked past me, through the doorless entranceway to my room and into my kitchen. "Is this all you got?" he said after opening a couple cupboards and finding only wide water glasses. He came back into the room, handed me a glass full to the brim with wine. "What are you on about?"

I drank before I spoke. "Tammy. Is she okay?"

"She's a kid, Paul. I thought you work with them all the time. They are always upset over stuff that doesn't matter."

But it had mattered. I had felt how much it had mattered. I had seen her in pain. But Nik, with his own child, was able to dismiss it. Like how my parents always dismissed me.

"I was more worried about you," Nik said. "You just took off."

"I thought I'd ruined everything," I said.

"You can't ruin everything with kids. They're still growing. They don't even know which way is up." As he spoke, Nik came closer. His hand circled around my hip and back and then over my ass. "Finish your wine," he said.

I couldn't fight it, Adrian in my mind, the loneliness, needing Mom and Dad, having no one, but Nik was here in my apartment.

I finished it.

"I know what you like," he said. "You can trust me. I'll do it right."

My brain turned off.

Maybe everything is about a lack of tenderness—all I knew as a child was a desire to be hugged, to be loved, which grew into a more perverse version of the same desire. Sometimes I wanted to tell people that I only wanted to be hugged before we began to sleep together, but I could never get those words out, and then it always turned into sex, all of that affection that I'd ever given out had always turned into sex, and I wanted it too, of course, as soon as I was touched. I wished I didn't.

And he did give me what I wanted. He grabbed my hair and pulled. He spanked my ass. He asked if he could put his arm around my throat and I said yes and he squeezed. He poured me more wine and I drank more wine. I lay in the dark beside him and I felt myself disappear. He touched me and I flinched and then I kissed him, let him kiss me, bite my neck, my shoulders. His arms were long and strong and could wrap completely around my body as he fucked me from behind. His smell wasn't like Trevor's, but it didn't turn me off either. It was enough as long as I didn't think, as long as I drank more. Sometimes I was me, but sometimes I was also somewhere else.

And I woke up that morning with Nik in my bed, pushing back my hair from my forehead, saying "Hello, hangover," and kissing me. And then I told him I wanted to fuck, and so we did.

✧

Adrian's birthday came on June 11, and then two days later it was mine. A month had passed since his death and it was time for me to go to Caledon again. My parents came to Toronto to pick me up, and then we drove in silence. I watched highway become suburbs become strip malls become country until we were turning up their driveway.

They left the TV playing in the background while we had cake and they gave me a couple presents—trinkets they had found in gift shops, nothing that suited me. Mom stopped to stare at the screen as a news story played. "What is it?" Dad said to her, cutting off his sentence to me abruptly. We'd been talking about work, what I was doing for money, but he felt what Mom felt and something about the way she was looking at the TV caught him.

"Another kid has gone missing," she said. "That's the third this summer."

"They'll figure it out," he said.

"But sometimes it's too late." As usual, they were two sides of the same brain arguing with each other. Sadness flickered over them, but I was unable to connect to the news story over the ache of my own discomfort at being home.

"Sorry, Lina," they said, attention now unified and focused. They handed me a card. Inside, it said they'd pay the $150 members' fee for a sculpture studio I'd been wanting to join since I moved to Toronto. I didn't have the space or materials to create what I wanted, and it seemed that going to a dedicated space would give me the time I needed to create.

They asked me, "Why don't you go back? School is always waiting for you.

"Teaching is a start, but you're so smart. You don't need to limit yourself to tutoring. You could teach in high school, in colleges, or university. It just takes a little hard work and dedication.

"Don't let your talents go to waste. We haven't heard anything about a new sculpture or painting in years."

My drawings and plans for The Lighted City burned brightly in my mind. I would never show them.

"Now you can't say you don't have anywhere to work on your projects."

Underneath it all was their anxiety about whether or not I was finally happy, whether or not everything was their fault, no matter how many times I told them it wasn't or avoided them the way they'd avoided me. Their bond, which had never had room for me, had grown even stronger as they aged and I moved out. They'd even gone into business together flipping houses, even though, in Caledon, people only bought land to flatten the houses on them and build something huge and traitorous.

And of course, now, with the funeral passed, they said nothing about Adrian.

I went to bed early, irritated and guiltily ungrateful, but once again, when I heard their footsteps take them into the bedroom, I climbed the steps from the basement and went to sleep on the living room couch. Like I had when I was a kid, I yearned for someone to come take me away. Being snatched seemed better than where I was, trapped in my childhood house, locked in my childhood self.

How It Happened
The Lighted City

The day everything happens is because Adrian is angry.

It's all my fault. I have a crush, a date to the prom. A quiet boy from my art class. He's one of the best artists in the class, and his work always has something to say. He's been walking around by my desk like we all often did, circulating through other people's work, seeing the progress come along, comparing our work to theirs. But more than that, we are seeing how everyone's style is falling into place, how each piece is more them than the one before it.

He looks at my piece that first month of my final year of high school, and he says, "Man, your stuff is always so ugly, I love it." We're doing self-portraits, but I make myself blue, my skin peeling, rotting on one cheek. I'm only following a feeling that if I don't put on paper will throb within me every moment, make my knuckles tear. "I mean, raw. It's good. You've got your own style."

He goes back to his own desk, covered by the beginnings of an idealistic portrait of himself. He scowls at it and gets up to get a new piece of paper from the wooden paper rack at the back of the room. Brings it back to his table and begins again.

I've never felt comfortable at school, never feel comfortable or safe anywhere except hidden away with Adrian. But in that class, something magical happens, beginning in the first semester. The students all grow familiar and comfortable with each other. A couple that sits at the front of the class hang their coats up against the window by their desks, bring vinyl snowflake stickers and stick them to the glass as we near winter. They are creating a home in the classroom. When I want a break from working on my portrait, I draw their set-up from behind them. Like the huts, I think, like The Lighted City, creating your own place to hide. But instead of cutting them off into isolation, their work creates a mood of comfy refuge that filters through the class. Students begin to drift into the art room when they are on lunch even, wanting an extra hour to do art, but also to feel that feeling throughout the day.

The boy I like in my class, he is my first real friend and later becomes my partner before I move to Toronto. I don't know how to be friends with someone without poking it into something more. Instead of needing me, he supports me and looks to me for gentle support in return. I haven't thought about what I will do or where I'll end up. I know my parents will pay for school if I don't choose somewhere expensive or too far away. And I don't really want to be like Adrian, hanging around doing nothing during the days since he graduated, although I'm scared to tell him I'm thinking about going to school.

"On Friday, instead of working on your projects, we'll have a visitor," our teacher tells us one day. "She used to go to school here and now she's at Sheridan's illustration program. Some of you might be interested in that." She looks out at all of us. Most of us had taken art year after year, but only a handful are considering it as something to pursue. A couple of people talk about graphic design, video game design. Others want to go to med school or become lawyers. Everyone has a dream.

"You'd be great at that," my friend tells me during lunch.

"Are you sure kids want ugly books?"

"It doesn't have to be like, children's fairy tales. Like, you could do covers for magazines or books for adults. Let's go to the library after school. For inspiration."

I get off five bus stops early with him and we walk to the library. He types on the computer they have there, so normal, so calm, searching for books like we do at the school library. I realize he comes here all the time. That outside of school, he has a normal life going to the movies and the library or seeing friends on weekends. I'd been to a couple sleepovers or birthday parties as a kid, when the other students invited everyone, but as the groups become more selective, I find myself on the outside. I am good at comforting my peers if they are sad or lonely, but I am too quiet to be a real friend. So, while him spending time with me is incredibly special to me, I am just another kid from school he's hanging out with—he has friends who are both boys and girls, and he seems open to people from all walks of life.

"Look, Paulina," he says once he's found the section of art books. "Look at all of this." He pulls out volume after volume of different anthologies of illustration. He goes to the magazine rack and brings down an assortment. "See how many different styles there are? You could do anything you wanted, as long as it worked with the story or magazine."

Making the imaginary real. I pick up a magazine. Or making the real imaginary. I don't say anything, but he sees the shift on my face.

"See? We should work on our applications together. And we'll have to do portfolios."

"You're going to go there too?"

"Well, yeah, I've always wanted to do kids' books. I know you think it's dumb."

"I don't," I say. "Not at all."

I go home with an anthology of illustration checked out and new library card. And a crush.

But it's more than a crush. When I'm alone, I imagine what he would say, imagine a life I can live with him. Play out scenarios where I can express my true feelings, all the different ways he could break my heart. But it's so different from The Lighted City, from the way Adrian and I imagine together. I feel a change—that yes, maybe I can be an illustrator, and maybe someone other than Adrian can love me, maybe there is worth in myself that I haven't quite uncovered yet.

I spend more time alone, more time drawing at school or with my crush, working on our portfolios. We make our appointments to apply with the guidance counsellor together, one after the other. More time away from Adrian. I'm finally becoming myself, not part of him. This is the first time I've ever felt that the care and love I have for Adrian is wrong. When I'm away from him, I feel myself slowly unwinding. It seems possible that maybe I can get better, that The Lighted City, our escape, needs to be more a state of mind, and that it can occur while I am alive. That I'll find my place.

I draw my crush a picture of us on the dance floor. Balloons make an arch in the background. I draw a few of our classmates in the background, the couple who transformed our class slow-dancing, the others each doing the dance I knew they would do. I draw it in his style, idealistic, beautiful. He looks at it and then looks at me and says, "Is this us at the prom?"

I'm so nervous my hands won't stop shaking. I sit on them and nod. "Sure, let's go. Of course, I want to go with you." And then he kisses me. My first real kiss.

How It Happened
June 2016

Back in Toronto after my birthday, I gathered my drawings and supplies and biked over to the sculpture studio to pay my fee and get a tour. For my membership fee, I was given unlimited access to the studio, use of the tools, access to slightly discounted supplies, my own locker, and a cubby made of two large plywood shelves. It was as good as I could get in Toronto—all the other shared artist spaces were too expensive or required an in. Although all of my friends from The Cave were artists, none were practising. Stef had stopped painting years ago when Wynn was little and she began teaching college. Kayla pretended that she'd shifted from installation art to acting, but never really did much of anything except work her day job. She listened to music, she danced. Of course, Trevor wrote, but he'd been able to turn his house into a safe haven for his writing, never needing to go out or have access to another space. It was different for sculpture. I needed a place where I could spread out and have that place only dedicated to my art. I could barely afford to have a place big enough for me to live in, crammed in an attic, my bed visible from the sink in the kitchen if I left the curtain open.

I lined my cubby with red and gold patterned paper I'd bought from a store in Chinatown for a couple dollars a sheet. I brought in a bunch of used books on contemporary sculpture that I'd picked up over the years from second-hand stores. But mostly I brought in what I'd collected: the barrette, a chain from a necklace, a pair of broken sunglasses, one of my old IDs, a burnt-out light bulb, pieces of glass beer bottles, a few bottle caps that I'd saved since I was a child. There were images I'd ripped from magazines, old plates with interesting patterns or textures, several stones. Anything I'd been drawn to— either here on the streets of Toronto, or even in Caledon as a kid—I'd saved, slipped into my pocket, and put into a clear storage box I'd kept in the corner of my room. I knew it was trash, but to me it was my treasure. As a kid, I'd felt the same way, as if I was salvaging something rare and important. I brought the box into the studio, but I wasn't sure what to do with anything. All of my ideas before had been about The Lighted City. Part of me had thought I'd build a magnificent tree, like our home base tree, out of all the garbage I'd saved. And then I'd set it on fire, and that'd be part of the sculpture too. I'd photograph it as everything melted and fell apart. Part of the sculpture would be that some parts would be left behind, charred but still intact, whereas other things would turn into smoke or a puddle of their previous self.

But after my last visit home, when I hadn't been able to sleep with the brightness of the moon, twisting and turning through nightmares of my past, I would have given anything to get away from my childhood, the images of trees burning, of fields, of insects and wildlife, of empty, lonely houses. I felt exhausted by it, wanted something different from my present. But my life now was explanations of light bulbs, my phone lighting up in the dark, pages written about me, an imaginary boy.

It all seemed connected to that past, too, but how? The pieces of my life in the present were searching for pieces from the past, trying to make connections. But it was irrational, wasn't it, that the present echoed the past, which echoed a child's imagination, which echoed what they were told about the present, which echoed another past, which echoed a different child's imagination, which echoed what they were told about their present and so on.

And I didn't know how to turn all this thinking into sculpture.

I spent a lot of time trying to get started, organizing my pieces, not really doing much of anything.

✧

I've never been able to do small, careful things with any sort of precision. Even my art was better done in grand sweeps, looked better if you squinted slightly, was better made of multiple parts that maybe didn't necessarily go together.

After a lesson at Tammy's mom's, I shredded cheese for Tammy's pasta. Both Nik and Magda were working late, so it was my job to make sure Tammy got fed before Nik came to pick her up to switch houses. She only ever wanted to eat cheesy pasta made with grated cheese, so dry with just salt and pepper. When I was a kid, I'd only wanted ground beef, taste buds turned off of anything else.

Tammy sat at the table. I asked if she wanted me to set a place for Colin, and she glowered at me. "You know he's not here," she said. "You'd be able to see him. And Rachel's not coming either. She's away all this week."

Ever since I'd pretended to let Colin come inside, I'd been on Tammy's bad side. She seemed to think I was an idiot. She'd decided she didn't like any form of pretend, and yet she still talked and wrote about Colin incessantly. I'd broken her trust, so she never shared with me directly, only through her work. Even then, she didn't want any collaboration or help coming up with ideas. Mine were tainted. She would only let me check the spelling mistakes. Then I had to pretend I hadn't read it. If I acted like I had, if I tried to talk to her about it, she'd shut down. Sometimes she cried, but mostly she didn't say anything. She seemed to want me to leave her alone.

What I'd learned from Stef's daughter, Wynn, is that you need to let kids grow in their own time. You have to let them be how they want, explore how they want, play how they want. This doesn't mean you don't watch them, that you don't pay attention, but you have to give them a certain amount of freedom to try out being different types of people. Right now, Tammy didn't want to talk to me. She wasn't cruel, she wasn't hurtful, she still did her work and was polite. But she was punishing me.

I grated and grated, watching her draw at the table from the corner of my eye. I pushed on the cheese, but the wrapper, slick with condensation, slipped from my grasp. My thumb slid hard against the grater. Pain for a second and then a numbness. Blood rose to the surface of the knuckle. I stuck it into my mouth before I cursed in front of Tammy. Before I made anything worse.

Cheese had to go into the garbage and I rushed to the bathroom for a Band-Aid, wrapped it around my thumb. I had the heady feeling of release I had when I ripped open my hands, the throbbing pain in my skin distracting me from the pain in my chest. I breathed in and out, splashed water onto my face and made sure I looked calm in the mirror, not wanting to frighten Tammy.

When I came out of the bathroom, Tammy was gone. The water bubbled on the stove. "Tammy?" I called out, but I didn't hear her or any sound from her iPad. The TV was off in the living room. I ran up the stairs and checked her bedroom and her mother's, but she wasn't anywhere.

The house was so big; there were so many places she could hide if she wanted to play a trick on me. "Tammy? It's not funny. It's almost dinnertime. Come on."

Still silence. That's when I noticed the back door was ajar.

Could someone have come and taken her, like those other kids? I was only away for a second, but bile rose in my throat as I imagined something terrible happening to her, Tammy being taken far away from her home, hurt—worse than hurt. I imagined the look on Nik's face when I told him Tammy wasn't here, gone, stolen. I raced into the backyard. "Tammy?" I shouted. "Tammy!"

As I came over the hill in her backyard to where it sloped down toward the ravine, I caught sight of a flicker of blond hair. Wind was whipping the trees at the edge of the forest and their branches bobbed. I ran to her, where she was sitting on the ground, at the edge where the fence was all matted down. "What are you doing? I was worried about you."

"I was going to see Colin, but it's too dark," Tammy said, and the sky was getting darker, ready to rain any minute.

"You can't run off when I'm watching you," I said. "I need to always know where you're going."

"Okay," she said happily, as if nothing had happened. She stood up, brushed the leaves and dirt from her jeans, and ran toward the house, not waiting for me to follow.

Inside, the noodles were boiled almost to mush. I took the pot off the burner, drained the noodles, mixed them with the cheese that was safe and clean.

She looked at my hands as they set down the bowl.

"You get hurt a lot," she said.

"Sometimes," I said.

She began to eat and I started on the dishes. My heart pounded in me rapidly. I tried to focus on the dishes, the smell of the soap, the repetitive task. I felt caught by her. Terrified I would do something else inadvertently wrong.

Nik came to pick Tammy up and take her back to his place. "Go get your bag," he said to her, and she ran upstairs, two at a time, to fetch her Peppa Pig backpack, stuffed with the things that were important enough to be ferried between houses. Once she was upstairs, he grabbed at my thumb. "What happened to you?" he said. "You all right? Were you upset?"

I was surprised Nik asked, since Trevor had never asked about my scars or when the skin was newly opened, even when it happened after we'd been in an argument. Other than the odd blunt child, Nik was the first person to notice, or maybe the first person not to let politeness override his curiosity.

"No, it was a cheese-grating accident," I said.

"Gross. I hope pieces of you didn't get mixed in Tammy's dinner."

I laughed. "Well, today went smoothly otherwise. The usual Colin stuff." I felt bad for lying, but knew that Tammy hadn't sensed my panic, didn't understand the fears I'd had when I saw the door open and her gone. I didn't know how to explain it to Nik. And despite the time we spent together, I was never totally sure how he'd react, whether he'd fire me or if Tammy would be in trouble. "And Rachel today, too, but apparently, she's away all week? She's always so specific in her games. 'One week,' she said, and held up her finger."

"She's always moving Rachel in and out," Nik said. "I think it might be her way of figuring out the divorce. You know, living two places at once, and needing to leave," he said. That was interesting to me—imagination not as escape but as a way to understand. "Can I see you tonight?" he asked as he handed me the money for the day.

"I need to go to the sculpture studio," I said.

"Sculpture studio? You've got to give me a better excuse than that."

"I just started," I said. "I'm trying to get things going with my art again."

"Okay, I get it, you don't want to see me."

"I'll be done by nine, home by nine-thirty. Come then."

He nodded and then laughed, showing all his teeth. Maybe relief at getting what he wanted. His eyes didn't look at me. "Okay, then," he said. And he didn't touch me, opened the door, said *bye* and then shut it behind me. The softness of its click, I couldn't tell if it was dismissive or intimate.

✧

That summer, when I entered the sculpture studio, my mind seemed alive with a new fire I hoped I wouldn't lose before finishing a sculpture or two. I began to create. One of the other members had sold me some old soapstone he hadn't wanted for half the price, and I began to go at it with the studio's rasps and chisels. The soft powder I carved away felt as if it could be massaged into me like moisturizer. Even though I used a ventilator, I still woke up in the middle of each night, coughing, my lungs heavy like they were coated with dust. But better to create than have my imagination twist in nightmares. A long crack appeared down the middle of the stone, about a foot across each way. I planned to cast spider-like hands in silver metal if I had the money. Some falling against the sides of the rock, spilling and collapsing like water.

That night, Nik came over. We ordered pizzas and drank wine and sat on my bed. We took off our shirts and our pants and lay together in our underwear. He squeezed me so hard into him, I felt like my dusty lungs would burst through into his with each breath. "I want to pound you," he said.

"Ugh, don't say *pound*."

"Bang, fuck, split you open."

Normally the act of being wanted turned me on. Even words like that could turn me on—I was drawn to their violence. Sex that was tender, despite maybe being what I needed deep down, sometimes made me have to run to the bathroom after, where I hugged the toilet, stomach rocking with anxiety. Or I'd be touched in a delicate way that would shoot me back from the person I was with. My body remembered something I didn't. His words, they couldn't do anything for me that night. After the studio, feeling free, creating something from those parts of myself I'd been ignoring for so long, I needed to be alone, and yet needed Nik, needed to be wanted, didn't want to be left. He danced a hand along my back and around the front of my chest to hold a boob.

"Stop it," I said. I moved away from him and went under the covers.

"What's wrong?" he said. "Is it me?"

"Don't think so," I said, although this had never happened with Trevor. Part of me thought that it was because Trevor was so different from Adrian, broad and tall with different colouring. And while Nik was blond, he had the same cold eyes as Adrian, blue eyes that always saw right through to what you were feeling. The same slender build. "I haven't been feeling great lately."

"Tell me. Tell me what's wrong." He spun around in the bed so we were lying head to toe. He grabbed my foot and pretended it was a telephone. "Hello? Is anyone there?"

Nik had already told me so much about himself, about the break-up, about his fears for his daughter. He'd text me any time he was down and had confided in me that he thought he might go on antidepressants if he didn't feel better once he switched companies. He constantly felt stuck, aimless, unhappy, although with me, he was constantly smiling and joking. But I understood his unhappiness, felt understood by it. So I told him about Trevor and how he'd betrayed me and wrote all my secrets like they were his own. I didn't tell him about Adrian, or about the gun, stowed in my backpack beside the bed where we lay, but I barely thought about the gun when I talked with Nik, and Adrian was gone and all I was ever left with was heartbreak anyway.

When I was finally done talking, he sat up and kissed me. He held my face, petted my tangled hair like I was his little cat. And then he kissed me again. He held me tight again, and I could feel him hard in his underwear.

"I think you might be wrong about this guy," he told me.

"What do you mean?" I said, and rolled on my side, away from him. I stared at my ceiling, wishing I'd thought to turn off the light. All of me was illuminated, even the bad parts.

"Maybe you didn't understand fully or something. I mean, I don't think that guy meant to hurt you ... He probably wasn't even thinking. Do you really think people are that calculating?"

"Yeah, I do."

"Are you that calculating?"

"I barely even know what I'm doing."

"Don't you see how that's ridiculous, then? You're not some wounded outcast. People love and care about you, and the people around you seem like they aren't really shitty people, they're just trying to figure everything out too."

I started to kick at the blankets.

He said, "If you think people are like that, I'd hate to see what you think about me."

"Why?"

"Well, people make mistakes. It's not always clear. Do you think I slowly figured out a way to leave my wife? It was something that just happened, and it was fucking horrible. Neither of us wanted it. And then you end up in something fucking new and you're like, how did I get here, and then that goes to shit too..."

"Fuck me," I said, mostly to get him to stop talking. I couldn't stand to hear him defend Trevor, who he'd never even met, who I loved at the same time I met Nik. Who I still loved with all of myself, if I stopped long enough to think about it.

He climbed on top of me, his dick hot against my ass. He fucked me hard and for a long time, and then we lay side by side in the dark. While it was happening, I thought of Trevor: his hands, his mouth, and I wanted him so much I thought I would cry, right then with Nik inside me. I wondered why Nik minimized what Trevor had done, why he made it seem like Trevor deserved more understanding from me. As if he didn't care about losing me to another man. He didn't seem to be jealous, not like Trevor, and definitely not like Adrian, who could be set off by thinking about me spending time with another of my friends.

Maybe, despite the fear I felt sometimes when with Nik, or the way everything had started, him appearing at my apartment, maybe there was something special. Maybe he just wanted me to be happy. Even if one day I escaped from him and found my way back to Trevor, where my heart always led me, maybe it wouldn't matter. Maybe, to Nik, none of it mattered. Maybe this meant he understood me.

Now

The moon wakes me. Its light comes through the window, and I know what it wants me to do, so I listen. I walk outside. My ears thud with the sound of my own blood, pumping through me with fear. Even in the moonlight, there are shadows of the most terrifying dark, cast by bushes and trees. I walk around the porch toward the back of the house, and then I start to walk to the forest, where it gets even darker. A quiver in my limbs means I won't be able to go much further, too afraid, but the closer I get to the woods, the closer I feel I'm getting to something real.

I creep into a shadow created by the branches of a maple tree in my parents' backyard. The darkness in every shadow seems to shift and move, darker spots that hover. The moonlight casts the backyard in a glow.

I know why it's brought me here.

Adrian is moving toward me, his long fingers playing with a rope. "How could you?" he says.

The rope is pulled taut in front of him now. His hands close into fists, each fist holding the rope, knuckles turning white.

I don't resist. My body goes limp, too afraid. I don't have my anger in me; it can't appear with Adrian. Instead, I tell him I am sorry.

He pulls my clothes off me.
And then fire, a tree, a burning blaze.

The light spills through my window and onto Trevor, sprawled in my bed. I forgot to close the blinds again. His morning face is like I remember it, eyes squinting, not willing to open even once he's awake. But his hand moves over and clasps mine, and I think maybe he knows that I've had a nightmare. Or maybe that's not what the hand means at all. "What's on for today?" he says, his voice all groggy.

I kiss his bare shoulder and then his cheek and crawl on top of him. I breathe in and out, and I focus on his face, on all the details that make him him, until the dream doesn't feel as real anymore. "I could make you breakfast?" I say. "Or we could..." And he flips me over and we begin again.

I do make breakfast. My classic cheap and easy meal, egg in the hole. I tear a hole in a slice of bread loosely with my hands. "What are you doing?" he says. "We aren't animals." He lays the second piece of bread on a plate and takes a glass and presses down with the open end. It cuts a perfect circle in the bread. Mine looks child-like in comparison, but I like it.

"Well, that one can be yours," I say, "and this one will be mine." I add them to the melted butter in the pan, crack the eggs, and fill up the holes. When they are done, we eat them in seconds, but we're content.

I begin to tell him about the treatment.

"Sometimes I think it's making everything worse," I say. "Like everything feels right up close at the surface like I can touch it and it's ruining everything."

"What do you mean?" he asks.

"Well, part of me feels like I'd already been doing so much better on my own, like I've got the teaching together, I've got the show coming up, I'm making things again. Most of the time, I feel proud of what I've been doing."

"You've accomplished a lot the last few years," he says. "I'm proud of you too."

I roll my eyes. "Thanks." I don't know how to feel about Trevor saying that. Does it matter for him to be proud of me for the things I accomplished without him? "Anyway, it all still bothered me sometimes, especially my sleep, or sometimes I'd feel jumpy for no reason. The worst was when I'd start having nightmares again, then it made it hard to sleep and I was always exhausted and that made me even more jumpy, and then being on edge would make me go to bed anxious and I'd have the dreams. Sometimes it seemed hard to break the cycle. So I thought the therapy would help.

"But it's been making me relive all of it. It's not like when you just go to talk therapy and talk about whatever you want. It's like going over terror again and again and again. And I feel like I have less control sometimes, over how I'm feeling. When I'd worked really hard to get control. Like this one client I had, Jocelyn?"

"That old lady, right?"

"I'm pretty sure you aren't supposed to say 'old lady,' Trev, but yeah, her."

"You were working together for years, weren't you?"

"Even before you left," I say. "We started right at the beginning of the pandemic. Anyway, at a showing she had, I was freaked out by one of her paintings. Like all of a sudden I was in a different place and terrified—when that hasn't happened to me too much in the past few years. And then I was just off. And Kayla and Stef didn't like her art and were saying things about it, and she overheard, and now I've lost her as a client.

"I've tried to distract myself a bit, but it bothers me. Every time I lose a client, I feel like I've failed. And of course, I worry about the money, but it's also like the world telling me that I should just give up. That I'm doing it all wrong."

Trevor puts his hands on top of his head. "Well, first things first, have you tried to get Jocelyn back?"

"Well, no. And it's about more than just getting her back. I feel terrible that I offended her. I don't want to hurt anyone... I want to do the opposite."

"So, heal? Look, one thing I've learned is that apologies are powerful. If you want to make things right with Jocelyn, just apologize. Maybe she won't hire you again, but at least you'll feel better about it."

"Apologize, eh?"

"Well, it worked with you, didn't it?" he says, and stands up and walks over to me, wraps me in a hug. "Imagine if I'd let you get away."

We spend the rest of the day making plans, exploring how we'll make a relationship work. Trevor still has at least one year left in his PhD, but the idea of being together and yet apart doesn't seem like it will work for us. "I guess I could come out there," I say. "If you still think that would be a good idea."

"Yes, absolutely. I'd love that. You could either get an apartment, or, if you wanted, you could come live with me. Or stay for a bit and then we can figure it out from there."

"Does Dalhousie have an undergraduate visual arts program?"

"I don't think so, but there's the Nova Scotia College of Art and Design close by."

"Right, NSCAD." I think about going back to school to finish what I started, wondering about the pieces I'd create. And then I could figure out what was next for me from there. "Let's do it," I say.

For the first time, Toronto's grip on me starts to loosen and I'm ready to go on an adventure—forward instead of around and around again.

As I walk Trevor up to the subway station, I tell him more about treatment. "We've been talking a lot about when I found those kids," I say. "The boy. And how I feel like it's all connected to this really real part of me, like who I was as a child. And how that childhood me is the same me who was unable to help them."

"What does it matter, what you did as a kid? Do you really feel like that kid is the same you? And what happened, it didn't have anything to do with it, Paul. It was happenstance. I felt terrible that you had to go through that, but it's not like it's all tied together."

"I guess it just feels that way sometimes," I say.

"A measure of a person doesn't just get set when they are young. Then, no one would have any hope. They'd be stuck in whatever circumstances they were born into."

"But isn't that the case, in a way? Some people, they have it easy, and even something small like having two attentive parents who nurtured your gifts or something, that's enough to set some people up for success. And then for others, it will always be more of a struggle, and there will always be more pain because of a whole variety of factors. Like, it's not easy. And the paths we take—it's not like we have a whole lot of choice. I wouldn't have been an artist if it wasn't for who I was as a child."

"I guess I'm talking about the idea of a 'good person.' A good person isn't born into the world—it's what you do. And I think the choices you make when you're an adult and have the full range of knowledge of what a person is and how you want to be in the world—that's a lot more important than what you did when you were a kid when you were still learning and making mistakes."

We reach the subway, and we're both freezing cold, but it's been worth it to get to talk a little longer.

I tell him, "I think you underestimate children."

How It Happened
June 2016

I had another tutoring client I began to see on weekends, a twelve-year-old boy who loved to paint. The brochure I'd put out with Trevor had worked, at least for me. I went through the different techniques and colour combining and gave him assignments, but he mostly wanted to paint and draw characters from TV. He scratched at pimples that were starting to come in at his hairline and put his head down on the table whenever I tried to talk to him about art history, which his parents wanted to make sure he learned. We eventually struck a deal—I'd show him how to draw one new cartoon character for every artist I taught him about. I finished every session with a strained debrief on the boy's progress and was never entirely sure if they'd have me back the following weekend. But it was better than entirely relying on Tammy. "Maybe one day you could help Devang with a project he's doing with his friends. Could be some new clients for you." And I smiled and looked grateful, even though I wasn't sure if anything more would come of our sessions.

✧

Adrian and I had once made our own kite out of paper. It didn't really catch the wind, but I'd told him that if we put enough glitter on it, the magic would bring it up into the air. We ran with it trailing behind us. In our minds, it was strong enough to pull us up and away from the ground. It could transport us to other worlds.

I tried the same thing with Tammy. Glitter was dusted all over smeared white glue that also got all over the paper tablecloth I'd laid down at her mom's—always kept more pristine than Nik's. We went outside and, holding my hand, Tammy led me down the hill to where the wire fence blocked off the entrance to the ravine. "Can I show you something?" she said. I hadn't even said *of course* before she led me to where the wire fence was matted down. A tree had fallen on it and pushed it to the ground. Now the fence was overgrown with grass and weeds, green and happy and resilient. "That's how I get in to see Colin. Can we go?" She was shivering. We should have brought a sweater now that the weather had changed. It had been cool all week.

I could see the ravine, where it sloped steeply down, studded with trees and shrubs, leaves and ground cover. Somewhere down there was water, but I couldn't hear it or see it. I knew that Tammy thought Colin lived all the way down, in the reeds.

"Your mom doesn't like that," I said. "And then we'd both be in trouble."

"No," she said. "No, only I would be, I promise, I promise you won't get in trouble. Can we please go down so you can meet Colin?" She spoke with an urgency that built to distress. I was worried about her.

"Let's grab some sticks for the kite and go back."

Tammy spoke very little for the rest of the day, but found two sticks, straight and strong. In her living room, we taped them to the back of the kite, reinforcing it. Then we added some kitchen twine.

"Will it fly?" she asked.

"Why don't we take it outside and try it out?"

We went back into the backyard and Tammy ran, trailing the kite behind her. I honestly hadn't known if the kite would take flight or not, but as soon as she started to run with it, I knew that it was too heavy to fly. All the materials were wrong—the paper, the sticks, the glue and glitter. All of it weighed the kite down. "Paul! It won't fly!" Tammy said, pulling it behind her, running faster and faster. "Why won't it fly?" She tugged at the string. Her bad mood was getting even worse.

"Look at it go!" I said. "It's taking off. It must be the glitter, I think it's magic."

Tammy stopped running. "There's no such thing as magic."

"That's not what I heard."

"Paul, magic is for babies. I'm not a baby."

She picked up the kite and walked inside. She threw it by the door and left it there.

Screwed up again, I thought, but when I went inside Tammy had turned on her iPad and was watching YouTube videos about building kites, ones that would actually fly.

"I think I know how now," she said to me when I sat beside her. The rest of the lesson, I followed Tammy's instructions. I corrected Tammy's spelling as she wrote down our materials: garbage bags, electrical tape, twine, and wooden dowels. Then we made a how-to guide with pictures and simple sentences underneath.

When we heard the key turning in the lock, Tammy grabbed both pieces of paper and ran to the door to greet her mom, shoving the pictures up at her hands, full of briefcase. "Mom, we are going to make a kite! A real one! And we made a whole plan."

"Well, we actually already made a kite," I said to Tammy and her mom, not wanting her mom to think we'd wasted the whole lesson on one activity.

"But it was fake!" Tammy said. "We are going to make a real one." She waited for her mom to take the papers from her.

"I think her drawing is getting better," her mother said, after she'd set her things down. "And did she write this herself?"

"I corrected the spelling," I said.

"Do you think any of it stuck?"

"I'm sure. When she's interested—"

Tammy ran back into the room with her iPad, video playing. "Look! We'll make one like this!"

"That's nice, honey, but I'm talking to Paulina now."

If Nik or I spoke to her like that, she would have cried or pouted for the rest of the afternoon. But she went to the living room table, where should could still see me and her mom talking, and sat down with her iPad, watching the video of the kite coming to life again.

"I think it would be a good idea for us to actually build it. If you could reimburse me the supplies, I could cut the dowels and everything at the sculpture studio so that we only need to assemble it here. Then maybe we could fly it one afternoon."

"You won't get a good enough breeze here," she said. "Maybe by the water."

"My friend has a kid around Tammy's age. Maybe she would like that, for us to go down to the water together one day instead of staying inside. It's turning out to be a wonderful summer."

"Actually, I've found it chilly, but whatever you want to do, I don't care," she said, and opened her wallet. "How much is Nik paying you these days?"

I took the twenties she offered me and shoved them in my pocket. Her high heels clicked as she walked toward the kitchen. I waved at Tammy and left.

✧

On the bike ride home, wind snaking up under my helmet and into my hair, pushing it away from my sweaty neck, I was filled with longing for Trevor. He wasn't even in my life anymore, except, like Adrian, he was always in me, whether we were together or on a break. I thought of his hands, his grey eyes, his shoulders that spanned from one side of a doorway to another. His eyes when he looked wounded, all of him wounded. The way he said *I love you* in the dark. I knew he would be happy if he knew I now went to the studio. If he thought I was finally taking my art and myself "seriously." But the way he took himself seriously was what had led to us being apart, those pages sitting in my mind's eye.

You can love someone and hate their guts. And I hated his guts, but I still wished the wind was his hands, my bike carrying me to him.

✧

A card was waiting for me in the mailbox, a red envelope. The return address was from Vancouver. I tore it open and a cheque for one hundred dollars fell onto my table out of a birthday card.

> *Niece,*
> *You are one of a kind*
> *creative, good,*
> *with a sharp mind.*
> *I hope your birthday*

is as swell as can be
because you are
so so special to me!

The inside of the card was filled with Aunt Dot's cursive.

Paul,

Thank you so much for coming to Vancouver last month and for honouring Adrian's memory with us. I'm sure it was difficult for you, as it was for us all, and I wish we'd gotten to spend more time together. I want to let you know that the offer to come live with us in Vancouver is always open. April and I would like for you to feel there is always another home out there open to you.

There are many things I wish I'd gotten to say while you were here. Things I wish I'd gotten to ask you. As you know, Adrian was abused for years and years, and I'm sure you wonder how I didn't pick up on it, why I didn't do anything. The person I thought I was living with, Jim, was different from the person he was, and I trusted him to be alone with Adrian. I was also going through a lot of my own struggles at the time, which I don't need to unload on you, and I know it's not an excuse. As a parent it was my responsibility to protect my child, to be aware of what was going on. They still haven't been able to find Jim. I did end up reporting him, once we were divorced, so the police would love to find him too. But I guess he disappeared off in the wilderness somewhere. Hopefully a bear got him, haha.

*I know it's hard to joke about these things, but sometimes
it's all I have. I miss Adrian so much. I miss the little boy he
was when he was a toddler, still happy and amazed by the
world, before we had to deal with any trouble with fights at
school or fires lit. Before I had to work so hard to contain
Adrian that I didn't have time to think about the why of it.
Why he was so angry, why he couldn't make friends except
for you, why he lit fires when he was out in the world but
created things when he was at home.*

*I've always wondered why you didn't come to me. I would
have believed you. I'm not sure what I did to make you think
I wasn't safe to tell. I love you like you are my daughter, Paul.
You could have told me.*

*I hope we can have more of a conversation about all of
this, one day, so that finally we can start to heal as a family.*

*I'm running out of room, so I'll sign off for now and say,
Happy Birthday! I love you so much!*

Aunt Dot

Underneath her signature one line was worked in. *Stay dry! April.*

I hugged my backpack to me and read the lines again. I knew
she'd blamed me for not telling her. Guilt rose through me, and I
began to rock. *I need the gun*, I told myself, *I need the gun. Why
didn't I tell someone? Why didn't I tell anyone? I let Adrian suffer. I
need the gun.*

I had to meet Tammy, Stef, and Wynn. But after that, I would
find a place, and then I would join Adrian.

✧

Tammy took to building the kite better than to reading, writing, or drawing. She spread her own instructions, the ones we'd made, in front of her and studied them. Then she lined up the materials on the ground. First, we needed to cut the garbage bags. Tammy needed me to help with this, and I cut as she gave me instructions, but she was able to do a bit on her own when it was a straight line, and I realized how much she'd grown in a month. Now she was coordinated enough to hold and cut. I didn't appreciate enough, then, how children grew and changed.

The hollow dowels I'd cut were laid down on the garbage bag, fastened with black electrical tape. Then the twine, attached to one end. Tammy took a leftover piece of garbage bag and cut it into a tail that was crooked, still good enough to flutter in the wind.

We took a cab to Stef's and picked up her and Wynn. The girls said *hello* shyly and then didn't speak for the rest of the ride, instead listened to me and Stef chatting about nothing—how hot the sun was, whether it would be too windy, how excited we were about getting the girls together, how lucky we were to get to spend a work day down by the water. Every so often we asked the girls, "Are you excited?" And they said *yes*, but refused to look at each other.

Wynn was two years older than Tammy, though so small for her age that she was often mistaken for younger. Tammy also held herself with much more confidence than Wynn, who wasn't insecure, just always seemed to be dreaming, as if the real world was what was fake and inside her mind was real. With her dark hair clipped close to her head, she seemed the total opposite of blond, proper Tammy, dressed in matching shorts and T-shirt, a Toronto Blue

Jays baseball hat that Nik must have bought for her. Stef used hand-me-downs. As well as being cheaper, she felt it to be the ethical decision with clothes that only fit for a few months, and Wynn was still too young to notice.

Once the kids were outside and we could see the lake, stretching out along Sunnyside Beach, Tammy began talking to Wynn first, showing her the kite, the different parts. Wynn, normally better at pretending than listening, did her best to follow along. "They're really trying," I said to Stef.

We joined the girls and took turns helping them run with the kite, angling it so it caught the wind. But each time, we grounded it, dragging the kite along behind us. Stef and I watched people flying kites on YouTube on the minuscule, cracked screen of Stef's iPhone, and then I held the kite and felt for which way the wind was coming. Stef held the roll of twine, Wynn watching at her side. When it pushed up and under, getting light in my hands, I let go, but the kite dipped and wobbled in the air. "Quickly!" I said to Stef, and she unrolled the twine, giving the kite more length, and it swept up into the air, diving side to side, but more stable the more twine Stef gave it.

"Paul! Look at how high it is!" Tammy said.

"It's so cool!" Wynn agreed. "Can I try?"

Stef handed the twine over to Wynn. "Five minutes and then you have to give Tammy a turn." Finally airborne, the kite skipped in the wind.

Stef and I left the girls to figure it out and went to watch them from a picnic table. We'd brought along snacks in two tote bags, hummus and ready-made sandwiches from the grocery store. "You seem to be doing well with Tammy now."

"Key word: *now*. She's just so different from the way I was, I think. Instead of me teaching her, I'm trying to keep up constantly. And after all that imaginary friend stuff, she doesn't trust me."

"She seems to trust you okay. And she definitely still likes you," Stef said. "But I'm surprised hearing about her imaginary friends now that I've met her. It doesn't make sense to me."

"What do you mean?"

"Look how she is." Stef gestured at the girls and opened a can of pop.

I watched Tammy and Wynn. Tammy held the kite now, and it caught the wind, fluttered up. "It's dancing," Wynn said, and danced on the spot.

"No," Tammy said, and adjusted the string with the seriousness of a captain steering. "Kites can't dance."

Kites couldn't dance because to Tammy they were things—and things didn't have life. She was not a child like me, like Wynn. She couldn't imagine something into reality.

Then what did that mean about her? To me, the kite danced in the air because it *was* dancing, like the grass swayed or the sky chose to be blue or the trees asked the girls to please, please stop playing with the kite and climb on up.

But to Tammy, a tree was a tree, the grass only grass beneath her feet. The sky was blue because, like I explained to her, it was the easiest colour for us to see. And that was all.

"My friend, Colin, he's trapped," Tammy said to Wynn. "He lives in the ravine, in the bottom. So he can never come up."

A boy at the bottom of the ravine. Tammy running off, playing at the edge of the forest, trying to get to Colin.

For Tammy, only real things were real, not the imaginary.

"What's wrong?" Stef asked. "You look like you've seen a ghost."

But Adrian wasn't there.

Instead, there was a boy at the bottom of the ravine. I could hear the blood pounding in my ears.

"I have to call Nik," I said. "I have to get Tammy back home."

✧

I followed Tammy as she scrambled down the steep escarpment. I could hear Nik stumbling behind me, snapping twigs and slipping in the mud under the fallen cedar debris. Off the paths, we could easily have stepped on a place sandy and loose from erosion and lose our footing. But I knew how to walk on a hill like that, how to stay calm and methodical, letting my feet feel for steadiness.

"Aren't there stairs around here? People walk through this ravine, it's not just wilderness."

"They're too far," I said. "Have you ever been down here? It's not easy to get around if you're not on a trail. We need to know Tammy's way."

As a child, I'd imagined myself as a mountain goat or someone who'd grown up living off the forest my whole life, and I felt myself slipping back into these thoughts. I wasn't myself anymore. I was someone who could do things without being afraid, I was a hero from a book, I was a protector, and I would save the day if Colin or whoever was in these woods was still in these woods. I couldn't possibly make a misstep, and if I did, I would catch myself and continue on until we found him. Tammy climbed down through the ravine in the same way. She grabbed branches to steady herself against the steepness and they bent as she pulled them with her. I apologized secretly to the trees, focused on them instead of my own heart. It was hurting again. It hurt so much.

I felt Nik fall against my back. "Careful," I said.

"Why are you being so serious?" he whispered. "There's not going to be anything there. It's a kid's dream."

"You don't understand." How could he? When I'd asked Tammy more about Colin, pressed her for details, she described him, what he looked like, the little shelter with the tarp where he was staying—she knew things about him that didn't make any sense if she'd made it all up. Nik had never lived the way we did, with knowledge that held too much weight. Sure, he'd had other problems, but he had Sunday mass and family gatherings, sports games with friends, walking around the mall to try to meet girls. I ignored him. "Watch Tammy," I said, because up ahead was a clearing.

I could smell my own anxious sweat, pungent with garlic from the hummus I'd eaten with Stef. It made me want to puke. What if I was wrong?

Tammy's feet led her, feet that had walked down that ravine when she wasn't allowed time and time again.

How It Happened
The Lighted City

I'm supposed to go to The Lighted City. We were supposed to go, together. But we've never planned it, despite Adrian trying. The longer it took to make it real, the more it seemed like maybe we didn't have to make it real. Maybe The Lighted City could remain a dream, something hopeful between two kids.

The day it happens, I'm not ready. Adrian says it's time for us to go. And he's always the one who tells me how it all works. Needs me to believe him, no matter how much of my imagination it costs. "The Lighted City needs you, Paul. It's always needed you more than it needed me." He has a can of gasoline. He must have had it for a while, but he's never told me that it will be time soon. It's supposed to be a plan between the two of us, but I end up tied to the tree alone.

When I get home from school that day, Adrian calls me. "I never see you anymore, Paul," he says.

"I know, I'm sorry, I've just been busy," I say.

"You're always busy. With *school*." He says the word like a curse. Adrian was kicked out of three schools, mostly for fighting or setting parts of the classroom on fire. And now he's too old to be a student in the day. Aunt Dot talks about him getting his GED, but the thought makes him rage. He says that he's done. It's time to go.

But he's never angry with me—I always do what he wants. "Please, Paul, it's been terrible here," he says. His voice cracks as he speaks. "It's always terrible."

"I'll come over tonight."

As I walk over, the sun glows on the horizon. May slowly fading into June. Days getting longer and longer.

We are together in the backyard, knowing Uncle Jim is inside. In our little shelter, I feel safe. Adrian leads me out there. "I made this new one for you," he says, like they all hadn't been for me. The sticks are bound together into a roof, rope used to tie them together with intercut braiding. The bottom of the hut has pieces of moss he must have cut from the forest. The walls are made of bundles of grass pulled from the yard. It must have taken him hours. "I had to do something while you haven't been around," he says. We sit facing each other, cross-legged. He reaches for me, for a hug. I pull back.

"I know," I say. "It's just—Adrian, do you ever feel like what you want is changing? Like you could be more than what we have here?"

"Like The Lighted City," he says. "I feel like it's time."

I feel fear prickling at the back of my legs. The beginnings of sweat. "No, I don't mean like that. Like I feel like I'm growing up. I don't think I'll have to live here forever. And you don't either. You could go to school, you could move away and get a job. We don't have to be trapped here."

. I've said things like this before. As I get older, the way to The Lighted City is more terrifying and, for Adrian, more necessary. As he's grown, more and more pathways have closed to him. He has a criminal record from a fire he set a couple years ago, and he has never had a job. Uncle Jim has left him alone since Adrian reached his height, and Adrian spends his days outside, dreaming of The Lighted City and constructing more shelters. "The Lighted City will free us from all of that. School, a job. Everything is a trap. The only thing that isn't is letting go."

"But maybe letting go, doesn't have to mean…what you mean."

"There's only one way out, Paul. Even if we pretend it's worth it to last longer. Either it happens to us or we can control it."

"But I don't want to. I don't want to die."

"Who is he?"

"What do you mean?"

"Where are all these dreams coming from?"

From nowhere, I begin to say, but he always knows more than me. He always knows more about me than I know about myself, knows my secret desires. It's how he's kept me with him, how our secrets are always bound together. He knows me too well.

"You have a crush on someone?"

"No," I say.

"Someone at school? Is that why I never see you?"

"Shut up," I say and try to push him. He's getting closer and closer.

"Do you think about him with me? Do you think about him when you're with me?"

I wish he hadn't asked me that. The love I feel for Adrian is the only thing that I think will ever kill me. But what he says is true. Thinking about other people is the only way I don't feel wrong any-more. I'm getting nightmares all the time. I need to feel free from all of it. So when I sleep at his house, or spend time with him in the backyard, and I feel his sour breath on my face, like he's been eating nothing but bread all afternoon, I do think about my crush. But not even about him, an amalgamation of different men who will one day love me. In this blend, the person he becomes is a person I truly desire, not just want to help, whose love is pure and free from any ties. This is what I want.

These things never make sense until you're in them, and even then, they're impossible.

And somehow you grow up and they remain the worst thing you've ever done. I always thought if only I did something different, loved him in the right way, it'd make him better and make me better too.

And that's when he starts yanking me by the arm, out of the fort, out into the long, tall grass that scratches at my knees, my calves. The ground hurts my feet, the dried grass so sharp against them. I look down at my body, shocked by it, by the limbs, by how they look, exposed out there underneath the night sky. He starts talking more about The Lighted City. How it's time for us to be together. I want to believe it's only a game.

But it's a plan we've had for so long.

We were going to tie ourselves to the tree. We'd set ourselves on fire. We'd die holding hands. Our spirits would be released from our bodies and go wherever they would go. We'd finally be able to be together.

I look down at my body and stop thinking. Stop being Paul. I leave my body.

When I come back in he's pouring gasoline all over me and my clothes are gone. So are his. The bark presses into my back. He's soaking my feet, my legs, my stomach, my hair in gasoline.

And then, I betray him. Instead of taking his love for what it was, the way I had before, I yell. I yell until someone comes. I don't even care that it's Uncle Jim.

How It Happened
2016

My therapist said that people can only ignore things for so long. That sometimes it's like a pot bubbling over, or like when you push down on a Bodum too fast and it all sprays out. That's why I punched things, that's why sometimes I'd go out and get so drunk I couldn't walk. "Talk to me," she'd say. "I'm here for you, Paulina. I'm here to feel with you."

But no one could feel with me, and sometimes I couldn't feel either. And that was the worst part, when my past opened up and sucked me in, and when I was in the middle of something scary, like walking down further and further into a ravine, where more and more branches blocked the sun, where I needed, needed, needed to feel.

The ravine behind Tammy's house was exactly how she'd described it. Every branch, the number of steps it took to get down. As Nik joked, I became more and more wary. The more accurate she was, the more I knew there must be a little boy down here, lost.

The reeds. Bulrushes grew up from swampy water, a stream running through bog-soaked mud. I stepped in it, soaking my shoe.

"Paul, this is fucking ridiculous," Nik said. "Seriously, it's time to go back. It's enough. I came and picked you up, ready to stop this stupid game, and now I've played along enough."

"Shh," I said, and grabbed Nik's arm. "Look."

Across the stream, behind a few more trees, was the start of a clearing. And I spotted it. Branches were lashed to the nearby trees and covered with branches of leaves, tied all together with rope. A little lean-to. The world shimmered around me. "There's Colin's house!" Tammy said.

When she spoke, the sick feeling in my stomach started again. "Someone else has been here," I said to her. "We need to be quiet."

"We should leave," Nik said, his voice now hushed.

Tammy showed me how she crossed the stream. A few thick branches were laid against the mud and water. Too heavy for a child to have placed. I went on ahead, went to the lean-to, poked my head around to where I saw sheets and a tarp piled underneath the shelter.

The first thing I saw was the sole of a shoe, the toe pointing up in the air, the foot attached to a leg covered in leaves. I backed away.

I touched my face and felt tears there. The tears stopped quickly, the way I knew how to stop them, so that my stomach churned instead and I began to gag and the pain in my chest had turned into something that felt hard and permanent and like it could rip right through me.

I turned to Nik. "Was it you?" Had Tammy and Nik always planned to bring me here? Was this what the job had been about? Nik texting me in the middle of the night, Nik in my bed, Nik standing under the streetlights, holding up my hand to examine my scrapes. I looked at Nik and started to walk away, blood flooding my ears, my heart pounding. The man in my dreams. Kayla warning me, "Everyone is lying to you, especially him," and everything in me always telling me not to trust.

"What do you mean?" he said, and I knew he'd break into a smile, showing me those crooked teeth, but then he sees the boy, too, the shoes. A tree was burning, somewhere. I smelled smoke. I'd always smelled smoke, hadn't I, constantly, all the time. I thought it was supposed to be the two of us together.

Not like this.

But here the tree wasn't burning, and Nik didn't break into a smile, and I couldn't see his blue eyes at all, and maybe they'd only been hazel, never blue anyway. A branch cracked beside me. I turned and I saw him. Adrian, watching me. He had wanted to see what I would do, a test.

"Someone's there!" I said to Nik. "Take her back."

He looked at me, desperate to understand, yet behind his eyes was fear. Tammy started to cry. Nick bent down and told her to get onto his back, then began to climb the escarpment again.

And then, everything began to go wrong. Or maybe everything had been beginning to go wrong from the moment I was born and I was always destined for this moment. I could have followed Nik and Tammy up the hill, I could have gone home, and then we could have called the police after I hid the gun somewhere safe.

Adrian began to walk toward me, and then I realized he wasn't there, only my memories, only the boy's body. I felt like I was being watched and scanned the trees, the brush, but my eyes couldn't focus. I heard Adrian's voice at my ear, *Now, now.*

My fear folded in, if only I could feel, and then the sickness in my stomach rose and became tingling along my skull, and I was pawing through my backpack for the gun, the gun I had loaded before I slipped it into my backpack today, my secret. I turned it toward myself, my finger on the trigger, and as I squeezed, I heard a yelp. I flinched and the bullet missed me, flew up into the air, through the trees' canopy.

I looked around. And then I saw the glint of a pair of glasses, two eyes watching me from behind a trunk. "Are you okay?" I called out. The glasses belonged to a girl, and she was alive. She ducked behind the trunk. "It's okay," I said. I slipped the safety back onto the gun and slid it, still warm, back into its canister in my backpack. "I thought I saw someone," I said, my voice gentle like when I was teaching. "But we should get out of here. Are you hurt?"

The girl came out from behind the tree. I guessed she was the same age as the boy in the lean-to. Her face was streaked with dirt and leaves were caught in her hair. She shook her head.

"Come on," I said, and walked over to her.

She backed away. "You were going to hurt yourself," she said.

"It was an accident," I said, but my mind was already thinking of the next time I'd be alone. The girl came closer to me. "I can carry you, if you want. I'll get you out of here." I hunched over, offering my back. The girl nodded and jumped on, wrapping her thin arms around my neck.

I began to climb out of the ravine, grabbing onto trees and brush to help stabilize us against the steep terrain. "My name is Paul."

"I'm Alexis." We continued to climb in silence. "I just wanted to find Bradley," the girl said.

"You must be a really good friend," I replied, but I wondered how much she had seen, if she'd also seen his body in the lean-to, if she'd seen who'd taken him. If she'd been brought there by them. "Have you ever had a secret, Alexis?"

"Bradley and I have some," she said. "About treasure."

"Have you ever had a grown-up secret?"

"No," she said. "But next year I'll be in the fourth grade."

"That is pretty grown-up." I hesitated, stumbled for a minute under her weight as my foot caught a root. "Whoa."

"Whoa," she echoed. I steadied myself and I felt both of our bodies relax as I gained my footing. I continued to climb.

"I need you to keep a secret about what you saw. Everything else, you can tell everyone, okay? Actually, it's important for you to tell everyone what you know, how much you know. But I need you to keep a secret for me about the gun."

"About the gun?"

"Yeah, that I have that gun."

"Oh," she said.

"I was trying to protect you," I said, another lie.

"Okay," she said. "Our secret."

✧

Nik was waiting with Tammy at the edge of the ravine when I finally climbed up. "Paul, what the hell was that? I heard a gunshot. Did someone shoot?"

"No, no," I said. "Nothing like that. I just found Alexis down there."

Tammy was holding Nik's hand, looking up at me. She looked shyly at the girl.

"There wasn't a gun," the girl said.

"Tammy," I said. I got down on my knees and reached for her shoulders so she would look me in the eyes. "Did you know? Why wouldn't you tell us? You knew he was down there and couldn't tell us? Instead, we had to find him? How could you do that to me?"

She didn't even seem present. When her eyes met mine, I couldn't feel her. Her beautiful, cherubic looks made her seem vacant, when normally she was alert and full of sharp intelligence. I could tell she was far away from me and Nik. Who knows what was inside her head.

"That's enough!" Nik said. "It's not her fault." He yanked Tammy out from between my hands and then I was lashing out at the trees on the edge of the ravine, punching at them, clawing at them. "Stop it!" Nik yelled. His hands were all around me and he pulled me away from the trees and brush. "Just look at yourself." My hands were sliced and scratched all over, bleeding. My arms were scratched almost the whole way up. The stinging from the cuts sang through my body and focused my mind again. Tammy and Alexis were hiding behind Nik. He made his body a barricade between me and them. "You can't act this way," Nik said. "Not in front of the kids. Not around Tammy. Keep away from her."

"It was a boy," I said.

"I know. But we're the adults here, get it? The police are on the way. Who's she?" He pointed a thumb behind him in the direction of Alexis.

"She knew the boy," I said. Alexis sat down on the grass. "I think she might have run away from home to look for him?"

"Hey," Nik said to Alexis. She flinched when he directed his attention at her. "Do you need to call someone? Do you know your home phone? Want to use my phone?"

She approached Nik suspiciously, before she took the phone from him. She wouldn't talk to either of us. And I didn't know if she acted like that because of what she'd seen or if she was a child I had been. One who knew too much.

That night and the days after come in patches. Silence from Nik. I lost track of how many times I spoke to the police. Just like when that man at the bar had roofied me, they didn't care what I had to say, didn't listen. They searched the forest, and while they found pieces of clothing and a man's blazer, they didn't find anyone else. They said they found a bullet, buried in leaves, and I said nothing, nothing about the gun. It became clear to me that I actually was a coward. I waited for the moment that Alexis would rat me out, felt guilty for telling her to keep a secret when who knew what else she was dealing with, but they never asked me about a gun. They asked if I needed to go to the hospital. Asked who had hurt me, my arms, my hands. I didn't know how to say the things I needed to say except to say I'd done everything wrong.

They asked me about my work with Tammy, if I'd ever met Bradley, which was what they kept calling Colin. "We thought he was imaginary," I kept saying, but it sounded strange coming from me. One of the cops even asked me, "Really, imaginary? Didn't you or her father wonder why she kept talking about him the way she did, saying he was real? Why did she go down there alone? How many times?"

I said I didn't know, that she wasn't my child. But I knew I was partly responsible. That I'd failed Tammy, somehow, in the same way I'd been failed. I'd always said my parents did everything that they could, but maybe there was something more that could have been done. Maybe I could have been talked to more, hugged more, made to feel that my games didn't need to be kept secret, made to feel like they were my family, not only Adrian.

Or perhaps I had been the one who failed. I was only five, but I should have told my parents what was happening to him as soon as he told me. I'd had a feeling that everyone knew. I didn't understand how they couldn't have known, even with Adrian making me promise to keep everything secret.

Now that I was older, I felt that I'd come from a family of monsters. That I'd started out not being one, but had somehow become one over time, that it had slipped into me the way I'd always been afraid it would.

They came to my house and picked me up and brought me in for more questions. "So, this kid was imaginary, you thought?"

"She said he lived in the ravine. Would you think there was a real kid?"

"Did you?"

"Well, that's why we went down there, because I had a hunch."

"And how did you know where he was staying?"

"Tammy brought us down there. She must have seen him before."

"And why did you think the kid, who first was imaginary, now was real? Did you know something about the kid?"

"No, I swear, that was the first time, the only time I'd ever seen him."

"Did you ever meet a man? Did Tammy talk about a man?"

"No, only Colin."

"Yeah, a man named Colin," they said. They flipped through their notes. "That's the kid's father."

"The kid?"·

"The boy you found. His father, Colin. You see him around?"

"No," I said. "Only the girl."

After I left that day, despite feeling sure of my answers while talking to them, I began to doubt myself. The more I walked toward home, the more I doubted. As I unlocked my front door and walked up my stairs, I doubted. How had I known that the boy wasn't imaginary? Why had I known there was a kid down there, while Nik had still thought it was all a game? Why hadn't Tammy known that she should have told an adult right away? Or was it our doubt — that we didn't listen to her saying he was real — had our doubt been what killed him or had he been dead the whole time? The kid had been missing only a few days. It didn't make sense. Colin wasn't even his real name.

But it was the name of a man. A man who had moved trees and set up a lean-to. A man who maybe had been scoping out a spot. Colin, covered in reeds at the bottom of the ravine.

For a moment, everything in my life twisted until it made perfect sense. Everything took on a significance—an empty folder, a locked door, texts in the middle of the night, news of a suicide, a gun in a tea tin, a manuscript left forgotten, collected pieces of trash from the street, a night stretching onward, a friend not looking back to see where I was going, the ember from a cigarette, a scar on an arm, an invisible friend.

Instead of the way things usually occurred in my life, pure chaos, an unorganized jumble, everything became connected in a logical order that I felt I hadn't seen before. An invisible friend, news of a suicide, a gun in a tea tin.

And then—an invisible friend, a gun in a tea tin, news of a suicide.

News of a suicide. It seemed this story would begin with Adrian's and end with mine and in the middle was the child. The child whose dead body I would never be able to forget. I knew I couldn't be trusted, I knew I was all wrong on the inside, wrong like Adrian, wrong like my uncle, wrong even like my parents. It was me. Somehow, I had done it.

Other pieces began to rearrange as well, like they had when I was a kid—needing to be hugged, Adrian telling me what happened to him night after night, my silence, my secrets, his breakdown.

There was even a particular way of squinting, like when looking at my drawings or sculptures, putting the pieces all together, that made me think that perhaps it'd been me who'd tied myself to that tree, that it'd been me who'd wanted to die that day, to set myself on fire the way Adrian and I had always planned. It didn't matter that it wasn't how things had happened. It was how things *felt*. All my fault.

The gun tasted so good as I put it in my mouth, my finger tapped the trigger lightly without pressing down. I had fired in the ravine—I could press it again. *Now*, I thought. *Now*.

Now

I don't want to feel like I'm making a rash decision because I'm in need. But I am in need. I want a future, need to feel like there is momentum in my life.

I don't want to hurt myself—I don't think so, at least—but I'm not convinced that starting things up with Trevor again isn't hurting myself. Even though things have changed with us over the years, friendships like ours are always better with a bit of distance. But since starting treatment, I'm scared most nights to sleep alone unless I put all the lights on, and when I'm close to Trevor, I worry a little less about death and think less about the things that have happened to me over the years. And maybe that's all some of us need, a warm body beside us.

I text Stef. *Can I come over? I need your help with some stuff.*

Her reply isn't like her, short and curt. *Sure.* She even includes a period. I feel uneasy, but I push it out of my mind. I'm too excited about the new possibilities with Trevor—the idea of going back to school within reach, maybe one day learning new ways to teach, to inspire art in others. To grow.

Before I leave my place, I turn on my laptop. Normally, Jocelyn and I would have a mid-week check in. I think about what Trevor said about apologies—about how if he hadn't apologized, maybe we would have lost touch with each other, and it's true. At one point, I had no intention of ever speaking to him again. Even though I'm embarrassed and not sure what to say, I start to write to Jocelyn.

Sunday, December 21, 2025
Jocelyn,
I wanted to let you know how sorry I am about your showing and the way the night went. While I know it's not an excuse, I haven't felt myself lately and I let this impact my behaviour. One of your paintings I hadn't seen before deeply moved me, and I was a little off for the rest of the night. I have been amazed to see how much you've created in the time we worked together. From your email, it seems that you don't feel I value you or your work. I just wanted to let you know that I do, and I'm looking forward to seeing what you do next, even if we aren't working together.
Paul

I press *Send* and then, before I can regret it, I bundle myself up in my winter coat and hat and head out to Stef's. On the bus, I read about the programs at NSCAD on my phone, trying to see which one would fit the work I've already done at Sheridan. Stef texts me to let myself in, and when I get inside, I see Wynn decorating a Christmas tree by the window. She waves at me, half-heartedly. She doesn't do anything with enthusiasm now that she's sixteen.

Stef's place looks different. Instead of tidy and punctuated with small, Wynn-related messes, blankets are scattered on the couches and pillows on the ground, half-eaten meals on the coffee table and barely touched mugs of tea gone cold.

Stef is on the couch, in purple sweats, her hair pulled back and deep circles under her eyes. She looks even worse than last time I saw her.

"Paul," Wynn says from the Christmas tree. "What do you think?"

The tree already has lights wrapped around it that blink. Wynn's in the middle of hanging ornaments. A few are scattered on the branches closest to her.

"Looks great," I say. "What kind of lights are those?" They are stumpy and flash brightly, not like the bulbs we had when I was growing up.

"I dunno," Wynn says. "Christmas lights?" I'm not used to her attitude yet. Just last year she still got excited to see me.

"Wynn," Stef says from the couch. "It says right on the box: LED. They are all LED these days."

"When your mom and I were your age, they didn't have lights like these," I say.

"Cool," says Wynn, meaning the opposite.

"Look at this," says Stef. She claps and the lights switch from blinking to static, solid multicolours. She claps again and they turn off.

"Mom, stop it," Wynn says. "You're ruining my flow state." Wynn claps and the lights go back to blinking.

I flop onto the couch beside Stef. "So . . . I saw Trevor," I say. "And we talked, and I think we're going to give a relationship a shot."

Stef doesn't have the energy to look surprised. "You are?"

"Yeah, like a real one. So I'm going to move to Halifax—soon, I guess. I can keep up with my clients out there, and I think I'm going to try to get into this school to finish my degree."

"You'll move out there?"

"Yeah."

Stef's mouth pulls into a thin line, and I know she'd frown if only she'd let herself.

I keep talking, already nervous about asking Stef for help. I need to ask her before I chicken out. "Can you help me go through the NSCAD website and see what I need to do to apply? I'm not sure if I'm too late for September or how to transfer my credits over or what." I pull out my laptop from my backpack. Stef gets up and walks to the kitchen. My stomach begins to sink. I'd thought Stef would be excited for me.

"Sure, I can help you. But I've got to tell you, you sound like Kayla, getting all ahead of yourself over a guy." She pulls out a canister of tea and puts the kettle on. From over by the Christmas tree, Wynn raises her eyebrows at me.

"But this isn't just a guy. It's Trevor. And it's not just about that; it's about actually doing something with my life."

"I just want to make sure you're thinking it through," she says.

"And maybe being like Kayla isn't a bad thing," I say. "I mean, she goes after what she wants, at least. And she seems happy with her job."

"And do I not seem happy?" she says. She starts to slam things around in the kitchen, and I notice how the dishes have built up. She actually seems like the least happy person in the world right now. "Is that what you're saying?"

"Stef, why are we fighting?" I ask and walk into the kitchen. "What's wrong?"

"Since I told you I'm pregnant, I've barely heard from you at all. And it's been rough, Paul. I'm sick all the time. And you only reach out when you need something? I need to be able to count on you as well, instead of you always running to me when you have a problem. Sometimes I need help too. And now you're going to leave?

"Last time he asked you, you decided not to go, but for some reason it's different this time? You don't think about how I'll cope? Or Kayla? Or what about your folks? Or Wynn?"

Wynn pops her head into the kitchen, looking very much like Stef used to when I first met her, a smile playing on her lips. "Um, I don't care if you leave to get some in Halifax. Have fun, Paul."

"Wynn, can you not say 'get some' to my friend? And let us talk. Alone."

"I'm sorry, Stef," I say. "But I don't think I'm doing anything wrong."

"Then go. I'll help you with the application, I promise, but not today. I'm not feeling well. Just leave."

And I go. Wynn waves at me from the window. Stef and I have never fought like this before. Maybe I have been selfish. Like with Jocelyn. I know I've only been focused on one thing: getting my life together. But maybe the side effect of that work and focus is that I've been letting down the people I care about most.

Outside, it feels extra cold. I was expecting to spend a bunch of time with Stef around the holidays, and now I'm not sure if she'll even want me around.

As I board the bus, I pull out my phone to text Stef that I'm sorry, but as I do, I get a series of texts from Kayla.

Whoa.

Heard the news.

I didn't think you had it in you.

Leaving.

Love!

I guess I was wrong then
about u & toronto
I guess there's a first time for everything ;)

✧

The next day, I have a session with Selina. "I find it interesting," she says to me, "that when you found those kids in the ravine, you actually managed to rescue one, but you still feel like you failed them."

I think about the words I'd said to the girl, Alexis. That I'd made her keep a secret. I don't tell Selina about the gun, but I say, "I think I could have been more comforting. I think the things I said and did, the way I reacted, made it worse."

"Well, I think it would be hard for anyone to react perfectly in that situation. What would you say to one of your friends if they were beating themselves up about the same thing?"

I think about Stef, who always tries to be perfect. How I wish she would relax, realize she's human. "That nobody can be perfect, I guess."

"Yeah, exactly," Selina says and adjusts her glasses on her nose. "Now, Paul, we've had about twelve sessions now, and usually we try to make this type of treatment short-term, so that you leave it with the skills to treat yourself. So I'm thinking we should wrap up in a week or two. There are a few things I'd like to revisit, to close some doors. But I wanted to see how listening to the recordings has been for you."

"I guess it has gotten easier lately. To listen. At the beginning, I kept disconnecting. But now I can listen without going away from myself. I think writing about it all helped too."

"That's amazing. This isn't a quick fix, you know. There might be times where things get a little worse again, where you might have more nightmares, or feel a little edgy. But I feel confident that you'll know the signs a little better, so that you can start to use these techniques."

I don't understand. I'd thought that working on one trauma would unlock another that would unlock another until I was free from all of it, weightless and at peace. That as I learned the tools to stare each piece of my past in the face, the rest would fall away. But does this mean I'll constantly have to go through this process, that my dreams will keep coming back, that I'll never be able to forget Adrian's face, his breath on my face? That I'll never be free from the moment I couldn't move, didn't know who I was? That I'll forever be sculpting The Lighted City, Adrian, that little boy left in the ravine? "What's the point then?" I ask Selina. "Why did we even do this?" But what I really want to know is if I'm constantly going to be repeating things: treatment, memory, my past. I want to move forward. To believe it's possible to move forward.

"I think it has helped," she says. "And it's to give you the skills, so that you know, no matter what happens in the future, you'll be able to handle it and process it."

"So, I won't have to feel bad forever?" I ask.

"No, Paul," Selina says, and smiles at me through the screen. "You'll be able to enjoy your life."

How It Happened
June 2016

I woke up in a king bed between Stef and Wynn. "Paul!" Wynn exclaimed, her eyes already open, and she climbed on top of me and gave me a hug. "Are you sad? Here is a big hug!" She rubbed her head against mine, her short brown hair prickling my ear. Stef woke up on my other side.

"You doing okay?"

"I think so," I said. I remembered a long time ago, when I'd had a nightmare and Mom had come to lie with me in my bed. I'd forgotten until this moment. She'd held me as I cried. What other comforting memories had I forgotten? What else had I failed to pay attention to at the time, not knowing I would need it as an adult? Stef gave my hand a squeeze.

"I'll make breakfast. Let's get up."

Derek was sprawled sleeping on the couch, children's toys scattered across the living room floor. His mouth hung open.

"Watch," Wynn said to me and walked over to him. She stuck her fingers right into his open mouth. He stayed asleep. She sniffed her fingers. "Ew," she said. Some things you have to learn from regret.

The smell of bacon finally roused him. "Hey, Paul," he said. "You doing okay?"

"Yeah, thanks for letting me stay here last night."

"Taking my spot in the bed!" he said, and laughed. He walked over to Stef and put a hand on her back. She smiled at him.

We all ate together around the table, like a real family. No one talked about what must have brought me here. What I remembered in fragments. Me sobbing into the phone with the gun on my lap. Stef showing up and putting it away. Asking me if I needed to go to the hospital. Me clinging to her like she was all I had. Her taking me home in a cab, while I said I couldn't, I was too afraid to die, but now how could I live. She had tucked me into her bed with her, held me until my breathing slowed.

After breakfast, Derek and I tidied up the living room together.

"You talked to Trevor lately?" he asked me.

"No," I said.

"You should," he said. I knew that's all he would say about it.

✧

Trevor was the one who wrote to me first. His email said that he'd cut out the parts from his novel that I thought were similar to me. That if I wanted, he'd throw the whole thing away. He said that what I had seen had been his rough notes, and he was sorry if, somehow, he'd gotten something wrong or that he'd hurt me by taking what I told him and putting it down on paper. He said he should have asked first. He said that he never really knew what he was writing or even thinking until it was down on paper, and so he tried to record everything he could. "But I'm human, Paulina, and I make mistakes. If I've hurt you, that's the worst mistake I could make."

I wrote him a kind email about it that surprised me with my own forgiveness and then found myself walking up the steps to his apartment where he wrapped me in his arms. I thought that if two people deserved each other, it must be us, compatibility or not. I knew that I was the only one who could ever love him, who understood that hole that existed in him. Perhaps it was wrong for me to want to patch it up with my own pain, to want to put my whole body curled in a fetal position into the parts of himself that he hated. He bent me over, kissing my face again and again as he fucked me, and I said his name. Afterwards, he held me and I rested my head on his chest. "We're always doing this," he said.

"I know," I admitted. "Maybe we just aren't ready." I didn't have to say for what.

"Yeah. We should pivot," he said, purposefully. "Try things from another angle. What do you think?"

I laughed. I sat up and hugged my knees. "Like what?"

"Friends?"

"Friends," I said.

"Like really good, real friends," he said. "No expectations, just someone on our side."

I smiled at Trevor, and although I loved him, I knew I was still tangled. "That sounds nice," I said.

The silence from Nik got to me. How we'd shared something so significant at the ravine that day, yet I never heard from him again. I did try to text him, once or twice, to see how Tammy was coping, but he never wrote me back, despite reading them.

But I still lived in Toronto, the big city where no one could ever get away from each other, and so, leaving Stef's one day, I passed Nik, Tammy, and a woman walking down the street, Tammy holding both of their hands between them. "Hello," I said, and stopped, ready to chat. "How are you?"

Nik looked at the store behind me instead of looking me in the eye. "Rachel, this is Paulina. She used to teach Tammy."

"Paulina, I've heard so much about you! How's your new job?" Rachel shook my hand and smiled at me with disarming openness.

"Oh, I don't have a new job," I said, and continued walking. I looked back to see Tammy waving bye to me, cheerful and even more confident than when I'd taught her. I smiled and waved to her too. I told myself she must not have understood about the boy down there. That maybe Colin was only imaginary after all. But maybe some children are resilient.

✧

I finally wrote back to Aunt Dot, on a page torn from my sketch-book.

I got your card, I wrote.

All I can say is that I'm sorry and that I also need to find a way to heal. I was only a child when I found out about Uncle Jim, or just Jim, because I do not want to say uncle *because he is no family to me. I loved Adrian and wanted to make things better for him. But I was afraid and didn't understand what was happening...I was only five when I first found out. I know I should have come to you. Or told my parents. I regret it so much. I was so afraid of being a bother or betraying Adrian, but I understand that it would have saved him, and that maybe it would have saved me too. I'll always hate myself for not speaking up.*

I put the letter in the mailbox and waited. As the days passed, the hate for myself reverberated through me, but I'd promised to call Stef if I felt like everything became too much again. I breathed, I walked, and I sketched. I'd started to dream of a new project.

Aunt Dot replied to my letter through Facebook. *My darling girl, I am so sorry. I am so so sorry. You were only a child. I didn't mean to put it on you at all.*

I typed back before I gave myself time to think. *Thank you.*

I'm sorry you felt you couldn't come to me back then. I hope you feel that you can now. I'll always have a place for you. I knew that she meant it, but felt drained by the exchange. That night, I slept for almost twelve hours.

At my parents', I waited for night to fall and then I slipped out the screen door, my backpack on my back. I'd left my shoes outside, their hungry mouths waiting for my feet. I ran down my road, then along Adrian's winding dirt road, the moon shining on me, keeping me safe. I wasn't afraid of night anymore. The bungalow. The field of long, dried grass. I climbed the wooden fence that bordered the property, and dropped over the other side. I cut through the grass. I could hear the frogs singing their summer song. *Mate with me, mate with me.* I ran to our home base tree. The tree that he'd tied me to, the tree where we were discovered together. The tree that was supposed to burst into flames, to become the centre of The Lighted City. A screech broke through the cool night, sounding human: a barn owl.

The gun was in my hand, and I'd always known I couldn't do it. I was so ashamed by the fact I'd never be able to. I would die as all people did, but either in a way I didn't see coming or slowly through illness. I'd never be able to control it. I shot at the tree, its limbs now lifeless and dead, once, twice, three times. The lights in the old house flicked on. Dad told me it was full of squatters, that the electricity had never been turned off. With shaking fingers, I took the old tin and put the gun away, in the hollow of the old tree, a secret again like it always should have been.

Now

The morning of the show, I have an email from Jocelyn. She hasn't replied to my email, but has forwarded a newsletter from *Strokes*, an online art magazine. The only words from her say, "That you?" There are pictures of me and the two other artists who will be showing at the gallery this weekend. Our names are printed underneath, and I imagine Jocelyn sending the email to me, a smile in her eyes.

In my headshot, taken by Kayla, I look into the distance as if there's something I really need to see. It was only a bird, but in the ones where I looked directly into the camera I appeared too tired or haunted.

Trevor helps me and Kayla load my structures into a van before we head over to the show. I still haven't heard from Stef. Kayla has been over a couple times and told me that Stef's doctor finally had her go into the hospital to get an IV treatment since she'd stopped holding down food or water. I sent flowers to her house, but still didn't hear anything.

At the gallery space, I go to my installation room. I arrange the huts in a circle. I lay down long, dried grass I've collected from

Caledon to form paths to each hut. The paths meet in the centre of the circle and then lead to the back door. Outside, in the middle of a puddle of water contained by a kiddy pool, I set up the tree. A bunch of branches I've glued and tied together to look like a trunk and dead limbs. On the pavement around the pool, I scatter more grass, leaves, trying to make the Toronto asphalt natural.

Then I go back inside to focus on the huts and the pieces that go inside. When it's all done, I go back outside and set the tree on fire. The light is reflected in the pool underneath.

A security guard hovers nearby with a fire extinguisher, just in case. My vision was to do it in the middle of the room, but not even my studio mate could be convinced. I just have to hope that the gallery goers will follow the path outside and watch the branches burn. Against the night sky, it does look powerful. And familiar.

And for a moment, above the burning tree, I can almost see one of Jocelyn's spirits, glowing.

People begin to filter in and walk around the installation. Some peer into the huts. In one, there is a pair of boy's tennis shoes, the same as the ones the boy was wearing when I found him in the ravine. In another one, children's drawings are taped to the wall. In another, there is a foot-tall plastic replica of Rodin's *The Kiss* that I've found online and then wrapped in twine. Two beings locked together.

I imagine Adrian walking through the exhibit, how he'd understand all the ways he's taught me and all the ways he's hurt me and how they've all led me to this place.

"It's a great piece," a voice says from beside me, and Jocelyn is actually here, attending the show. "This time I get to be the one drinking wine at *your* opening," she says, and toasts into the air.

"It's good to see you!" I say, and I'm overcome. I don't know how to express the relief I feel at seeing her, my gratitude.

She gives me a little smile and shakes her head. "I had to see what all the fuss was about." I know then that we won't talk about the emails and things also won't go back to the way they were, but maybe I'm okay with that. Things are changing, and, finally, I'm changing too.

I go with Trevor and Kayla outside while they smoke, and as I shiver, Trevor tucks me inside his open coat. "You guys make me want to barf," Kayla says, and then waves at a figure approaching from down the street. "Speaking of barf!"

"Stef!" Trevor says and untucks me from my warm cocoon. He gives Stef a hug. "I heard the news from Derek. Congrats! Are you feeling better?"

"I finally got a prescription," she says. "Took me going to the hospital for them to believe my morning sickness was as bad as it was, but at least it's helping now. Am I too late for the show?"

"Not at all," I say. "I can bring you around, if you want."

"Sure." We leave Trevor and Kayla to finish their cigarettes, and walk inside. "Thanks for the flowers. I've been a wreck."

"No worries," I say, and bring her around the gallery. "It must have been horrible to be at the hospital." We look at some of the other artists' work first, explore.

"Honestly, at least they made me feel better there. It was worse before. I was barely getting through each day."

I reach my hand out to her. "I'm sorry, Stef," I say. "Are we good?"

Stef stops and turns to me. "Paul, we're always going to be good. It doesn't matter how mad we get at each other," Stef says. "If we're close, there will be times we don't see eye to eye. But that doesn't matter with family, and Paul, you are my family, okay? After all this time, there's very little you could do that would make me want you out of my life. Please remember that."

I start to tear up. Family. "I'll try to be there for you more, about the baby. I got a little wrapped up…" I want to tell her everything I've been going through with Selina, and I know that I will. That I'll go over after work one day before we leave, and I'll tell her all of it, right from the beginning. Maybe I don't need to hide this part of myself from the people I love.

"We're cool," she says. "You can still be family in Halifax, I guess. But Wynn will miss you, no matter what she says."

We go into my installation room and I let her walk around without me, so I don't have to see her reaction. You can start to see her bump coming in, life growing in her.

My parents finally arrive. They wear N95 masks on their faces, but still hug me. Dad walks straight to my installation room, and Mom wanders a bit. Today they seem less united than usual, but she catches up to him and holds his hand as they stroll through the exhibit. "Good job, Lina," Dad says, resting his hand on my shoulder, and his touch does not make me flinch.

I FaceTime Aunt Dot on my phone and show her and April around the gallery. "You'll have to take pictures," she says, "We can't see well."

"I will," I say.

The tree has burned down to ashes that float in the water. Kayla, Trevor, and Stef go to a nearby bar to catch up while I clean up what I can from the showing before coming back tomorrow. The ashes swirl in the water, and this is my art too. Allowing what was to become something new.

Alone in the gallery, I realize that no matter what happens, I need to see who I become.

I see the rest of my life stretching before me then, everything that will eventually come to be. I will get to the point that I don't think about Adrian as much, that I don't resent people I know for their happy, uncomplicated childhoods. Maybe I will further dedicate myself to things that grow—volunteering at a community garden, or continuing to teach. I will also dedicate myself to my own growth, commit to the person I'll become. This promise glimmers in front of me, in the water, so briefly but so clearly, like something I can touch.

An image of myself, cooking in the kitchen, peeling carrots, children of my own, laughing and playing in the living room. The hope it would take to have children. I could have that in me.

An image of myself, alone, by a lake, looking across the water, trying to catch sight of a blue heron. Forty-six and feeling the weight of Dad's passing. I look down at my phone and Mom is calling. She has been calling a lot lately. She doesn't know who she is without Dad. I know I will never have this problem of hers again, not like I did when I was with Adrian. It is another thing I have outgrown, although this grief has brought everything up again, like air bubbles expelled from the mouth of a bullfrog. I do not pick up her call. I continue to look for the heron.

Older still, my wrinkled hands dive into clay. I feel an overwhelming sense of love—for the material, for my hands that are still strong, for the process it takes to create something beautiful. A crowd of ten-year-olds surround me. I explain how to spin the wheel and create a bowl. I walk around, watching my students work.

I wrap the whole of myself around these future memories, and then, as soon as I feel I'm able to grasp them, they're gone. A perfect, simple future. To live a life like that, it wouldn't make me fear death or desire it. But as with all good things, if you think about them too hard and for too long, they disappear. And this future disappears, leaving me only in the present.

Acknowledgements

Play exists in huge debt to its editors: I couldn't have gotten *Play* into the world without you. Linda Pruessen, I learned so much from you, both as a writer and an editor, and everything you've taught me has made me a better writer. Catriona Wright, thank you so much for reading *Play* at such a busy time and providing notes and suggestions. Your thoughts helped me see the book clearly and believe in it again. You are one of the truest friends I have. Meg Storey, thank you so much for your early developmental edits and helping turn a mess into a book.

Sofia Mostaghimi, thank you for being the best BFFL and surfing these writing waves with me; for helping me map *Play*'s structure on bristol board and printing drafts and bringing them to the hospital for me to mark up; for going on a writing retreat with me when I was still using my cane and struggling to get around (where half the time was spent watching *The Fosters* and half the time writing); and for *always* talking to me about friendship and play.

Thank you to my early readers of chapters and bits: Nadia Ragbar, Cheryl Runke, Andrew Battershill, and Menaka Ramen-Wilms.

To my family, Ken, Beata, Lila, Lukas, and Mom and Dad: I love you so much. Thanks for always supporting this writing dream of mine and for having good conversations. Michelle, Vince, and Zoë: honourary fam forever!

Craig, thank you for being my home. For allowing my heart a place to be at peace. Olive, I wish you a childhood filled with love and play. I promise to pay attention and to listen. I love you, my family.

Play and my writing time was supported by the Ontario Arts Council's Writer's Recommender Program and the publishers who recommended *Play*; the Canada Council for the Arts; and the Writers' Trust Woodcock Fund. Thank you to Spencer Gordon and Naben Ruthnum for their support during the Woodcock application process and to James Davies for reaching out and suggesting I apply. I urge all writers who are going through life-changing hardship to apply to the Woodcock Fund: they want you to keep writing. Don't give up!

Thank you to Hazel Millar and Jay MillAr. It's been amazing to see Book*hug Press grow since I first published with you in 2015 and to be putting out my third (!!!) book with you. And thank you so much to Marilyn Biderman of Transatlantic Agency for working on my behalf to find *Play* a home.

The type of therapy that Paul is engaged in with Selina is based on Cognitive Processing therapy, a trauma-informed version of CBT tailored for people living with PTSD and C-PTSD. For more information, see the manual *Cognitive Processing Therapy for PTSD* by Patricia A. Resick, Candice M. Monson, and Kathleen M. Chard, which lays out the protocol. Thank you so much to my colleague and friend, Anita Corsini, for introducing me to this therapy for PTSD and unlocking both something for my novel and something for my own treatment.

Thank you also to Dr. Jenkinson at Sunnybrook Hospital for fixing my pelvis and then seeing what else I needed.

Paul, her friends and family, and her story are all works of fiction, but her pain is very real. I hope that this book allows people to talk a little more openly about their own experiences with stigma-laden trauma. This book is for all of you who are trying to come to terms with your life experiences and who are trying to heal. I see you. Your effort is valued.

PHOTO: ANGELA LEWIS